CW00684379

# AN EYE FOR AN EYE

# AN EYE FOR AN EYE

## ALAN J. MURRAY

*Mill City Press, Minneapolis*

Copyright © 2015 by Alan J. Murray

Mill City Press, Inc.
322 First Avenue N, 5th floor
Minneapolis, MN 55401
612.455.2293
www.millcitypublishing.com

All rights reserved. No part of this publication may be reproduced, stored in a retrieval system, or transmitted, in any form or by any means, electronic, mechanical, photocopying, recording, or otherwise, without the prior written permission of the author.

ISBN-13: 978-1-63413-199-5
LCCN: 2014920226

Cover Design by Biz Cook
Typeset by James Arneson

*Printed in the United States of America*

*This book is respectfully dedicated to the men and women of America's armed forces and intelligence services, who were the inspiration for this story.*

*An eye for an eye makes the whole world blind.*

**~ Mahatma Gandhi**

## AUTHOR'S NOTE

This is a work of fiction. All persons, places, things, and events in this story are a product of the author's imagination, and any similarity to real-world people, places, events, and organizations is purely coincidental. Although some real-world events and organizations are mentioned in this story to enhance authenticity, they are not intended to describe or portray real-world persons, tactics, beliefs, or policies.

# CONTENTS

# 1. TAKEN BY SURPRISE

*Aldgate Ward*
*East London, United Kingdom*

"Hurry, he's coming! Get ready!" the leader whispered.

Alerted by the sound of approaching footsteps coming from inside the house, the small group—all of them sheathed in black fatigues—melted into the evening shadows as they took up their assigned positions near the doorway.

Fumbling for his keys, Jamal opened the door to his apartment and stuck his right foot part way out, feeling for the familiar top step as he went. What happened next was the last thing Jamal expected, so he never saw it coming.

"Now!" the group's leader shouted.

Without warning, the night around Jamal suddenly exploded in a barrage of thunderous shouts. From every direction, flailing hands thrust from the darkness and grabbed him. Jamal was overwhelmed and confused by the rapidity of the attack. Before he realized what happened, he was fully subdued. Taken completely by surprise, he let out a fearful scream. In an instant, a large, burly hand swiftly covered his mouth and stifled his cry.

"Quickly! Place the tape over his mouth!" he heard one of them yell.

"The bag! The bag! Come on, get it over his head," another one barked.

In less than a minute's time, the attackers bound his hands, gagged him and slipped a black cloth hood over his head. Standing on the top step to his flat, he struggled unsuccessfully, writhing as if a large animal caught in a leg hold trap as he attempted to break his captors' grasp. The more he fought to break free, the tighter they gripped. After two or three minutes, he simply gave up the fight. It was pointless. Jamal panted heavily, trying to catch his breath. His heart was racing, pounding loudly against his chest. His mouth was dry with fear. He tried to swallow, but could not. His bladder had let loose and Jamal felt a warm trickle running down his right leg. Although he tried to stop the flow of urine, fear blocked his efforts. The disgusting sensation continued unabated.

*I am going to die. May Allah have mercy on my soul.*

Jamal had not seen any of his assailants before they seized him. He couldn't tell how many there were, but he guessed there were at least four in the group. It was dark and the streets in this section of Aldgate on London's eastern edge were a dimly lit maze of small alleyways that spilled over into neighboring Whitechapel. That had made it easy for his attackers to spring their assault.

Jamal listened carefully, hoping that the commotion had attracted the attention of some neighbors. However, like most city dwellers, even if they did see or hear the racket, the neighbors would very likely ignore it for fear of reprisal or of becoming victims themselves. Jamal was sure his captors knew this and were taking advantage of his neighbors' predictable "see no evil; hear no evil" apathy. Unfortunately, he was right and no one rushed to his aid. He was at the mercy of his captors, whoever they were.

# 1. TAKEN BY SURPRISE

A torrent of questions swirled around inside Jamal's mind like kaleidoscopic images falling over one another as he attempted to make sense of the chaos. *Who are they? What have I done? What do they want? Where will they take me? Will they kill me?* However, his attempt to answer them only added to the confusion.

Jamal tried to scream for help, but the tape over his mouth muted the sound so that it was nothing more than a muffled grunt. The black cloth hood covering his head was tight around his neck. With his hands bound behind his back, there was no way that he could remove it on his own. The bag's dank, musty smell meant that Jamal wasn't the first captive to encounter it. The rancid odor of sweat and other bodily secretions trapped inside the covering was nauseating. Jamal tried to cough but choked instead.

Two captors stood on either side of him, arms locked together, which made him feel like a cow moored to a stanchion. Jamal couldn't move. The image of a tethered animal before the slaughter flashed through his mind. He shuddered as a wave of fear and desperation swept over him.

Jamal grew increasingly impatient as thoughts raced through his mind. *What's next? Come on—finish it!*

In the distance, the sound of a motor grew louder. Some kind of vehicle was approaching, rumbling down the dark, narrow street. Jamal strained to hear, hoping to tell by its noise whether it was a car, truck or small van Jamal listened intently, but the cloth bag over his head made it difficult. As hard as he tried, he wasn't able to pick out any identifiable characteristics, so he couldn't be sure of its type. However, he was sure of one thing: that it was coming for him.

# 2. NIGHT HAWK

*Szczytno–Szymany International Airport*
*Near Stare Kiejkuty, Poland*

Flight 602 was a non-scheduled "business" flight from London's Northolt Airport to Warsaw's Frederic Chopin Airport in eastern Poland. In actuality, Northolt was a small RAF airfield on the city's north side. Though used primarily for government and diplomatic traffic, it wasn't unusual for an occasional civilian jet to land or takeoff from there. The long-range Learjet 35A aircraft designated Flight 602 was registered to Acworth Marketing, a Texas-based U.S. corporation, whose address was simply a post office box in the heart of Houston's central business district. Typically, seven passengers occupied the mid-size corporate jet's plush leather and burled walnut interior. Tonight though, excluding the two pilots in the cockpit, there were only three other people on board.

The jet's exact destination was Szczytno-Szymany International Airport in northeast Poland, the only airport designed for domestic and international air traffic service in Warmia-Mazury province. However, the Polish Transport Ministry listed it as "temporarily closed to air traffic." In reality, it was one of several military facilities used by the U.S. as a staging area for the ongoing counterinsurgency efforts in Iraq and Afghanistan. The airfield was located roughly ten kilometers from the village of

Stare Kiejkuty and once served as a military airfield in northeastern Poland.

During World War II, it was a staging base for the German Luftwaffe to conduct bombing raids against Warsaw. The airstrip's importance grew during the Cold War since it was one of several able to handle the large Soviet-made military planes of the Warsaw Pact. After the collapse of the Soviet Union, the airport's significance gradually diminished and its relevance was all but lost— that is, until now. Launched by the Americans in 2002, Operation Enduring Freedom thrust Szczytno-Szymany International Airport into prominence once again.

The airport served as a gateway to a Polish intelligence training school near the village of Stare Kiejkuty, located about twenty kilometers from Szczytno-Szymany International Airport. The complex was a Soviet-era compound once used to train Communist agents and assassins. Still operational, the Polish army now ran the school. Unbeknown to the outside world, there was something else far more secretive taking place behind the barbed wire and chain link fences of the Polish-run intelligence complex at Stare Kiejkuty.

The CIA operated an interrogation and short-term detention facility for suspected al-Qaeda and Taliban terrorist suspects there. Stare Kiejkuty was part of a network of secret facilities or "black sites" scattered throughout Eastern Europe used for covert activities. Prisoners whom the CIA or British MI6 captured using extraordinary rendition were secretly flown to this site—or others like it—for interrogation and temporary detention.

The CIA's Counter Terrorist Intelligence Center, or CTIC, at Langley conducted these clandestine flights. To mask the program, detainees bounced from one site to another, and were never held in one place long enough to attract unwanted attention. It was a simple concept and it worked.

The Learjet 35A aircraft bore no markings except for a small FAA N-number registration on its tail and was painted Juneau white, hence its nickname, "Snow White." When fully loaded with seven passengers, crews jokingly referred to it as "Snow White and the seven dwarfs." Two of the passengers on board this flight were CIA officers. They were escorting a detainee captured the night before to Stare Kiejkuty for "low level" interrogation. That was the kind reserved for detainees who, when captured, showed some interest in cooperating with the CIA and MI6 afterward, most often as an informant inside a terrorist cell.

The Learjet 35A neared the end of its flight plan route, Frederic Chopin Airport in Warsaw, but did not descend to land. Instead, it streaked onward through the nighttime sky some one hundred and fifty kilometers north of the capital toward its secret destination. It was early November and the weather in this region of Poland was typical for the time of year. A blustery north wind accompanied a low overcast and white flecks of snow swirled through the air. Though closed, Polish air traffic controllers cleared the Learjet for an ILS/DME approach to Runway 02 at Szczytno-Szymany International Airport. The jet landed, rolled to the end of the 7,000-foot runway and turned left onto taxiway Echo.

The crew taxied southbound and followed taxiways Alpha-3 and Alpha-4 to the parking stand marked "1." No other aircraft were on the ramp and there was no marshal to guide Snow White into place. The pilots had flown into Szczytno-Szymany many times during the last few months on similar missions, though, and were familiar with the layout. A small, camouflaged military truck was waiting when the Learjet came to a stop. The captain shut the engines down and the copilot went back and opened the cabin door. The two CIA officers and their black-hooded charge climbed down the steps and quickly walked to the waiting truck. They got in and the truck drove away, fading into the cold winter night.

〈●〉

IT WAS a short thirty-minute drive from the Szczytno-Szymany International Airport to the complex at Stare Kiejkuty. After a brief stop at the main gate, the truck entered. Once inside, it rumbled along, passing two watchtowers before it turned off the road and stopped in front of a nondescript, gray cinder block building. The CIA officers climbed out with their prisoner and whisked him through the entrance. They kept his hood on and wound their way through a series of narrow corridors to a small, cell-like room. One of them opened the door while the other ushered the detainee into the room. The agents plopped the prisoner down on a metal chair in the middle of the room and stood next to him, resting their hands on his shoulders.

A few seconds later, another man entered the room and approached the trio. He stopped two feet from them and studied the prisoner for a long moment. Suddenly, the man grabbed the detainee's black hood and yanked it off his head. Not expecting it, the startled prisoner jumped up from his seat but the two CIA men held him down. Free of the hood, he looked about the room and tried to get a better glimpse of his captors, but the bright lights made it impossible. The man bent low, brought his face close to the detainee's, and stared at him in silence.

After a long pause, the man straightened and lit a cigarette. He took several drags and exhaled in one slow, deep breath. A cloud of bluish smoke filled the room and hung in the air. The man looked directly at the prisoner and addressed him in a low, rather menacing voice, "Hello, Jamal."

# 3. WON'T TALK?

*CIA Interrogation Site*
*Stare Kiejkuty, Poland*

*Jamal. He knows my name!* Jamal, hands bound behind his back, sat helplessly in the center of a windowless room that was the size of a large closet and, except for the chair and table, was bare. The gray painted walls were made of concrete blocks and the floor was a cement slab. Bright lights on the ceiling angled down toward the middle of the room where Jamal sat. Jamal stared at the man who stood directly in front of him, and waited for his next move. *Will he beat and torture me? Will he kill me instead?*

The man took several more drags from the cigarette pinched between his fingers and then dropped the butt on the floor. He placed his heavy black boot over the stub and ground it out with a back-and-forth motion as if he was squashing a bug. The cloud of bluish smoke he exhaled drifted toward Jamal and hung over his head. Jamal coughed.

"Smoking is bad for you. Did you know that, Jamal?" the man sneered.

Jamal looked down at the floor and did not respond.

"Let's not get off to a bad start, you and me," the man cautioned. "I'd like you to call me Tony. How does that sound?"

Jamal continued to look down and remained silent.

Tony stepped closer and lit another cigarette. "Jamal, I am your friend. Others here wanted to hurt you. However, I convinced them to let me talk to you first. I assured them that you would cooperate with me and tell me what they wanted to know." He paused and rubbed his chin. "They told me it wouldn't work and that their way was better." Tony walked to the small table and sat on its edge.

"Don't prove me wrong. Don't make a liar out of me, Jamal."

Tony lit another smoke, took a deep drag and exhaled in Jamal's face. Jamal coughed once more.

"What do you say, Jamal? Will you help me?"

Jamal slowly raised his head. He stared at Tony for a long moment and then answered. "Why? Why should I help you?" he shouted, "You're just like all of the other Americans and Brits!"

"But you see, Jamal, that's where you are wrong. *If* I were like the other Americans and Brits, as you say, then by now I would have cut off your scrawny balls and stuffed them in your mouth like grapes. However, I haven't done that, have I?" Tony jeered

Jamal stared at Tony, his eyes smoldered with defiance.

"But," Tony hissed, "That doesn't mean I won't." He flicked his spent cigarette butt onto the floor and ground it into shreds with his heavy boot.

"You won't harm me," Jamal shot back, "I'm worth more to you alive than dead."

"Don't be impressed with your own importance, Jamal," Tony snapped. "You're just a little fish in a very big pond. You're nobody. Your family probably doesn't even know you're missing."

Jamal glared at him. "I have divorced this life. I don't care about my family and they understand," Jamal replied. "Kill me then. Go ahead—I welcome martyrdom. Kill me!" he shouted.

Tony slid off the small table and leaned down, crowding Jamal's face. "Oh no, Jamal. Not so easy or so fast. That would be just what you and your Muslim brothers want. No, Jamal, you won't die a martyr. Not here, not now—in fact, maybe never."

Tony straightened, lit another cigarette and looked at Jamal. "I'm afraid we're not getting off to a good start, Jamal. Don't you agree?" Tony mocked.

Jamal turned away. "You're not my friend—don't pretend to be. You're just one of them—another infidel."

"That's not polite, Jamal, "Tony warned. " In spite of your rude behavior, I'm going to prove that I really am your friend," he continued, "I'm going to tell you the fastest way to get out of this shit hole."

Suddenly the door to the interrogation cell flew open and a large man burst into the room. Jamal spun his head toward the door. The oversized hulk's all black leather jacket, boots, shirt and pants looked more like executioner's garb than street clothes. This man, also a Caucasian, spoke English as well. He began to shout at Tony.

"Goddamn it, Tony!" he yelled, "I knew it wouldn't work. I told you he wasn't going to cooperate."

"For Christ's sake, Ray," Tony countered, "It takes time. We've only been at it for a few minutes. I know I can get him to talk."

"Bullshit," Ray shot back, "He's not going to talk this way. I think we should save ourselves a lot of time and drag him down the hall."

Tony froze and his eyes widened. "No, Ray. Not that—not yet! Give me some more time—just a couple of hours. I know Jamal will come around. Let me try."

Ray marched over to Jamal and bent low, their faces inches apart. "Listen to me, you Koran-kissing piece of shit," he growled, "You've got two more hours to open up and spill your guts, hear? If by then you haven't told us what we want to know, it's down the hall with you. Believe me, you'll wish you had cooperated with Tony. Oh, and one more thing, Jamal. I'm giving you more time for one reason, and it's not because I like you—it's because I like Tony. Got it?"

Ray straightened himself and grabbed Jamal by the collar. He tugged hard and yanked Jamal up from his seat. Jamal's shirt tightened around his neck and he gasped for air. Ray kept him suspended for a few seconds and then plopped him back in the chair. Jamal coughed as he caught his breath. Ray didn't say anything else. He spun around and stormed out of the room, slamming the door behind him.

Jamal looked up, his face ashen, eyes wide with fright. Beads of perspiration clung to his forehead. Tony walked to the center of the room and sat on the edge of the table. He stroked the back of his neck and let out a heavy sigh. Tony leaned toward Jamal and spoke in a low, soft voice. "Ray wasn't kidding," he whispered, "I've seen him beat people until they're senseless. I've also seen him kill prisoners like you with his bare hands." Tony sat back. "But for you, Jamal, he's got something else in store. Ray won't kill you—that's what you want. What he has in mind will make you wish you were dead. Trust me, I know." Tony lit another cigarette and inhaled deeply.

Jamal closed his eyes and shuddered. After several seconds, he opened his eyes. He swallowed hard and turned to face Tony.

"Now, one more time, Jamal," he said, "Can we be friends? Will you help me?" Tony leaned closer to Jamal's face and whispered, "Last chance."

# 4. DEATH TO THE UNBELIEVERS

*The Presidential Palace*
*Tehran, Iran*

A light rain was falling in the darkness that was beginning to slip over Tehran as the sleek black Mercedes Benz sedan arrived at the gate of the Iranian presidential palace. Inside, except for the driver, sat the only other occupant, President Azar Farahani. Farahani stared intensely through the rear passenger window into the coming night. His black, deep-set eyes did little to hide the rage that was burning deep within his soul. Years had passed since the first Gulf War and much had changed in the region. It had been only two weeks since the Americans had launched a nuclear missile at the Revolutionary Guards Safe House located near Varamin, some forty kilometers southwest of the capital.

The U.S. strike was in response to an Iranian-planned biological attack against America emanating from Cuba. The safe house was in actuality a three-story villa cleverly built in a way so that it blended into the mountainside to which it clung. A hardened facility that could withstand a blast from airdropped bombs, it was virtually undetectable from the air or ground. Hidden deep underground was a bunker that would protect its occupants from a nuclear detonation on the surface above—or so the Iranians thought.

After coming to power in 1979, the Council of the Islamic Revolution regularly held important meetings there. It is where clerics and followers of Ayatollah Khomeini charted the course of the new Islamic Republic of Iran. Here they drew up plans to fight the eight-year long war against Iraq. Here they hatched the idea for developing a nuclear weapon and delivery system capable of reaching Iraq, Israel, Saudi Arabia, Moscow and eventually, Washington. In addition, here they initiated a plan to infect hundreds of Cuban "refugees" with smallpox, knowing that as they streamed toward south Florida in a flotilla reminiscent of the 1980 Mariel boatlift, the Americans would come to the rescue. That would be their undoing.

However, because a defection by a scientist at Havana's Center for Genetic Engineering and Biotechnology and sheer luck, the Americans discovered the plot just days before its planned launch. The result was a swift and unprecedented response from Washington. In the aftermath of the attack, it was obvious that U.S. intelligence had pinpointed the exact location of the safe house in Varamin. A submarine-launched nuclear missile had vaporized the mountainside command bunker and killed everyone inside, including President Farahani's trusted aide, Iranian Revolutionary Guards minister Moshen Rafiq-Doust, who was the mastermind behind the plot. The force of the U.S. response took the Iranian regime by surprise.

Farahani had just come from a meeting with the Supreme Leader of the Islamic Republic of Iran, Ayatollah Shahzad Ali Shirazi. The meeting had gone exactly as President Farahani had hoped and expected. The ruling cleric's position was clear, and Farahani agreed with it. Within hours following the U.S. strike against the safe house in Varamin, Shirazi said in remarks broadcast on Iranian state television, "Some people say that the U.S. president is not prone to calculating the consequences of his actions, but it is possible to bring this kind of person to wisdom." The meaning of his remarks was quite unambiguous and could only suggest one thing: If the United States were to attack Iran, the country would respond by striking U.S. interests all over the world. When, where, and how? That was for President Farahani and his ministers to decide.

As the car approached the gate, a pair of uniformed police officers wielding submachine guns emerged from the guardhouse. To provide an added measure of security, two small Russian-made armored vehicles flanked the road on either side of the gate. The car came to a stop and the driver lowered the window. He held up his identification card for the guards to see. One of them bent over for a closer look and then glanced toward the back seat.

"Good evening, Mr. President," he said and then looked back at the driver, motioning him to proceed. They snapped to attention and saluted. The gate opened and the Mercedes sped inside past two Iranian-built Zulfiqar main battle tanks toward the palace. Military vehicles and anti-aircraft missile batteries dotted the grounds and the palace itself was ablaze with light. The country wasn't at war—at least not yet. The president of the Islamic Republic of Iran had a long, but hopefully promising, night ahead of him. It was time to exact revenge.

As the car approached the portico, President Farahani remembered the words from the Koran that Ayatollah Shirazi had left him with earlier that evening, "We decreed for them a life for a life, an eye for an eye, a nose for a nose, an ear for an ear, a tooth for a tooth, and a wound for a wound." That is precisely what Farahani hoped to plan for the Americans—a sharp, stinging retaliation in kind—an eye for an eye. *Truly, this plan will have the blessings of Allah*, he thought.

The notion of such an outcome caused a twisted, rather perverse smile to spread across his otherwise featureless face. As the sedan came to a stop in front of the presidential palace, Farahani recalled the white Arabic script that appeared eleven times on the top and bottom edges of the Iranian flag. It simply said, "*Allah Akbar*," or "God is great."

# 5. NOTHING TO FEAR

*The White House*
*Washington, D.C.*

Although there were only minutes before the televised address to the nation, Robert K. Brewster, the President of the United States, sat behind the large wooden desk, cradling his head with one hand. Eyes closed he periodically rubbed both temples with his thumb and forefingers. The strain of the past few days was beginning to show. Brewster hadn't slept much at all. In fact, no one in his Cabinet had, either. His face could not hide the worry he felt. This was a very dangerous situation. When briefing reporters and talking to his Cabinet and members of Congress, Brewster tried his best to hide it. If public perception was any indication, he had been successful in his efforts so far.

Two weeks earlier, President Brewster's world had changed when he gave the order to launch the Trident missile that successfully destroyed the Iranian command bunker south of Tehran. In the minutes that followed the launch, leaders implemented the Continuity of Government, or COG. In accordance with the plan, several high-ranking and key US government officials raced to various locations—many of them underground bunkers—to insure their safety and the continuation of governmental operations in the event of a retaliatory strike by Iran or some other rogue state aligned with them.

The Secret Service hadn't taken any chances in protecting the president, either. The threat was too great and the consequences too devastating. Within minutes of ordering the missile launch, Marine One lifted off the South Lawn of the White House, presumably carrying the president and bound for Mount Weather, a highly secure bunker facility in the Virginia foothills west of Washington, D.C.

In reality, the Secret Service rushed President Brewster to Andrews Air Force Base from the White House's West Wing in a custom-built, heavily armored Chevy Suburban nicknamed the "War Wagon." At Andrews, Brewster boarded an E-4B airborne command post, a specially equipped Boeing 747 code-named "Looking Glass" that had been flown in from Offutt AFB in Nebraska during the night. After remaining aloft for several hours, Looking Glass landed back at Andrews under cover of darkness with an F-16 fighter escort. Brewster quickly returned to the White House in the War Wagon without the usual contingent of Secret Service and military escort vehicles with red and blue lights flashing and sirens wailing. Once there, he took command from the Situation Room located on the ground floor of the West Wing.

Now, Brewster sat quietly behind his desk trying to gain the strength and composure to face a troubled nation and its citizenry and thought about his many predecessors and their own trials. The president recalled that James Madison fled to Virginia as the British burned the White House during the War of 1812. Next, he tried to imagine how Abraham Lincoln felt as he learned of the Union's defeat at Manassas, only a few miles from the White House. Brewster wondered how Franklin Roosevelt reacted when told of the surprise attack by the Japanese at Pearl Harbor.

He put himself in Harry Truman's shoes when he made the decision to drop the first atomic bomb on Hiroshima. Brewster took comfort in the words President Roosevelt used during his first inaugural address in 1933, "the only thing we have to fear is fear itself."

Brewster's new second-term Chief of Staff, Paul Mc-Cormick, leaned over his boss's left shoulder. "Mr. President, you're on in five," he said in a soft, reassuring voice.

The president turned toward him and forced a smile. He gripped his hand, giving it a confident squeeze. "Thanks, Paul."

The threat of an attack by the Iranians or another extremist Islamic group was great so the televised address would originate from the Situation Room. Of course, viewers would think that the president was in the Oval Office. The Secret Service had insisted on these measures since the Oval Office's windows faced the South Lawn of the White House. Even though they were made of special, bulletproof glass, given the circumstances, the risk to the president was too high.

An elaborate backdrop that looked exactly like the Oval Office had had been constructed and placed in the Situation Room. To make it seem real, a body double would be at Brewster's desk in the Oval Office while he was actually speaking to the nation from the Situation Room in the basement below the West Wing of the White House. To anyone observing from the outside, that would make it appear as though the broadcast was originating from there.

Although the Countersniper Team—uniformed Secret Service officers with machine guns and hand held Stinger anti-aircraft missiles were always protecting the president at the White House—for added security, several M1117

Armored Security Vehicles and anti-aircraft batteries had been placed around its grounds.

As a further precaution, the Federal Aviation Administration recently imposed a twenty-five nautical mile no-fly zone around Washington for all commercial and general aviation aircraft. U.S. Air Force and Air National Guard F-16's with shoot down orders patrolled the skies over the nation's capital around the clock. The nation's seat of power had been cordoned off and the White House itself had become an impregnable fortress—and for good reason.

A voice from behind the camera announced "One minute, Mr. President." Brewster wiped his brow, took a large sip of water and then cleared his throat. "Dear God, give me strength," he said to himself quietly.

The White House Communications Office producer raised his right hand and extended his index finger, waving it back and forth to get the president's attention. Once he caught Brewster's gaze, he looked squarely at him saying, "Mr. President, you're on in five-four-three-two-one-now." His right hand arced downward so it was pointing directly at the man behind the desk in the "Oval Office."

Right on cue, Brewster began:

*"My fellow citizens, as you know from my address to you two weeks ago, America's naval submarine forces launched a nuclear missile in a pre-emptive strike to prevent the Islamic Republic of Iran from carrying out a deadly biological attack against our nation originating from the island of Cuba, ninety miles from our shores.*

*This unprovoked act of terrorism had only one purpose: To cripple and kill as many innocent Americans as possible in an attempt to bring our mighty country to its knees. Thanks to the heroic actions of a few brave and gallant citizens, the plot was uncovered in time to prevent it from occurring. The American response was swift and measured. Iran paid a high price for its decision to plan and execute such an attack.*

*Nonetheless, our nation considers the Islamic Republic of Iran to be a clear and present danger. I have been in consultation with my entire Cabinet, including the Secretaries of Defense, State and Homeland Security.*

*The risk of a retaliatory strike against America at home and its interests abroad by the Islamic Republic of Iran remains high. The terror threat level is at red.*

*Please be assured that the federal, state and local government and public safety officials everywhere are working tirelessly around the clock to protect our nation and each one of you from harm.*

*In the coming days and weeks, I would urge you to go about your normal, daily routines but remain vigilant. Report anything suspicious or out of the ordinary to your local or federal law enforcement agencies right away.*

*If we succumb to fear, then our enemies will claim victory. If we stand steadfast and resolute as one nation, undivided, then our enemies shall have no power over us, and we will have won.*

*As your president, I appreciate your courage, your conviction, and your unwavering support. May God bless each and every one of you, and may God bless the United States of America."*

The red light on the TV camera in front of the president went out. Brewster turned his head toward the producer looking for the "on air" light to be sure that they weren't still live. Too many public officials made embarrassing comments before realizing that they were still broadcasting. He remembered Ronald Reagan's now infamous 1984 blunder at the height of the Cold War when he joked around during what he thought was a voice-level test before his regular Saturday radio address to the nation. "My fellow Americans," Reagan announced, "I'm pleased to tell you today that I've signed legislation that will outlaw Russia forever. We begin bombing in five minutes." *Certainly, this was no time for that kind of mistake*, Brewster thought.

The president rolled back away from the desk as McCormick approached.

"Well, Paul," Brewster asked his Chief of Staff, "how did it go?"

"You laid it out pretty well for the American people, sir. I think it was right on the mark," he replied.

"Good, Paul," Brewster nodded. "I hope so."

"You'll know for sure when you read tomorrow morning's *Washington Post* headline, Mr. President."

"That's exactly what I'm afraid of," he sighed. "Paul," the president continued, "I want a meeting of the National Security Council first thing in the morning. Make it for eight o'clock—no seven-thirty sharp. We'll hold it in the Roosevelt Room."

"Yes, Mr. President. Will there be anything else?"

"No. Just make damned sure everyone is there. I don't want anyone absent," he said emphatically.

"Very well, sir. I'll get right on it."

"Thanks, Paul," Brewster responded. He turned and walked toward the door of the Situation Room, a pair of Secret Service agents close behind him. "I'll see you in the morning," he called over his shoulder.

# 6. A HAPPY REUNION

*U.S. Naval Submarine Base*
*Kings Bay, GA*

As the President of the United States finished his televised address to the nation, Navy Commander William C. Murphy picked up the remote control and turned off the television set. He placed it back on the coffee table and leaned back on the small sofa, turning toward his sweetheart.

"Well, Susan," he asked, "What did you think of the president's remarks?" looking at her rather quizzically, trying to gauge her sense of approval.

Like millions of other Americans tonight, he and Susan had tuned in to hear their president talk about the events of the past few weeks. Bill Murphy's perspective on what had occurred was far different from every other viewer tonight. For it was the submarine he commanded, the USS *Wyoming*, that had launched the nuclear missile Brewster referred to in his speech. Now back in Saint Marys, Georgia following the end of the combat patrol and extensive debriefing, Bill Murphy and the entire crew were taking advantage of refit, the time between patrols when the outgoing crew would get come much needed "R&R" and then begin the train-up for their next long period at sea.

"I don't know," Susan shrugged. "Brewster wasn't that convincing to me. I got the sense he knows more than he's telling us."

She crossed her legs and leaned forward a bit, planting her elbow on her thigh so she could rest her chin on the back of her hand. As a veteran reporter for the *Washington Post*, she had been around long enough to know when public officials weren't forthright in their speeches to the public.

"How 'bout you, Murph?" she asked pensively.

Murphy dropped his head slightly and stroked the back of his neck with the palm of his hand. He looked up and exhaled with a long, worried sigh.

"I agree with you, Susan," he nodded. "I feel the same way. As my father used to say, 'Still water runs deep.' The president seemed very preoccupied to me. I think there's something else going on, too."

"Should we be worried? Should we change our plans then?" Susan asked.

"No, I don't believe that's necessary," Murphy said. "With the heightened state of security everywhere, I'm sure there's no cause for concern."

"Maybe I should call the cruise line first thing in the morning just to be sure," Susan said. "It's a four-hour trip from here. I wouldn't want to drive all the way down to Fort Lauderdale only to find they've canceled our sailing for some reason."

"Well, if it will make you feel better, go ahead," he replied.

Susan smiled and took his hand. "Thanks, Murph. Better to be safe than sorry," she said.

Murphy smiled back approvingly. He leaned over and pecked her softly on the cheek.

Susan glanced at her watch and stood up. "It's not quite eight o'clock yet. Let's go over to the Oyster Shack and have a quick dinner. We can finish packing when we get back. There'll be plenty of time."

"Good idea, Susan," Murphy said as he rose from the sofa. "I am a little hungry now. I don't want to stay up too late, though. We've got a long day ahead of us tomorrow."

# 7. BACK IN THE SADDLE

*The U.S. Embassy*
*London, U.K.*

Allan Anderson left the modest flat he rented on Argyle Street, which straddled Camden Town and Islington just north of London proper, and headed for his office at the U.S. embassy. This neighborhood of tree-lined streets, located a few city blocks from the River Thames and its famed London Bridge, was peaceful and idyllic. Allan liked the area because it was convenient to the embassy and offered a wide variety of nightclubs and restaurants. As another advantage, it was popular with other diplomatic mission employees and, above all else, was affordable.

From Allan's neighborhood, it was a short ride on London's underground train system, dubbed The Tube, to the stop nearest the embassy, which was Bond Street. Conveniently, his flat was a brief stroll from the King's Cross station. Once there, he would take the Victoria line southbound to Oxford Circus, change to the Central line, and go westbound one stop, exiting at the Bond Street station. A ten-minute walk down Duke Street and along Brook Street would take Allan directly to the embassy gate located at 24 Grosvenor Square.

As he entered the King's Cross station from the street level this morning, the added presence of extra uniformed police officers and squad cars once again reminded him of the heightened state of security that existed throughout the city. Allan knew firsthand the reason why. He had been directly involved in thwarting a terrorist attack against the U.S. that the Iranians had planned to launch from Cuba. As a result, the probability of retaliation was great. After his harrowing experience in Cuba, he couldn't wait to get back to the relative safety of the embassy and his normal routine. He was a CIA analyst, not a field operative. He was damned lucky to be alive. A chill ran up his spine as he thought about it.

Minutes later, The Tube deposited him at Bond Street. He scurried off the train and took the escalator up, exiting onto the street. He glanced around and noticed several police officers, some with bomb-sniffing dogs, scanning the area for any potential threat. Allan dodged the usual swarm of morning commuters heading into the station as he began walking briskly toward the U.S. embassy.

"Allan! Allan!" a voice behind him called.

Allan turned around to see a middle-aged man a few feet behind him. He held a briefcase in one hand and waved at Allan with the other as he broke into a quick gait to catch up with him.

"Wait! I'll walk with you," the man shouted.

"Oh, great," Allan muttered under his breath. "Just what I need this morning."

Allan didn't stop walking but did slow his pace a bit to allow the man to close the gap between them. Allan turned around again and cringed slightly. As if right out of central casting, the man's outfit seemed to scream, "Hey, I'm a U.S. government agent!" He was dressed in a dark gray suit, black shoes and belt, and white shirt with a conservative blue and white striped tie. The blue in the man's necktie

tie matched his eyes. He had closely cropped curly, sandy brown hair. His name was William Blanton, although he preferred the more familiar "Bill."

Bill Blanton was in his mid-forties. He worked for the FBI as its counterterrorism liaison to the British Security Service, MI5. Since the U.S. continued to share information with the Brits and the French, the FBI tasked Blanton to work closely with MI5, the French Secret Service and Interpol. He worked in the New York field office until his reassignment to the London embassy some six weeks earlier.

Blanton quickly caught up with Allan.

"Jesus Christ! Look at you!" he exclaimed, slapping him on the back a couple of times.

Then he extended his right hand waiting for Allan to respond in kind. Allan hesitated for a moment, but eventually took Blanton's hand and shook it.

*This crazy ritual is more like a frat party than a chance meeting of two civil service professionals*, Allan thought.

"Way to go, hot shot!" Blanton beamed. "How the hell did you manage to do that over there? Was that a stroke of luck, or what?" he asked, referring to Allan's recent involvement in foiling the Iranian-planned Cuba terrorist plot.

Allan shrugged. "Actually, it was pretty easy," he replied nonchalantly. "First, they started shooting at us. The rest is history, as they say." He cast a feigned smile in Blanton's direction.

"Well, you'll have to tell me all about it. I want to hear the whole story from start to finish. I'll bet it's fascinating," Blanton said. "Can we get together for lunch today?"

"I'm sorry, Bill," Allan replied. "Not today. I've got lots of catching up to do."

"Maybe tomorrow, then?" Blanton pressed.

"Nope," Allan shot back. "Flying back to the states in the morning. I'm going to meet my sister, Susan, in Florida for a Caribbean cruise. I figure I need a break after all I've been through."

"Too bad. Guess it'll have to wait until you get back."

"Afraid so," Allan answered, trying to sound disappointed.

By now, they had completed the ten-minute walk from Bond Street to Grosvenor Square and had arrived at embassy gate. Allan glanced around. A lot had changed here during the last few days, too. In addition to Marine guards patrolling the perimeter fence on the inside, the Metropolitan Police had machine gun-wielding officers stationed every thirty feet or so all the way around the block on which the embassy compound was located. Concrete construction barriers in the street turned the wide thoroughfares into narrow, one-way lanes that would make it very difficult for a bomb-laden truck or car to get close enough to the embassy to pose a major threat. Only service or official vehicles could go beyond a certain point, and all underwent a thorough search.

A queue had been set up outside the main entrance for embassy staff and other employees to go through as they entered for work. Official staffers went to the left and local nationals and contract employees to the right. Inside the embassy's main entrance, a small tent-like structure housed screening equipment and the personnel who operated it.

"See you later, Bill," Allan called to his walking companion.

"Okay," he replied. "If things change and you can do lunch, let me know."

Allan forced a smile and nodded. *No way*, he thought. *Something about him rubs me the wrong way.*

Allan made his way in turn to the head of the line and walked through the gate, presenting his State Department ID to the Marine guard standing on the other side.

"Over there, please, Mr. Anderson," he ordered, gesturing toward a small folding table on one side of the tent.

Allan looked around. The equipment reminded him of an airport screening area. Positioned midway between the entrance and the exit was a large, doorframe type of structure that Allan guessed was a metal detector. Piled on another table was a collection of handheld metal detection wands. Dressed in "chocolate chip" camouflaged fatigues and flak vests, six tall, ruggedly built Marines with automatic rifles faced inward and were strategically positioned at even intervals all around the outside walls of the tent. Allan knew why they were there. It was obvious. While there was only one way in, there were two ways out. One was under your own power on your own two feet; the other was in a black body bag. The U.S. government wasn't taking any chances.

After a careful check of his credentials and ID, a Marine conducted a thorough search of Allan's briefcase and directed him to walk through the metal detector. Allan held his breath. Silence.

*Thank God*, Allan thought as he walked out from between the uprights. *I hate those things.* He exited the tent and headed for the main entrance.

Once inside the embassy, the Marine guards greeted him.

"Good morning, Mr. Anderson," one of them said.

Allan looked up and recognized the guard immediately. "Hello, Corporal," Allan replied.

Two guards were on duty at the main security checkpoint this morning. One was a more senior Gunnery Sergeant and the other, a junior Lance Corporal named Chang. The sergeant checked Anderson's official State Department photo ID as Chang examined Anderson's briefcase and had him pass through another metal detector. Next, Corporal Chang waved a radio frequency sniffing wand over Anderson and his briefcase. Chang was checking for electronic bugs or tracking devices surreptitiously planted on Anderson or his belongings.

When given the all clear by Corporal Chang, Anderson waved his ID near an electronic sensor, which would permanently record his name along with the date and time he did so. This was the way the embassy security staff would know who came and went and when they did so. It also gave the security staff the ability to track and pinpoint an employee's location anywhere in the embassy at the touch of a button. Allan clipped his ID badge to his shirt pocket and headed for the elevator.

He pushed the button and stepped inside. Just before the doors shut behind him, he heard a familiar voice shout, "Don't forget about lunch. Call me!"

The elevator doors clunked shut and Allan closed his eyes, slowly shaking his head from side to side. *Yeah, right*, he thought.

# 8. AMPHIBIOUS ASSAULT

*The Persian Gulf*
*South of Basra, Iraq*

The silvery glow of the half-moon that hung high over-head played across the waves of the Persian Gulf south of Basra. With each undulation, the shimmering light revealed dozens of large, hulking forms that hugged the water's surface. A few thousand meters in front of the dark shapes, the sound of breakers rolling into the marshy shoreline broke the nighttime silence. Accompanied by an eerie calm, a light breeze stirred the salty air. It was 03:00 UTC March 20, 2003. The Coalition's main amphibious assault force for the invasion of Iraq was in position and waiting for the "go" order.

Painted up with camo and outfitted with issued load bearing equipment, PO1 Tracy Owens was like the other Navy SEALs sitting in two-dozen CRRCs (Combat Rubber Raiding Craft). Although lightly armed, years of rugged training combined with finely honed skills made these men a formidable fighting force. Three hours earlier, several two-man SEAL swim teams went ashore to secure the beachhead and neutralize any of Saddam Hussein's Republican Guards that happened to be in the vicinity. After the landing zone was secure, Owens and the rest of the assault team in the CRRCs would go ashore to begin the fight.

Despite the events that lay ahead, the night was almost pleasant, with two-foot breakers and eighty-one degree water. Although total darkness with no ambient light from the moon would have been ideal, the wave and water conditions were a plus. The SEALs practiced for such a landing countless times before. In addition to the SEALs, units of the Special Boat Service (SBS) Royal Marines and the British 3 Commando Brigade Royal Marines would support the attack against Iraqi positions on the al-Faw peninsula. Their primary mission was to secure the nearby oil fields and prevent their destruction by the Revolutionary Guards. More importantly, they would secure access to the port of Basra for follow-on forces and equipment.

At 10:15 p.m. EST., President George W. Bush announced in a televised address to the world that he had ordered an "attack of opportunity" against targets in Iraq. That was precisely the moment the two-dozen black inflatable F470 CRRCs simultaneously roared to life and sped away from the safety of the landing craft toward the marshy shore. Each boat was steered by a specially trained coxswain. Sitting next to him was an assistant coxswain who relayed hand signals from the other boats.

Crouched low to minimize their surface signature, the other occupants in each boat, all Navy SEALs, waited for the CRCCs to make contact with the shoreline. PO1 Tracy Owens glanced over his shoulder and watched as their mother ship, the USS *Bataan*, and her nearby landing craft melted into the darkness. He turned around and hunkered down as salt spray from the CRRC's wake splashed onto his goggles. Owens tightened them to keep the salt water from running into his eyes. He squinted and peered into the night in an attempt to distinguish the beach up ahead from the murky water that surrounded the CRRCs.

The boats raced on, the drone of their 65-horsepower motors sounding like a squadron of Sopwith Camels flying in formation. Foam earplugs dulled the roar as Owens continued to scan the horizon, hoping to see the shoreline emerge in the distance. Suddenly, as if by magic, a few meters ahead a faint, but discernable, line separating the black water from the night sky became visible. Owens quickly glanced at the coxswains behind him. The sailor with his hand on the tiller craned his neck to get a better view of the landing zone while his assistant rapidly telegraphed hand signals to the boats closest to them. Owens swiveled around and looked at the two CRRCs on either side of him. He clenched his fist and pumped it up and down in the air a few times. SEALs in the boat on the left and the right quickly acknowledged Owens' gesture. The sixteen men of Golf Platoon, Sea Air Land Team Eight (SEAL 8) were ready.

The steady vibration of the propeller masked the random thump-thump of the reed stalks whacking the underside of the CRRCs. The coxswains did not slow down as the twenty-four CRRCs carrying the SEALs bore down on the beach. Saddam Hussein had ordered the marshes drained in the mid-1990's following the first Gulf War. Now remnants of stout reeds interspersed with new growth poked up through the sand and ohal low water here and there. The roaring outboard motors drowned out the sound of the reeds slapping against the thick, black rubber hulls. Owens stared straight ahead, as the dingy beach came closer. Suddenly, the CRRC lurched as it contacted the shore and slid a few meters onto the wet, sandy landing zone. The coxswain quickly cut the motor and the SEALs flew out of the boat. They fanned out a few meters apart, took up crouching firing positions, and waited. In the still night air, the only sound heard was the gentle lapping of the shallow waves against the reeds and soft sand.

Owens turned to one of his teammates, PO2 Michael Kidd from Eugene, Oregon. Owens gave him a thumbs-up and Kidd returned the gesture. They were best of friends. Owens and Kidd met in BUD/S (Basic Underwater Demolition/SEAL) training at Coronado and went through it together as swim buddies. The rigors of SEAL training had forged a special bond between them. They supported each other through the program from start to finish—the old "cooperate-and-graduate" approach. It had worked. In the three years since BUD/S, they had become inseparable, both on duty and off. Tonight, they would have another opportunity to put the cooperate-and-graduate method to the test.

Before Owens could turn back around, the silence erupted in a blinding flash and a loud explosion. A mortar round had hit the beach one hundred meters to their left. The concussion knocked Owens off his feet and he lay on his back trying to catch his breath. He quickly spit out a mouthful of wet, salty sand and rolled onto his belly with his Colt M4A1 assault rifle trained in the direction of the mortar fire. Owens heard the telltale *ka-whump* as another mortar round left its tube and arced over the reeds and sand toward their position. Darkness made it difficult to pinpoint the launcher's exact position. Although mortars were not accurate weapons, the bang and flash from a nearby impact could still be lethal or, at the very least, cause traumatic injury. The second round landed almost one hundred meters to their right.

*Should we run or stay?* Owens' mind raced as he tried to decide. There was no easy answer. If they stayed put, the Iraqi mortar might find its mark by bracketing fire. If they ran ahead for cover, a sniper could pick them off or another incoming mortar round might tear them to pieces. Owens made his decision.

He signaled to Kidd with his hand, indicating that they would run forward toward the mortar tube. Owens reasoned he would force the Iraqis to make a choice: Adjust their mortar to try to take him and Kidd out, or continue to focus on the larger force that was behind them on the beach. Owens was betting that the Iraqis would choose the SEALs behind him and Kidd. That would give them a chance to get close enough to knock out the mortar tube with hand grenades.

Owens raised his hand and gave Kidd the move out signal. Side by side, they sprinted up the beach toward a clump of reeds where Owens believed the mortar tube was located. They hadn't gone more than ten meters when Owens heard the *ka-whump* of another mortar round leaving its tube. Owens expected the projectile to fly over their heads and land on the beach behind them. They continued to charge the reeds when suddenly, unexpectedly, a large mound of sand and salty earth beneath their feet erupted in a searing flash and deafening explosion. The mortar had found its mark.

Owens came to in a daze and tried to focus. There was a loud ringing in both ears and his vision was blurry. A trickle of blood oozed from his nose. He looked around on the beach near where he was lying, frantically searching for Kidd. About five meters away, a crumpled body lay face down in the sand. Owens began to crawl toward it. With each move, a sharp, stabbing pain shot through his right leg and traveled up his side. Shrapnel had ripped through his thigh just above the knee. He continued to crawl toward his teammate even though the steady jolts of pain made him wince and cry out.

Owens reached the twisted body and rolled it over. It was Kidd. Owens reached for Kidd's carotid artery searching for a pulse. There was none. Desperate, he placed his hand on the other side of Kidd's neck and felt again. Nothing. Owens clutched his best friend's mangled form and hugged it tightly. As he sobbed and heaved, Owens slowly uttered the SEAL code he and Kidd had both sworn to uphold, "Loyalty to Country, Team and Teammate…Teammate…Team—"

That was the last thing Navy SEAL PO1 Tracy Owens remembered about the amphibious assault against Iraqi forces in Basra that night. Medics found him lying unconscious next to Kidd's body. Quickly evacuated to a fleet hospital ship where his condition was stabilized, Owens was flown to Landstuhl Regional Medical Center in Germany and then on to Bethesda Naval Hospital just outside Washington, D.C. for treatment and recovery.

Navy doctors determined that Owens wasn't suffering from Post-Traumatic Stress Disorder, anxiety or depression. In fact, his condition wasn't severe enough to warrant a medical discharge. Instead, they told Owens that the painful memories were something he would have to deal with—perhaps for the rest of his life. After several weeks of close observation and evaluation, his team of doctors declared him fit for duty and he returned to his unit.

Still, Owens' post-combat experience hadn't been an easy one and the specter still haunted him from time to time. True to his namesake—Tracy was of Irish and Gaelic origin, and meant warlike—he was a fighter. That, according to his doctors, was precisely why during the years following that terrible night on the beach at Basra, he had managed to keep his head on straight.

{ ● }

"That will be all for now, Owens," Commander David Atkins remarked. Atkins was a Navy Medical Corps psychiatrist responsible for monitoring the mental condition of SEALs assigned to Owens' unit. Periodic visits with each SEAL—especially combat veterans like Owens—insured that only the fittest SEALs remained in the fighting force.

"I'd say you're continuing to deal with things quite well," Atkins added. "I'm very pleased. Thanks for recounting the beach assault again. I think talking about it helps, don't you?"

Owens nodded. "Yes, but it doesn't make it any easier, doc. Maybe one day I'll be able to put it completely out of my mind."

"Maybe. Time has a way of making things better," Atkins replied encouragingly.

Owens stood to leave. Atkins joined him and they walked toward the door. Atkins turned the handle and smiled at Owens. "See you in a month."

Owens smiled back at Atkins. "In a month," he repeated. Owens swung the door open and added with a wink, "Unless I go to war, of course."

# 9. CAN YOU HELP ME OUT?

*Saint James Square*
*London, U.K.*

Bill Blanton sat quietly on a black wrought iron bench in a distant corner of the park. Arching over him in the late autumn sun, the nearby branches of a bare, gnarly oak tree fanned out above him like the arms of a large patio umbrella. He glanced at his watch. It was a few minutes after two. A half an hour before, he had hopped The Tube to Baker Street and emerged in front of Regents Park. Situated in northwest London, the park was a very popular spot for city residents and tourists alike, and offered a variety of fun and leisure activities.

The famous London Zoo was on its north side while another section boasted a boating lake surrounded by well-manicured gardens brimming with cultivated flowers. The park provided a very tranquil setting for visitors. It was also home to Regents College, which attracted many foreign students. Inside Regents Park was the biggest mosque in London, the London Central Mosque. On Fridays, the main Muslim day of worship, the mosque was usually overflowing with worshippers from all over London and beyond. That was the reason Bill Blanton was here—he had arranged to meet one of them.

Blanton sat on a park bench reading the morning edition of *The Daily Telegraph*. He wasn't sporting his usual dark suit and crisp white shirt. Instead, he wore a blue button down Oxford shirt and lightweight Cardigan sweater complemented by khaki slacks. He had even ditched the trademark sunglasses. Today Bill Blanton looked more like a tourist or Londoner rather than an FBI agent. Moreover, that was the point—to blend in with the dozens of other people who were circulating through Regents Park this afternoon.

Blanton's perch was a stone's throw from the London Central Mosque. From his vantage point, he could see the mosque's gold dome and signature minaret tower protruding above the trees. In front of him, an expanse of soft green grass unfolded like a living room carpet. On either side of his bench, a few remaining clumps of white and pink cleomes mixed with yellow snapdragons reached for the afternoon sky. He looked up from his paper briefly and watched children frolic about as they ran in between the many picnickers whose blankets dotted the lawn.

Blanton gazed at the mosque's distinctive minaret as he recalled comments made at an anti-terrorism task force meeting he attended a week earlier at the U.S. embassy. A senior FBI anti-terrorism official from Washington had called the mosque a recruiting ground for al-Qaeda and the French secret services liaison described it as an incubator for Islamic extremism. As the FBI's counterterrorism liaison at the embassy, it was Blanton's job to obtain information to help thwart an attack against the U.S. or its allies. The U.S. and British governments authorized Blanton to use any legal methods to do so. This afternoon he was going to employ one of the oldest of them—an informant.

Blanton glanced at his watch and then snapped his newspaper open to the "Arts and Features" section again.

He returned to an article that reviewed an upcoming film entitled "The Counterfeiters." Based on a true story, the film detailed how a group of concentration camp prisoners who were all expert forgers or printers, took part in a Nazi operation to produce hundreds of millions of counterfeit dollars and pound notes in a plan to destabilize the Allies' economies.

The article went on to conclude that luckily for Britain and the United States, the war ended before the Germans could flood the European continent with their fake currency. *Nothing new*, Blanton thought as he continued to read. Within the last few years, Iraq, Syria and even North Korea had devised similar schemes. Fortunately, the Secret Service and the FBI were able to uncover them in time and nix the operations before they wreaked havoc.

Blanton turned the page and started to scan the backside for another interesting article but a man's voice speaking in English interrupted him.

"Excuse me. I am from Cambridge and seem to have lost my way. I am looking for the zoo. Can you give me directions, please?"

Blanton lowered the newspaper to see a modestly dressed man who appeared to be in his mid-thirties standing in front of him. The bespectacled man wore a neat but scraggly, black beard. He was dressed in a simply light gray sport coat and matching trousers that ended at top of his plain black shoes. Tucked neatly into the trousers was a white, long sleeved shirt with an open collar. Blanton noted that the man wore no jewelry—not even a wedding ring—even though Islamic law allowed a plain silver one.

Blanton recognized the man as his contact and hurriedly folded the newspaper and laid it on the bench beside him. He sized the man up for a few seconds before he spoke.

"I'm from Liverpool, but I do know the zoo is located on the park's north side. May I recommend the Giraffe House?"

Over the last six months, the two had met dozens times following Blanton's posting to London by the FBI. Even so, they went through the same ritual and verbal exchange every time. Their meetings were hardly clandestine. Rain or shine, they always met at the same bench in this corner of Regents Park on Friday afternoon after midday prayers. Their encounters never lasted long either—usually fifteen or twenty minutes—which was just enough time for a quick exchange of information.

The instructions for the meetings were simple. Blanton's contact would approach him saying he was from Cambridge and was looking for the zoo. Blanton was to respond by telling him that although he was from Liverpool, he knew the zoo was on the north side of the park. Blanton was to recommend the Giraffe House to him. That way, each one would know nothing was out of the ordinary and could be certain there was no compromise. If either of them used a different, pre-arranged phrase, it would signal that it was too dangerous to go ahead with the meeting.

"I was hoping you'd say that," the man replied. "May I sit?"

"Yes. Please do," Blanton said, gesturing toward the other half of the bench. He quickly sat down next to Blanton.

Long before the emergence of al-Qaeda and Osama bin Laden as major threats to the United States, the FBI organized a special counterterrorism office in New York—the Joint Terrorist Task Force (JTTF)—to gather intelligence and investigate early terrorism cases. After 9/11, that effort took on a special significance. As one of the agents first assigned to the JTTF, Blanton found himself swept along during the group's meteoric rise to national prominence.

From the FBI's perspective, perhaps the most significant factor in the progress of investigations and preventing future attacks was the appearance of several al-Qaeda defectors who provided key details on the structure and operation of the terrorist organization. Sitting on a park bench beside Blanton this afternoon was one of them—Jamal al-Afsar, code named "Sinbad."

Over the past several years, Sinbad and defectors like him had provided the FBI and CIA with a treasure trove of information on the inner workings of al-Qaeda. Piecing together the knowledge that they gathered revealed much about its staffing, operations and finances. As former—in some cases, current—associates, they were able to provide operational details regarding planned attacks. Sinbad's value to the FBI and the CIA lay in one simple, yet important, fact: he was one of those current associates.

Sinbad was born to poor Muslim parents in a small mountain village in northwest Yemen in the early 1970's. His mother died when he was a youngster. Sinbad's father was unable to care for him and his many siblings so he enrolled him in the *madrasah* at the local mosque. The *imam* took him in and Sinbad spent his early years learning the Qur'an from wooden tablets. He excelled at his religious studies. The *imam* recognized Sinbad's potential for learning and arranged for him to transfer to another *masadrah* in neighboring Saudi Arabia. There he enrolled in advanced courses, including in Arabic literature and English, as well as science and world history.

Sinbad received a scholarship to King Khaled University in Abha, the capital of Asir province in southwestern Saudi Arabia, and graduated with a degree in Islamic studies. Afterward, he applied for continued study at Oxford University in England. It was there his beliefs began to change. At first, the change was subtle, but after several weeks, it grew more pronounced. Eventually, the change became menacingly radical. Then something happened to Sinbad—something so severe, so frightening, that it choked out the militant feelings that once raged inside him. It was then that he decided to help the Americans by providing information about Islamic terrorists to them. He never revealed details of that incident to Blanton. Likewise, Blanton never asked Sinbad why he had turned against his Muslim brothers. Apparently, it didn't matter, as long as each man got what he wanted from his regular encounters.

Blanton began, "So, what have you got for me today?" He never addressed his contact by his first name or his code name—for security reasons, they both preferred it that way.

"Something very interesting has come to light," Sinbad answered. "I'm quite sure you will find it helpful."

"Really?" Blanton replied curiously. "What might that be?"

Sinbad leaned closer to Blanton and lowered his voice. "The Islamic student discussion group I belong to at Oxford passed out some leaflets at Wednesday night's meeting. I brought one of them for you. It's entitled 'The Rotten Fruits of Democracy.'" He handed it to Blanton.

"What does it say?" Blanton asked. "Is there anything ominous in it?"

"Well," Sinbad replied, "yes and no. It seems to be a very innocuous document at first. But, when it's read through a couple of times, it's easy to see that it's full of hatred for the Kuffaar (non-Muslims) and there's a very clear message in it."

"So, what's the message?" Blanton responded, trying to hide the impatience in his voice.

Sinbad cleared his throat. "It's a recruiting tool. The leaflet labels say the University of Oxford Da'wah (evangelism) Society produces them, but I don't believe they do. They carry a cell phone number to call 'for more information about Islam.'" He paused for a few seconds and then continued. "But, when I called the number, it was answered by someone claiming to be from al-Muhajiroun."

Blanton cocked his head slightly, a quizzical look on his face. "The same al-Muhajiroun organization from Tottenham, north London?" he asked.

Sinbad shifted his position a bit, turning toward Blanton. "Yes, the very same group that aimed to establish a 'global Islamic state' before being banned under the U.K.'s Terrorism Act 2006."

Blanton leaned back against the park bench and contemplated what Sinbad had just told him. He stroked his face and then let out a deep breath.

Throughout the 1990's, thousands of men from around the Muslim world were recruited by organizations like al-Muhajiroun to join the Taliban in its fight against the Northern Alliance in order to establish an Islamic state in Afghanistan. Recruits went to *mujahideen* basic training camps in Afghanistan and Pakistan. Those who excelled became part of the larger jihad that targeted the United States and its allies. Men who accepted that offer received advanced or even specialized training, such as in explosives and bomb making.

"You're right, that is helpful information. What I really need is a name. Do you know who was passing out the leaflets? Is he a student? Does he worship at one of the nearby mosques?" Blanton pressed.

"I'm sorry. I'm afraid I don't know." Sinbad replied.

"Omar Bakri-Muhammed, the cleric originally behind al-Muhajiroun, fled London before he could be arrested is now in hiding somewhere in the Middle East—Lebanon at last report. This development means that someone else has taken over the organization and is trying for a comeback." Blanton explained. "I really need a name. Can you help me?" he pleaded.

"I'll do what I can," Sinbad replied. He stood up and turned to leave. "But I won't make any promises."

# 10. THE FIRST CASUALTY OF WAR

*The White House*
*Washington, D.C.*

The windowless Roosevelt Room across from the Oval Office regularly served as a meeting room for the National Security Council, or NSC. The NSC was the president's principal forum for considering national security and foreign policy matters. The president chaired the National Security Council, so today was no different—except for the crisis the nation currently faced. That was evident by the dozens of uniformed Secret Service agents in body armor and Marines in full combat gear stationed in the corridor outside the Roosevelt Room.

Present for the meeting this morning were the Vice President, the Secretary of State, the Secretary of the Treasury, the Secretary of Defense, Secretary of Homeland Security, and the Assistant to the President for National Security Affairs. The Chairman of the Joint Chiefs of Staff and the Director of National Intelligence were also there along with Paul McCormick, the president's chief of staff. No one was absent and for good reason—McCormick had made that point very clear to the NSC members.

President Brewster cleared his throat and took a sip of water from a small glass before he began. He glanced around the room, studied the group briefly, and then spoke.

"Gentlemen, we are faced with a crisis of unparalleled proportion. Our nation has faced serious threats during its two hundred plus year history, but today's situation, I dare say, is the gravest one we have had to confront yet." Brewster paused and looked around the table at each of the National Security Council members in turn and continued. "We know what *has* happened. To protect our nation and our allies, we must now focus on what *will* happen."

After his introductory remarks, Brewster did not waste any time getting right down to business. He looked directly at the secretaries of defense and intelligence, and then turned to his homeland security chief. Certain that he had gained their full attention, Brewster leaned forward.

"You three are probably in the best position to shed some light on this situation. Let us talk first about threats here at home and then threats abroad. Which one of you would like to begin?" he asked, referring to any possible retaliation by the Iranians.

David Carter, the Secretary of Homeland Security, led off.

"Mr. President, based on assessments by the FBI, CBP and TSA, the threat of an attack inside the U.S. remains high. The good news is that our elevated threat level screenings at all airports for domestic and arriving international flights will in all likelihood prevent a repeat of a 9/11 style attack. The bad news is that other portions of our transportation infrastructure—bridges, tunnels, rails, highways and ports—remain vulnerable."

"So what exactly are you saying, David?" the president asked. "Make it simple."

"I'm sorry, sir," Carter continued, "What I mean is that it will be almost impossible to patrol every bridge, tunnel, rail station and sea port. The risk of an attack on one of those facilities by a single suicide bomber or a series of coordinated attacks by several bombers is high. Given the escalation of events over the past few weeks, I believe it's inevitable."

"Options?" Brewster asked, looking around the table at the NSC members.

Before anyone else answered, Carter resumed the discussion where he left off.

"The best thing we can do, Mr. President, is to continue to conduct thorough pre-boarding screenings for air passengers. We've added more air marshals to domestic and international flights. CBP has stepped up its surveillance of our border with Canada and Mexico. The FBI and ATF are working closely with state and local law enforcement agencies to share information and intelligence. The FBI, along with the CIA and NSA, is continuing to monitor incoming and outgoing phone and electronic communications," Carter explained. "We're doing everything possible to deter, detect and prevent an attack," he added.

"To sum it up then," Brewster responded, "It's not a matter of *if*, but a matter of *when*."

"I'm afraid so, Mr. President," Carter answered. "It's a waiting game now."

Brewster stroked his face a couple of times and ended with a heavy sigh.

"Well, let's turn to threats abroad. Who would like to begin?" he asked.

Secretary of Defense John Ellis spoke up.

"Mr. President," he began, "the Shahab-3 missile poses the most serious threat abroad from the Iranians. It is believed to be single-stage, liquid-fueled, scaled-up version of North Korea's Nodong missile. The Shabab-3 is sixteen meters long and can carry a 1,000-kilogram payload. It has a range of 1,300 kilometers, making it capable of hitting U.S. interests in Iraq, Afghanistan, Pakistan, Kuwait, Saudi Arabia and Israel."

Brewster sat back and let out a deep breath. He looked at his Director of National Intelligence, James Conroy.

"Jim, what do you think about that?"

"Well, Mr. President," he responded, "I have to agree with John. According to our sources, the Shabab-3 would be the most serious threat to our interests in the region. The Iranians have no nuclear capability yet, so the missiles would be fitted with conventional warheads. Although the distance from Tehran to Tel-Aviv is 1,598 kilometers, the Shabab-3's 1,300-kilometer range is still a cause for concern."

Brewster turned to Ellis. "What do you recommend?"

"I would suggest stationing Patriot batteries in all areas within the range of the Shabab-3, including our allies Saudi Arabia, Pakistan, Kuwait and Israel, but particularly in Iraq and Afghanistan," Ellis offered.

"Do we have enough Patriot launchers and crews?" Brewster asked.

"Actually, sir, we don't" Ellis replied. "But, the Iranians don't have that many Shabab-3 missiles, either. I think by carefully analyzing and assessing the threat, we can maximize the protection of our forces and allies with the Patriot batteries that are available."

Brewster turned to Conroy and peered at him over the top of his glasses, "Jim?"

"I agree with John, sir. It's not ideal, but given our anti-missile resources, it's the best we can do—placement based on the highest risk of attack."

Brewster sat back in his chair. It was clear that he was processing what Ellis and Conroy had just told him. After a long moment, he leaned forward and looked at Secretary of State Adrian Ashe.

"Contact the ambassadors of Pakistan, Israel, Saudi Arabia, Afghanistan, Iraq and Kuwait and get their government's permission to station Patriot missile batteries in their countries," he directed Ashe. "Do you anticipate any problems, Adrian?"

No, not exactly, sir," Ashe replied. "But if I may offer a suggestion, perhaps it would play better for the press and world opinion if the U.S. received requests to station Patriot missiles on their soil directly from these countries rather than the other way around. It's a shaded difference, Mr. President, but an important one."

The president leaned forward across the conference table, looking first at Conroy and then at Ellis before turning to Ashe. "Very good, Adrian—I almost forgot—truth is often the first casualty of war."

The president turned and looked at his chief of staff. "Paul, as soon as you hear from Adrian that everything's been arranged with—make that requested by—all of the governments on the list, set up a press conference."

Before McCormick could answer, Brewster stood and started for the door of the Roosevelt Room. "That will be all for now, gentlemen," he said. "I expect updates in writing from each of you on my desk first thing tomorrow morning."

# 11. ON THE ROAD

*Naval Submarine Base*
*Kings Bay, Georgia*

Although it was six thirty-three in the morning, the late November sun hadn't edged above the horizon yet. In the half-light of dawn, a few lingering stars hung in the sky overhead. The steel blue Jeep Grand Cherokee rolled down USS Henry L. Stimson Drive toward the base's main gate. In the back were two large suitcases tossed there a few minutes earlier by the vehicle's driver, Navy Commander William C. Murphy.

Murphy turned toward his traveling companion, Susan Anderson, and smiled. "This is going to be a great trip!" he quipped. "I don't know about you, but I really need this."

She placed her hand on his leg. "Murph, I'm sure you do. That goes for me, too. It's been a rough few weeks for both of us."

He nodded. "It sure has," he sighed.

Murphy slowed the Jeep to a crawl as it approached the main gate. Concrete barricades arranged in an obstacle course fashion partially blocked the exit lane. A similar, but more complex, array stood on the entrance side of the gate. Bluish white light from large, portable floodlight carts illuminated the area. Pairs of Marines in full battledress with M-16's at the ready stood a few feet apart. Humvees and M1117 ASVs flanked the brick and glass guard building. Murphy switched to the parking lights and rolled the driver's side window down.

In recent years, especially after 9/11, security at U.S. military installations worldwide increased. However, due to the heightened risk of a retaliatory attack by Iranian agents or Islamic sympathizers because of the pre-emptive missile strike by the U.S., security at Naval Submarine Base Kings Bay was extremely tight. Part of the reason was simply that it was a U.S. military base. The other, more important reason, had to do with its mission and the fact that the sub responsible for launching the strike against Iran—Murphy's sub, the USS *Wyoming*—was homeported at Kings Bay.

A Marine motioned the Jeep to move forward. Murphy crept about twenty feet until the Marine raised his hand and signaled Murphy to stop. The Marine approached the vehicle while another Marine walked around the Jeep with a flashlight and looked in the windows. Two more guards kept their weapons pointed toward the ground in the direction of the vehicle. Murphy slipped his military ID from the plastic sleeve and held it out for the Marine to see.

The Marine studied it for a few seconds and then looked at Murphy. Satisfied, he bent lower to get a better view inside the Jeep and focused on Susan.

"Wife, sir?" he asked.

"No. Traveling companion—girlfriend, you might say," Murphy responded with a faint smile. "Off on a short holiday together."

The other Marine made his way around the vehicle and gave a nod.

"Very well, sir," the first Marine acknowledged. He handed Murphy's ID back to him. "Drive carefully and have a nice day, sir," he said, popping a crisp salute.

Murphy returned the salute, drove through the gate and turned left onto Crooked River Road. In six miles, they would be joining Interstate 95 for a long, southward trek to Port Everglades.

Murphy looked at Susan. The new security procedures were very rigorous and extremely thorough, even for an old salt like him. However, Susan was new to military life and its routines.

If the gate check experience bothered her, she didn't let it show. Still, he decided to offer an explanation—just in case.

"Pretty tough back there, Susan. But the Marines are just doing their job," Murphy offered. "The new procedures are very thorough—even frustrating—but it helps to keep the good guys in and the bad guys out."

"I know," she replied. "I'm glad security has been stepped up. In spite of what the president said last night, I don't think we've heard the last of the Iranians. It scares me a bit."

Murphy turned to look at her, nodded in agreement, and then quickly changed the subject.

"We'll be near Saint Augustine in an hour or so," he said. "Let's stop there for some breakfast. Sound good?" he asked.

Susan leaned her head against Murphy's shoulder. "Sounds great," she said with a yawn. "Wake me when we get there."

〈 ● 〉

The drive from Naval Submarine Base Kings Bay in Saint Marys, Georgia to Port Everglades near Fort Lauderdale was three hundred and seventy miles. According to the

GPS in Murphy's Jeep, it would take five hours and thirty-nine minutes, not counting stops for gas and food. Their cruise ship, the *Southern Star*, would be boarding between 2 and 4 p.m. and set sail at 5:30 p.m.

*That should work out well,* Murphy thought as he glanced down at Susan. She had been sleeping for almost an hour. It was a few minutes before eight and they were nearing Saint Augustine. Murphy decided this was a good time to stop and get a bite to eat along with some much-needed coffee. He nudged Susan to rouse her from her nap. She opened her eyes and sat up.

"Are we there yet?" she asked with a laugh.

"We passed Port Everglades two hours ago. I decided we'd go to on Key West instead," Murphy teased with a chuckle.

"I know you're kidding," Susan said wryly. "Really, where are we?"

"We're near Saint Augustine. I saw a sign that said 'Food – Next Exit' about two miles back. Are you hungry?"

Susan yawned and stretched. "Hungry, yes. But I think I need coffee more than I need food."

Murphy glanced in the rear view mirror and reached for the Jeep's turn signal lever. "Good. We'll get off at this exit then." The vehicle drifted into the far right lane as it left the Interstate.

"Keep your eyes open for any place that looks good, Susan." Murphy brought the Jeep to a stop at the end of the exit ramp. "I'm hungry and want a real breakfast this morning," he added.

"I guess that means Starbuck's and Dunkin' Donuts are out then, right?" she teased.

"Afraid so," Murphy replied, feigning disappointment.

"Over there, Murph!" Susan shouted. "How about the Plantation House?" She pointed toward a structure adorned with graceful white columns on the opposite side of the highway.

"Great. The Plantation House it is," he answered. The Jeep darted across the street and into the restaurant's parking lot. Murphy maneuvered into one of the spaces and brought the vehicle to a stop. He turned off the engine and looked at his watch.

"Well, Susan," he advised, "Only four and a half more hours to go."

"That makes me feel better," Susan said with a big laugh, "because it could be six and a half!" They both laughed loudly. Murphy put his arm around Susan and pulled her close to him and they strode toward the entrance.

The host promptly seated Murphy and Susan at a table for two in a corner of the dining room. The restaurant was nearly full and the wait staff scurried between the tables to keep up with orders. Not long after they sat down, a young woman in her mid-twenties arrived holding a coffee pot marked "Decaf" in one hand and an unmarked coffee pot in the other.

"Good morning. I'm Mary," she announced cheerfully. "Coffee, anyone?"

"I thought you'd never ask," Susan joked. "Regular, please!"

The server filled Susan's cup and turned to Murphy.

"And you, sir?"

"Certainly. Make mine regular, too," he replied.

Mary filled Murphy's cup and smiled. "I'll be back for your order in a few minutes," she said, and then dashed off.

Murphy picked up a menu and opened it. After a few seconds, he closed it and placed it back on the table.

"That was easy," he said. "It'll be the usual for me—two eggs over easy, corned beef hash, and whole wheat toast. I'm even going to have the grits. I don't get a breakfast like that every morning when we're out on patrol. How about you?"

"My usual, too," Susan beamed. "Blueberry pancakes and a fresh fruit cup on the side."

Murphy snickered. "You call that breakfast? There's hardly anything to it!"

"I've got to watch my girlish figure," Susan chided, wagging her finger at him.

Murphy nodded, not daring not to pursue it any further. "As you wish, my dear."

Susan reached into a large padded mailing envelope that she had carried in from the Jeep with her and removed the contents. She sorted through the pile and quickly pulled a folded four-color brochure from the stack. Susan opened the brochure and scanned it for a few seconds. She looked at Murphy.

"You don't mind if we go over the brochure and itinerary while we're having breakfast, do you?" she asked.

"Not at all," he answered. "It's probably a good idea."

Susan returned to the brochure and began to read the front panel quietly to herself.

"The Sovereign Cruise Line offers 2-night cruise vacations from Fort Lauderdale to Nassau-Paradise Island, Bahamas aboard the SS *Southern Star*. This cruise is the perfect short getaway and makes a great addition to any Florida vacation.

The 2-night cruise vacations leave every other day from Port Everglades at Fort Lauderdale, Florida to Nassau-Paradise Island, Bahamas. Your ship, SS *Southern Star*, leaves at 5:30 p.m. (boards from 2 p.m. – 4 p.m.) on the first evening and spends the next day in the Bahamas before returning back to Florida by 10 a.m. on the third day."

Susan looked up at Murphy and caught his eye. "Hey, Murph, did you know the name of our cruise ship is the *Southern Star?*" she asked. "Sounds a bit enchanting—even romantic—don't you think?" she said, winking at him.

Murphy smiled. "Certainly enchanting, and definitely romantic because we'll make it romantic," he suggested, returning the wink.

Susan studied the brochure again and looked up once more.

"Here's something that will interest you, Captain Murphy," she proclaimed. "And I quote, 'The SS *Southern Star* is a 574-foot deluxe ocean liner with over 288 spacious staterooms. She has a passenger capacity of 512 and carries an international staff and crew of 260. The vessel's cruising speed is 19 knots and her gross tonnage is 21,667 tons.' What do you think of that?"

"It's a relatively small vessel as cruise ships go," Murphy answered. "There are many on the open seas today that carry three or four thousand passengers in one sailing. They're out for days—even weeks—at a time. I think that the *Southern Star's* small size and relatively large crew for her passenger load means we'll really enjoy our three days onboard."

"I agree," Susan said. "Listen to this, 'Amenities include fabulous, live entertainment, fine dining in one of our two special restaurants, a multilevel casino, several cocktail lounges, a card room, full service spa, and deck pool. On-board the SS *Southern Star*, you'll experience the very best with classy ambience, attentive service, exceptional food and deluxe cabin accommodations.'" Susan stopped reading and looked at Murphy. "Welcome aboard!" she giggled.

Their server arrived just as Susan placed the brochure on the table.

"Perfect timing," Mary observed. "Now, what can I get for you?"

# 12. NATURE OF THE THREAT

*The White House*
*Washington, D.C.*

Usually, National Security Council meeting attendees assembled in the Roosevelt Room well ahead of time waiting for the president to arrive. This morning was different. President Brewster sat at the oval oak table long before any of the NSC members arrived. He hadn't slept much and got out of bed a little after 3 a.m. After he had showered and dressed, Brewster took the elevator from the second-floor residence of the White House down to the Oval Office, gathered up a stack of papers, and walked across the hall to the Roosevelt Room.

Brewster preferred to sit at the head of a long, wooden table in front of the fireplace near the doorway. That placed him under an imposing oil portrait of former President Theodore Roosevelt as a Rough Rider on horseback in Cuba. The first to arrive for the NSC meeting was Secretary of State Adrian Ashe. Followed by a senior aide, Ashe entered the Roosevelt Room without knocking. Surprised to see Brewster already seated at the table, he stopped in mid-stride. Ashe cleared his throat and managed to get a get a few words out.

"Mr. President, you're here early this morning," he stammered.

Brewster remained focused on the papers he was reading and did not look up. "Adrian," he acknowledged tersely.

Ashe walked softly toward the table and gently laid his briefcase on it. His aide quietly sat in a chair against the wall. Neither of them said a word. Soon, the other NSC members began arriving. Each walked into the Roosevelt Room and the surprise of seeing the president already seated at the table registered on their faces. As they filed through the door, one by one they offered a greeting of some kind—"Good morning; Hello, sir; Mr. President." Like Secretary Ashe, Brewster's reply to each of them was also curt. Silently, they took up their places around the table.

Sensing it was time to begin, Brewster glanced at his watch. He looked around the room and took special note of those seated at the table.

Dispensing with the customary "Good morning, gentlemen," Brewster began.

"Let's not waste any time and get right down to business. I don't like the recent developments of the past two days any more than you do," he said, referring to public statements by the Iranian government that radical Islamists had declared their intention to harm U.S. interests around the globe and that there was little they—the Iranian government—could do to prevent it.

"So let's cut right to the chase," Brewster continued, "I want a candid, accurate assessment of the threat. No conjecture, no hyperbole, and most of all, no goddamned excuses." The president lowered his head and peered over the top of his reading glasses to emphasize his next point. "Am I clear?" he asked sternly.

Heads nodded as Brewster surveyed the group. "Good," he huffed. He leaned back and clasped his hands. "Well, then, who's first?"

Secretary of Defense John Ellis spoke up. "I'll take it, sir."

"Please, John," Brewster acknowledged, "Go ahead."

"Mr. President," Ellis declared, "I'm confident that our overseas military bases and facilities are relatively well protected against any threat that the Iranians pose, including from Shabab-3 missiles. I have ordered all U.S. installations worldwide to implement Threatcon Alpha procedures in anticipation of an imminent terrorist attack."

Brewster tried to pin him down. "John, you say we're ready for an attack against our military installations by Iran or groups that it sponsors. Will they, in fact, attack our bases abroad? Do you think that's their game?"

"Actually sir, I don't," Ellis responded.

"What then?" Brewster shot back.

Ellis jabbed the tabletop with his index finger to emphasize his point. "I believe the real threat is here at home."

Brewster raised his eyebrows. "You mean inside our borders—somewhere inside the United States?" he scoffed.

Ellis stood his ground. "I'm afraid so, Mr. President. Right here at home—and not our military bases, either."

"Why here, John? Why here and not overseas?" Brewster pressed the defense secretary.

"Two reasons, sir—terror and targets," Ellis replied.

The president leaned forward. "Explain," he demanded.

"It's rather simple, sir," Ellis began. "An attack here similar to the subway bombings in London or the train bombings in Madrid will kill and injure scores of

Americans—the targets—and the results will be chaos and fear—the terror. That's what they're after. It's not necessarily about their ideological cause. It's more about our emotional aftermath."

Brewster sat silently and contemplated Ellis' remarks for a long moment. He leaned back again and looked at the Secretary of Homeland Security.

"David," Brewster asked, "do you agree with John?"

"Yes, Mr. President," Carter replied. "Unfortunately, I do."

Brewster leaned forward again, the worry evident on his face. "How so, David?"

"Their objective is to point out how vulnerable ordinary Americans are right here at home, regardless of how many procedures and measures have been implemented to protect them," Carter explained. "These groups will stop at nothing to turn Main Street into 'maim street.' For them, that's the big payoff."

"Then the threat *is* at home rather than abroad. Is that what I heard?" Brewster asked.

"More specifically, what is the most likely scenario?"

Carter continued, "We believe it will be another hijacked commercial airliner, sir."

"An airliner?" Brewster snorted. "With all of the procedures that have been implemented since 9/11, how the hell are they going to hijack an airliner? Somebody, tell me!" he begged.

David Carter answered. "We don't believe that the hijackers will attempt to seize the aircraft and fly it into a building like they did on 9/11. Again, since their motives are targets and terror, just by creating pandemonium in the cabin, they will succeed." Carter paused before continuing. "So many passengers travel with cell phones, they are counting on someone making a call from thirty-five thousand feet as soon as they commandeer the cabin. The next thing you know, the audio from that cell phone will be broadcast around the world on CNN."

"Hold on a minute!" Brewster snapped. "Earlier you said that they would stop at nothing to turn 'Main Street into maim street,' to use your words. An airliner doesn't fall into that category."

"You're right, Mr. President," Carter acknowledged, "It doesn't. Here's the problem. That terrorist action—the hijacking of an airliner—will be just the beginning. From there, things will escalate. We believe that after this first incident there will also be major attacks on our other transportation systems or in large public places—bombings similar to the ones in London, Madrid, Sydney and Paris."

"If so, what can be done about it?" Brewster asked.

Carter leaned forward and looked directly at Brewster. "Vigilance and deterrence go hand in hand, sir. The TSA is already conducting more rigorous, pre-boarding screenings for air passengers. We have added more air marshals to domestic and international flights." He paused briefly, looked at Conroy and Ellis, and then turned to Brewster again. "Mr. President, we are doing everything we can," Carter continued. "And I do mean everything," he added.

Brewster sat back and let out a deep breath. He looked at his Director of National Intelligence, James Conroy.

"Jim, you've been very quiet this morning. What do you think about David's remarks?"

Conroy rubbed his chin briefly and the spoke. "CBP has stepped up its surveillance of our border with Canada and

Mexico to prevent these cells from infiltrating. The FBI and ATF are working closely with state and local law enforcement agencies to share information and intelligence, particularly that involving the purchase of large quantities of ammunition or bomb making materials. The FBI, along with the CIA and NSA, is continuing to monitor incoming and outgoing phone and electronic communications. We've even brought the National Reconnaissance Office into the loop," Conroy explained. "Like DHS, our agencies are doing everything possible to detect and prevent an attack."

Brewster pushed his chair back from the table. "How come I don't feel convinced? I heard what you all said, but something is missing. And if I'm not convinced, then what about the American people," he asked. "How do you suppose they feel right now? Do you think they're worried?" Before anyone could respond to his question, Brewster answered it himself, "I do."

Brewster sat back in the high-backed, leather chair and clasped his hands. After a long moment, he looked around the table and let out a heavy sigh.

"What is it about these tinhorn regimes—Cuba, North Korea, Iraq and now Iran—that makes them so troublesome, creating crisis after crisis for us and our allies to deal with?" he asked.

"I can answer that, Mr. President." It was Secretary of State Adrian Ashe, who until now had said nothing.

"Please, Adrian. Enlighten us."

"Of course, Mr. President," Ashe responded. "During my many years of teaching at Harvard, I studied events that were considered to be major turning points in world history—assassinations, uprisings and rebellions, the emergence of radical political movements, economic upheavals, military coups, the birth of new religions or cults. They all had one thing in common." Ashe stopped speaking.

Brewster leaned toward him, "And that was?"

Ashe first adjusted his glasses, then looked directly at the president and resumed his discourse. "The founders of every great revolution began by clinging to the power of an idea. In the end, in order to survive when that idea failed, they desperately clung to the only thing they had left—*power*."

## 13. THE DEMON IS BACK

*Naval Amphibious Base Little Creek*
*Near Virginia Beach, Virginia*

Jolted awake by the loud thud of a nearby explosion, Tracy
Owens clenched the twisted bed sheets between his fists.
He sat up quickly and listened for a few seconds. Except
for the occasional sound of a passing vehicle somewhere
in the distance, it was quiet. Owens shuddered and beads
of sweat broke loose from his forehead and fell to his bare
chest. He glanced at the alarm clock on the nightstand
next to the bed. The bright red display said, "3:28 A.M."

"Arrrrgggghhhh!" he screamed.

Owens' head flopped back against the pillows. He
closed his eyes and recounted his last few minutes of
sleep. It was dark and there was wet, salty sand all around
him. He was running—running fast and hard. His heart
was pounding and he was out of breath. Suddenly there
was a loud explosion and a blinding, crimson flash. He
felt himself spinning around and around as he fell to the
ground. Next, Owens saw himself cradling the body of
his best friend and fellow SEAL, Michael Kidd. Owens remembered exactly where he was—on the beach
in Basra during that terrible night. He abruptly opened
his eyes and sat up again. A cold sweat clung to his face
and chest. Owens shook his head and began to sob. The
nightmare was back.

Owens got out of bed and made his way to the bathroom. He flicked the light switch and opened the white medicine cabinet on the wall above the sink. Owens reached for a small, brown plastic pill bottle labeled "Take 1 tablet by mouth one time daily as needed. Sertraline 50mg" and tore it from the shelf. He twisted the cap loose and shook one of the oblong blue tablets into his palm. Owens started for his mouth but stopped midway. He stood motionless and stared at the pill cupped in his trembling hand. After several seconds, Owens slid the tablet back into its plastic container and replaced the lid. He returned the brown bottle to the medicine cabinet and slowly closed the door. Owens hung his head and let out a deep, heavy sigh. He had won another battle with his demon.

( ● )

Naval Amphibious Base Little Creek was a small inlet on the southern shore of Chesapeake Bay located midway between Cape Henry and Norfolk. The Little Creek site offered SEALs varied terrain and settings for training, including sandy beaches, mudflats and woodland training areas. Three miles of beach on the Chesapeake Bay and nearly one mile of beach on the Atlantic Ocean provide a realistic environment for other hands-on training in support of amphibious operations. The parent command of the East Coast SEAL Teams, Naval Special Warfare Group 2, was responsible for their coordination, management and training. As usual, Naval Amphibious Base Little Creek near Virginia Beach bustled with activity this morning.

Little Creek was home to SEAL Teams Two, Four, Eight, Ten, and SEAL Delivery Vehicle Team Two (mini-submarines). At least two of the teams were always forward deployed to support operations in Iraq and Afghanistan. Now, SEAL Team Four was fighting Shiite and Sunni insurgents in Ramadi, Iraq while SEAL Team Ten was in Kabul, Afghanistan slugging it out with the Taliban. Owens' team, SEAL Team Eight, and another team, SEAL Team Two, were both back in the states for some much-needed down time. However, there was never any real R&R. A couple of days with back home family and friends were all any of them could expect. Training and preparing for the next deployment is how they would spend the rest of their stateside time at Little Creek.

PO1 Tracy Owens turned off Cove Road and skillfully maneuvered his shiny black Triumph motorcycle into a parking space near a sign that read "Motorcycle Parking Only" and cut the engine. He popped the kickstand down and carefully leaned the bike to the left until it came to rest. The cycle was his pride and joy. Owens bought it the same day the medical board released him from Bethesda Naval Hospital after he recovered from the injuries he sustained in a mortar attack during the invasion of Iraq in March 2003. The bright, shiny chrome handlebars and exhaust stacks complemented the Phantom black and Sunset red lacquer on the fuel tank and fenders. He removed his helmet and swung his right leg over the motorcycle onto the pavement like a cowboy dismounting his horse. Owens didn't waste any time and quickly made for the front door of Building 3853.

Morning roll call for Golf Platoon, Sea Air Land Team Eight (SEAL 8) was at 0630 hours sharp. Owens glanced at his watch. He still had ten minutes before morning formation. He quickly darted into the locker room and found his locker. He spun the dial and opened the door. Owens placed his helmet on the top shelf and hung his black leather cycle jacket on the hook below it. He closed the locker door and bolted for the main deck.

Owens entered the large open space amid the three hundred or so other men who made up SEAL Team Eight. He made his way over to Golf platoon and took his place in line at parade rest. The platoon chief, a rugged looking E-7, named Hartman, was busily checking faces in the formation against names on a clipboard. Hartman finished and nodded to Golf platoon's CO, Lieutenant Warner, to indicate that all of his SEALs were present. Hartman and Warner pivoted around and came to parade rest.

"SEAL Team Eight, Ah-ten-shun!" the senior enlisted man, Master Chief Howe, barked.

A loud *ta-tunk* filled the hall as nearly six hundred heels came together at once. The men stood rigidly at attention as SEAL Team Eight's commander, a career Navy O-5 named Pierce, marched smartly across the deck and wheeled around coming face-to-face with Howe. Pierce and Howe exchanged salutes and a brief status report. Howe took a step to the right, did an about face, and took a step back to line up with his CO.

Pierce paused for a few seconds then ordered, "Stand at ease!"

Like a perfectly choreographed stage performance, hundreds of legs and arms moved in unison to the more relaxed stance Pierce had commanded.

"Gentlemen," Pierce began, "As you know, three weeks ago the president ordered an attack against

Iran. That attack, carried out by one of our submarines, neutralized the immediate threat. Nevertheless, the risk of a retaliatory strike against America at home and its interests abroad by the Islamic Republic of Iran remains high. The national terror threat level is at red.

Effective immediately, all shore leave is cancelled. No absences will be granted to personnel for anything other than a family emergency, childbirth, hospitalization, serious illness, or bereavement.

All, I repeat all, SEAL Team Eight personnel are subject to twelve-hour alert and twenty-four hour ship out. Have your duffel packed with all first-line gear and ready to go. Make sure that all legal documents and NOK notifications are up to date. Review your immunization record and get any needed boosters by COB today. Ensure that your personal and team weapons are cleaned, inspected and ready for action.

Platoon leaders have additional information that they will brief separately. That is all."

Pierce paused for a few seconds to let his remarks sink in. He then looked left, right, back to the center of the formation, and came to attention.

"SEAL Team Eight, Pah-rade-rest!" he barked. "Ah-ten-shun! Officers, take charge of your platoons," Pierce bellowed next. He spun around and marched off the deck to the right. Chief Howe also spun around and followed, close on Pierce's heels.

One by one, the lieutenants all released their platoons to the senior enlisted man in charge.

"Golf platoon, dismissed," Lieutenant Warner shouted.

The sixteen SEALs in Golf platoon did an about face and broke ranks. They started for the exit when Hartman called out, "Owens, hold up!"

Owens stopped mid-stride and turned to face Hartman.

"Yes, Chief. What is it?"

"Owens, you really look like shit this morning," Hartman remarked. "Didn't sleep well last night?"

"No, Chief," Owens sighed, "I had the nightmare again."

"I was afraid of that," Hartman replied. "I think we need to talk. Let's go to my office."

Platoon Chief Erik Hartman was from New Braunfels, Texas. His blond hair, blue eyes and chiseled face hinted at his family's German heritage. Built like a brick shit house, Hartman excelled as a football player and wrestler in high school—and it was easy. Standing at six feet, three inches, he weighed two hundred and thirty-six pounds—all of it hard muscle. Known to his SEAL teammates as "Rock," Hartman was also handsome and intelligent.

Hartman graduated from high school and enlisted in the Navy. After Basic, he went to Master-at-Arms (MA) training. Because of his weight, size and strength, Hartman was a good candidate for that law enforcement and security specialty. He enjoyed the work and received recognition from his command numerous times for outstanding performance. Hartman often remarked that after three years in the Navy, he woke up one morning to the realization that the Navy needed him to become a SEAL. That is exactly what he did.

Hartman excelled at that, too. He participated in several SEAL-led operations, including Operation Enduring

Freedom in the Philippines in which SEALs were involved in the capture of a key Abu Sayyaf Group (ASG) terrorist leader. In 2006, a U. S. federal court indicted Khadaffy Janjalani, the ASG commander, for his alleged involvement in terrorist acts against United States nationals and added his named to the FBI's Ten Most Wanted Terrorist list.

Days later, an eight-man SEAL strike team that included Hartman landed on Jolo Island in the southern Philippines to hunt Janjalani down. For six grueling days and nights, the SEALs crisscrossed an area of dense jungle searching for Janjalani and always managed to miss him by an hour or two. Eventually, Hartman outsmarted Janjalani and his small band of men and captured the entire group singlehandedly. That campaign earned Hartman the Bronze Star Medal with a "V" for valor "while engaged in an action against an enemy of the United States." Khadaffy Janjalani found out the hard way what the men of SEAL 8 already knew—Rock Hartman wasn't someone you messed with.

Hartman and Owens walked fifty yards down the long corridor and stopped in front of a plain metal door with black letters "SEAL 8 – Golf Platoon – Platoon Chief" on the glass. Hartman opened the door and Owens followed him into the small room. Hartman gestured toward a chair in front of a standard Navy-issue gray metal desk.

"Have a seat."

Owens sat down and Hartman moved to the other side of the desk and sat. He leaned back in his chair and studied Owens for a few seconds before he spoke.

"Okay, Tracy," Hartman said. "Tell me what's going on. How bad is it?"

# 14. CANCELLED FLIGHT

*Washington-Dulles International Airport*
*Dulles, VA*

The hotel shuttle bus jostled along in morning traffic. It carried Allan and other guests for the short twenty-minute ride to Washington-Dulles International Airport. Allan had arrived at Dulles on a British Airways flight from Heathrow the day before. He had selected a late morning departure from London because it would put him in Washington just after 3 p.m. A delayed flight would still have allowed him plenty of time to get to his nearby hotel and settle in. That was important, since he had planned to catch an early morning flight to Fort Lauderdale, where he was to join Susan and Bill Murphy for a three-day cruise to the Bahamas.

Allan was still tired from spending eight hours and fifteen minutes in the air—not to mention getting up early to be at Heathrow three hours before his trans-Atlantic flight's scheduled departure. Because of the heightened tensions between the U.S. and Iran, the TSA ordered increased security measures—including tighter baggage and passenger screenings—for all inbound flights to the U.S. At Heathrow, long queues began at the ticketing kiosks and snaked through the terminal to the screening checkpoints. As countless passengers filed past, teams of rifle-toting soldiers and armed Metropolitan Police officers had scanned the crowds and kept a watchful eye. Even with these extra precautions, Allan's flight departed London on time.

The hotel shuttle bus dropped Allan off at Dulles' main terminal just before 10 a.m., nearly two hours before his flight's scheduled departure time of noon. Allan had flown in and out of Dulles numerous times before and was very familiar with the terminal's layout. Like Heathrow, heightened check-in security procedures were evident here, too. Allan noted that there was a much larger police presence, including the addition of K-9 units—presumably to detect explosives in carry-on luggage rather than smuggled contraband, such as cocaine or marijuana.

Just inside the terminal's entrance, Allan stopped and grabbed his cell phone off his belt and hurriedly dialed a number. A few seconds later, a woman answered.

"Hey, Sis!" he exclaimed, "How are you?"

He listened for a moment and then replied. "Right, I arrived yesterday afternoon, just like my message said."

Allan listened again and responded. "No, that's fine, Susan. I knew you were getting up early to begin the drive. That's why I didn't want you to call me last night. Sure, I'm glad you understand."

The exchange between Allan and Susan continued for a few more minutes. "I'm at Dulles and just about to check-in. Where are you? What's that? Near Saint Augustine. You just stopped for breakfast."

"My flight leaves at noon and I should be arriving in Fort Lauderdale a little after 2:30 p.m. I can be at the port by 3." Allan told her.

"Yes, I know. Boarding cutoff time is 4 p.m.," he repeated.

"How's Bill?" Allan continued. "Good, I'm looking forward to seeing him, too."

"All right. Drive safely. See you in a few hours," he smiled.

"Love you, Sis!"

Allan clipped the cell phone back on his belt. He extended the handle to his large bag, slung his carry-on's strap over his shoulder, and began to walk toward the ticketing area. Allan scanned the signs above the check-in desks for one that read "Mid-States Airlines." He saw a sign a few yards ahead with a logo that consisted of the airline's name in large blue letters superimposed across big silver wings. Allan promptly walked to the queue, checked bag in tow, where two-dozen passengers were in line ahead of him. He noted that the four Mid-States check-in stations were all staffed and the line seemed to be moving, albeit slowly.

When it was Allan's turn, a ticketing agent motioned him to approach the counter. He tugged on his large piece of luggage and stepped to the position. Used to the routine, Allan stood his wheeled bag upright and dropped his carry-on to the floor. He reached inside his sport coat and retrieved his flight itinerary and ticket receipt from the pocket. Although Allan had paid the fare from Dulles to Fort Lauderdale online before leaving London, he was not able to get an e-ticket and print a boarding pass. Due to the new security procedures, he was required to present himself at Dulles and show a type of government photo ID in order to get the actual ticket issued.

The ticketing agent, who was a hefty woman in her mid-fifties, looked like she could have been a prison matron. She wore a dark blue skirt and a white blouse topped off with a red, white and blue scarf around her neck. The silver nametag on her blouse said, "Martha Hale." Her stern face showed no emotion, not even after Allan managed a cheery "Good Morning." She was all business.

"Name and destination?" she demanded.

"Anderson, Allan Anderson. Fort Lauderdale," he replied. He held his itinerary out for her.

She glanced at it briefly, typed a few keystrokes, and then looked up at him. "I show you booked on Mid-States Flight 340, departing at 11:58 a.m.," she said.

"Yes, that's correct," Allan confirmed.

"ID please," she ordered.

Allan presented his U.S. passport to the agent. She took Allan's passport from him, jotted down some information, and then handed it back.

"Number of bags checked through to Fort Lauderdale?" she asked.

Allan placed his luggage on the scale. "One."

Martha Hale looped a destination tag around the bag's handle and moved it to the conveyor belt behind her. From there it would descend to the screening area below the terminal where it would be x-rayed, pass through an explosives detection chamber, and then on Mid-States Flight 340. Martha stapled Allan's luggage claim stub to his boarding pass envelope and handed it to him.

"Flight 340 departs from Gate B14. The passenger screening area is to your left. Thank you for choosing Mid-States Airlines for your air travel today, sir. Have a pleasant day," Martha said with a barely perceptible smile.

Allan smiled back. "Thank you."

Constant reminders of the increased security threat blared through the terminal's public address system. These warnings repeated every few minutes and sounded like a broken record. "Ladies and gentlemen, the Transportation Security Administration would like to remind you…Do not accept items or carry-on luggage from strangers… Monitor your carry-on luggage and personal belongings at all times…Report any suspicious activity to the nearest law enforcement officer…"

During the walk to Concourse B, Allan noted there were several two-man teams of heavily armed police officers dressed in combat boots, body armor, and black fatigues stationed every few yards apart. *They look like they're ready for anything*, Allan thought as he strode past.

Allan negotiated the maze of stanchions and nylon webbing that led to the checkpoints. Every second or third passenger set off the alarm because of the lower screening device sensitivity that reflected the increased threat. Allan managed to get through without setting off any buzzers or lights. He made his way to gate B14 from the main terminal via the moving sidewalk. It had taken him fifty minutes to get this far. Allan noted that Mid-States Flight 340 showed "On Time," and would begin boarding in thirty minutes.

Allan sat down, leaned back, and snapped the morning newspaper open. Front-page headlines cited the increased tensions between the U.S. and Iran. Lately, especially after the pre-emptive strike against Iran by the U.S., it was difficult to pick up a newspaper and not see articles devoted entirely to that subject. Allan scanned the captions one by one, "U.S. Airlines Step Up Security Checks," "Nation On Alert," "Government Tracks Terror Suspects," and "Experts Question Country's Anti-terror Preparedness." He settled on a topic and began to read.

# AN EYE FOR AN EYE

Allan was still reading front-page articles when the gate attendant's voice came over the public address system. "Ladies and gentlemen, this is a boarding announcement for Mid-Sates Airlines Flight 340 with service to Fort Lauderdale. At this time, we invite all passengers traveling with small children or special needs to board now. We would also like to welcome our Elite Status passengers to board at this time as well. We will begin boarding by rows in just a few minutes. Thank you."

Hearing his row number called, Allan made his way the gate. He showed his ID and boarding pass to the gate agent. She waved him past and he started down the jetway. Flight 340 was a Boeing 737 and Allan had a window seat near the back of the airplane. He much preferred an aisle, and something farther forward. However, by the time he purchased his ticket, there were only a few seat choices left. He was stuck in the very last row on the right side, seat 31F. The only good thing about it—if there was anything good about being in the very last row—is that there were only two seats on the right side of row 31, compared to three seats for every other row section.

Allan drew closer and noted that a large man with a crew cut already occupied the adjacent aisle seat, 31E. Allan smiled and said, "31F." The man stood and stepped into the aisle. "Thanks," Allan quipped. He stuffed his carry-on bag in the overhead compartment, slid into 31F, and sat down. He fastened his seatbelt and went back to reading his newspaper. Other passengers continued to fill up the seats all around them. A few minutes later, the flight attendants began making cabin announcements.

The 737 bucked slightly as the tug began to push it back from the jet way onto the ramp. Allan looked out the window and watched an orange-vested wing walker guide the Boeing 737 backward away from the concourse. The tail of the airplane swung ninety degrees to the right and the jet came to a stop. The overhead lights flickered off and then quickly back on as the pilots started the aircraft's engines.

Allan turned to the man seated next to him and noted that he was carefully studying every passenger now aboard the airplane. Allan decided to strike up a conversation.

"Hi, I'm Allan Anderson. I didn't get your name."

The man was dressed in a sport coat, open collar shirt and slacks. He glanced at Allan briefly but did not extend his hand. "Jones, Jack Jones."

Before Allan could respond, the man again focused his attention on the passengers. The Boeing 737 began to roll across the ramp and the flight attendants began the litany of cabin safety announcements.

Allan tried once more, "Do you live in D.C.?"

Without looking at Allan, Jones replied, "I do. Like most people here, I work for the government."

Allan continued, "So do I. But I work overseas."

"State Department," Jones said matter-of-factly.

"Right," Allan acknowledged. "How'd you know?"

Just a hunch," Jones replied.

"Good guess! And you?" Allan asked.

"Nothing important—a low-level Justice Department job," Jones shared.

"Been there long?" Allan wondered.

Jones turned toward Allan, "Almost five—"

He cut his answer short when the airplane abruptly swerved off the taxiway and zigzagged to a stop. Jones remained seated. Squinting, he quickly scanned the cabin fore and aft and then crouched down to get a good view out the cabin windows. Allan peered out his window and could tell that the 737 had stopped on the ramp directly in front of the control tower.

He turned to Jones, "Do you think everything's okay?"

Jones kept his eyes riveted on the forward part of the cabin and hesitated before he answered. "I'm not sure, but I hope so," he replied in a hushed voice.

Allan tried to sound upbeat. "Maybe it's a mechanical problem and we'll be on our way as soon as it's fixed."

Suddenly, a woman's loud, piercing scream drowned out the murmur of other voices. Startled, Allan looked up to see a young man—probably in his late twenties—standing in the aisle near the mid-cabin exit row holding what looked like a cell phone in his upraised hand. This man had black hair, dark sunken eyes and a swarthy complexion. The clothes he wore were nondescript—jeans and a plain T-shirt.

A fearful thought raced through Allan's mind, *Jesus H. Christ! He has a bomb!*

Allan continued to watch him when, without warning, another man in the front of the cabin—this one dressed in a black windbreaker—stood up and turned to face the agitated man with the cell phone gripped tightly in his hand.

Another though flashed through Allan's mind, *Goddamn! There are two of them!*

Allan caught movement out of the corner of his eye. He glanced down and saw Jones reaching inside his sport coat with his right hand. Allan cocked his head slightly to get a better view. Jones started to withdraw a pistol from its holster.

"S-h-h-i-i-t!" Allan exclaimed in a barely audible whisper. Jones didn't look at Allan—perhaps he hadn't heard him. *Maybe he was lying earlier—maybe he's one of them, too*, Allan thought.

The man in the very front of the cabin took a couple of steps toward the passenger with the cell phone.

"Stop! Stay where you are or I'll blow us up!" he shouted in heavily accented English. "Don't come any closer! I am not afraid to die!" The passenger waved the cell phone back and forth and the man froze.

Allan held his breath and glanced at Jones, who focused on the passenger with the cell phone. Jones had worked the automatic pistol out of its holster and he gripped it in his right hand.

*What's he going to do?* Allan wondered. *Is he going to kill someone?*

He waited for Jones' next move. Allan's muscles were tense and his breaths were shallow. Perspiration beaded up on his forehead. He tried to swallow, but his mouth and throat were dry.

Suddenly, the man in the front of the cabin took another step toward the passenger with the cell phone. As soon as he noticed the movement, the apparent hijacker turned his head toward the man in the windbreaker, and opened his mouth to speak. Before the thug could utter a word, Jones sprung to his feet, leapt into the aisle, and leveled his weapon. A loud, muffled crack accompanied a bright orange flash from his pistol. A clean shot to the head had found its mark. The passenger with the cell phone fell backward and crumpled lifelessly to the floor. Immediately, dozens of panic-stricken passengers crouched low in their seats and began to scream.

Weapons in one hand, and badges held high in the other, Jones and the man in the windbreaker both shouted, "Federal Air Marshals! Federal officers! You are safe! Stay calm! You're all safe!" Jones quickly surveyed the passenger compartment looking for any accomplices while the other air marshal quickly advanced on the terrorist to make sure he was dead and no longer a threat to anyone onboard.

Allan's head slumped to his chest and he let out a deep breath. Beads of perspiration plopped into his lap. He was in shock from what he had just witnessed and began to feel queasy. He reached into the seat pocket in front of him and after a brief search, found what he was looking for. Allan removed the long, narrow paper bag, quickly opened it, cupped it over his mouth, and vomited.

# 15. A LONG DAY AHEAD

*The White House*
*Washington, D.C.*

Although he normally knocked before entering the Oval Office, Paul McCormick burst through the door, a plain-clothes Secret Service agent on his heels.

"Mr. President!" he shouted.

Brewster looked up, startled by the intrusion. "Yes, Paul. What is it?"

McCormick tried to catch his breath. "Sir, there have been numerous incidents at major airports around the country. All have occurred within the last twenty minutes."

Brewster put his pen down. "What kind of incidents, Paul?"

McCormick quickly glanced at a single sheet of paper inside a folder stamped "Urgent Threats" in big red block letters and then blurted out the answer. "Involving commercial airliners, sir," he panted. "Several carriers reported that passengers—either foreign nationals of Middle Eastern descent or U.S. citizens with ties to the Middle East—interfered with the operation of those flights on the ground."

Brewster leaned forward. "Go ahead, Paul. What are the details as you know them?"

McCormick stepped closer to the president's desk. "According to reports from the TSA and Federal Air

Marshals Service, lone passengers on commercial flights originating from six east coast airports—Boston, New York, Pittsburgh, Dulles, Atlanta and Miami—created disturbances in the cabin by standing up while the aircraft were taxiing for takeoff from the terminal. These passengers did not comply with instructions from crewmembers or Federal Air Marshals to remain seated. In all cases, the disruptive passengers held a cell phone in their hand during the disturbance, perhaps suggesting that it was a bomb detonator. Air marshals shot and killed one. The other five have been apprehended and are in custody."

"Any airborne threats or anomalies?" Brewster probed.

"None that we know of. As a precaution, the FAA has implemented a ground stop at all U.S. airports. We alerted the European Aviation Safety Agency and aviation authorities elsewhere around the world. Additionally, air traffic controllers sent coded transmissions to the crews of all airborne domestic flights that advised them to take extra precautions both in the air and on the ground."

"Good. What about our air defenses, Paul?"

"The chairman of the JCS has informed us that F-16 interceptors have been scrambled and will be providing high cover around those airports where these incidents occurred. Additionally, the—"

"Stop right there, Paul," Brewster interrupted. He leaned back and closed his eyes.

"Is everything all right, sir?" McCormick asked.

"Give me a moment to think," Brewster replied. After a few seconds, he opened his eyes and sat upright.

"Before we go any farther," he suggested, "Let's get David Carter on the phone."

"I agree, sir," McCormick replied, "Maybe DHS has some additional information they can pass along."

"Oh, and get my press secretary geared up, too. I want to be ready to make a statement," Brewster added.

McCormick reached for the speakerphone on the president's desk and lifted the handset. He began to speed dial Carter at DHS but was interrupted by a loud knock at the Oval Office door. Before Brewster could respond, the door flew open and six heavily armed, uniformed Secret Service officers streamed into the room. One ran around the president's desk to the window that faced the Rose Garden and South Lawn. He quickly drew the heavy, deep blue, floor length drapes shut. Another officer joined him at the window. Weapons at the ready, two more men took up positions near the door. The remaining pair quickly rushed to the center of the Oval Office and flanked the president on both sides.

"What's all this about?" Brewster asked. "Is there something else going on that I should know about?" he demanded.

"Not at all, sir," the squad leader answered, "Just a precaution until we have a better understanding of the situation."

The plain-clothes agent cocked his head, put his finger to his radio earpiece and listened for a few seconds.

He straightened and addressed the president, "I've just received a communication from the chief of the White House security detail, Mr. President. These measures are necessary to insure your safety until we have clarity. I hope you understand."

Brewster lowered his head and rubbed the back of his neck. He looked up and let out a deep breath. "Of course."

McCormick removed the handset from the speakerphone again and pushed the speed dial button labeled DHS. On the second ring, a voice answered with, "Carter here."

"David, Paul McCormick. I'm with the president in the Oval Office. I'm going to put you on speaker."

He pushed the button labeled Speaker and returned the handset to its cradle.

"You're aware of the commercial aircraft incidents?" McCormick probed.

"Yes. My staff and I have been following it from here," Carter replied.

"What can you tell us that we might not have gotten from TSA and the FAA?"

"Reports are still coming in from the TSA field supervisors at the airports involved,"

Carter explained, "But from what we can tell, these incidents appear to be part of a coordinated operation."

The president jumped into the conversation, "How so, David?"

"Well, sir," Carter went on, "All of the flights were scheduled to depart from major east coast airports at twelve noon, give or take a couple of minutes. They all involved a single male passenger in his mid-twenties. The perpetrators were all of Middle Eastern descent—foreigners or U.S. citizens with ties to the region. Each of them waved a cell phone wildly about during the incident, suggesting they had a bomb. However, law enforcement didn't find evidence of explosives or weapons on them or in their luggage. Federal Air Marshals shot and killed a perpetrator who was aboard a flight departing from Dulles. The rest—five in all—were subdued by air marshals and are in custody."

Brewster pressed his Homeland Security chief for more information. "What is the FBI's take on this, David? Was it a real threat or was this a just dry run designed to test our procedures and response? Or instead, was its purpose to rattle an already nervous public and ratchet up anxiety?"

"That's a good question, Mr. President. It might be one, the other, or even both. Interfering with a flight crew is a federal offense under the Air Piracy statutes, and special agents from the Bureau just arrived on site and are interrogating the men now. At this point, though, it's simply too early to provide you with a definitive answer."

"Let me be more specific," Brewster shot back. "Will there be a second wave today or perhaps tomorrow? Will they try it again, but with real explosives the next time?"

There was a brief pause before Carter responded. "That's what the Bureau's agents will be trying to find out, Mr. President. I'm afraid that we don't really know. My personal opinion is that it's an attempt to rile the public and nothing more," he offered. "I think the Iranians are behind it—they are still reeling from the missile attack of a few weeks ago. However, I don't believe they're foolish enough to order their foot soldiers to hijack one of our airliners or worse yet, blow one up."

"Look, goddammit," Brewster fumed, "I'm sure this story is already being aired on CNN. The public will be looking to us for answers and more importantly, for some assurances that the skies are safe for air travel. I want you to put every available DHS resource on this immediately. First, we need to know whether this is a credible threat or not. Secondly, in any case, find out who is behind it. Last, tell me if can we expect more of these kinds of incidents or—heaven help us, something much worse—in the coming days? Work your people around the clock, if that's what it takes. Am I clear on that, David?"

"Yes, Mr. President, quite clear," Carter acknowledged. "Will there be anything else, sir?"

"No, David. That will be all."

Brewster punched the speakerphone off and the line went dead.

He turned to McCormick, "Get Conroy over here. Have him bring a couple of his top intelligence staffers with him. And cancel my schedule for the rest of the day."

McCormick nodded. "Right away, sir."

Brewster stood and made for a side door, the two heavily armed uniformed Secret Service agents close behind. "I'll be in there," he announced, referring to the small dining room next to the Oval Office, the only room in the West Wing with a television set. "I want to see what CNN is saying about all of this."

McCormick watched the trio's exit, Brewster in the lead. "Very well, Mr. President."

Brewster took a few steps and stopped. He turned to face McCormick. "Oh, and one more thing, Paul," he snapped, "Don't plan anything for the rest of the day. I'm afraid it's going to be a long one for all of us."

# 16. A CHANGE OF PLANS

"The traffic on I-95 is pretty light for a weekday," Murphy observed.

Susan was quick to agree, "Yes, and I'm glad. Many people are still at work, so I'm sure that the rush hour volume will be heavier. We'll already be at the port by then."

"Suits me just fine," Murphy quipped.

Susan glanced at the clock on the Jeep's dash. It read 12:48 p.m. "I wonder how Allan's doing—he should be in the air right now," Susan noted. "He said his flight would arrive at 2:30. I think a cab ride from the airport to Port Everglades will take about ten minutes."

"Assuming his luggage made it on the airplane, we will probably see him there at—say around three," Murphy added.

"Where are we now?" Susan asked. "How much longer?"

"According to the GPS, we've just passed Stuart," Murphy replied. "It says we have another hour to go. Looks like we're right on schedule."

"It's the top of the hour. Mind if I get some news?" Murphy asked.

Susan reached for the Jeep's radio. "Of course not."

She turned the knob, selected AM, and pressed Search. Instantly, the sound of a radio station blared through the speakers.

"Good afternoon, I'm Russ Smith at the news desk in Miami," the announcer began. "Here are the latest world and national headlines.

Today, the government of Iran announced that recent economic sanctions imposed by the world community following the U.S. missile attack against it have provoked outrage in the Middle East, fueling a new wave of Islamist anger. IRNA, the Iranian news agency, quoted President Azar Farahani as saying 'there is little his government can do to prevent retaliatory attacks against American interests around the world, including on the U.S. mainland.' So far, there has been no reaction from the State Department of White House.

In other news, the Department of Homeland Security is continuing to investigate the disruption of commercial flights at six major east coast airports earlier this morning. According to a department spokesperson, after the planes began taxiing for takeoff, a lone passenger on each flight stood up, shouted wildly, and waved a cell phone—thought to be a bomb detonator of some kind.

The incidents, which occurred at airports in Boston, New York, Pittsburgh, Dulles, Atlanta and Miami, appear to have been coordinated to coincide with a twelve-noon departure time. According to the Department of Homeland Security, the men were all either killed or apprehended by Federal Air Marshals and undergoing questioning by authorities now. The spokesperson reported that none of the passengers or crewmembers on the affected flights suffered any injuries during the

incidents. We will continue to follow this developing story for you.

Keep it here for more news right after this break…"

Susan reached up and snapped the radio off. She turned
to Murphy, her face ashen white.

"What time was Allan's flight scheduled to leave Dulles? Didn't he say 11:58 a.m.?"

"Yes, I think that was it," Murphy responded. "Do you
suppose his flight was one of those affected?"

"God, I hope not," Susan stammered. "He's probably in
the air. Otherwise he would have called."

"Not necessarily," Murphy suggested. "If he happened
to be on one of the affected flights, there's a very good
chance that air marshals ordered all of the remaining
passengers to surrender their cell phones during the incident—just in case there was a bomb on board. That would
prevent an accomplice from detonating it."

"What does that mean, Murph?" Susan asked. "If he
can't call us, how will we know?"

"Unfortunately, Susan, until we actually see him at the
port or he gets a chance to call us from Dulles, we won't."

Susan slumped down in the seat. "If the flight was cancelled, he won't make the sailing, Murph."

"Yes, Susan," Murphy replied, "I know."

Susan looked out the window and said nothing for the
last thirty miles of their trip. Murphy didn't say anything
either. Near the Fort Lauderdale-Hollywood airport, he
took the exit for I-595 and followed ramp onto the east-
bound spur. According to the GPS, they were less than
three miles from Port Everglades. It was 1:01 p.m. but
Murphy decided against turning on the radio to get an

update on the attempted ground hijackings. I-595 ended and became Eller Road, a two-lane divided highway that led to cruise ship passenger terminals. Murphy maneuvered the Jeep along the access road toward the entrance gate.

"Hey, look at that," Murphy remarked, referring to a long line of brake lights ahead. "Must be about twenty cars in front of us."

A slow flying police helicopter swooped low overhead and circled back toward them.

"What do you suppose is going on?" Susan asked. "Do you think it's related to the commercial airline incidents?"

"I'm sure it's just routine," he suggested. "Similar to what we're doing back at Kings Bay. Remember this morning?" He brought the Jeep to a standstill.

"I hope so," Susan responded glumly, "I don't want anything else to pop up and ruin our trip."

Murphy and Susan made it to the entrance gate twenty minutes later. Murphy noted there were four Broward County Sheriff's patrol cars parked near the gate—two outside the fence and two inside. A pair of deputies stood near each car. Armed with shotguns, they wore bulletproof vests. Murphy saw a deputy with a leashed dog—a German Shepard—next to the gate. He was wearing thick, bulky gloves that extended to his elbows. In addition to a big, bulky vest that resembled a baseball plate umpire's, he wore a helmet with a Plexiglas face shield.

Susan saw him too. "Why is the canine officer dressed that way?" Susan asked curiously.

"I think he's part of the bomb squad—he and the dog are searching vehicles for explosives," Murphy surmised. Susan didn't respond.

An armed port security guard motioned them to stop. Murphy rolled down the driver's window.

"Good afternoon, sir. Ma'am," he said, bending down to see Susan. "What cruise line are you departing on?"

"Sovereign Cruise Lines. The SS *Southern Star*," Murphy answered. "She sails at 5:30."

"May I see your tickets and some identification—preferably a passport—please?" the guard demanded.

Susan reached down and grabbed the large envelope on the seat beside her. She opened it and fished around for a few seconds. She produced two passports along with tickets for the SS *Southern Star* that the cruise line had mailed her. She handed them to Murphy, who handed them to the guard. He scrutinized the passport photos and then stared Murphy and Susan for a few seconds. He studied the tickets and after long moment, tucked them in the passports.

"I'd like you to pop the rear hatch, sir. Then I'd like both of you to step out of the vehicle and stand over there." He pointed to a pair of orange traffic cones roughly ten feet from the Jeep.

Murphy glanced at Susan first, and then opened the door and stepped out. Susan opened her door and climbed out. They both made their way over to the traffic cones. The deputy with the German Shepard approached the Jeep. He led the dog around the vehicle first in one direction, and then another. Each time, he paused near the rear hatch, where the luggage was. He walked over to the gate and ordered the dog to sit and stay. Then he wheeled a large device that looked like an automotive floor jack up to the Jeep. It had lights and large, round mirrors on it so he could inspect the underside of the vehicle. He pushed it under the Jeep and rolled it around—first near the front, then the sides, and finally, the vehicle's rear end.

He pulled the device out from under the Jeep and walked over to his dog. "It's okay," he called to the guard.

The guard motioned Murphy and Susan toward him.

"Thank you, sir. You may reenter your vehicle and proceed to the mid-port garage for parking. Your ship will depart from terminal number twenty-two. Follow Eller Drive straight ahead. It turns into South East 10th Avenue. You will see a parking garage on the left and the terminal will be in front of you at the circle. Drop your bags off first and then park. It will be much easier. Have a nice trip."

Murphy closed the rear hatch. He and Susan climbed back in the Jeep and crept thought the gate.

"Boy," Susan exclaimed, "For routine, that was pretty damned thorough!"

Murphy shook his head. "I have to agree, Susan. That's much tighter security than what we experienced at Kings Bay this morning."

Susan turned to Murphy, "Do you—"

The ring of her cell phone interrupted her.

"Hello, this is Susan."

"Allan!" she shouted, "Where are you? Tell me you're in Fort Lauderdale."

Murphy looked at Susan. The expression on her face changed to a frown as she listened.

"I'm sorry, Allan. So sorry," she sighed. "Bill will be disappointed, too."

"Yes, I know," she said, "It could have been much worse—you could have been hurt or—"

She didn't finish the sentence. "Thank God you're all right. That's important."

She listened and then said, "Okay, we'll call you to-night. You must be tired, so it will be early. I love you, too. Bye."

Murphy was just pulling up to the front of terminal twenty-two. Susan laid her cell phone on the seat. Murphy parked the Jeep near the curb between some other vehicles in the loading zone and turned off the ignition. He leaned over, put his arm around Susan's shoulder and gave her a gentle squeeze. She looked up at him, sadness in her eyes.

"I'm sorry, Susan," he sighed, "It's not a good way to start a weekend get-away, is it?"

She shook her head, "Uh-uh."

"At least Allan's okay," he added. "One less thing to worry about, right?"

Susan nodded and he gave her another squeeze.

Murphy reached for the Jeep's door handle. "Well, let's unload the bags. Now that we've come this far, we don't want to miss the *Southern Star* when she sails, do we?"

Susan reached for the other door handle with a sigh. "I hope nothing else goes wrong," she groaned.

# 17. NOBODY'S HOME

*Camden Town*
*London, U.K.*

An ordinary black car came to an abrupt stop in front of the modest building at 814 Argyle Street in Camden Town. Two men climbed out and hurried to the entrance. Each was dressed in a dark suit and wore a double-breasted Gabardine trench coat over it to help ward off the November drizzle. At the top step, both stopped, and the driver hastily surveyed the street. Satisfied that no one had followed them, he nodded and the pair quickly entered. Once inside they stamped the rain off their overcoats and rubbed their hands together to shake the chill.

"Lovely weather isn't it, Travis?" the driver quipped, a tinge of irony in his voice.

"Ah, William, so it is," he replied with a twisted smile. "I believe it was Browning who wrote, 'Oh to be in England now that April's there.' Trouble is, winter's nearly upon us and April's been with us for most of our summer."

"Can't change it, now can we?" Travis shrugged. "All right then, let's get on with the job."

William nodded in agreement, "Sure thing."

Number 814 Argyle Street was a two-story apartment building that contained four units—two flats were located on the first floor and two on the second. The men walked down the hallway and stopped in front of the door marked

"2." All of the tenants were single professionals who worked day jobs, so there was little chance that anyone would be home or might return soon.

Travis pointed toward the entrance. "William, keep an eye out. Let me know if you see or hear anything at all," he said in a hushed voice.

Travis turned his attention to the door lock. It was a typical arrangement consisting of a handle with an inset lock and a separate deadbolt located about two feet above it. First, he tackled the handle. He produced a small, flat metal box from his raincoat pocket. Travis opened the box and carefully studied the lock and keyhole. After a few seconds, he selected one of the master keys and worked it into the lock. He bumped the handle a couple of times with his fist to jiggle the pins into position. Travis turned the key and heard the tumbler pins click as the lock gave way.

"One down and one to go," he said softly.

William kept his eyes focused on the entrance and did not turn to look at Travis, but acknowledged with a soft-spoken, "Good."

Travis quickly turned his attention to the deadbolt. That would be a more formidable challenge. If he was not able spring the deadbolt, they could not gain access to the flat. Worse, there was no way for Travis to relock the bottom one again—although the apartment's owner probably would not notice.

Travis examined the deadbolt, looking closely at the keyhole for telltale clues about its design. They were in luck—the deadbolt had a single-sided key entry with a flip switch on one side, not one that required a key on both sides of the lock.

"Looks like this will be an easy one," Travis whispered.

Using a simple technique that employed a wire shim and a modified screwdriver, Travis first slid the paperclip-type shim carefully into the keyway. Then he pushed the long, narrow screwdriver into the notch alongside it and wriggled it around. He gave the screwdriver a couple of good twists and in less than a minute was rewarded with a muffled thunk as the plug gave way and the bolt retracted into the lock.

Pleased that he had easily defeated the door locks, Travis turned to William and smiled, "We're in."

William joined him as Travis quickly opened the door and the two slipped inside.

"Nice to know you haven't lost your touch, Travis."

"It's all the practice lately," he agreed. "Well, let's get to it. No time to waste."

The flat was a modestly furnished one-bedroom affair. Even so, in this section of London an apartment this small would be costly. Most of the tenants in the Camden Town-Islington neighborhood were professionals who worked for one of the nearby foreign government embassies.

William pulled a digital camera from his trench coat. "I'll start the photo shoot," he announced. "Want me to get it all?"

"Yes, and make sure you don't disturb anything. We don't want to tip him off."

"Right-oh. I'll be careful." William turned on the camera and began snapping pictures of the apartment from various angles.

"While you're doing that, I'm going to have a look around," Travis said. "We need to find just the right spot."

William continued to take photos. "Sure thing. Let me know when you're ready."

Travis donned a pair of latex surgical gloves to mask his fingerprints and walked through an archway into the kitchen. One by one, he opened the cupboards and surveyed the contents.

"Nothing out of the ordinary in here," he called.

"Right," William replied. "I'll be in the bedroom."

Travis returned to the sitting room and strode to the entertainment center. He peeked in a drawer below the television set and then opened a storage cupboard near the base.

"Just the spot," he called to William. "I'm going to install it here."

Travis unplugged the television set and other electronic components in the cabinet from their power strip. He coiled it up and stuffed it into the outer pocket of his trench coat. Then he withdrew an electric multi-socket cord from his other overcoat pocket, inserted the dangling plugs into it, and connected it to the wall outlet. The power strip looked ordinary enough, but in fact, besides being fully functional, it contained a very sensitive radio-microphone. Voice-activated, it could transmit to a receiver up to 1,500 meters away. It would be perfect for monitoring conversations that took place in the entire apartment from anywhere along the nearby street.

"All set," he updated his partner. "I've tested the unit, and it checks out fine."

"I'm still in the bedroom," William responded.

"I'll be right there," Travis called.

He walked straight through the doorway and into the bedroom. It was a small space furnished with a wood-framed double bed, dresser and armoire. A small closet off the room revealed the usual assortment of shoes, shirts, neckties and suits.

William was busily clicking away.

"Did you get it all?" Travis asked.

"Almost. Just a few more close-ups."

Travis bent low and glanced at a framed picture on the dresser.

A handwritten inscription read, "With all my love, Meredith."

"Who's this?" he wondered. "Any idea?"

"Haven't a clue," William answered. "I have a couple of shots, though. And a good close-up, too."

"Excellent. We'll run the photo when we get back," Travis replied. "It will be important to find out who she is and what she does. That may be useful later."

"Agreed. I'm finished," William stated.

"Good enough."

"And you?"

"Not quite. One more place to check." Travis ducked into the bathroom and quickly surveyed the surroundings. He emerged after a few seconds. "Not there either."

Travis pointed to the dresser. "I think the best place is right over there." He stepped to the dresser and placed his hand on a small box made of inlaid wood.

"Will this do?" he asked.

William drew near and Travis opened the box. He peered inside, "Yes, I think so."

"Good. Do you have a photo of it closed?"

"Absolutely," William confirmed.

"Very well, then. When I'm finished, snap another few, will you?"

"Sure thing," he responded.

Travis reached inside his raincoat and produced a small cloth bag. He loosened the black velvet pouch's drawstring and shook the contents free. Six pea-sized cut diamonds spilled into the box and settled on top of cufflinks and other jewelry. He gently nudged the gems in among the other items so no one would see them when they opened the box.

Travis turned to William, "Look good?"

"If I hadn't seen you dump the stones in there a minute ago, I wouldn't know," William nodded.

"Nothing like an anonymous tip about stolen property to provide a reason to question someone, right?" Travis quipped through a sly smile. "We're so bloody good!" he grinned.

William bent low and took a few more close-up photos of the box and its contents, the diamonds barely visible in the lens. He closed the lid and straightened. "That's it. I've got all I need."

"We're finished then." Travis said, glancing at his watch. "We've been here sixteen minutes. Time to go."

William slipped the camera into his trench coat pocket and they started for the door.

Suddenly, there was a loud knock. A young woman's voice called out, "Hello, it's Meredith. Are you there?"

The two men froze, barely breathing. Travis placed his finger over his pursed lips. With a simple nod, William signaled that he understood. Travis pointed to his hip and then reached inside his trench coat. He retrieved his cell phone and carefully checked to be sure that the ringer was in the off mode. William did the same and gave his partner a thumbs-up signal.

The two men had every legal right to be in this particular apartment. Current law required that the British Home Secretary sign a warrant before police or MI5 officers could conduct covert intrusive surveillance and place electronic bugging devices inside residences or private vehicles. The team had such a warrant, tucked in William's trench coat pocket. However, to produce it for the young woman at the door if she decided to enter the apartment would not only be embarrassing to the two men and the British government, but would compromise the entire undertaking. Fearing the worst while hoping for the best, they stood there motionless, and waited.

After another couple of knocks, a smallish sheet of paper floated under the door. Travis and William listened intently to the footsteps as the woman made her way down the hallway and let herself out. Travis walked quietly to where the paper lay, bent down, and picked it up.

"It's from a small spiral notepad," he concluded. "Something she carried in her purse, I'd say." Travis examined the page closely then looked at William. "She jotted a quick note. It's signed 'Meredith.' Could she be the same Meredith whose picture we saw on the dresser?"

"We didn't get a look at her, so we can't be sure. Still, there's a very good chance she's the same girl," William replied.

"What do you make of it?" Travis read it aloud, "Allan, I'm worried about you. We must talk, but don't call me. Best if you stop by to see me at work. Meredith."

"Odd, I should think. Let me have a listen once more." Travis read it aloud again.

"Yes, definitely odd. Do you suppose she is trying to tell him something or perhaps warn him?

"Could be," Travis mused. "But warn him about what? She can't possibly know any of this."

"No, I suppose not. But then again—" William stopped in mid-sentence. "Of course, that's it!" he exclaimed. "She works at the embassy; I'm sure of it. I remember her name—Meredith Wilson—from the LE staff roster," he said, referring to the list of locally employed, or LE, staff.

"If she's an LE, then what are you suggesting? That she's heard or seen something?"

"Precisely. It's quite possible—no highly probable— that she heard or saw something."

"We'd better let Singleton know straight away."

"I agree—we've no time to waste. Let's get to it."

William opened the door and checked the hallway. Satisfied no one was watching, he stepped into the cor- ridor. Travis carefully placed the note on the floor near its original position and followed his partner through the door, closing it behind him.

# 18. BE CAREFUL WHAT YOU WISH FOR

*Terminal 22, Port Everglades*
*Ft. Lauderdale, FL*

The area in front of Terminal 22 was bustling with activity. Every few minutes another vehicle stopped near the curb as the *Southern Star's* passengers arrived and offloaded their luggage. Porters swarmed around dozens of baggage carts and heaped suitcase after suitcase on to them. Full carts went to the screening area as empty ones quickly took their place. Although it appeared somewhat chaotic, the system was actually quite efficient. Murphy and Susan trotted around to the back of the Jeep. Before Murphy could get the key in the lock, a pleasant, white-gloved porter greeted them in slightly accented English.

"Good afternoon," he said with a broad, gleaming smile. "I'd like to welcome you to the *Southern Star*. My name is Ben. It is a pleasure to have you as our guests on this cruise."

Susan was the first to reply. "Well, thank you, Ben. We're looking forward to it."

"Yes," Murphy added, "we certainly are."

"May I help you with your bags?" Ben asked.

"Please do," Murphy answered. "Do we need new tags? We filled out the ones Sovereign Cruise Lines sent us a few days ago and attached them to our luggage."

"Let me see," Ben replied with another big smile. "It will only take a couple of minutes."

He reached into the Jeep and lifted the two heavy suitcases out one at a time, and placed them on the concrete a few feet away. "May I see your passports and tickets, please?"

Murphy and Susan handed the porter their tickets and U.S. passports. Ben inspected the luggage tags and compared the information to that on their travel documents. He withdrew a small notebook from his shirt pocket, scribbled a few lines, and then slipped it back into his shirt.

"Everything is in order, Mr. Murphy and Miss Anderson," he beamed. "I will be happy to see that your bags are moved through the screening area and then delivered to your stateroom."

"That would be wonderful, Ben, "Murphy nodded. " Thank you." Susan's smile signaled her agreement. Murphy thrust a closed hand toward Ben. Like a true veteran, Ben quickly reached for the neatly folded dollar bills in Murphy's hand.

"That's very kind of you, sir," Ben said with his characteristic smile and a slight bow of his head.

"You are most welcome," Murphy responded.

"As soon as you park your car, you can proceed to the passenger check-in point to your right," Ben said, pointing toward the pier.

"Over there?" Murphy referred to a kiosk with a large sign affixed to it that read, "All Departing Passengers Report Here First."

"Yes, that's it," Ben said. He lifted the two bags and started to carry them toward a nearby baggage cart. "I'll see you on board," he called.

"Pleasant fellow," Susan remarked.

"Yes, he was," Murphy agreed. "Do you suppose every member of the crew is like that?"

"I sure hope so," Susan giggled. "I'm ready to be waited on hand and foot."

Murphy smiled. "Yes, your Highness. Is there anything I can get for you?" he teased.

"Funny!" she shot back. "You know darned well that I'm really not spoiled. I don't need extravagant trappings like champagne, strawberries and caviar. I can get along without the caviar just fine. So there!" She giggled again.

Murphy winked at her. "Whatever you say, your Majesty."

She bobbed her head from side to side, mocking him. It was his turn to laugh.

"We'd better get going," she said. "I'll wait here while you park the Jeep."

Murphy nodded and pecked her on the cheek. "Great. It should only take a few minutes." He spun around and walked to the driver's door. A few seconds later, he jumped in and drove away.

The six-story Mid-port Parking Garage was located within walking distance of Terminal 22. Renovated a few years ago when other facilities at Port Everglades underwent expansion, the project added three additional floors and doubled its parking capacity to 2,000 spaces. Murphy eased the Jeep into the entry lane and crept up to the ticket dispenser. Murphy reached for a large green button labeled "Push For Ticket." The sign next to the device read "$15 per day." *A bargain at twice the price,* he thought. Murphy extracted the ticket from the slot and the barrier arm swung up. He drove through and began to wind his way around the garage, climbing upward as he went.

On the first level, he passed a Broward County Sheriff's deputy seated in a golf cart. He then drove by another deputy who was on foot patrol on the third level. By the time he had found a parking space on Level 5, he had seen three more Sheriff's deputies who were patrolling the parking garage. Murphy cut the wheel sharply to the left and brought the vehicle to a stop.

The space was perfect—it was on the inside to protect his Jeep from the weather.

Murphy switched the ignition off and placed the ticket on the dashboard in plain view. He got out of the vehicle, closed the door, and activated the locks with the remote control. Murphy made a note of the parking space on a slip of paper and tucked it in his wallet. He turned and made for the elevator.

A few minutes later, he emerged from the elevator on the ground level and exited the parking garage. Murphy quickly walked toward Terminal 22 in search of Susan. Her flowing blond hair hung in the autumn breeze and made her easy to spot, so it didn't take him long. She was standing near the check-in kiosk craning her neck and scanning the crowd. Once Susan spotted him, she bounced up and down, and frantically waved a hand back and forth.

"Over here!" she shouted. "Murph, over here!" she called.

Murphy raised a hand and waved back, to let her know that he saw her. She acknowledged and moved toward him with outstretched arms. Murphy met her and gave her a warm embrace. "I told you that wouldn't take long," he quipped. He wrapped an arm around her shoulder began to walk toward the kiosk. "Let's go get checked in, shall we?"

"Good idea," Susan replied. "We've been going since five this morning. I'm beginning to feel tired." She yawned to make her point.

"Me too," Murphy agreed. "I wouldn't mind unwinding a bit myself."

"As soon as we get on board and settled in our stateroom, I can find out what's going on with Allan," Susan said. "I'm worried he won't make it here in time."

"Let's get to it, then," Murphy responded, picking up the pace.

"Oh," Susan remarked, "Ben came back by while you were parking the car. He said that ship's concierge had assigned him to be our cabin steward and that he looked forward to serving our needs during the cruise. That was nice, don't you think?"

"Yes, I do," Murphy smiled, "he seems very attentive. And I'll bet he's already left a bottle of chilled champagne and fresh strawberries in our stateroom."

"There you go again," Susan joked. "You just can't let it go can you?" She batted him gently with her hand. "I'm sure Ben knows better than that—even if you don't," she laughed.

"By the way," she added, "he has an unusual accent. Where do you suppose he is from? Any idea?"

"No, I'm afraid not," Murphy replied. "He speaks English rather well, but you're right— he does have a slight accent. I can't place it though. Most cruise ship employees are foreign nationals, so that's to be expected, I suppose."

Oh well," Susan shrugged, "it doesn't really matter. I was just curious that's all."

Susan and Murphy had made it to the check-in kiosk and were standing in front of the attendant's window. "Time to get our passports and tickets out for boarding," Susan said. She fished around inside her purse and produced them. She smiled at Murphy and then handed the stack of documents to the agent. Susan bobbed back and forth like a schoolgirl who was making her first field trip. "Here we go. I can't wait!" she exclaimed. "It's going to be an adventure."

"Be careful what you wish for, Susan," Murphy winked, "you just might get it."

# 19. STRAWBERRIES AND CHAMPAGNE

*Port Everglades, Aboard the* Southern Star
*Ft. Lauderdale, FL*

The boarding process was surprisingly easy given the thorough search Susan and Murphy underwent earlier at the Port Everglades entrance. The agent took the documents from Susan. First, he scrutinized their passports and tickets and verified their identity. Next, he crosschecked their names against the *Southern Star's* passenger manifest. Finally, the agent scanned the latest TSA terrorist watch list and determined that their names were not on it. Satisfied, he generated two laminated passenger identification cards bearing their names, ship, date of departure, and destination.

The agent smiled and handed the cards to Murphy. "Here you are, Mr. Murphy, an ID for you and one for Miss Anderson. Please keep these with you at all times," he instructed. "Are there any questions?"

Murphy and Susan both shook their heads. The agent handed the passports and tickets back to Susan.

"Very well, then." He pointed to a small glass and metal structure a few yards away. "You may proceed to the screening station over there." It was hard to miss—a large sign that said Passenger Screening hung above the entrance. The agent continued, "Once you've passed through the metal detector, you will be able to board the *Southern*

*Star* and make your way to your stateroom. Your luggage will be waiting for you there. Thanks for cruising with us and enjoy your trip!"

Murphy whirled Susan around and started toward the passenger-screening lounge. "So far, so good!" he beamed. "That wasn't difficult at all."

Minutes later, they moved through the metal detectors and met their carry-on bags on the other side. The pair claimed their hand luggage and walked down the aisle that ended in front of the last checkpoint. An armed Sheriff's deputy with a rather serious-looking German Shepherd at his side surveyed the approaching passengers from behind dark sunglasses.

"It reminds me of airport security," Susan said. "Don't you think so?"

"I don't know," Murphy chuckled. "I travel by sea everywhere I go, remember?"

"Oh, you know what I mean," Susan chided. "Stop kidding around."

Murphy gave in. "Yes, you're right. After 9/11, the cruise lines adopted similar passenger screening procedures. It would be very difficult for a passenger to sneak a weapon or a bomb aboard." He glanced at Susan who gave him a reporter's inquisitive look. "Every piece of checked baggage is subjected to a rigorous analysis. First, it's matched to the passenger manifest. The x-ray machine and bomb-sniffing chamber are next. Any unusual signature or discrepancy results in closer inspection by hand."

"How do you know that?" she wondered.

"Mmmmm. Let me think," he stalled. "Oh, that's right! I read about it in the *Washington Post*," he blurted out.

Susan's frown signaled the end of her amusement with Murphy's jokes.

"I'm sorry, Susan," he apologized. "I remember reading about it in an Office of Naval Intelligence paper shortly after 9/11. The International Maritime Organization, which is part of the U.N., introduced the International Ship and Port Facility Security Code. At the same time, the U.S. created the Maritime Transportation Security Act. That's how these procedures came about." Murphy paused briefly and then concluded with, "Aren't you glad you asked?"

"You don't really want me to answer that, do you?" At first, Susan tried to hide her reaction, but the smirk on her face grew wider until she exploded with a sidesplitting laugh.

"What's so funny?" Murphy demanded. "You don't think I made that up, do you?"

"No, of course not," she laughed some more. "Nobody could make that up—except for you, Commander."

This time, Murphy frowned.

"Okay," Susan sighed, "that makes us even." She leaned over and kissed him on the cheek.

"Thank you," Murphy responded softly.

"That is until next time," Susan whispered in his ear.

"Humph," Murphy grunted, which made Susan giggle.

The agent who was operating the boarding door signaled for Susan and Murphy to approach. She took their documents, compared them to their newly issued ID's, then returned their passports and tickets and waved them through. That was the easiest part of the entire boarding process.

The electric door swung open and it was like walking onto a movie set. The first thing that Susan and Murphy noticed was the elegance only a ship from a bygone era could boast.

"Wow!" Susan mouthed. Murphy glanced around at the polished teak and gleaming brass fixtures and smiled.

Launched by Queen Elizabeth II in 1964, the *Southern Star* was a gracious dame with nuances and curves that made her quite different from ships that were more modern. Their prefabricated hulls and boxy, space-efficient superstructure designs maximized the passenger count with revenues in mind. The *Southern Star*, on the other hand, was a cruising ship designed with passengers in mind.

Susan and Murphy walked up the gangway and marveled at the sights. When they reach the top, the ship's captain, who was dressed in a crisp white uniform, greeted them as they stepped onto the boat deck.

"Good afternoon," he said warmly. "Welcome aboard the *Southern Star*. I'm Captain Jensen. It's my pleasure to have you along."

Susan and Murphy both nodded and smiled approvingly. "Thank you so much. It's nice to meet you," they replied.

Jensen pointed to another officer standing a few feet to his left. "The ship's purser will direct you to your stateroom. I hope you enjoy your stay with us."

Murphy and Susan approached the purser and showed him their IDs. "Let's see." He scanned the clipboard and instantly found their names on the passenger manifest. "Ah, yes. Mr. Murphy and Miss Anderson. You will be staying in cabin 533. Let me give you a map."

The officer produced a diagram of the *Southern Star's* decks and quickly drew a series of lines with a bright yellow marker. He pointed to a red dot. "We are here. Simply follow the yellow line along the boat deck, down one flight of stairs to the promenade deck and your room is halfway down on the right side."

"You mean starboard, don't you?" Susan teased.

The purser smiled. "Yes, of course starboard. Most passengers prefer left and right. You must be a sailor."

"No, but my companion is. He's in the Navy," Susan beamed.

"Interesting," the purser mused. "Me, too. At least I was. Landing signal officer on a carrier—the *Kennedy*. Evan White's the name."

Murphy extended his hand. "Murphy, Bill Murphy. I'm a sub driver." Susan leaned close to White. "Captain of a boomer," she whispered loud enough for Murphy to hear. He glanced at Susan, frowning slightly.

White raised his eyebrows. "Now that's impressive. Maybe we'll get a chance to swap war stories over dinner."

"I'd like that," Murphy nodded approvingly. "I'd love to hear about carrier ops from an LSO. I always wondered how those flyboys managed to plop a jet on a soap bar floating in the middle of the ocean." He laughed and White joined in.

White shook Murphy's hand. "Welcome aboard and enjoy your stay." He handed Murphy a key and smiled at them.

Susan and Murphy turned and strolled along the boat deck tracing their path on the map. They walked by a block of suites and meeting rooms and continued aft past the lifeboats and shuffleboard courts. Wide, open promenades that extended to the base of the funnel recalled the best in postwar British marine architecture. Being on the *Southern Star* was almost like being on a floating museum.

Down one flight of stairs and along the starboard side's covered promenades, just as the purser instructed, brought them to cabin 533. L-shaped with a double bed, it varied slightly from the other outside units in this section of the *Southern Star*. Those particular staterooms had two twin beds, but the tradeoff was less living space. Unlike cabins on the lower decks that had portholes, each of the rooms on the promenade deck featured a rectangular picture window that looked out onto the walkway.

Murphy slid the brass key into the lock and turned it. The tumblers made a distinctive click. Murphy opened the door and entered the stateroom. Susan followed following close behind. The furnishings were simple, yet elegant. The decor included burled walnut effect wood, double full-length mirrors and reproduction oil paintings. The art deco bathroom was full of brass and tile. The appointments complemented the best features of the *Southern Star*.

"Isn't it wonderful?" Susan exclaimed.

Murphy nodded approvingly. "Very nice. Better than the *Wyoming*," he said, referring to his submarine quarters.

Susan walked over to the small credenza.

"What this?" she asked.

Murphy turned to look. "What's what?"

"This," Susan answered. "Come and look, Murph."

Murphy walked to the credenza. Sitting squarely in the middle of it was an ice bucket that held a bottle of Asti Spumante. Two crystal champagne flutes stood next to the ice bucket. Beside them was a large silver bowl filled with fresh strawberries topped with a mint sprig. Lying in front of the ice bucket was a small envelope.

"Did you do this?" Susan demanded.

"No," Murphy shrugged, "I don't know anything about it."

Susan quizzed him further. "Are you sure?" she insisted. Murphy shook his head and shrugged once more. Susan picked up the envelope and opened it. "All right, then, "she said. Susan withdrew the note card and read it aloud. "I understand you have a fondness for strawberries and bubbly. Have a wonderful stay! Ben."

Susan looked at Murphy. She placed a hand on her hip and cocked her head. "How did he know that?"

Murphy shrugged. "I'm not sure," he replied innocently.

# 20. THE NEXT MOVE

*Milbank District*
*London, U.K.*

Thames House, home to MI5's Joint Terrorism Analysis Centre or JTAC, was an older office-building complex in Millbank on the bank of the River Thames. Adjacent to Lambeth Bridge and a short distance from Westminster Palace, Thames House was almost directly across the River Thames from the new headquarters of its sister organization, MI6 at 85 Vauxhall Cross. Lambeth Bridge, one of several crossings in central London, was a busy east-west span that carried traffic and pedestrians over the River Thames.

Thames Houses' architecture was quite unremarkable from a distance. However, once up close, passersby could easily see that sculptures decorated the Portland stone facade. Completed in 1930, the structure stood as one of the finest buildings of its kind in the British Empire. Prompted by the need for more space in the mid-1990's, MI5, the British Security Service, refurbished the entire complex of buildings for its new quarters. Thames House's pale yellow roof was the color of English farmhouse cheddar and earned it the nickname "The Wedge" from MI5 staff and employees.

The drive from Anderson's flat in Camden Town to MI5 headquarters at Thames House was about six kilometers.

London city traffic was the usual stop-and-go because of volume and fender benders. The black car weaved in and out of traffic like a skier winding his way down the slopes. A horn blared from behind as another driver unsuccessfully attempted to cut them off.

"Bloody hell!" Travis cursed, "Where did these blokes learn to drive? This isn't the English countryside!"

"Tough crowd on the streets today," William acknowledged. "Good thing we haven't far to go."

Travis nodded, "Almost there, thank goodness."

The car skipped along Whitehall, which turned into Abbingdon Street and then Millbank Road. The street names were confusing, to say the least because they quite often changed at each major intersection. Thames House was located at the corner of Milbank and Horseferry Road. Travis steered the car into the turn light at the traffic signal opposite the parking deck entrance. A few minutes later, they had secured a parking space and had made their way to the elevator. Once inside the main building, Travis and William went straight to Singleton's office.

Their knock brought a simple "Come." James Singleton, director of MI5's Joint Terrorism Analysis Centre, sat behind his large, imposing desk. He peered over his reading glasses as the pair quickly marched in. Furnished exclusively with traditional pieces and no modern accessories, Singleton's office was somewhat anachronistic. However odd it seemed, that style was a perfect match for Singleton's personality.

"Sit," he commanded. "What have you got? Give it to me straight away," he instructed.

As the chief of one of Britain's most important multi-agency intelligence organizations, he was famous for his tough debriefings. True to form, Singleton grilled the agents as though they were suspects under interrogation. The back-and-forth volley between Singleton and the agents continued relentlessly for more than thirty minutes. Finally, the barrage ended.

"Well, we can't just bring him in for questioning—he's a U.S. citizen working for the State Department," Travis objected.

"You're quite right, we can't. However, there is another way—his girlfriend. We can use Meredith Wilson to get at him," Singleton explained. "There's no prohibition against doing that."

The two agents glanced at one another and then Travis responded. "Yes, Mr. Singleton. You are quite right, indeed. Shall we ring her up later?"

"No, thank you. Now is fine." he replied. Singleton opened a large notebook on his desk, slid his index finger half way down the computer printout and stopped. "I've got it," he proclaimed as he lifted the handset and dialed her home phone number.

"Miss Wilson, my name is James Singleton. I work for the British government and I am calling about an acquaintance of yours, Allan Anderson. I am afraid that Mr. Anderson may be involved in a matter related to national security and we will need to ask you a few questions. It is rather urgent, so would you mind coming by today?"

# 21. DEAD IN THE WATER

*In the Miramar Café*
*Aboard the* Southern Star

Commander William Murphy, Susan Anderson and half a dozen other early birds sat around a table in the *Southern Star's* Miramar Café. A bright bouquet of flowers accented the crisp white linen cover, which was dotted with festive, pastel-colored china. Like sentinels, two tall silver carafes—one for tea and the other for coffee—stood in the middle table as if guarding the bowls of fresh fruit and baskets of bread and pastries set out beside them.

Customarily, the ship's officers made it a point to mingle with the passengers at every opportunity, especially during mealtime. For this morning's breakfast, that function fell to the vessel's purser, Evan White, whom Murphy and Susan met while boarding in Fort Lauderdale.

White entered the café, removed his saucer cap, and tucked it under his left arm. He stood near the host's station and scanned the dining room, displaying a cheery smile as he did so. After a moment, he locked onto Murphy's table and began to move in that direction. Purser White slowly wound his way toward Murphy's party, nodding and exchanging pleasantries with many of the passengers as he went.

"Good morning, folks. How are you?

"Lovely morning, isn't it?"

"Nice to see you."

"Beautiful day."

Eventually, he reached his intended destination. "Mind if I join you and your company of friends?" White asked Commander Murphy.

"By all means," Murphy replied through an inviting smile. He stood and made a gesture toward an open seat next to him.

White nodded graciously. "Thank you, then. It will be my pleasure." He settled into the plush chair and reached for the coffee carafe. He poured himself a cup and raised it as a toast to the group.

"Good morning, everyone," White said. "I'm delighted to join you."

Purser White introduced himself to the circle. He recounted his stint in the Navy, discussed his career with Sovereign Cruise Line, and told them how long he had been serving aboard the *Southern Star*. In turn, the passengers provided White with a brief rundown of their own backgrounds—where they lived, their career or line of work, whether this was their first cruise, and so on.

"What an interesting group," White remarked. "I am so pleased to make your acquaintances."

"Me, too," and "Likewise," they replied in a chorus.

"Well, then, don't let me interrupt any longer," White implored. He reached for a breadbasket. "Blueberry muffins are my favorite, so I've have to try one," he quipped. He selected a plump one, broke it in two, and took a bite. "Mmmmm," he smiled. "Almost as good as the ones my grandmother used to make—almost."

Shortly afterward, the chitchat resumed. Murphy and White hit it off at once and swapped tales, each giving the other a glimpse into his Navy career. Susan chatted buoyantly with Mercedes, the middle-aged woman seated beside her who was a New York City advertising agency executive. The others around the table smiled and nodded as they became engrossed in a myriad of topics.

The group had been enjoying small talk over their croissants, muffins and coffee when things inexplicably changed for the worse. Murphy was the first to notice it and cocked his head quizzically. Normally, the *Southern Star* would be plowing through the water at nineteen knots when underway, but instead, she was at a standstill.

Unsure of the cause, he leaned close to White. "We seem to be dead in the water," he whispered. "Am I right about that?"

White straightened in his chair, looked to his left and then to his right   He strained to detect a sound or some other indication that the *Southern Star* was still underway. The furrows on White's brow, combined with the frown on his face, provided Murphy with the answer to his question.

"We're stopped, aren't we?" Murphy asked in a hushed voice.

White acknowledged with a quick nod, "Afraid so."

No one else around the table was aware of what White and Murphy realized. The conversations kept going—in fact, the lilt of bubbly small talk and laughter filled the Miramar Café this morning.

Sensing a bigger problem, White motioned toward the café entrance with his head.

"I think we should have a look," he suggested quietly. "Must be some kind of trouble."

Murphy replied softly, "I agree."

"Let's make our way to the bridge then," White suggested under his breath.

Both men stood, feigned a smile, and excused themselves. They quickly exited through the café's main entrance and made for the ship's bridge.

Murphy and White had barely backed away from the table and slipped out unnoticed when suddenly, three men burst through the kitchen door into the café. Black ski masks hid their faces, so it was difficult to tell much about them. However, the AK-47 Kalashnikov assault rifle each one menacingly pointed at the passengers in the dining room spoke volumes about the trio's intentions.

"Don't move! Don't move!" one of them shouted.

A few passengers screamed in shock and disbelief. "Quiet! Quiet! Stay in your seats!" another masked intruder commanded.

Susan and Mercedes, the ad exec she was chatting with moments before, exchanged furtive glances. Although neither one spoke, their looks were nonetheless easy to interpret. The pair's raised eyebrows and dropped jaws were unmistakable expressions for "Oh shit!"

# 22. READ BETWEEN THE LINES

*In the Miramar Café*
*Aboard the* **Southern Star**

For nearly 30 minutes, the captors subjected the passengers in the Miramar Café to a torrent of insults, threats and taunts. Susan was becoming angry and impatient. She hoped the rant would stop, even if only briefly. She got her wish when the terrorists paused to gulp some water down.

In a daring, uncalculated move, Susan jumped up and waved her arms high above her head. "Wait! Wait! I'm a reporter for the *Washington Post!*" she yelled. "I can get your message out. My newspaper can tell the world."

Her shouts immediately attracted the attention of the group's leader, a tall, swarthy man whose dark eyes were sunken deep into his bearded face. He spun around and trained his AK-47 on her. Susan froze and slowly lowered her arms to her side. Her eyes grew wide and the color quickly drained from her skin. The leader studied her while he kept the Kalashnikov pointed at her. For a few tense moments, neither one moved or spoke. Then he raised a hand and motioned for her to approach him. He kept the assault rifle cradled in his right arm, trigger finger at the ready.

Oblivious to the intense gaze of the other passengers, Susan shuffled toward the man and kept her eyes fixed on the weapon's large, adjustable front sight. Her legs trembled and her entire body shook as she crept closer. Susan stopped about fifteen feet from the man. Without warning, he suddenly thrust the rifle's muzzle toward her. Startled, Susan instinctively jumped back as gasps and screams erupted from the onlookers. She slowly raised her hands to shoulder level and swallowed hard. The loud gulping sound she made broke eerie silence that hung over the dining room.

The leader swung the AK-47 toward one of the tables. "Sit," he commanded in a harsh, authoritative voice.

Susan edged slowly toward the table, slid a chair out a few inches, and poured her shaking frame into it.

"Tell me more," he ordered. "I want to know about this newspaper connection."

Susan stared at the steel blue gun barrel aimed at her chest. Once more, she swallowed hard and cleared her throat. "It's simple, really," she stammered. "I cover foreign affairs for the *Washington Post*. I can contact my newspaper and convince them to run a front-page story. All you have to do is tell me what you want to say."

"How do I know you are telling the truth?" he demanded. "Who says you're not a spy working for the CIA?"

Susan gestured with her hand, "Look around you," she said. "I am a tourist just like these other people. I am on vacation—just taking a holiday. That's all."

The leader shook his head. "I am not convinced. I know the trickery of the CIA. You think I am easily fooled, no?"

"I know it's hard for you to believe what I am telling you," Susan sighed. "But if you want me to help you tell the world your demands, you are going to have to believe me."

"No!" he bellowed angrily. "You Americans are all alike!"

He thrust the Kalashnikov toward her. Susan shrank back in the chair and cowered.

"You are an agent of the Great Satan! Perhaps I should kill you now and be done with it," he cursed.

Susan glowered back at him. "If that is what you truly believe, then perhaps you should! It will spare me the fate of the others."

The leader moved to the table and bent low, his dark eyes inches from Susan's face. "A defiant one, I see," he hissed. "In my country, a woman such as you would be punished for her insolence."

"But I am not in your country," Susan shot back.

"No," he growled, "and it is lucky for you."

Susan did not respond. Instead, she turned her head away from the leader's stare. He straightened and backed away from the table.

"Look at me," he ordered. Slowly, Susan turned to face him.

"You cannot be a CIA agent," he declared confidently. "None could be so brazen or as stupid as you. Rather than calculating and cunning, you are reckless. Some would say I am crazy, but I believe you," he nodded.

Susan did not change her expression and continued to stare at him. She held her breath while he formulated his next remark.

After a long moment, he spoke. "So, what will you tell your newspaper?" he asked. "Will you have them print our demands exactly as we state them?"

"Of course," Susan replied. "But in return, I want something, too."

"You are hardly in a position to bargain," he snapped.

"Then I won't contact my newspaper and your story will never be told," Susan shot back defiantly. "Instead, the only thing that the world will read is about your capture by the U.S. military."

"Arrrggghh!" the leader growled   He raised the weapon and aimed it directly at Susan's head. "Stupid woman," he shouted. "You anger me!"

Susan did not flinch. "Unless you intend to kill all of us in order to make your case, I want all of the passengers on this ship released unharmed," she demanded.

"But you are all enemies and the Koran says, 'slay them wherever you catch them.' Maybe I should kill you along with the others now," he snarled. "What do you think?"

"Wouldn't that go against the teachings of Muhammad?" Susan asked pointedly.

The leader cocked his head and narrowed his eyes as he considered her question. Without giving him time to formulate a response, Susan quickly fired another verbal salvo at him.

"The Koran says Muslims can retaliate if attacked, but they may not launch unprovoked violence. Peaceful prescriptions balance many of its passages about warfare. In other words," she reasoned, "if your enemies let you be and do not make war on you and offer you peace, Allah does not allow you to harm them."

"What you say about verses from the Koran is true," the leader nodded. "But how does it apply to you and the other Americans?" he asked.

"Because we are not soldiers," Susan replied. "Like me, the others on this ship did not attack your country. We are just ordinary people—innocents—who have been caught up in these events. Harming us won't promote your cause. Instead, it will have the opposite affect and earn you world condemnation," she added.

The group's leader studied her briefly. "I'll consider your demand," he replied. "I make no promises. I will wait to see what kind of response you get from your newspaper."

"Fair enough," Susan agreed. "I will prepare something for you to review using my laptop computer. First, I must alert my editor. Do I have your permission?"

"Make it quick," the leader snapped. "No tricks, either," he warned.

Susan nimbly typed a brief, carefully worded text message on her phone. She had assured the group's leader that she would relay his demands to the *Washington Post*. Instead, this particular communication would go to one of her close contacts at CNN. It was very short and said all it needed to.

Susan quickly reviewed the few lines on the device's display that read, "Aboard cruise ship *Southern Star* near Bahamas. Have been hijacked by terrorists. Demands are unknown. No claim of responsibility. Need DOD response ASAP. Disseminate as required." Satisfied it would do the job, she pushed Send.

# 23. BREAKING NEWS

*Dania Beach Hotel*
*Ft. Lauderdale, FL*

Allan sat in the dining room at the Dania Beach Hotel, a few blocks from the Fort Lauderdale-Hollywood International Airport. After a series of delays, including interviews by FBI agents regarding the attempted hijacking of his flight from Dulles, Allan arrived in Fort Lauderdale around midnight the day before. Still a bit shaken from the ordeal, he hadn't slept well. To top it off, he missed the *Southern Star's* scheduled sailing. By now, Susan and Bill were half way to the Bahamas without him.

Allan considered hopping a flight to Nassau and joining them there for the short cruise back to Florida. It didn't take long for him to conclude that it wasn't worth the extra hassle or expense. He would simply wait for them in Fort Lauderdale. The hotel had a lovely pool, workout room, Internet, and was within walking distance of the beach. Even though a tropical storm was beginning to form near the Bahamas, forecasters didn't expect it to affect Florida's Atlantic coast or the islands for a few more days. With any luck, Bill and Susan's cruise would escape the rain and wind.

For now, Allan was content to enjoy a late morning breakfast. Allan gulped his morning coffee and began to read details of the *Miami Herald's* front-page account of the hijacking incident.

# Hijacking Attempt Foiled Near Nation's Capital

Dulles, Virginia (AP) — An incident aboard a Mid-States Airlines jet yesterday in which a Federal Air Marshal shot and killed a passenger was "by all appearances a terror attack," the U.S. Department of Homeland Security said in a statement.

Mid-States also said there had been an attempted hijacking. However, Washington-Dulles airport officials downplayed the incident, which occurred Friday afternoon on a flight from Washington-Dulles Airport to Fort Lauderdale, Florida

Department of Homeland Security officials said Federal Air Marshals on board the jet averted a hijacking. They did not blame the incident on ground security, which is under the responsibility of Transportation Security Administration. They noted that TSA personnel had followed established screening procedures.

A TSA spokesperson made it clear that the man did not manage to board the jet with a weapon. The airline's deputy general manager, Patrick Kelly, also said the hijacker had no weapon when shot and killed by federal law enforcement.

The TSA emphasized that stringent security measures are in place for all flights to and from U.S. airports, including both domestic and international departures and arrivals. All passengers are checked with hand-held metal detectors and must empty their pockets.

A government statement said the passenger, whose name has not been released, did not raise suspicions at the airport, and was allowed to board the jet with the other passengers after screening. "His actions were not spontaneous," the statement said. It noted no similarities with the September 11 attacks and the man's motive was not known. Federal law enforcement agencies continue to pursue several leads both here at home and abroad.

The Federal Air Marshal who fired the fatal shot stated that the hijacker waived his cell phone and failed to respond to his commands to drop it. When the hijacker lunged toward the Federal Air Marshal, the officer fired, killing the assailant instantly. No passengers were injured.

"From what we know now, we can say that there is no doubt that there was an attempted terrorist attack here. There was an attempt to hijack the plane," Mid-States General Manager Arthur Shapiro said.

Unofficial sources report that just two hours after the incident, police and Homeland Security agents converged on the hijacker's apartment in a Virginia suburb near Dulles, just outside Washington, D.C., and searched it. A laptop computer and other items were seized, but no other details of that raid have been released to the public.

Personnel close to the investigation said that this incident appears to have been part of a wider plot to bring down U.S. passenger aircraft or at the very least, disrupt air travel in major cities around the country. Due to recent tensions between the U.S. and Iran, extra security measures have been instituted at all U.S. airports.

In Washington, lawmakers from both parties were quick to react, expressing concern and saying that even though security has been significantly tightened after 9/11, more should be done to protect the flying public. President Brewster is expected to issue a statement regarding the hijacking incident from the White House later today.

Allan laid the newspaper on the table and stared out the window for a long moment, replaying the events of yesterday in his mind. He was there and watched the entire incident unfold in front of him. Allan had been sitting next to the Federal Air Marshal who killed the hijacker. A number of thoughts raced through his mind. *What if the hijacker had fired first? Would he have missed the air marshal and hit me instead? What if he had a bomb and exploded it? What if we had taken off? Would he have flown us into the White House or Capitol building?*

Allan stood and made his way to the breakfast buffet. He picked up a plate and began to move down the serving line. He glanced up at the wall-mounted television to see the screen suddenly change from CNN's morning news program to a static shot that simply read "BREAKING NEWS." The banner dissolved to a CNN studio reporter, but Allan couldn't hear what she was saying. He continued to watch and noted that there was a map of Florida and the Bahamas on the screen. *Perhaps they're talking about the tropical storm*, Allan thought.

Allan continued to watch as the camera zoomed in on the map and Allan saw a red "X" on the map northwest of the Bahamas islands. A few white letters were under the X. Allan couldn't see them well from where he was standing, so plate in hand, he moved closer. Allan got to within a few feet of the television and was able to read the text. Allan said nothing. He simply stared at the text on the television screen near the red X, "U.S. cruise ship hijacked by terrorists near Bahamas Islands." The color drained from his face as the food plate slipped out his hand and crashed to the floor.

# 24. DANGER, DANGER

*On the promenade deck*
*Aboard the* **Southern Star**

The *Southern Star's* fully covered promenade deck offered passengers a variety of dining and entertainment venues. It was home to several shopping and video arcades and housed the lower level of the ship's casino. The Miramar Café, located furthermost aft, doubled as a buffet during the day and a colorful nightclub after sundown. Now, however, it was neither.

White and Murphy wasted no time as they scurried along the promenade deck toward their destination, the *Southern Star's* bridge located amidships. Ship's purser Evan White led the way with Bill Murphy close behind. Though they were unaware of the situation unfolding in the café, the veteran sailors sensed that something was amiss and were determined to find out exactly what was wrong.

"Evan, we couldn't have run aground," Murphy suggested. "This far northwest of Nassau, the water's probably at 10 fathoms."

"Quite right," White agreed. "I don't know what to make of it. Must be serious though, because no one from the bridge watch called me in the Miramar Café to alert me of a problem," he added.

Murphy shook his head. "Hmmm. It sure is puzzling. No noise, no lurch, no clue."

"That's why I want to get up there right away," White said, pointing in the direction of the superstructure as they both hurried along.

White and Murphy had yet to encounter a single soul. The ship had only a few dozen guests and a reduced crew on board for her three-day sailing because of a tropical storm forecasted to pass menacingly close to the Bahamas. The low clouds were thickening and becoming more ominous. Even so, the expected storm squalls and torrential rains were hours away. It was early morning and a weekend to boot so, except for the breakfast group in the Miramar Café, the other passengers were still inside their cabins.

A few minutes after they exited the dining room, White and Murphy reached the main stairwell located just aft of the superstructure. To reach the bridge, they would have to climb six flights of stairs, going past the boat deck, where most of the *Southern Star's* A and B cabin suites were located, and continue on to the uppermost level, the bridge deck, where the ship's heated pool and Jacuzzi were found. From there, they would have to duck through a watertight door in the bulkhead and make the trek aloft on the last two flights of stairs to the wheelhouse.

Designed to accommodate leisure passengers, rather than sailors stationed on a naval vessel, the stairways on a cruise ship as the *Southern Star* were wide enough for both White and Murphy to scamper up them side by side.

"I'm used to walking up these damned things," White puffed. "Obviously, age is catching up with me."

"I know exactly what you mean" Murphy managed to reply with a grimace. They bounded out of the stairwell onto the boat deck, turned the corner and continued their ascent up the next flight, although their paced had slowed somewhat. White and Murphy were halfway between the boat deck and the bridge deck when five quick, deafening blasts of the ship's horn punctuated the morning quiet and stopped them in their tracks.

*Hunnh-Hunnh-Hunnnh-Hunnh-Hunnh*

"What the hell was that?" a startled Murphy demanded.

"I don't know," White responded, shaking his head. "Ship's horn, but it doesn't make sense."

Murphy briefly lowered his eyebrows in thought. "Wait! Maybe it does," he replied. "That's the signal for danger. ' Blast quick five to stay alive.' Remember?"

"You're right. That's it!" White exclaimed. "Someone on the bridge is signaling danger."

Murphy hesitated and then asked, "Do you *really* think we should try to get up there for a closer look?"

"I don't think we have any choice, do you?" White shrugged.

Okay, then. Let's go," Murphy nodded. "We'll go slowly and quietly. I'll follow you, Evan."

White gave a thumbs-up and began creeping up the last two flights of stairs leading to the bridge deck with Murphy only inches behind him. The signal from the *Southern Star's* horn was deliberate and unmistakable and it could mean only one thing: Whatever had caused the ship to stop moving also placed it in imminent danger. In a matter of minutes, White and Murphy would know why.

# 25. DAVID AND GOLIATH

*The White House Situation Room*
*Washington, D.C.*

Not wanting to be late for his own meeting, President Brewster darted from the Oval Office into the corridor. With two Secret Service agents in tow, he bounded down the short flight of stairs just past the West Wing's Cabinet Room—Brewster preferred the flight of steps over the elevator located near the Vice President's office—and headed for the White House Situation Room. Now on the ground floor almost directly beneath the Oval Office, he scurried through the lobby, made his way down a few more steps, and entered the briefing room on his right.

After the failed Bay of Pigs invasion, President Kennedy constructed the first Situation Room, once a Truman-era bowling alley. Rather than the bunker-like complex buried far below the White House that much of the public imagined, the Situation Room was a large, 5,000 square foot area consisting of the watch room, a videoconference center and a briefing room. Aides and staffers, including those who operated it around the clock, referred it simply as The Woodshed.

Used so much by Lyndon Johnson during the Vietnam War that he kept his Oval Office chair there, other presidents did not place a lot of emphasis on the Situation Room until recently. George H. W. Bush, Bill Clinton and George

W. Bush all found the capabilities and resources located there to be invaluable in light of fast-changing conditions around the world. President Brewster and his administration relied on the Situation Room even more. Daily terrorist threats and numerous regional conflicts required constant monitoring in order to protect American citizens and the nation's interests at home and around the world.

Brewster burst through the door of the Situation Room with the two Secret Service agents still at his heels. The president wasted no time. "Seats, please," he barked as the assembled cabinet members stood. Ordinarily, this meeting would take place in the Roosevelt Room. Today was different. Things had grown worse during the past few hours. It was important for the decision makers and key advisors to have up to the minute intelligence at their fingertips. Those resources were only available in the Woodshed's conference room.

Brewster took his place at the head of the elliptical table beneath a large Presidential Seal that hung on the wall behind him. The president's haggard look and a grumpy expression portrayed the enormous strain he felt.

The president clasped his hands and leaned forward. "Nothing," he said, "Nothing," repeating the word for emphasis, "could have prepared us for this. It has caught us completely off guard and completely by surprise. The nation's airport security is topnotch. Coordination between federal, state and local law enforcement agencies is unparalleled. Our commercial planes and the flying public are safer than ever. But while we were busy looking one way, al-Qaeda was coming at us from a different direction—one that we completely overlooked simply because we didn't expect it."

Brewster looked around the room. "Before I even ask the question, ladies and gentlemen, you already know what it is. However, my question is not what's important; your answer is." The president paused, "So, what the hell are we going to do about this?"

The room was deafeningly silent. No one moved. No one spoke a word. Although a sound absorbing "whisper wall" replaced the mahogany paneling in 2006, there was an eerie air in the Woodshed. Seconds turned to minutes as Brewster waited for a response.

Finally, the president answered his own question. "There's only one thing we can do, and that is to show those bastards what we're made of!"

He turned to Secretary of State Adrian Ashe first.

"What's the status of our requests—I mean arrangements—" catching himself "to place Patriot batteries in Pakistan, Israel, Saudi Arabia, Afghanistan, Iraq and Kuwait?"

"As expected, Mr. President," Ashe answered, "the leadership of each country welcomes U.S. support and protection. They are as worried about how this situation might unfold as we are and it is very troubling to them. After all, Iran is in their backyard and can foment unrest seemingly at will. On top of that, there is the nuclear weapons question. That big unknown has everyone nervous—even us, as you know. To that end, I have assured the various ambassadors that we will stand by them no matter what."

"Thank you, Adrian," Brewster replied. "Anything else?"

"No, sir," Ashe responded.

"Very well, then," the president said. He looked to his left. "Jim, it's your turn. What have you got for us?"

"Mr. President," the director of national intelligence began, "as we all know, it's been very difficult—make that impossible—to find out exactly what's going on down there. The SS *Southern Star* is incommunicado and cut off from the outside world. In other words, nothing in and nothing out—except for that text message from the reporter."

"Nothing at all?" Brewster scoffed. "I find that hard to believe."

Conroy frowned. "There hasn't been any radio contact either, sir. The Coast Guard has been monitoring all maritime frequencies since the hijacking occurred. They've heard nothing either. Apparently, the perpetrators have control of the ship's radio room. Quite possibly, they've disabled or destroyed it."

"For Christ's sakes, Jim!" Brewster shouted, frustration showing through, "Just what the hell are we supposed to do? Sit here and wait?"

Conroy looked down at the table and stroked his forehead. After a few seconds, he looked up at Brewster. "I've discussed this with my deputy sir and we've come up with a plan. It may not sound like much, but it's the best we can do. We're fighting a low-tech war in a high-tech environment. They've got us stumped—our advanced weapons and capabilities just don't fit this kind of scenario. Unfortunately, I think they damned well know it. It's a lot like the Biblical story of David and Goliath—and we're Goliath. A smaller, less sophisticated enemy cleverly used a crude, but effective, method of attack to knock us off our feet. We haven't been out gunned; we've been outsmarted."

Brewster leaned toward Conroy. "What's the plan, Jim? What do you have? I just hope it's good."

"Do you remember the Mariel II smallpox plot from a few weeks ago?" Conroy asked.

Brewster nodded.

"One of our best, a former covert ops specialist, was instrumental in bringing that to a successful close and getting our people safely out of Cuba and to the United States," Conroy continued. "He has lots of experience in extricating agents and other high-value assets out of tight spots—black holes we call them." Conroy paused.

"Go on," the president instructed.

"Well, Mr. President, since neither the Army's Delta Force nor the FBI's Hostage Rescue Team has any off the shelf plans for this sort of thing, I'd like to put our man to work on it right away. We figure if he is that good at taking people *out* of impossible spots, then he might come up with a way to put some people *into* one. We'd like him to develop a plan to insert a special team on the SS *Southern Star*." Conroy finished and waited for the president's reaction.

Brewster didn't respond. He sat back and studied Conroy for a long moment.

"We really don't have any other choice, do we, Jim? There simply aren't any more options available, are there?"

"No, Mr. President, I'm afraid not," Conroy replied. He glanced at Secretary of Defense John Ellis.

Ellis took the cue and spoke out in support of the Intelligence Director.

"Jim's right, Mr. President," Ellis said. "We're not going to be able to surround them and shout 'come out with your hands up' like the sheriff in an old John Wayne western."

"Very well," Brewster replied. He looked at the other cabinet members. "Any objections?" he asked. They shook their heads.

The president turned to his director of national intelligence, "What next, Jim?"

"Let's get our man on the phone—I'd like him to hear it from you, sir," Conroy replied. "I'd like you to tell him how important this is. I'm sure he already knows that—we all do. However, the added emphasis from you, Mr. President, will convey true urgency."

Brewster nodded, "Get to it then."

"Oh, there's one more thing, Mr. President."

"Yes, Jim?"

"This one isn't in the rule books—our man will need carte blanche. He's going to have to think outside the box and he's going to need a PD to get things done," Conroy said, referring to a presidential directive, an executive order issued by the president with the consent of the National Security Council. A presidential directive had the full force and effect of law and it was sweeping in the extent of its authority and scope. It was the same as uttering the words "Open Sesame."

Brewster nodded his approval and gave Conroy a thumbs-up gesture. "Get him on the phone. There's no time to waste."

Conroy lifted the handset on the secure communications console in front of him and pushed several numbers on the keypad. "I'll put it on speaker, sir." He punched a blinking red button and returned the handset to its holder. The sound of two crisp rings filled the small conference room. After the third one they heard, "Special ops section, Peter King here."

# 26. ASSUME THE WORST

*On the boat deck*
*Aboard the* Southern Star

Morning had come to the *Southern Star* as a thick, gray overcast that blanketed the entire sky from east to west. Although it was daylight, the late November sun was noticeably absent, resulting in an eerie pall that hung over the ship as it drifted helplessly. For White and Murphy, the pale light would act as a cloak to help them avoid detection. Because of the approaching storm, the wind had freshened and now averaged fifteen knots with peak gusts to twenty knots. Also in their favor, the noise from the stiff breeze spilling over the bow and tumbling around the superstructure would help to mask their advance toward the ship's bridge.

The *Southern Star's* bridge was the nerve center for all command and control functions about the ship. From this position, the captain or officer of the watch could manage all of her navigation and propulsion systems, machinery and boilers. The bridge also provided a common platform for the ship's alarms, communications equipment and controls for other systems.

One aspect of bridge design that would normally be a plus was the superb visibility that provided occupants with a clear view of the sea ahead and abeam. Typically, from the ship's conning position in the center of the bridge, it was possible to survey a huge arc that spanned from 125 degrees port to 125 degrees starboard. For White and Murphy, though, that might prove to be a disadvantage as the two made their way aloft.

Ship's purser Evan White and U.S. Navy Commander Bill Murphy stood huddled together outside the hatch that provided access to the last, two flights of stairs leading to the bridge. In hushed voices, they planned their next moves.

"I'm bothered by the horn blasts," White whispered. "Only one series—how come we've heard nothing else?"

"I'm not sure. We have not heard any gunfire, and I would say that is positive. But by itself, that isn't a very good indication of whether the crew has been overpowered by intruders or not," Murphy replied in a low voice.

"Intruders?" White repeated with a scowl. "How could intruders get aboard this ship?" he scoffed. "All of the passengers were screened before they boarded and had to pass through metal detectors." White paused briefly and then continued. "Every piece of luggage was X-rayed and passed through a sniffer. I don't see how."

Murphy was silent for several seconds and then responded, "What if the intruders weren't passengers. What if they were—"

White cut him off. "Crew?" he interjected. "You think that some of the *Southern Star's* crew is behind this?" White shook his head. "I find that hard to believe. I think you're wrong, Bill—dead wrong."

Murphy stared at White. Neither man spoke as each one considered the possibility that someone on the inside—members of the crew—had taken over the ship. The only sound present was the rhythmic *clank-clank-clank* of halyard clips striking flag poles anchored near the ship's swimming pool.

White broke the silence with a heavy sigh, "Bill, I'm afraid you may be right. Most of the crew is new and has never sailed on this ship before."

"Surely the cruise line did background checks?" Murphy asked.

"Of course," White shot back. "But how thorough do you think they were? Probably not like the ones we were subjected to in the Navy."

"Probably not," Murphy replied, nodding in agreement.

"Damn!" White cursed. "Well, let's get on with it."

"Right. We can't come up with a plan until we know what's happened," Murphy responded.

"Okay, here's what we'll do—no, make that what *I'll* do," White proposed.

Murphy raised his eyebrows and cocked his head slightly. "What you will do?" he chided, emphasizing *you*. "This isn't a one man show!"

"Bill," he countered, "I'm part of the ship's crew, so they might expect me to show up. If I did, it wouldn't seem out of place. You, on the other hand, are a passenger. If you showed up on the bridge, especially if you were accompanying me, well..."

"I see your point," Murphy acknowledged. "You just want me to stay here, then?

"Yes, that's probably best. If I don't come back down or you hear gunfire..." White paused for a moment "...then you can assume the worst."

"Very well, Evan," Murphy replied. "Good luck and for God's sake be careful!"

White reached for Murphy's shoulder. "Thanks," he said, gently squeezing his partner.

White moved toward the hatch. A large sign on the door read "NO ENTRY - AUTHORIZED PERSONNEL ONLY." White reached the entryway and, one by one, slowly unfastened the four pivoting latches, or dogs, at each corner, being careful not to make any noise while he did so. Next, he grasped the locking lever with both hands and pushed it upward with a quick, but silent, jerk. The pins that held the hatch closed retracted and White swung the door open inch by inch until it was just wide enough for him to slip inside the compartment. He turned toward Murphy, gave a reassuring thumbs-up and faded from sight.

# 27. THE CLOCK IS TICKING

*CIA Headquarters*
*Langley, VA*

Peter King reached across his desk and picked up the phone. He answered the call with his customary greeting, "Special ops, Peter King here." King recognized the voice at once—it was the Director of National Intelligence.

"Good morning, Mr. Conroy," King continued. *Based on the developing situation with the Southern Star, it was anything but good*, he thought privately.

"Peter, I need your help." Conroy paused. "So far, no one else has been able to analyze this hostage situation and provide me or the president with acceptable options."

"I understand that, sir," King replied. "What would you like me to do?"

"Give it to me straight," Conroy demanded. "What do you think our chances of ending this successfully? By that, I mean by without loss of American lives."

"I'm afraid the assessment isn't at all good. It will be very difficult to board the ship without the terrorists noticing. The *Southern Star* is a small vessel as cruise ships go. It will be nearly impossible to insert a rescue team by helicopter," King admitted.

"What about a nighttime operation?" Conroy asked. "Does that change anything?"

"No, sir, it won't. The ship has been stopped and although her engines are probably running at idle to keep the generators operating, the noise from an approaching Pave Low helicopter will be loud enough to alert the terrorists," King explained.

"What then?" Conroy pleaded, "We have to find a way to get a team on that ship. We're running out of time."

"Yes, of course, Mr. Conroy," King replied. "We haven't completely run out of time, but the clock is ticking. What makes this situation different is that the group behind the incident has made no demands of any kind."

"Yes, it is puzzling, isn't it?" Conroy acknowledged.

"It is," King went on. "Usually, these types of actions are for a cause—they want prisoners released, ransom money paid, immunity from prosecution, or some kind of humanitarian aid for Arab refugees. With this one, though, we simply don't know what we're up against."

"Anything we can draw on from previous ops conducted by us, the British or Israelis?" Conroy asked.

"I've already reviewed several recent terrorist episodes and compared them to the *Southern Star* incident. They don't have much in common except for one, which is strikingly similar, but with a twist."

"Which one?" Conroy wondered.

"Do you remember the October 1985 hijacking of the Italian cruise ship *Achille Lauro* by Palestinian terrorists?" King asked Conroy.

"As a matter of fact, I do. Go on," Conroy instructed.

"I know the details of this incident firsthand—I was working out of our Cairo office at the time," King recalled. "The *Achille Lauro* was on a twelve-day Mediterranean cruise with about 680 passengers and a mostly Italian and Portuguese crew of about 350. She had left Alexandria in Egypt and was heading for Port Said, its next Egyptian port of call. Short of her destination, the captain sent out an emergency radio message stating that the ship was under the control of a group of armed men," King recounted.

"Yes, I do remember that incident," Conroy acknowledged.

"The next day," King went on, "the hijackers demanded the release of fifty of their Palestinian Liberation Front (PLF) comrades imprisoned in Israel. They threatened to kill passengers, starting with the Americans, unless the authorities met their demands. The hijackers also threatened to blow up the vessel if a rescue attempt was mounted or if anyone tried to capture them."

"How many hijackers were there?" Conroy asked.

"Only four, but heavily armed," King answered. "They were all Shiites, part of the Palestine Liberation Front, a splinter group aligned with Arafat's PLO."

"Four? Only four?" Conroy responded in amazement. "And we couldn't manage to get a goddamned team on a ship that size or get the crew or even some of the passengers to overpower them?"

"No," King explained, "Most of the passengers had disembarked at Alexandria to go on a sight-seeing trip to the Pyramids, followed by a trip to Port Said. They were to rejoin the ship and sail on to Ashdod, an Israeli port seventy miles south of Tel-Aviv close to the Gaza Strip. Apparently, the four hijackers had intended to remain incognito until the cruise ship docked at Ashdod, but a ship's steward discovered them—only then did they seize the ship. Consequently, in addition to the crew, there were only some sixty to eighty passengers—a dozen of them Americans—left on board the *Achille Lauro*. That made the job of hijacking the ship and taking hostages easy for such a small group of terrorists. It also made it very easy for them to control the situation."

"What were the details surrounding the rescue of the passengers?" Conroy asked.

"Since the *Achille Lauro* was an Italian flagged vessel, the Italian government was running the show. It wasn't clear exactly which group they were dealing with, so it was difficult thoroughly assess the threat. The Pentagon was urging President Reagan to brush aside diplomatic protocol and launch a U.S. led military rescue effort. Even then, those suggestions were difficult to plan and implement. It would take some time just to get all the various forces—including Navy SEALs, army commandos, helicopters, ships, and so on—in place. Another problem for the planners and decision makers," King disclosed, "was how to assess the likely reaction of the hijackers to a military assault."

Conroy pressed King for more, "What was the outcome?"

"The Syrians turned the ship away from the port of Tartus, and in response, an American passenger was killed and his body thrown overboard. In the end," King suggested, "it was the Egyptians who spoiled the deal. Egyptian authorities permitted the *Achille Lauro* to dock in Port Said and gave safe passage to the four terrorists, intending to turn them over to the Arafat's PLO."

"As I recall, though, they didn't get away," Conroy said.

"No, you're correct," King replied. "The EgyptAir jet carrying them first to Algiers was intercepted by Navy F-14's and forced to land in Sicily. Italian authorities arrested the hijackers, and since the *Achille Lauro* was an Italian registered ship, they claimed jurisdiction. All four hijackers were subsequently tried under Italian law, found guilty and given long prison terms."

"So you believe this is similar. In what way, Peter?" Conroy responded.

"Similar, yes. But there's a twist," King suggested.

"How so?" Conroy wondered.

"A few months before this incident, a TWA passenger jet bound for the U.S. was hijacked by Palestinians in Athens, Greece. The terrorists diverted it to Lebanon and held the passengers hostage for more than two weeks on the airport tarmac in Beirut. This incident also involved the killing of an American, a U.S. Navy diver, and the hijackers subsequently escaped."

"Yesterday, there was an incident at Dulles in which an armed passenger was shot by a Federal Air Marshal during what was believed to be a hijack attempt," King stated.

"Wasn't it?" Conroy asked.

"No, I don't believe so, sir," he asserted. "I contend that it was a distraction—a ruse."

"For what?" Conroy demanded. "Why go through all of that planning and risk having one of their operatives killed or captured?"

"That's the twist—instead of an airplane hijacking followed by a ship hijacking, we've got what *appears* to be an airplane hijacking followed by a ship hijacking."

"They—whoever this group is—wanted us to think that they're next move was going to be hijacking an airliner again, just like 9/11, especially since it occurred near the nation's capital. Obviously, it wasn't," King surmised. "They intended to commandeer that cruise ship—the *Southern Star*—all along. By faking an airliner hijacking, they caused us to ramp up airport and airline security and in effect, look the other way. We diverted law enforcement manpower and resources—all of our attention—to something that was never going to happen in the first place."

"I'll be damned!" Conroy exclaimed. "We thought that these two incidents were separate, unrelated events. We failed to connect the dots again. Son of a bitch!"

"It seems so, Mr. Conroy," King conceded. "It seems we missed again."

Conroy's deep sigh whooshed through the earpiece. "The president is going to be very, very unhappy when he finds out."

King said nothing and instead waited for Conroy to speak.

"Thanks, Peter. Call me as soon as you have something—anything—I don't care how ridiculous, how daring or how impossible it sounds. I don't care if it's two o'clock in the morning. I want to know—I have to give the president something concrete he can act on—and soon. Understood?"

"Yes, Mr. Conroy," King responded. "I understand."

The receiver on the other end clicked and the line went dead. King returned the handset to its cradle, leaned back in his chair, and closed his eyes. After a few seconds in thought, he took a deep breath and let out a heavy sigh. King rubbed his eyes briefly and opened them again. *Time to call in another marker.* He leaned forward and reached for the phone. *I just hope I can get in touch.*

# 28. RIGHT PLACE, RIGHT TIME

*Room 303*
*On Vacation*

Jack Stanton fumbled, feeling for the cell phone on the nightstand next to his bed. Once in hand, he answered it. "Stanton, "he managed in a gravelly voice.

"Jack, who do you think this is?" Stanton instantly recognized the caller. It was his old friend, Peter King.

"Judging from the surprise nature of the call, there's only one possibility," Stanton replied. "You're the only person who reaches me at the most inconvenient moments." They both laughed.

Stanton continued, "But do I dare ask the reason you're calling me this time?"

"Three guesses and the first two don't count," King teased.

Stanton played along. "Peter, for Christ's sake! It's barely morning. Do you suppose I can think clearly after being roused from a sound sleep?"

"Okay, Jack. I'll cut right to the chase—I need another favor," King responded.

"Didn't I do something like that for you a few weeks ago? You haven't forgotten so soon, have you?" Stanton kidded.

"No, Jack, I haven't. That's precisely why I'm calling you now. We've got a situation—a very serious one." King explained. "I've been asked by my boss to come up with a solution and I'm going to need your help."

"Well, it can't be another incident involving a newspaper reporter and one of your little spooks trying to escape from Cuba, can it? We recently took care of something like that together, remember?"

"No, Jack. I wish it were that easy," King answered. "This scenario makes that one look like a walk in the park. Nope—we're facing at something a hell of a lot more difficult than that."

"How so?" Stanton asked.

"So difficult that the neither FBI's Hostage Rescue Team or the Army's Delta Force can handle it. They haven't got a clue. Nobody knows what to do. Hell, I don't even know what to do—and I'm the guy who's got to figure it out," King confessed. "That's why I'm calling you at ten in the morning. I'm hoping you can put that tactical brain of yours to work."

"You're kidding, right?" Stanton asked. "You mean the FBI's HRT and the Army's Delta Force can't handle it?"

"No, I'm not kidding, Jack. I wish I were," King sighed.

"All right then," Stanton replied, "tell me what the hell's going on?"

"It seems that several Al-Qaeda operatives have somehow managed to commandeer a cruise ship off the Bahamas," King explained.

"A cruise ship? A big goddamned cruise ship?" Stanton snorted. "What else? What do the bastards want? Do we know yet?"

"We don't know what their demands are, Jack," King continued. "But we do know that all one hundred and twenty passengers on board are Americans."

"You know where this is going, don't you?" Stanton asked King. There was no reply.

"Do we have contact with anyone on the ship by cell phone or radio?" Stanton asked.

"No, not really," King replied, "at least not yet. Nothing we can classify as reliable."

"What possible options are being discussed?" Stanton asked. He then rattled off several possibilities, "Rappelling onto the deck from Blackhawks? Approaching by motorized raft and climbing up the side? Organizing the passengers and crew to retake it from within?"

"Yes, Jack. We've initiated analysis and planning for each of those options. In my opinion, it seems like the odds of a successful outcome aren't good for any of them," King offered.

"I agree with that assessment," Stanton conceded. "Chances of rescuing the hostages without substantial loss of life probably aren't good."

"I was afraid you'd say that, Jack," King sighed. "But I appreciate your honesty. This is a very, very tough situation."

"So exactly where is this cruise ship and what is its name?" Stanton asked.

"She's forty miles northwest of Nassau. Her name is the *Southern Star*," King replied.

Neither man spoke during a very long lull. That prompted King to say something. "Jack, are you still there? The connection hasn't faded has it? Can you hear still me?"

Stanton finally spoke. "Jesus H. Christ!" he exclaimed.

"What's the matter Jack? Is everything all right?" King prodded.

"I'm not sure, Peter," Stanton replied. "You're not going to believe this when I tell you. At the last minute I decided to take a short vacation and I'm on that goddamned ship."

Now it was King's turn for silence. After a very long moment, he reacted to what his friend had just revealed.

"Son of a bitch!" King shouted. "You're right, I don't believe it. However, this may be just the solution I've been looking for."

"Funny thing," Stanton replied, "I always seem to be there just when you need me most. Which one of us do you suppose is the lucky bastard?"

"Obviously, Jack, it's you!" King teased. "Here's your chance to win another medal. Hell, you might even get a promotion when it's over."

"Thanks. I'll try to remember that when the shooting starts," Stanton joked before continuing. "Seriously, Peter, here's what I need you to do. Run the passenger list to find out if there's anyone on board that I could use—current or prior military, former federal agent, police officer—anybody with skills."

"I'm way ahead of you, Jack. My people are sifting through the passenger data as we speak," King replied. "I've got my contacts at the Bureau and ICE going through the crew list, too. Maybe we can find someone in that group who can help you. At the very least, perhaps we can figure out who's behind this."

"Good," Stanton replied. "See if you can come up with the military's OPLAN, too. I don't need the details right now—just an overview."

"Okay, Jack. Will do." King acknowledged. "Call me back in one hour," he instructed.

"You got it. One hour." Stanton ended the call and set the cell phone down on the nightstand. He rubbed his face with both hands. *Jesus H. Christ! How the hell are you going to get out of this one, Stanton?*

# 29. CRYPTIC CODE

*On the bridge deck*
*Aboard the* Southern Star

The set of steps leading from the bridge deck up to the bridge itself was more like a ladder than a staircase. They were much steeper and narrower than the ones found on sections of the *Southern Star* frequented mostly by passengers. Installed on the superstructure above the passenger decks and areas below the water line where the boilers and machinery were, this type of stairway took up less room and only needed to accommodate one person at a time. Their nearly vertical, seventy degree slope, open risers and treads that were only foot and a half wide and four inches deep were the reason handrails that ran from the top to bottom were affixed to each side of the stairs.

Although White had been on the *Southern Star's* bridge many times before, it wasn't his normal duty station. As the ship's purser, White had an office located on the Atlantis deck forward of the main stairwell near the Shore Excursion Office. He handled crew and passenger manifests, payroll, daily activity schedules, routine reports and the like. His role was purely administrative, though, and he had no command or control authority. Purser Evan White was the officer responsible for ship's clearance and processing of legal documents with port authorities, so it wouldn't be unusual for him to make his way to the bridge when the ship was underway. That's exactly what he was counting on.

White firmly grasped the ladders' handrails and began the steep ascent. He silently coached himself through the slow, deliberate motions he was performing with his feet and hands as he made his way aloft.

*Easy does it...one foot at a time...hold on tight so you won't slip...that's it, now on to the next tread...*

White strained to identify any sound that would give him a clue about what was happening some thirty feet above him inside the wheelhouse, but heard none, and that made him wonder even more.

*Are the captain and bridge crew alive? How many intruders are there? Did anybody get a distress call out?*

Although it was well past daybreak, clouds obscured the sun so the cramped ladder space was stuffy and very warm. Even though the *Southern Star* wasn't moving under her own power, the generators were still online and providing electricity. The HVAC system was one of the essential services that operated off the main electrical grid, so everyone aboard was still enjoying the comforts of conditioned air—everyone except Evan White. Beads of perspiration from White's brow slid down his forehead, past his cheeks and plopped onto the front of his uniform shirt as he worked his way upward.

*Almost there...just a few more...keep going.* He repeated the mantra to himself, rhythmically moving his hands and feet as he did so, propelling himself upward and closer to his objective.

The bridge, like every other important compartment aboard the *Southern Star*, was fitted with a watertight hatch. White knew that it wasn't open because he didn't see any light coming from the wheelhouse. Once he reached the top of the ladder, he wasn't sure what his next move would be.

*What will I do when I get there?* White wondered to himself.

To gain access to the bridge's control room, first White would need to unfasten the dogs on the closed hatch and then open it by raising the locking lever. That was sure to attract the attention of the unwanted occupants and the result, although unknown, was also unpredictable. Isolated from Bill Murphy, who was still on the bridge deck below, White would have to make that decision entirely on his own.

As he neared the top of the ladder, a strange sound caught his attention. The tinny noise reminded him of a woodpecker's tapping, but it had a deliberate cadence.

*Ting, Ting, Ting—Ta-Ting, Ta-Ting, Ta-Ting—Ting, Ting, Ting*

White remained motionless and cocked his head, hoping to hear the distinctive pattern again. His reward came in the form of two more bursts, which were identical to the first group.

*Ting, Ting, Ting—Ta-Ting, Ta-Ting, Ta-Ting—Ting, Ting, Ting*

*Ting, Ting, Ting—Ta-Ting, Ta-Ting, Ta-Ting—Ting, Ting, Ting*

Suddenly, a raucous commotion erupted from behind the hatch that was a mere three feet from his face. White froze and held his breath, not knowing what would come next. He heard two distinct voices, each one shouting loudly in Arabic. Then, accompanied by muffled grunts and groans, someone dragged a heavy object across the floor. After several minutes, the shouting stopped and quiet returned.

*What the hell was that?* White wondered.

Several possibilities—none of them good—raced through his mind. White gripped the ladder's handrails even tighter than before.

*I have to get below and tell Murphy what I heard...maybe he could figure it out.*

White was about to begin his descent, but paused. He recalled the sound that preceded the scuffle.

*Was it some kind of coded signal or message?*

White closed his eyes and played the sequence over and over again in his mind. After a couple of minutes, he nodded and opened his eyes.

*That's it! Ting, Ting, Ting—Ta-Ting, Ta-Ting, Ta-Ting—Ting, Ting, Ting is Morse code for Dit, Dit, Dit—Dah, Dah, Dah—Dit, Dit, Dit or S—O—S. One of the crewmembers on the bridge was sending us a distress signal!*

Evan White was satisfied that he knew all he needed to. He loosened his grip on the ladder's handrails and began his descent, though at a much quicker pace than for his climb.

# 30. A VERY LONG DAY

*Aboard the* **Southern Star**
*Near Nassau, Bahamas*

Jack Stanton sat on the edge of his bed thinking about the phone call from Peter King. He stood and shuffled over to the credenza. Stanton plugged a small coffee maker into the wall socket, placed a paper filter into the basket, and dumped a packet labeled "Special Blend" into the waiting holder. Next, he filled the glass carafe with water, poured it into the wide opening, and pushed the red ON button. Within seconds, the sound of percolating coffee dribbling into the glass pot filled the room. Stanton made his way to the divan, plopped down, and closed his eyes. After all, it was still early. *So much for sleeping in,* he muttered.

Luckily, for him, there was no Mrs. Stanton to contend with—he never married. Entering the Army after graduating from the Virginia Military Institute in 1980, he had never found the time to become romantically involved. He had dated off and on but never developed a serious, long-term relationship with anyone. For Jack Stanton, the Army was his first love and he was forever married to his career. That arrangement suited him just fine—his career was all that mattered.

It was quite a career, too. Jack Stanton had a razor-sharp mind, and could analyze things with computer-like speed and logic. He was a brilliant tactician, too. Stanton had proven himself as a young captain in 1990 on the "March to Baghdad" during the first Gulf War. His Military Police company was escorting a handful of captured Iraqi soldiers to a holding area when two Soviet-made Iraqi T-72 tanks appeared out of nowhere.

In most situations, the first thing to do is to deploy to cover. Then, after taking up a defensive position, the next thing to do is to engage the enemy. With sand dunes and flat terrain in every direction for as far as the eye could see, running for cover was next to impossible.

Jack Stanton remembered his old football days at VMI. In an instant, he decided there was only one thing to do and it had to be done fast. He would split the company into two elements and send them off in different directions at breakneck speed, ninety degrees apart. One minute later, each of the two vehicles in the elements was to begin weaving back and forth in a scissor-like movement that would make it hard for the tank crews to acquire and fire on the HUMMVs carrying the prisoners.

From start to finish, in typical Jack Stanton fashion, the analysis, formulation, and communication of the plan to the rest of the Military Police company took no more than two minutes. The First Sergeant and one platoon sergeant would go with the vehicles. Stanton and the other platoon sergeant would stay behind with LAWs, or Light Anti-tank Weapons, and attempt to neutralize the T-72s before they could fire on the HUMMVs that were carrying the Iraqi prisoners.

It was a brilliant tactical success. The T-72s had turned nearly 180 degrees away from each other to acquire and track the HUMMVs that had begun swerving back and forth. When they turned, that left Captain Stanton and his platoon sergeant in a position where the tank crews could not see them, as they lay flat on the desert sand. Better yet, the T-72s left their broad side—the weakest portion of an armored vehicle—completely exposed to Stanton and his platoon sergeant. The LAWs that Stanton and his platoon sergeant let fly quickly found their mark. Two violent, crimson fireballs appeared as the ammunition and fuel inside the T-72s exploded.

Captain John H. Stanton received the Silver Star "for gallantry in action against an enemy of the United States while engaged in military operations involving conflict with an opposing foreign force."

Eventually, his career led him to the G-3 of the 58th Military Police Brigade at U.S. Naval Base Guantanamo Bay, Cuba. What would have been an unusually boring assignment, guarding suspected al-Qaeda prisoners, turned into another one of those opportunities in which only someone of Jack Stanton's mettle could excel.

A few weeks earlier, Jack Stanton had helped his friend Peter King with another impossible scenario. A deadly bio-terror plot against the United States had been uncovered in Cuba. Iran was planning to launch an attack using Cubans infected with a deadly strain of smallpox and set adrift in the Caribbean to mimic the Mariel Boat Lift of 1980.

After alerting U.S. authorities, the assets—a CIA analyst from the London Embassy; his sister; a *Washington Post* reporter; a CIA in-country asset; and a defector—sought refuge and made their way by car from Havana to Guantanamo Bay. Cuban intelligence was on to them, however, and picked up the trail near Santiago, some fifty miles away from Guantanamo.

Traveling in a vintage 1958 Lincoln Coupe that belonged to the Cuban defector, the group raced toward safety and, with the aid of a satellite phone and Peter King, managed to stay ahead of the Cubans who were pursuing them in a Soviet-era BTR-152. That is where Jack Stanton's spur of the moment tactical brilliance saved the day again. Fortunately, for everyone involved, Stanton was on night patrol in the southwest corner of GITMO with Command Sergeant Major Pete Matthews, his fellow hero from the T-72 Gulf War incident.

In order to gain entry to the Naval Base, the driver of the Lincoln rammed the perimeter fence at full speed. The car careened through the wide break in the steel mesh, bounced and swerved, and came to a stop inside the compound. Anticipating the entire sequence of events, Stanton and his top NCO had positioned their two M1117 ASVs on either side of the fence near the gap where the Lincoln had penetrated it.

As soon as the BTR-152 was about fifteen meters from the opening in the fence, Stanton gave the order to move out. The M1117's 260-horsepower diesel engines roared to life, catapulting the six-ton armored vehicles forward with a jolt. The ASVs' Cummins diesel engines and Allison six-speed automatic transmissions enabled them to go from zero to thirty-two kph in less than five seconds. That was about the length of time Colonel Stanton figured it would take the ASVs to contact the BTR-152 broadside. The two ASVs, each weighing more than six tons and traveling more than thirty-five kilometers per hour, struck the left and right midsection of the BTR-152 simultaneously. The impact crushed the vehicle as if it was an empty beer can and instantly killed the Cuban soldiers inside.

Once the four assets were safely in the hands of Stanton and his team, a military transport flew them from Guantanamo Bay back to the U.S. mainland. Soon afterward, Stanton decided he needed a brief vacation. A two-night, three-day cruise in the Caribbean on the *Southern Star* seemed like the perfect getaway.

"Some goddamned vacation," he snorted.

Jack Stanton stood and made his way to the credenza for a much-needed cup of coffee. *This is going to be a long day*, he thought. *A very long day.*

# 31. SOS

*Near the bridge deck*
*Aboard the* Southern Star

Bill Murphy impatiently glanced at his wristwatch. Ship's purser Evan White had been gone for exactly twenty-seven minutes, although to Murphy, who was anxiously awaiting his return, it seemed like an eternity. Adding to Murphy's uneasiness were the loud voices he heard coming from the bridge a few moments earlier. He was positive that they were a foreign tongue, which be believed to be Arabic. If that were true, rather than a mere possibility, it made the likelihood that a band of terrorists had hijacked the *Southern Star* a near certainty. Murphy's eyes focused on his wristwatch again. Twenty-nine minutes had now elapsed since White slipped into the compartment and began his ascent toward the bridge. Murphy was worried.

*Come on, Evan!* Murphy silently pleaded. *Damn it. Hurry up and get down here!*

Murphy was about to look at his wristwatch when Evan White emerged from the hatch. White stepped onto the bridge deck, took a few short steps, turned around, and fell back against the bulkhead. Murphy could see that White's normally crisp uniform shirt and trousers were soaked. Murphy quickly went over to him.

"Evan," Murphy whispered, "what the hell happened?"

White shook his head. "It doesn't look good, Bill" he replied. "I'm pretty sure the ship's been taken over. I couldn't open the hatch to the wheelhouse to confirm it, but there was a scuffle and I overheard voices yelling in Arabic—at least I think it was Arabic."

"I heard the shouting, too. And I agree; it was Arabic," Murphy concurred. "How many of them?" he asked.

"Two. I only heard two voices, so I think there are just two on the bridge," White answered.

"Anything else?" Murphy asked.

Yeah," White responded. "It's the damnedest thing. I had just reached the top of the ladder when I heard tapping on the deck floor above me. I wasn't sure what to make of it, but I think it was a signal from one of the bridge crew. I believe that they were sending us a warning,"

Now very interested in White's explanation, Murphy drew closer. "How so?"

"I'm convinced that it was Morse code." White began. "I heard the sequence three times. The taps were evenly spaced and had a distinctive rhythm. No way could they have been random. Whatever its meaning, the tapping was intentional," he added.

Murphy probed further, "What were the Morse code characters?

"Dit, Dit, Dit—Dah, Dah, Dah—Dit, Dit, Dit," White replied.

Murphy gazed at White for a moment before he responded. Like every other current or former Navy officer, these two also understood Morse code. Perhaps that's exactly what the person who tapped out a message on the bridge's deck floor was counting on.

"That's 'S—O—S' in Morse code for sure," Murphy acknowledged. "Sent three times, you say?"

"Yes," White responded. "After the third series was sent, the brouhaha began."

Murphy rubbed his forehead for a few seconds, then turned around, stepped back and propped himself against the bulkhead next to Evan White.

Murphy leaned closer to White. "That's a game changer," he said in a low voice. "And from here on out," he added, "it's going to be a very different kind of game."

# 32. RULES OF THE GAME

*The White House Situation Room*
*Washington, D.C.*

"Okay, John, let's have it straight and simple. I don't want anything except the facts."

"Of course, Mr. President," Secretary of Defense John Ellis replied. He cleared his throat before continuing. "Launching the SEAL team from NAS Little Creek in Norfolk is the easy part. The Air Force will use a C-130 Hercules to transport the men and their equipment. It's a relatively short flight. The problem, though, is getting them from the landing airport to Kings Bay so they can board the USS *Florida*, a submarine specially equipped for this type of operation."

"How so?" Brewster probed.

"There isn't an airport close by that can support the weight of the Herc. The civilian field at St. Marys is long enough—5,000 feet. However, I'm afraid that the asphalt would crumble beneath its landing gear. It's not designed for that much airplane. The nearest airport that can handle a C-130 is Jacksonville International, some thirty miles south. Another option is the former Navy Air Station at Cecil Field, east of Jacksonville. However, it will take longer to get the SEAL team to Kings Bay by road because it's not close to the Interstate like Jacksonville International. We considered a few other airports, but they aren't much better than St. Marys—they're either too small or too far away."

"You mean one of our key submarine bases doesn't have a civilian or military airfield closer than 30 miles away? Did I hear you correctly?" Brewster asked in a raised voice, his frustration coming through.

"I'm afraid so, Mr. President," Ellis answered timidly. "We're just going to have to work around it."

Brewster glanced toward Paul McCormick. "Make a note of that, Paul," he jabbed his index finger at the chief of staff. "I want to talk with the Senate's Defense Appropriations Committee chairman as soon as we're through here. We must address this issue. Do you agree?"

McCormick nodded and jotted a few lines on a legal pad.

"Put the Armed Services Committee chairman on the list—he might as well hear my concerns, too." Brewster added. McCormick kept his head down and continued to scribble. "Got it, Mr. President." McCormick laid his pen down and looked up.

Brewster swiveled toward the opposite side of the conference table and refocused his attention on Ellis. "Well, what are the options then," he demanded.

Ellis reached for a pushbutton remote control, "I'm going to bring up the video portion of my briefing on the display to your front, sir." The lights in the Situation Room dimmed and a monitor the size of a large screen TV sprang to life. A map that combined satellite imagery with roads and other manmade features appeared. It looked similar to Google maps, but the resolution was much sharper. It was also real time—there were no static images—so the viewers saw everything as it actually was.

The user could overlay other data such as law enforcement and intelligence information, and zoom in to the point where it was possible to read the headline on a newspaper held in someone's hands.

Feeds from the Department of Homeland Security's VECTOR network provided real-time camera images from hundreds of airports, train stations, ports, bus terminals and major highways around the country. In addition, it was possible to review signals from security cameras in major government buildings and offices throughout the U.S. with the push of a button. Like a scene out of *1984*, Big Brother was definitely watching.

The first image to appear was a bird's eye view of the Kings Bay Naval Submarine Base. A pushpin marked the center of the military installation. Ellis moved the cursor across the screen so it hovered over the symbol. A small window detailing the facility's name, coordinates, time, and other key information popped open. Ellis worked the remote control and zoomed out so Brewster and the others could see the area fifty miles around Kings Bay. Major highways, secondary roads, natural features such as rivers, and other bodies of water, were clearly visible. Built up areas—cities, towns and even small villages— formed a mosaic of browns among the green splotches of the surrounding forests and farm fields. Thin, white grid lines crisscrossed the display and provided a latitude and longitudinal point of reference.

"Mr. President," he began, "Our sub base at Kings Bay is located in the center of the map here," referring to a circled-x under his mouse pointer. "Jacksonville International Airport, or JAX, is thirty miles south." Ellis dragged a yellow line down the screen from the center of the map to another pushpin denoted by the number 1. "It's our best bet. The airport provides easy access to Interstate 95 and has an area adjacent to the commercial cargo ramp where we can perform the offloading operation. The Hercules can land and have the entire SEAL team package on its way in less than thirty minutes. If conducted at night, it will go unnoticed and undetected."

Ellis looked at Brewster, as if he expected the question. He wasn't disappointed.

"All right, John, if that's our best option, then what airports have you crossed off the list as unsupportable?"

Ellis dragged the cursor over another symbol and zoomed in. "Cecil Field isn't as close to the Interstate as Jacksonville International, so we ruled that one out." Ellis slid the cursor up the screen and stopped. "As I mentioned before, Mr. President, St. Marys won't accommodate the landing weight of the C-130. Brunswick-Glynco Jetport can handle the C-130's weight, but at fifty-five minutes driving time, it's no closer to Kings Bay than Jacksonville." He moved the cursor up the screen again. "The only military airport we considered, Hunter Army Airfield in Savannah, can easily accommodate the C-130. However, it's almost two hours away from Kings Bay by road. Therefore, Hunter AAF is off the list. That brings us back to Jacksonville International. Hands down, JAX is our best choice."

Brewster opened a manila folder and quickly flipped through the first few pages. He looked up at Ellis. "John, there's an Air National Guard facility at Jacksonville. Why wouldn't we offload there instead of the commercial cargo ramp? Unless I'm missing something, it seems to me that it would be more secure and less likely to arouse any suspicion. After all, we don't want to tip our hand."

# 32. RULES OF THE GAME

"That's an excellent question, Mr. President. We considered that option in our initial planning. The security team ran various 'what-if' scenarios and determined that it would be easier to avoid detection if the C-130 were to park on the civilian side and conduct the offload there. Since so many people and vehicles traverse this ramp, they concluded that the plane and its pallets would blend in better there because those activities would be quite typical. The Air National Guard operation is different. They are a tactical fighter wing that provides air defense with F-15E Strike Eagles from Homestead. Their apron is small and near the intersection of both main runways. More importantly, it is visible from the main passenger terminal, making it susceptible to surveillance. The planners opted for a remote corner on the other end of the airport, Air Cargo Ramp 3. It's perfect—isolated, not lighted and not visible from the main terminal. The SEALs will be transported to Kings Bay in nondescript rented vans and their equipment will follow in two unmarked rented trucks."

"Very well," Brewster replied. "I was sure you had considered it, John. However, I had to ask."

Ellis smiled faintly, "I understand Mr. President. Thank you for bringing it up." The secretary of defense looked down at the conference table for a few seconds. He took a deep breath and exhaled with a sigh.

Brewster sensed something was unsaid. "What is it, John?"

Ellis raised his head and turned to Brewster. "There is one more thing, sir. Our SEALs are the best and they have trained for every mission, every contingency we could come up—except for this one. We never thought anything like this would happen. Nobody is ready for this scenario—not the FBI, not Delta Force, not the SEALs. There is no time to stage it for a practice run, either. Once they leave the *Florida,* they're on their own. They will be making up the rules of the game as they go. I'm sorry, Mr. President." Ellis did not sit down. Instead, he remained standing and waited for a response from the commander in chief.

All eyes in the room now focused on the president. Robert K. Brewster did not respond. He simply stared at the secretary of defense for a very long time.

# 33. DIVERSION OR DIVISION?

*The U.S. Embassy*
*London, United Kingdom*

Bill Blanton already new some of the details before he read the *Evening Standard's* online version of the day's latest terrorist scare. The embassy's watch officer had alerted him as soon as the story broke. Once Blanton arrived at the embassy, he received a brief report summarizing the incident. Nonetheless, scanning headlines and checking accounts were still an excellent way for Blanton to learn more about the dozens of events occurring every day around the world. Now that most major newspapers throughout the globe had their own websites, it was far easier to do. When added to CNN's twenty-four hour breaking news coverage, it was a much simpler way for him to keep up with ever changing situations.

Blanton scrolled down through the text starting with the late day headline.

## Bomb Blasts Rock Northern Spain

Madrid, Spain – Four bombs exploded in northern Spain on Saturday—including one outside a bank—causing damage but no injuries, regional Interior Ministry officials said. A caller earlier warned about the explosives, saying he was speaking on behalf of Basque separatists.

The armed Basque group ETA has been fighting for decades for an independent Basque homeland in northern Spain and western France. The group ended a self-imposed cease-fire in December 2006 with a deadly bombing at a parking lot at Madrid's international airport. Since then, ETA regularly has detonated bombs, often after phoning in warnings. More than 800 people have died in Basque violence. As for any connection between ETA and Islamic extremists, it is widely accepted that al-Qaeda has a large presence in Spain. An unnamed U.S. terrorism expert said looking for partners like ETA would be at the top of al-Qaeda's list. "We know that the majority of people in Spain oppose the wars in Iraq and Afghanistan," he said. "It is highly probable that ETA has been infiltrated by the al-Qaeda network," he added, "which brings with it the chance that they are finding success recruiting within ETA."

Blanton lowered his head and stroked the back of his neck a few times. He pushed the chair away from the desk and stood. He picked up his coffee cup and walked over to the window. Blanton's fifteen-foot-by-fifteen-foot embassy office was typical. A single tall, window framed with simple drapes looked out over the London cityscape. The usual office furniture filled the room—an oak desk; one upholstered side chair; a small, matching oak credenza behind it; and one four-shelf bookcase, which was placed against the wall. A picture of the president hung on the wall behind the desk and an American flag flanked the small credenza. Small and neat, Blanton's office had an air of officialdom.

Blanton gazed out the window eastward across the London rooftops. In the distance, he could see the finial-topped dome of St. Paul's Cathedral against a backdrop of the River Thames. Sir Christopher Wren, one of England's most gifted architects, designed the present-day replacement for Old Saint Paul's, gutted in the Great Fire of London in 1666. The massive stone cathedral took more than thirty-two years to complete and still stands today, over four centuries later. Two towers at the west end, one housing a large clock and bells and the other only bells, flanked the church's three hundred and sixty-five foot tall central dome. Like peaks in a far off mountain range, St. Paul's prominent features stood out in the urban skyline.

A sudden knock at the door interrupted his thought. "Come," Blanton commanded. The door opened and he turned to see Meredith Wilson, his administrative assistant, standing there.

Blanton smiled. "Good evening, Meredith."

"Good evening, sir," she responded cheerfully.

"What brings you in?" Blanton asked.

"I thought with the bombings in Spain today there might be lots of work and you'd need my help," she explained.

"That's very kind of you, Meredith," Blanton replied. "I wasn't going to call you in as I'm sure most of it can wait until morning. But, since you're here, you might as well settle in for a bit and we'll see."

"I'd be happy to, Mr. Blanton." Wilson smiled, moved toward her desk, and sat down. "Let me know if I can do anything," she quipped.

Moments later, Blanton walked to the doorway and leaned his shoulder against the frame. He kept his coffee cup in one hand and jammed the other one in his pants pocket. Wilson sensed his presence and looked up.

"You've heard the news, Meredith. What do you make of today's events?" Blanton asked.

Indicating that she didn't fully understand his question, Wilson cocked her head to the side. "How so?"

"I mean don't you think it's strange that these bombings in Spain today were low key? They didn't cause any injuries and did very little property damage. One of them simply exploded in the sand on an empty ocean beach," he explained. "Why bother?"

"You've got a point, Mr. Blanton," she agreed. "I'm rather sure that these terrorists—part of ETA I think the BBC said—could have done something large and deadly if that was their intention."

"Precisely," Blanton continued. "Large and deadly, assuming that was their real intention. They've demonstrated their capability to do that in several previous incidents. So why do this and why do it now?"

Wilson shrugged. "Those are great questions. I'm afraid I don't know either."

Blanton straightened, removed the hand from his pocket, and nodded. "Maybe we can find out."

Wilson looked at him skeptically, "How?"

"Meredith, search the files and see if you can come up with any other incidents similar to this that occurred the same time as some other attack or incident. Don't limit your search to the U.K. or Europe. Do a worldwide search and check for things that happened a day before and a day after these events," Blanton instructed. After a brief pause he added, "There has to be some significance to these bombings in Spain."

"Do you think this is a diversion, Mr. Blanton?" Wilson asked pointedly. "Is that what you're suggesting?"

"That is exactly what I am suggesting, Meredith," Blanton answered. "The attacks in Spain could be a diversion, or they could even be a low key sympathetic attack on another front—a divisional response, if you will. They might appear unrelated, but they could be linked."

"I'll get right on it, Mr. Blanton," Wilson replied. "However, I'm afraid it will take a while."

Blanton looked at his watch. It was nearly six o'clock.

"In that case, why don't I send out for some food then—how about good old pub fare? Shall we make it fish 'n' chips?" he asked.

"Splendid," Wilson giggled, "Just what I was fancying!" She immediately went back to her computer keyboard and began typing again.

"Good then," Blanton smiled, "fish 'n' chips it is. And I won't forget the extra malt vinegar for you this time!" He walked to the phone on his desk and lifted the receiver. Blanton paused before dialing the number as a strange thought flashed through his mind. He turned and looked out the window at St. Paul's Cathedral again. After a few seconds, he shook his head, reached for the number pad and began to dial.

# 34. MORE INFO

*Dania Beach Hotel*
*Ft. Lauderdale, FL*

Still stunned by the CNN news story about the hijacking of the *Southern Star*, Allan sat quietly in his hotel room thinking about the morning's events. Although the other major news outlets were now covering it, the details were still sketchy. Allan didn't really know any more now than he did when the news first broke. He had tried to call Susan's cell phone several times since then, but couldn't get through. Allan wasn't sure why and had considered several explanations. Perhaps it was due to the tropical storm that was swirling around out there; or maybe Susan's cell phone battery was dead; then again, she might have simply turned her phone off; or—heaven forbid—it could be something worse. It was the "something worse" possibility that really bothered him.

Allan decided he would call Meredith, partly because he needed a friend to talk to right now, and partly because since she also worked at the U.S. embassy, she might know something. CNN's top of the hour headlines didn't shed anything new on what was happening, which only added to Allan's frustration. The local time was a few minutes after 1 p.m. and it was five hours later in London, just after six in the evening. If Meredith went out for the day with friends, she'd certainly be back home by now. Allan turned the television's volume down and reached for his cell phone. He dialed the number to her flat and he held his breath. Her answering machine picked up on the fifth ring. "Hello, this is Meredith. I'm sorry I can't take your call right now, but if you leave your name and number, I promise I'll call you as soon as I can."

"Damn!" Allan shouted. He dropped the phone and fell back against the bed, exasperated.

Suddenly he sat up, snatched his cell phone and quickly dialed another number.

On the second ring, a pleasant voice answered. "Good evening, you've reached the embassy of the United States in London. I'm Meredith Wilson. How may I help you?"

Surprised that he had been able to reach her, Allan didn't respond right away.

"Hello. May I help you?" Wilson asked. There was no answer. After a moment, she pressed the caller again, "Hello. Are you still on the line?"

Allan regained his senses and blurted out, "Hi, Meredith. It's Allan. I've been trying to reach you and couldn't. I'm so happy—no, glad—that I've finally located you."

"Allan, what's wrong? Are you all right?" she demanded. "You sound frightened. Are you hurt or in trouble?"

"Meredith, you're not going to believe what happened today—or what happened to me yesterday," he began. "I don't know where to start."

"I'm sure it's okay, Allan. Everything's going to be fine," Wilson reassured him. "Why don't you tell me what's going on."

"Sure," Allan sighed. "Sure."

"Have you seen the news yet?" he began. "I mean did

you hear about the attempted airliner hijacking here in the states?"

"Yes, I did," Wilson replied. "I read the newspaper account just this morning. Why do you ask?"

"That's what you're not going to believe, Meredith," Allan said. "I was on that airplane. That was the flight I was taking to meet Susan and Murph in Fort Lauderdale."

"Oh, my!" Wilson exclaimed. "Then you saw the shooting?"

"I did. I saw the whole thing," Allan explained. "One of the Federal Air Marshals was sitting right next to me."

"Were you scared?" she asked.

"It all happened so fast it wasn't until it was over that I realized how frightened I was," Allan admitted. "The worst part," he went on, "is that it could just as easily happened in the air rather than on the ground."

"Yes, I suppose so," Wilson added.

"That's what was so troubling," Allan said. "I'm surprised that this terrorist—assuming that's what he was—made it through airport security. TSA was extremely thorough with their screening procedures."

"You were able to catch another flight to Fort Lauderdale in time to meet your cruise ship, right?" Wilson asked.

"That's the other thing you won't believe, Meredith," Allan replied. "I missed the *Southern Star's* departure by a few hours because of all the delays at Dulles. However, I wasn't worried. I thought I'd simply hop a short flight to Nassau and meet the ship there, and sail back to Florida with Susan and Murph."

"If you're not on the ship right now, then what happened?" Wilson wondered.

"That's it, Meredith," Allan choked, "the *Southern Star* has been hijacked. The story is all over CNN and the major networks. Everybody is assuming that a terrorist group is behind it. So far, though, there hasn't been any claim of responsibility or communication from the ship."

"I'd ask if you were kidding, Allan, but I can tell from the tone of your voice that you're not. I'm so sorry," Wilson responded. "Have you tried to reach Susan?" she asked.

"That's what worries me," Allan answered. "I've been trying all morning and can't get through. I'm hoping it might be the tropical storm or a dead phone battery."

"I'm sure that Susan will call you as soon as she can," Wilson said reassuringly. "She's a very smart woman, you know."

"Yes, I know that, Meredith," Allan sighed. "Thanks for trying to put a good face on it and cheer me up."

"By the way, it's Saturday night. What are you doing at the embassy?" Allan asked curiously.

"There were bombings in Spain today," Wilson explained. "No casualties, but lots of damage. Very strange, I'd say. I thought Mr. Blanton might be here running it down, so I came in to see if he needed any help."

"Then I'm glad I reached you tonight. Have you heard anything at the embassy about the cruise ship hijacking?" Allan asked.

"No, I'm afraid not," she replied. "Mr. Blanton thinks the blasts in Spain were a diversion of some kind. He said that they could have killed dozens, but placed far from major population centers instead. He's got me running down similar incidents that occurred over the past couple of days around the world on the outside chance they might be related to these bombings."

"That's interesting," Allan replied softly. "Maybe the bombings in Spain and the airplane incident near Washington were a diversion for something bigger—the *Southern Star* hijacking."

"That's brilliant, Allan!" Wilson shouted. "I'll let Mr. Blanton know."

"If you don't mind, Meredith," Allan responded, "I'd like to tell him myself—I've also got a couple other things I'd like to talk to him about. Put him on the line, please."

"Sure thing," she replied. "Call me as soon as you hear from Susan, won't you?"

"Will do," Allan answered. "Keep your fingers crossed," he added, trying to sound upbeat. Allan closed his eyes as Meredith put him on hold. *It's going to take a lot more than that*, he thought, *a lot more*.

# 35. SHOOT, MOVE, COMMUNICATE, AND SURVIVE

*Aboard the* Southern Star
*Near Nassau, the Bahamas*

*Shoot, move, communicate, and survive.* Jack Stanton sat on the edge of the bed in his stateroom aboard the *Southern Star* and recalled the basic skills required of every Army soldier. He knew them well—they were part of every fighting man's training since World War II. Although the tools used had changed considerably over the past seventy years, the tenets remained the same. Field Manual No. 7-21.13, *The Soldier's Guide*, spelled it all out in very exacting language. Ingrained into Jack Stanton's fiber from the time he first set foot inside the Virginia Military Institute as a cadet, today shoot, move, communicate, and survive would become the basis of any plan he developed.

Stanton moved from the bed to a large, stuffed chair on the other side of his berth. He plopped down and gulped the last of the hot coffee from his cup. The phone call he had received earlier from his old friend at the CIA, Peter King, was troubling him. King had instructed him to call back in an hour, promising some much-needed information about the terrorists and passengers—and more importantly, the military's rescue plan. Stanton closed his eyes. *"Well, Jack, you're in one hell of a jam now. No weapons, no backup and no ideas. King better come up with something useful."*

*What to do?* Stanton's mind raced as dozens of options sped through his consciousness. Stanton recalled some of actor Clint Eastwood's best on-screen lines from the film "Heartbreak Ridge" when Eastwood, playing the role of Marine Gunny Highway, grunted the best way to beat adversity to his men, "You're Marines now. You adapt. You overcome. You improvise. Let's move. Four minutes! We move swift. We move silent. We move deadly." *That's it,* Stanton thought, *Improvise, adapt and overcome. It's the only thing to do. I just hope there are a few passengers I can count on—otherwise, I'm up the creek without a paddle.*

Stanton opened his eyes and glanced at his wristwatch. It was almost time to call Peter King back. He stood and walked to the credenza and poured another cup of coffee. He turned around, leaned back against the wall, and took a couple of sips from the mug. *Well, better get on with it—it's now or never.* Stanton retrieved his cell phone from the nightstand and returned to the stuffed chair. He sat down and dialed Peter King's number at Langley—he was right on time.

King answered Stanton's call the instant he heard it ring. "Hello, Jack. You're militarily punctual, as always."

"I've got nothing else to do. I'm on vacation, remember?" Stanton joked.

"Don't worry. You'll have plenty of things to keep you occupied very soon, Jack. I promise you," King responded.

"I can't wait," Stanton smirked, trying to add levity to the conversation. "What have you got for me?"

"Let's start with the terrorists. Here's what we know, Jack. ICE and DHS ran the photos and profiles for the entire ship's crew through Interpol's database and found matches for a handful of them on its terrorist watch list.

We're quite certain there's only a small number—perhaps eight to ten in all. We believe that they are well-armed and smuggled weapons and explosives aboard the *Southern Star* just before she sailed from Fort Lauderdale. Both CIA and DIA are attempting to link them to a particular group so we can better understand their background, training and motives. So far, no group has claimed responsibility, nor have the terrorists themselves made any demands. NSA is continuing to monitor the usual militant Islamic websites and Al Jizira broadcasts for developments. Hopefully, we'll learn more about them and what they want during the next several hours."

"Peter, are you sure about the number?" Stanton asked. "It's a real critical piece of information."

"Yes and no, Jack," King hedged. "We're sure there are at least eight to ten—that was confirmed by the matches against the Interpol database. What we don't know is if there are any new recruits taking part who aren't yet on the watch list. Nor do we know if there are any other participants—like crewmembers—who might be involved because they are being paid to or are being coerced in some way."

"For Christ's sakes, Peter!" Stanton snapped, "I can't develop an effective plan unless I know what I'm up against—and neither can you for that matter."

"Jack, settle down," King shot back. "I understand that just as well as you do, and you know it. The problem is that the bastards have outsmarted us again. We were looking in the wrong goddamned place—airport, bus, and train terminals. Our increased security measures after 9/11 were very predictable. Since they knew what we *would* do, it was easy for them to figure out what we *wouldn't* do. Once more, we failed to connect the dots and, surprise!"

"Sorry, Peter," Stanton apologized. "You're right. Getting all wound up over what happened and why won't change anything. More importantly, it won't resolve the crisis at hand, will it?"

"No, Jack. It won't," King agreed. "We've got to put our heads together and come up with something that will gain us valuable time and allow us to learn more about the terrorists until the cavalry arrives."

"Right you are, Peter!" Stanton replied. "What about the passengers? Anybody who can help?"

"As a matter of fact, yes," King said, "and you're going to like this next bit of information."

"Go on," Stanton insisted.

"One of the passengers is an active duty Navy officer named Murphy. He's on leave and on board with a woman companion—a *Washington Post* reporter. Murphy is an Annapolis graduate and from what I've been told by the Pentagon, quick thinking and very sharp," King explained. "He's a sub commander—a boomer skipper. His boat, the *Wyoming*, is the same one that launched the preemptive Trident strike against Iran a few weeks ago. Of course, we don't know if that's just a coincidence or part of the plot."

"I don't know either. But this whole thing sounds like pages ripped right out of a Hollywood screenplay," Stanton mused.

"Yeah," King answered, "it sure does—and you have a leading part. Here's your chance for real fame and fortune, Jack."

"Gee, thanks," Stanton replied sarcastically, "just what I've always wanted."

King continued, "We'll need you and Murphy to link up and devise a way to distract the terrorists just before the military rescue begins—that will be critical. I'll have more information about the OPLAN for you in another hour, so call me then. Got it?"

"Got it. One hour," Stanton acknowledged. He closed the cell phone and dropped it into his lap. Stanton closed his eyes groaned. *Shoot, move, communicate. That's the easy part. There is one more important thing I still have to figure out—how to survive.*

# 36. MAKE IT SO

Director of National Intelligence Jim Conroy began the midday briefing. "Mr. President, I'd like to provide you with some background regarding a similar terrorist situation that occurred in October of 1985. Perhaps you recall the hijacking of the Italian cruise ship, *Achille Lauro*. You may also remember that during the incident, a U.S. citizen was murdered and his body thrown overboard."

"Yes, Jim, I do," Brewster nodded. "I also remember that it was something of a botched job, complicated by politics and second-guessing on the part of the several countries involved."

"You're quite right, Mr. President," Conroy replied. "Let me give you some of the more important details. Under international law, the U.S. was within its rights to board and seize a vessel under the control of pirates, but Italian Prime Minister Bettino Craxi wasn't convinced. Fearing an international incident or reprisal from terrorist elements aligned with the PLF or the PLO, Craxi balked and failed to go along with the idea."

"What then," Brewster asked.

"Well," Conroy continued, "Craxi was only too happy to have the Egyptians permit the *Achille Lauro* to dock in Port Said. The Mubarak government likewise was happy to hand the four hijackers over to Arafat and the PLO. Nobody wanted to deal with the real issue: delivering swift, uncompromising justice."

Brewster leaned forward. "So how did the U.S. become involved, Jim?"

Conroy paused briefly and then responded. "This is the way it played out, sir. At 5:30 p.m. on Thursday, October 10, President Reagan was aboard Air Force One, returning to Washington, D.C. from a speaking engagement in the Chicago area, when word reached him that the *Achille Lauro* hijackers were getting away. Despite Egyptian President Mubarak's claims that the terrorist group had left Egypt, Israeli intelligence provided evidence to the contrary that showed they were still on an airbase outside Cairo. U.S. intelligence personnel were able to eavesdrop on calls made to and from Mubarak's office and learned that the Egyptians were planning to fly the hijackers out on a special flight to Algiers. Acting swiftly, they were even able to obtain the aircraft's identification and a flight plan."

Conroy paused until he was sure the president had kept up with the explanation.

"So far, so good, Jim," Brewster nodded. "Go on."

"Very well," Conroy took his boss's cue and continued. "Military advisors proposed intercepting the aircraft and forcing it to land at a NATO air base in Sicily. Reagan authorized the carrier USS *Saratoga*, patrolling the Adriatic Sea, to put seven F-14 Tomcats into the air. Their orders were to divert the Egyptian aircraft to a NATO base at Sigonella, Sicily. The appearance of the Navy fighters unnerved the EgyptAir pilot, who compliantly altered course for Sicily. To our advantage, he had no way of knowing that the American pilots had orders to refrain from shooting down the Boeing 737 without a directive from the president."

"Did that work? Brewster asked. "Were we able to apprehend the perpetrators?"

"Not exactly, sir," Conroy replied. "Initially the Italians were not inclined to cooperate, scrambling their own warplanes to prevent a landing at Sigonella. However, after a call from Reagan, Italy's Prime Minister Bettino Craxi gave permission to land. This is where things became a bit sticky. The American plan was to load the Palestinians onto a U.S. military aircraft and transport them to the States. But when American troops encircled the EgyptAir 737 they found themselves surrounded in turn by Italian soldiers and Carabinieri (Italian national police)."

"A stalemate of sorts," Brewster interrupted.

Conroy nodded. "Exactly, sir. To complicate matters, also on EgyptAir 737 was Abul Abbas, mastermind of the TWA aircraft hijacking and subsequent killing of a U.S. Navy diver. President Mubarak's government decided to send Abbas back to Lebanon along with the cruise ship hijackers and let Arafat deal with the repercussions of the dead serviceman and *Achille Lauro* passenger."

Brewster pressed him for more details and asked, "How did the Italian government react?"

Conroy responded, "They didn't give in. When Reagan called Craxi this time, he wouldn't budge. The terrorists faced a slew of charges, including premeditated murder, kidnapping and hijacking. Italy had decided that since the *Achille Lauro* was an Italian vessel, Italian courts should try the hijackers. The Italian leader refused to let the U.S. military take the fugitives into custody. Abbas and his fellow terrorists would remain in Italian hands instead."

"And?" Brewster prodded.

"It was a mixed bag of outcomes, Mr. President," Conroy replied. "The U.S. continued to pressure Italy to turn all five terrorists over to them. However, Arafat threatened Craxi with 'uncontrollable reactions' if the Italians turned Abbas over to the Americans. Craxi's government caved in to Arafat's threats. Italy refused a U.S. request to extradite the terrorist leader and soon freed Abbas. The only positive note in the entire affair was that in 1986 after a highly publicized trial, the four *Achille Lauro* hijackers were convicted and sentenced to long prison terms."

"Jim, as I recall, there were some repercussions, right?" Brewster asked.

"The political aftershocks were not long in coming," Conroy replied. "The Mubarak government demanded an apology from the U.S. for intercepting the EgyptAir flight and forcing it to land in Sicily. President Reagan vowed he never would issue such an apology—and he never did. The Italian coalition government of Prime Minister Craxi collapsed amid controversy as key members abandoned it for what they viewed as an anti-Israel, pro-PLO stance. And, in the cruelest irony of all, Yasar Arafat, having himself condoned the hijacking of the *Achille Lauro*, accused President Reagan of an 'act of piracy' by intercepting the EgyptAir 737."

Brewster stroked his chin. "So where does that leave us?" he asked.

This time, Secretary of State Adrian Ashe took the president's question. "Mr. President, the *Southern Star* is drifting in international waters some sixty miles northwest of the Bahamas. Since the vessel is under the control of pirates, international maritime law clearly gives us the right to act. To be sure, the Bahamas are part of the British Commonwealth and the British will stand with us. Consequently, we won't have to worry about bringing our case to the U.N. Security Council or World Court in The Hague before we proceed."

"Very well," Brewster nodded. "Now on to other matters." He turned to Secretary of Defense John Ellis. "John, what do your contingency planners say? Have they come up with any viable options yet?"

"Mr. President," Ellis began, "they are still assessing the situation and evaluating several options. They have ruled out a number of possibilities, including a nighttime air assault by helicopter. They've also scrubbed plans for a seaborne rescue. Both are too risky because the terrorists could easily spot those efforts and that would give them time to react, perhaps killing hostages or blowing up the ship. The most plausible option developed so far uses one of our new guided missile subs to transport SEALs close to the *Southern Star's* position. Once there, our forces would launch the rescue operation. Plans call for a nighttime assault that begins with an underwater SEAL deployment."

"How is that coming?" Brewster asked. "Are we ready to execute the plan?"

"Yes and no, sir," Ellis answered.

Brewster raised his eyebrows and peered at Ellis over the top of his glasses. "Yes and no," he repeated. "What the hell does that mean? Either we're ready or we're not."

"I'm sorry," Ellis responded. "Let me clarify that. We have a sound plan in place. The USS *Florida* and a SEAL team are at Kings Bay awaiting your orders. Once they sail, they can be on the scene in a matter of hours. Getting the submarine and the SEALs *to* the *Southern Star* is the easy part. The piece we haven't figured out yet is how to get them *on* the *Southern Star*."

Brewster scowled, his disappointment evident.

"I know it sounds far-fetched, Mr. President," Ellis went on, "but this is a ship, not a building or a rock wall. There aren't any doors or hatches at the water line. The SEALs will have to scale the side of the ship somehow, but they will have to do it without tipping off the terrorists. That's what we're working on. We've never planned for a scenario like this so we've never trained for it. We're making up the rules as we go."

Director of National Intelligence Jim Conroy spoke up. "It's not as bad as it seems, Mr. President. The good news is that I have one of my very best people working on it. I am confident that he can come up with an acceptable solution in short order. In fact, I'm so confident sir, that I'm willing to take a gamble."

Brewster removed his glasses and leaned forward. "Go on, Jim. I'm all ears."

Conroy paused briefly and then leaned forward as well. "Mr. President, I'm certain that if you give the order for the *Florida* to get underway, by the time she reaches the *Southern Star*, he will have come up with a way for the SEALs to successfully board her."

Brewster put his glasses on and leaned back in his chair. He looked at Conroy and then Ellis. "Gentlemen, I don't have to tell this because you already know it: The stakes are extremely high. Like President Reagan, I'm not concerned about the political ramifications—I could give a damn. I'm more concerned for the lives of the passengers and crew. It's high time we put barbaric acts like this to an end. Make it so."

Ellis and Conroy responded in unison with a resounding, "Yes, sir."

Brewster stood to leave. "I want hourly updates around the clock until this mission is completed," he instructed sternly. "Understood?"

Ellis and Conroy nodded, "Understood."

Brewster started for the door and stopped. He turned part way around and looked at the secretary of defense and director of national intelligence. "Good luck, gentlemen. I think you're going to need it—lots of it."

# 37. DÉJÀ VU ALL OVER AGAIN

*Dania Beach Hotel*
*Ft. Lauderdale, FL*

Allan's frustration turned to fear. A few weeks earlier, he found himself in Cuba where he managed to help Susan escape after she learned of a dastardly plot concocted by the Iranians to launch a bioterrorist attack against the United States from the island. Allan, Susan and two Cuban nationals eluded Castro's secret police and soldiers by making their way through the countryside in the middle of the night to the U.S. Naval Base at Guantanamo Bay. A machine gun bullet from an army truck that gave chase struck one member of their party, a CIA operative named Angel, who died instantly. Allan, Susan and the other Cuban, a biological researcher named Dr. Vega, narrowly avoided capture, imprisonment or execution. Once safely inside the compound at Guantanamo Bay, they were flown back to the U.S. mainland within hours.

There was only one thing Allan could do now, and that was the same thing he did when Susan was in danger in Cuba weeks before. Allan would turn to the only person he could trust, the only man he knew could help in this situation, Peter King.

Allan snatched his cell phone off the bed and quickly dialed a number. He had committed it to memory because his Uncle George, a.k.a. Peter King, had forbidden him to write it down. It was an unlisted government number that gave him direct access to his uncle's office inside the CIA's headquarters at Langley. His uncle had explained that the phone number wasn't really a direct link to his office. For security reasons, when dialed, the number connected the call to a switch that routed it to a reflector and then to CIA headquarters. The random pairs of numbers and switches changed at regular intervals and provided a basic level of communications security. All sensitive conversations used authentication and voice encryption. Even so, Allan's uncle warned him to use it only for emergencies. Allan nodded as the phone on the other end rang. *This is an emergency.*

On the third ring, there was a distinct click and Allan heard the voice on the other end say, "King here."

"It's Allan. Have you got time to answer a few questions?" he asked. "I think something's happened to Susan and I need to know what's going on. Is there a situation of some sort involving a cruise ship?" he blurted out in a single breath.

"Okay, Allan, slow down," King responded. "Now, what's this all about?"

"I'm in Fort Lauderdale. I was supposed to meet Susan and Bill here for a weekend cruise to the Bahamas. I missed my flight from Dulles because of an attempted hijacking or some other type of incident. I just saw a news story on CNN about their cruise ship, the *Southern Star*, being taken over by terrorists," Allan explained.

"Well, I'd say that pretty much sums it up, Allan," King replied. "You stated the facts accurately."

Allan pressed his uncle, "But there has to be more, right?"

"Yes, Allan, there is more, to be sure." King paused. "I'm afraid at the moment, we don't know what that is," he continued.

"I hope you're kidding. You are, aren't you?" Allan asked sheepishly.

"No, Allan, I'm afraid I'm not," King replied somberly.

Allan didn't respond right away. After a few moments, he spoke, "The agency, the FBI, Interpol—somebody has to know what is happening! There are Americans aboard that ship—and one of them is my sister. I find it hard to believe that we didn't see this coming or don't have a clue what it's all about."

"Allan, I know it's troubling, especially since Susan is aboard that ship," King said. "Agencies at all levels of government are using every resource available to determine who is behind this and what they want. I can tell you that this has the president's full attention and he has made it his highest priority."

"Well, we can't just sit back and wait for something to happen!" Allan snapped. "I might be just a CIA analyst rather than a field agent, but I'm not stupid."

"I agree with you, Allan, but calm down," King admonished. "Look, we're pulling out all the stops. Don't repeat this, but I've been given a PD and have taken a lead role in supporting the U.S.'s response."

"When you say 'response,' do you mean rescue effort?" Allan asked.

"Precisely," King answered.

"What do you know that I don't?" Allan quizzed his uncle.

"Here are the elements we do know," King began. "There are six to eight terrorists of Middle Eastern descent who posed as members of the *Southern Star's* crew. The perpetrators apparently smuggled the weapons and explosives they have at their disposal on board while the ship was preparing for her voyage. The terrorist group is a small cell affiliated with a London-based organization, al-Muhajiroun. Their leader, the radical Muslim cleric Omar Bakri-Muhammed and his followers advocated the development of a 'global Islamic state.' They are quite active in recruiting on campuses in and around London, particularly at Oxford," King explained.

"Hmmm," Allan responded. "I'm familiar with that group. One of the FBI's counter-terrorist agents recently assigned to the embassy—a fellow named Blanton—asked me what I knew about them. It seems he's been pursuing leads provided by one of the group's members. I do know that Bakri-Muhammed reportedly fled London to avoid arrest. Blanton was trying to identify who had taken over and was directing al-Muhajiroun's activities."

"Well, there you have it, Allan," King chuckled, "You knew more about this than you first thought. But you can also see just how complex these sorts of things can be."

"But I still don't get it," Allan said with puzzlement. "Why would a small, seemingly insignificant group like that want to take over a cruise ship with just a few American passengers on board?"

"Why not?" King shot back. "For them, it makes perfect sense. Except for the *Achille Lauro* incident, which didn't actually begin as a hijacking, something like this is a first. It's also a way for them to gain recognition and support from other militant Islamic groups and their backers, like Iran. Lastly, it is a warning to the non-Muslim world that no aspect of Western life is safe from their jihadist activities and goals."

"In other words," Allan replied, "it fits the classic definition of terrorism, which is any criminal act performed for a political purpose where such acts contain violence, the threat of violence or fear."

"Exactly," his uncle replied. "You've got it right."

"But that still doesn't address the reason I called you," Allan sighed. "How are we going get Susan and the others off the ship? I feel so damned helpless."

"If you want to help," King replied, "there is one very important thing this calls for and you're just the guy to get it for me. I need someone I can count on and someone already on the ground in Fort Lauderdale. There's no time to waste, so that someone is you, Allan."

"Of course. I'd be glad to help," Allan offered. "What is it?"

"I 'd like you to go to the Sovereign Cruise Lines office at Port Everglades and look at the *Southern Star's* blueprints and deck layout. I need to know every important detail about the ship's passageways, wheelhouse, engine room, entertainment lounges and dining rooms. Things like the number of doors and windows, how long the corridors are, distance between the larger entertainment and dining rooms, her height above the waterline. There may be other elements later on, but that will do for now."

"How will I get through the gate at the port now that the *Southern Star* has sailed," Allan asked. "I don't have a valid ticket. Even if I did, I'm sure the cruise line's not going to let me review the *Southern Star's* blueprints and layout just because I ask to."

"Leave that to me," King responded. "Remember the Presidential Directive I mentioned earlier?" he asked.

"Yes," Allan answered, "but how will that help me."

"A PD has the full force and effect of law and this one gives me carte blanche under the president's authority to do whatever I deem necessary to plan and complete this rescue mission," King explained. "It's as if I'm the new sheriff in town and you're now my chief deputy."

"If you say so," Allan replied.

"Trust me, Allan," King responded confidently, "by the time you get to the entrance gate everything will be in order. There will be a DHS car and Homeland Security escort officer waiting for you. You will have unrestricted access to all information on the *Southern Star*. As soon as you gather what we need, call me back on this number. I'll have instructions on where to send it and by what means. Any questions?"

"Nope," Allan answered succinctly. "Understood."

"Very well, then," King replied. "Time is critical, Allan, so get to it." There was a distinct click and then the phone connection went dead.

Allan pivoted around, picked up the room phone and dialed the front desk. "Hello, this is Mr. Anderson in room 116. I need a taxi to take me to Port Everglades right away."

# 38. FORTUNE FAVORS THE BOLD

*Underway in the Atlantic*
*South of Kings Bay, GA*

The USS *Florida*, guided missile submarine SSGN 728, was underway. Hours earlier, she left her berth at Naval Submarine Base Kings Bay and slowly made her way down the narrow entrance channel. She glided five miles along the marshy Georgia coast, slid past Drum Island, and reached the St. Marys Entrance, a wide expanse of water where the St. Marys and Jolly Rivers emptied into Cumberland Sound. Dotted by Cumberland Island on one side and Amelia Island on the other, it marked the beginning of a straight, eight-mile long channel that led east to the Atlantic Ocean. Once the *Florida* was safely off shore, she slowly slipped below the surface and out of sight.

Although the *Florida* carried her normal crew complement of seventeen officers, fifteen chief petty officers and one hundred and twenty-two enlisted men, today was different. In response to the hostage situation unfolding on the *Southern Star*, she was transporting other personnel as well. Under direct orders from the president, SEAL Team Eight was on board the submarine. Already the *Florida*'s Special Operations Forces (SOF) mission command center was a beehive of activity as the SEALs prepared for a rescue effort.

The *Florida* was a very special boat. In 2004, the *Florida* underwent an extensive, two-year conversion from a "boomer" that carried ballistic missiles to her present configuration. She remained essentially the same as when she was a boomer. The *Florida* still measured 560 feet long with a beam of forty-two feet and a displacement of roughly 18,750 tons.

Her SSGN conversion involved modifying the twenty-four Trident II D-5 nuclear missile launch tubes to carry one hundred and fifty-four Tomahawk cruise missiles and installing diver lockout chambers and landing pads for an airlock-like Dry Deck Shelter (DDS). The DDS housed the SEAL Delivery Vehicle (SDV), a small submersible that could carry up to six SEALs and their equipment. The *Florida's* refurbished midsection now included extra berthing and storage for sixty-six Special Forces personnel and the SOF command and control center. In addition, upgrades to the submarine's communications and sensor capabilities incorporated a command post called the Joint Task Force Connectivity Center.

Complemented by a variety of advanced, high-tech devices such as underwater robotic vehicles and even drones for aerial operations, the SSGN was a modern war-fighting machine. The Trident SSGN's design focused on four key mission requirements: stealth, payload, versatility, and endurance. The most important of these was stealth.

Modernization plans called for the installation of the Advanced SEAL Delivery System, or ASDS, which was still under development on some SSGN's. It was a new generation mini-sub intended for the covert movement of up to eight SEALs and their combat gear to and from hostile shores. Although an SSGN with the ASDS mounted had to restrict its speed, in an emergency, the submarine was capable of traveling as fast as twenty knots.

A sophisticated Battle Management Center (BMC) gave the SSGN a unique joint operations center capability to support SOF mission planning and execution. Located just aft of the submarine's control room, the BMC contained as many as thirty workstations with large screen displays for support briefings and operational graphics. Printing capabilities were available using the submarine's local area network and existed throughout the BMC and SSGN. During the final stage in the conversion process, the *Florida's* S8G nuclear reactor underwent an engineering refueling overhaul that would last for the remainder of her service life. Following successful sea trials, the USS *Florida* returned to operational service in May 2006.

Since the *Florida* was capable of achieving a submerged speed of more than twenty-two knots, she could cover a distance roughly equal to that between Washington, D.C. and Atlanta, Georgia in twenty-four hours. It would take only half that time for her to be on station in the waters off the Bahamas.

Commanded by Scott Davis, a Naval Academy graduate and career Navy officer, the former SSBN was a fearsome vessel even without her Trident nuclear missiles. Commander Davis recently bragged to one of his Annapolis classmates and close friends—a boomer skipper named Murphy, who captained the *Wyoming*—about her prowess. During a lunch at the Kings Bay Officer's Club one day not long after Davis joined his boat and her crew at the submarine base, he and Commander William C. Murphy, skipper of the *Wyoming*, were comparing notes in between bites of the daily special.

"Ever since I was first briefed on the capability of the SSGN," Davis began, "I continue to be impressed with what the *Florida* and her sister boats can do. In addition to her advanced torpedoes, she's equipped with one hundred and fifty-four Tomahawk cruise missiles. The latest Ticonderoga-class guided missile cruiser the Navy commissioned, the USS *Port Royal*, only has a normal complement of eight. Of course, a cruise missile is one hell of a weapon, so just one or two can do the job."

Davis took another bite of his Turkey Club sandwich, swallowed, and went on. "Here's another thing, Murph. Did you know that the SSGNs are the same length as the AEGIS missile cruisers? Both are five hundred and sixty feet long. Actually, the Ticos are seven feet longer,"Davis smiled and then raised the sandwich to his waiting lips. "But when you're packing the kind of fire power these platforms are, what's a few feet between friends?" Davis chuckled and bit into the sandwich again. "Good lunch today, don't you think?"

"Yes, the sandwich is quite good—one of my favorites—and the French fries are great, too," Murphy replied. "Go on, Scott. Tell me more."

"With a lot of borrowed technology and some new stuff, too, the SSGN is really like a submerged guided missile cruiser," Davis explained. "We've got Tomahawks and torpedoes just like the Ticos do. However, we can disappear and stay submerged for months at a time just slinking around the deep, silently waiting until our next assignment. Granted, the oceans are vast, but it's still hard to hide a five hundred and sixty-seven foot long surface vessel—even one that weighs almost nineteen thousand tons! That's the SSGNs chief advantage—stealth."

"I see your point," Murphy agreed. "I never looked at it quite that way for boats like yours. But of course, on boomers, we count on the same thing—being able to avoid detection."

Davis took the last bite of his sandwich, wiped his mouth with a napkin and looked at Murphy. "And here's the clincher. When we put an entire SEAL team on board the boat, we are suddenly transformed into a versatile, go anywhere, do anything, kick-ass, war-fighting machine. I really think I'm going to enjoy this command tour."

"Sounds like the Navy combined the best of everything into one neat package, giving you lots of combat capability," Murphy replied. "And, unlike our deterrent patrol missions which are all pretty much the same, you get to do something different on each deployment."

Yes, quite right," Davis nodded. "That aspect of it has a certain appeal, too." He slid a white envelope across the table in Murphy's direction.

"I want you to have this, Bill. Consider it a gift from the *Florida's* new crew and me."

Murphy picked up the envelope and smiled. "Thanks."

He opened it and removed a cloth patch emblazoned with the *Florida's* crest and motto. Typically, this insignia adorned the crew's blue duty coveralls that they wore at sea. Set on a background of brown and rust colored squares, the patch depicted a submarine on the water's surface that was wedged between two opposing dolphins, one gold and the other silver. Other images included Neptune's trident, a Tomahawk missile in a clenched fist, over a yellow silhouette shaped like the state of Florida. In the center, arranged in a circular fashion around the patch's symbols, was a Latin inscription, *Fortes Fortuna Adivat*, the *Florida's* motto.

"I never was very good at Latin," Murphy confessed. "What does it say?"

"It was chosen specifically for the *Florida's* conversion by DOD's Heraldic Branch. I think it's very fitting for the times," Davis replied. He traced the motto's words with his index finger and translated it for Murphy, "Fortune favors the bold."

# 39. GET THOSE BASTARDS

*Port Everglades Main Gate*
*Ft. Lauderdale, FL*

The white and blue Chevrolet Impala from the Hollywood Taxicab Company sped along the access road toward Port Everglades. Allan sat quietly in the back while the driver, a middle-aged Hispanic man who had introduced himself as Juan, tried to make small talk.

"Boy, that sure is something about the cruise ship hijacking, isn't it?" Juan remarked.

"You mean the *Southern Star*?" Allan responded. "The one drifting near the Bahamas?"

"Yep. That's the one," the driver answered. "I don't think they know what's going on yet, do they?"

"I only know what the news reports on the television have said," Allan replied. "I don't think there have been any new developments. Details are still rather sketchy."

"I feel sorry for all of those passengers," Juan said. "It's going to be tough to rescue them, especially with that tropical storm out there."

"I'm sure our government is doing all it can," Allan offered. "I wouldn't be surprised if they're planning some type of a military operation to free the hostages."

I sure hope so," the driver sighed. "We don't need another 9/11 type of tragedy caused here in the U.S. by a bunch of crazy terrorists."

"No, we sure don't," Allan agreed.

"I guess that just proves it's still a dangerous world out there," Juan lamented.

The taxi wound its way along Eller Road, a two-lane divided highway that led to cruise ship passenger terminals. Four Broward County Sheriff's patrol cars parked near the entrance gate—two outside the fence and two inside. A pair of deputies stood near each car. Armed with shotguns, they wore bulletproof vests, and helmets. Allan saw another deputy who was holding a German Shepard on a leash standing next to the gate. He was wearing thick, padded gloves that extended to his elbows. In addition to a big, bulky vest that resembled a baseball plate umpire's, he wore a helmet with a Plexiglas face shield.

"What's all this about?" Juan asked.

"Extra security. Probably has to do with the cruise ship hijacking," Allan surmised. "Looks to me like they aren't taking any chances."

Juan glanced up in the rear view mirror at Allan, "Do we need to go in there?"

No, that won't be necessary. Someone is meeting me here," Allan explained.

Juan raised his eyebrows, "How are you going to get past this? Are you a cop or FBI?"

"No, not exactly," Allan replied. "I can't say."

"Never mind," the driver replied. "I was just curious. It's probably better that you forget I asked."

An armed port security guard motioned them to stop. Juan slowed the car and it came to rest beside the gatehouse. He rolled down the driver's window and looked up at the guard. The officer kept one hand on his holstered service weapon as he spoke to Juan.

"Good afternoon," he said, bending down to see Allan. "Please shut off the car and place the keys in plain view on the dashboard," he instructed the driver.

Juan quickly complied.

"Now, please keep your hands on the steering wheel where I can see them," the guard added.

Satisfied, he resumed his questioning. "What is the nature of your business?"

Juan motioned with his head toward Allan on the back seat. "I'm just dropping off the gentleman as he asked."

The guard scrutinized Allan for a moment. "And your business, sir?"

"My name is Anderson, Allan Anderson," he replied. "I believe someone should already be here to meet me."

"May I see some identification?" the security guard asked.

Allan had anticipated that request and offered the security guard his maroon cover official U.S. passport. Allan did not have diplomatic credentials like some of the high-ranking London embassy staff. As a citizen-employee of the United States assigned overseas, he carried this type instead. It was different from the one the majority of Americans received and was distinguishable from other versions both by its maroon cover and by the capital letters OFFICIAL that appeared above the capital letters PASSPORT.

The security guard took the document from Allan's hand and opened it. He spent several seconds reviewing the data and then compared the photo on the passport's inside cover to the man who had identified himself as Allan Anderson. Satisfied, the security guard straightened and motioned for someone who was standing just inside the gate to approach the taxicab.

The guard bent low and nodded at Allan. "You may get out now, sir. We've been expecting you."

"Thanks," Allan replied. He leaned close to Juan. "How much do I owe you?"

Juan turned and gave Allan a rather puzzled look. Allan could see the bewilderment in the driver's gaze. Juan suddenly smiled and said, "See. I knew you were a government agent. Tell you what. If you're going to help catch those terrorists and rescue the passengers, nothing. It's on me," he beamed.

"Let me at least buy your lunch," Allan insisted. He thrust a folded twenty-dollar bill into Juan's hand.

"Okay, deal," Juan replied.

Allan opened the taxi's rear door and stepped onto the pavement. The man who had stood just inside the gate walked over to Allan.

"My name is Burns," he said with outstretched hand. "I'm your DHS escort officer. Nice to meet you."

Burns was relatively young, in his mid-thirties, clean shaven with brown hair and wore sunglasses. He was wearing a navy blue windbreaker that had a U.S. Department of Homeland Security logo on the left breast. Large, white block letters on the back of the jacket read DHS FEDERAL AGENT.

Allan shook Burns' hand. "Allan Anderson. Thanks for meeting me here. I have a lot of work to do. Shall we get to it?"

"By all means," Burns answered. "Here. Put this on," he instructed.

He handed Allan a DHS identification badge. In addition to Allan's name, photo and other key information, it featured a wide, red stripe that ran diagonally across it.

Bold black letters at the bottom of the badge read NO ER – PD.

"This will give you unrestricted access to anything inside the Port Everglades terminal area, including information about the *Southern Star*. No escort required," Burns explained. "It's by direction of the president."

"Sure thing." Allan took the ID from Burns and quickly clipped it to his shirt.

"Follow me." Burns turned and walked toward the entrance and the waiting DHS staff car.

Trailing Burns by several steps, Allan also started for the gate.

"Good luck!" a voice from behind called. "I hope you get those crazy bastards! Kick some ass!"

Allan turned to see Juan's fist high in the air as he made a thumbs-up gesture with it.

"Thanks!" Allan shouted back. He continued to follow Burns toward the DHS vehicle. *It's going to take more than luck*, Allan thought, *one hell of a lot more.*

# 40. TRUE KNOWLEDGE

*Terminal 22, Port Everglades*
*Ft. Lauderdale, FL*

The black DHS Crown Victoria carrying agent Burns and Allan rushed from the main entrance gate near the Port Everglades Administration Building toward Terminal 22. A large car, the Police Interceptor model Burns was driving featured a 250-horsepower power V-8 engine, heavy-duty transmission, and a host of other features that set it apart from its family-oriented cousin found in auto dealer showrooms around the country. One of them was a highly specialized fire suppression system designed to deploy chemicals to suppress or even extinguish a fire. In the event of a crash, it would automatically deploy once the vehicle had come to rest. That would provide more time for the occupants to escape. Another option called for the installation of ballistic door panels so the front doors could serve as shields to offer protection from incoming projectiles.

Allan tried to make small talk. "I'll bet this baby moves," he remarked.

"I wouldn't know for sure," Burns replied. "I've never used it in pursuit. Some of the other field agents have, though. They tell me this thing has got some muscle."

"Judging from the size of the hood, I'd say there's a pretty big engine under there," Allan continued.

"The Crown Vics used for police work have a 250 horse V-8," Burns stated authoritatively.

Allan paused briefly and then laughed aloud.

Burns look at him quizzically. "What's so funny?" he demanded.

"Why is it that an unmarked law enforcement vehicle always looks like a law enforcement vehicle?" Allan asked. "They've just got that look. You know what I mean: wide stance, big tires, black or dark blue paint, tinted windows, stealthy antennas."

"Yeah, I guess you're right," Burns agreed. "I never really thought about it, though."

The Crown Victoria they were riding in was no different. As an unmarked federal law enforcement vehicle, it had the usual complement of red and blue warning lights with two behind the front grille, two contained in a rear-window deck unit, and two installed in the front marker lights and rear taillight lenses. Even with dark tinted windows, they were still visible through the Crown Vic's glass. The four-inch stub antennas on each rear quarterdeck near the trunk lid and the GPS antenna on the roof were dead giveaways. If a casual observer needed additional confirmation, all he or she had to do was look at the license plates. Dark blue letters that read "DHS U.S. Government" and the vehicle's identification number would be enough.

It was less than a half-mile drive from the gate to Terminal 22 and the ride took under a minute. Burns stopped in front of the rather nondescript concrete building. The port authority had done their best to make the structure appealing to cruise line passengers by placing palm trees and hibiscus shrubs in well-manicured gardens around it.

While the soothing island look improved its appearance, the facility still lacked any striking design features and resembled a three-story office building instead.

Burns shut off the car and removed the keys from the ignition. He turned to Allan and simultaneously reached for the door handle.

"Come on, let's go," Burns commanded. He stepped out of the staff car and began to walk briskly toward the building's entrance.

Allan opened the passenger door, slid out, and quickly caught up with him.

"I've been instructed to take you to the Sovereign Cruise Line offices," Burns told Allan. "They have been directed by DHS to provide whatever information you need. We have a secure communications system in place so you can talk to anyone, anywhere in the world. One of the technicians will be able to help you do that—just ask."

"Thanks," Allan replied.

"You've obviously got connections," Burns quipped. "I've never worked with anybody who's had a PD before."

"Don't blow it out of proportion," Allan replied. "I'm just a low level 'go for.' I doubt you'd be overly impressed by my resume and background, Mr. Burns."

"If you say so," Burns chuckled.

They had reached the entrance to Terminal 22. Except for the two Broward County sheriff's deputies who stood by the doors, no one else was in sight. Although passengers who arrived for other departing cruises were on board their ships, all traffic in and out of Port Everglades ceased. Vehicular traffic in and out of the port stopped as well. In nearby conference rooms, dozens of FBI agents were questioning Port Authority employees who were on duty at the time of the hijacking. Port Everglades was in lock down mode.

One of the deputies, a sergeant, greeted them. "Good afternoon, gentlemen. May I see some ID?"

"Certainly," Burns replied. He pointed to his badge, "I'm agent Burns with DHS. This is Mr. Anderson. He's with the CIA."

Allan tugged at his ID and pulled it closer to the deputy. The officer first studied Burns' ID badge and then turned his attention to Allan's credentials.

"Burns and Anderson," he called to the other deputy. "See if they are on the access roster."

"Just a minute. Let me have a look," the second police officer responded. He scanned a typed page on the clipboard he was holding. After a few seconds, he looked up at the senior deputy.

"Yep, got them both on the list," he nodded. "They're good to go."

"You may proceed," the sergeant announced.

"Very well," Burns acknowledged. He turned to Allan, "Let's go!" Burns opened the door and held it. He motioned Allan to enter with his other hand. Allan darted through the doorway into Terminal 22's lobby and Burns quickly followed.

Burns jabbed an extended finger upward. "Sovereign's offices are on the third floor. We'll take the elevator. It's this way."

Burns started toward the elevator with Allan in lock step right next to him. He put his arm on Allan's shoulder. "Well, now what?" Burns asked.

"That's a good question," Allan sighed. "I don't really know what I'm looking for," he confessed.

"You're kidding, right?" Burns snorted. "You CIA guys have this already figured out. You're just pulling my leg," he insisted.

Allan stopped walking and turned to Burns.

"I only wish that were the case," Allan responded soberly. "That's the way it is in this business, Mr. Burns. More often than not, we don't not what we're looking for until we actually find it."

Burns stared at Allan and shook his head.

"I know that sounds crazy," Allan added, "but it's the nature of intelligence gathering and analysis. You're right; it does seem to be a contradiction. It defies logic and is something we all wrestle with."

Burns shrugged. "I don't get it. I thought you guys had it wired. Based on what you're telling me, most of the time the CIA doesn't have a clue."

"I wouldn't characterize it like that," Allan replied. "It's a very detailed, complicated process. Often times, there is no defined beginning or ending point."

"So it's hit and miss," Burns suggested.

"In a sense, yes," Allan conceded. "Information isn't deemed useful until after it's been verified, analyzed, and applied appropriately. Only then will its full value be realized."

"Nope. It still puzzles me." Burns scratched his forehead. "How do people in your agency sift through all the information you collect to figure out what's important and what isn't and what fits and what doesn't?"

"That's a great question. Let me share a quote from Confucius with you," Allan offered. "Maybe that will help explain it."

"Sure, go ahead," Burns agreed.

Allan took a deep breath and then spoke slowly, "When things are investigated, then true knowledge is achieved; when true knowledge is achieved, then the national life is orderly; and when the national life is orderly, then there is peace in this world."

Allan paused so Burns could process what he had just heard and then started for the elevator. "Okay, Mr. Burns," Allan grinned, "let's go uncover some true knowledge."

# 41. THE NEXT MOVE

*Milbank District*
*London, U.K.*

James Singleton, director of MI5's Joint Terrorism Analysis Centre, puffed on a fat cigar. Seated opposite him in his office were the two case officers who had just delivered their report. Singleton drew a breath and then exhaled. A cloud of thick, bluish smoke spewed from his pursed lips and floated upward. Singleton leaned back in his overstuffed, black leather chair and twirled the stogie between his thumb and forefinger like a baton major. The room reeked of stale smoke. He mulled over the material and then looked across his large, imposing desk directly at the agents.

"What about the girl, this Meredith Wilson?" Singleton asked intently. "Do we know anything that would be more helpful than the points you just outlined?"

Singleton tipped forward and carefully set the smoldering cigar in a heavy glass ashtray on one corner of his desk. He was a large man whose prominent facial features were set on a heavy frame. Large jowls hung low on either side of his mouth and above them, his flat, spade-like nose pointed upward to a brow creased from years of deliberation and worry. His large, bulging eyes were usually red and puffy, and topped off with bushy eyebrows. Given his usual style of dress and speech—a three-piece suit, bow tie, watch fob, and the always-polite Queen's English—he could easily have been a throwback to another era. Singleton looked like he had stepped out of a photograph taken in Britain during the 1940's—so much so, that when people met him for the first time, they often remarked that he reminded them of Sir Winston Churchill. It was something he had become accustomed to and rather liked.

William responded to Singleton's question first. "We've done a thorough background search and so far, haven't turned up anything unusual or suspicious in her past. Her current contacts don't link her to any known or suspected Islamic extremist group."

"A review of her financial transactions and bank accounts don't suggest anything either. No irregularities whatsoever," Travis interjected. "Furthermore, we checked with the Home Office and noted that she hasn't left the country in almost six years. That trip wasn't unusual—she took the Chunnel Train to Paris during the New Year's holiday."

"I agree with William," Travis added. "She's a low level U.S. embassy employee. She does not have access to the kind of information that makes her a threat to our operation. We don't believe she is in a position to compromise anything."

Singleton plucked the cigar from the crystal ashtray, inhaled, and sank back in his chair. James Singleton had entered Britain's intelligence services after he graduated from Oxford in the 1960's. He had grown into his job during the height of the Cold War when nations like Britain, the United States and the rest of the free world faced the threat of the Soviet Union's ICBMs and its possible overrun of Western Europe.

Singleton had seen it all, from the rise and fall of Communism to the emergence of Islamic extremism. He witnessed the crumbling of the Berlin Wall and the collapse of the World Trade Center towers. For nearly five decades, he had been a loyal foot soldier in Her Majesty's intelligence service. Singleton steadily rose through the ranks, from analyst to agent, station chief to branch chief, to his current position as head of MI5's Joint Terrorism Analysis Centre. The mantel clock on the credenza chimed the hour. Singleton removed the cigar from his mouth and extended his lower lip in thought.

"Did you know that it is difficult to make a piano sound like anything other than a piano, no matter how badly it might be played?" he remarked.

"Sir?" William asked quizzically. "I don't understand."

Singleton leaned forward. "It's not that straightforward. Somehow, the information is getting out. It simply does not add up—we are missing something. Whoever is responsible is either very good or very lucky."

At that, he smiled briefly and then sank back to enjoy another puff on his cigar.

"Then what about this Blanton fellow?" Singleton asked pointedly. "Can he be trusted? I get the sense from your earlier reports that he is someone who also bears close watching. Do you agree?"

"Yes, sir," Travis nodded. He glanced at William, prompting him for a reply. William quickly took the cue.

"Sorry, Mr. Singleton," William responded. "I couldn't agree more."

"Do you suppose he is working for the al-Muhajiroun terrorist group or some offshoot of it?" Singleton wondered. "These organizations are well financed and flush with cash. I hate to say it, but money—especially when offered in very large sums—makes people do things that are otherwise inconceivable. An American government employee is not well paid—even with the promise of a lifetime pension after retirement."

Singleton raised a thick finger in the air like a conductor who was attempting to get his orchestra's attention. He wiggled it back and forth for a moment as if to write a sentence in the space above his desk and then spoke.

"Remember the Kim Philby affair?" Singleton asked. William and Travis nodded.

The KGB had been very successful at recruiting spies in Great Britain before World War II. Known as the Cambridge Spies, four men who met at Trinity College, Cambridge University in the 1930's—Kim Philby, Guy Burgess, Anthony Blunt and Donald Maclean—managed to penetrate the British government at the very highest levels and serve the Kremlin for over thirty years. This gave the KGB unlimited access to the British government's secrets at many levels and provided a window on virtually every aspect of Her Majesty's realm.

Now in his seventies, Singleton remembered it all too well. Working for MI6, the British Secret Intelligence Service at the time, he was the case officer who intercepted a communiqué from Philby that tipped off Burgess and Maclean that their nest of spies was under surveillance. Although Singleton's subsequent investigative work resulted in two secret trials, Philby was cleared of disloyalty and—to Singleton's and everyone else's surprise—was allowed to go on working for MI6. Despite that, Singleton continued to suspect that Philby was a traitor and never gave up. He pursued his suspicions relentlessly and hoped to unravel the espionage ring, but by the time he was close to breaking the case, it was too late.

Kim Philby disappeared from Beirut in January 1963, after telling his wife he would meet her at a diplomatic dinner party that evening. He never did. Philby surfaced in Moscow weeks later and it was only then that MI6 learned the real extent of his perfidy. For decades, Philby and the others—Burgess, Blunt and Maclean—had been working as double agents, passing sensitive information to the KGB. What stunned British intelligence even more was the discovery that Philby held the rank of general in the KGB. Perhaps that was the reason for Singleton's next remark.

"Contrary to what most would think, enemies are predictable whereas very often, friends are not," he admonished. "Consequently, it is best to keep one's enemies close and one's friends even closer." Singleton paused briefly to let his remark sink in before continuing. "Based on your reports and our discussion today, if you are ruling out Miss Wilson, then I believe you should focus all future efforts on Mr. Blanton instead. However, don't completely discount Miss Wilson. Keep an open mind, gentlemen."

William, the pair's senior case officer, acknowledged Singleton's instruction. "As you wish, sir."

Singleton gazed at William and Travis through his watery eyes. "Well and good," he affirmed with a nod. "Let's not waste a moment, then. Best get on with the task."

William and Travis stood to leave and made for the door. Singleton leaned back in the large, overstuffed chair. He puffed on his thick cigar again and exhaled another cloud of bluish smoke.

"Keep me posted," he called after them. "I want to know of any new developments right away. There is much at stake here."

# 42. ROUND 'EM UP

*Aboard the USS* Florida
*Sixty Nautical Miles off the Florida Coast*

Lieutenant Brian Timmons, the SEAL team operations officer, sat next to a large digital communications console in the *Florida's* dimly lit Battle Management Center (BMC). Located just aft of the submarine's control room, the thirty foot wide by forty foot long BMC supported special operations mission planning and execution. The BMC contained some thirty workstations and included large screen displays for support briefings and operational graphics. Once the rescue mission was underway, it would serve as the nerve center for SEAL Team Eight's very important operation.

Minutes earlier, a chirping alarm had altered Timmons to an incoming priority message. Timmons and the operator, a petty officer named Watson, watched intently as the words scrolled across the screen. The streaming text abruptly stopped and Timmons carefully read the bright lines on the monitor in front of him.

MSG #0445884Y7873DDYTHRFJ    UTC 1342Z

PRIORITY FLASH//LEVEL ONE

CLASSIFICATION TOP SECRET

FROM JCS J-3 PLANS/OPS

# AN EYE FOR AN EYE

FOR COMMANDER SEAL TEAM EIGHT, CAP-
TAIN USS FLORIDA

REF OPLAN ALPHA-FOUR-ZULU//OPERATION
SECOND LIGHT//

SECTION I

BY ORDER OF THE PRESIDENT OF THE UNITED
STATES SEAL TEAM EIGHT AUTHORIZED RE-
PEAT AUTHORIZED TO EXECUTE OPLAN AL-
PHA-FOUR-ZULU OPERATION SECOND LIGHT.
LAWFUL USE OF DEADLY FORCE IAW RULES OF
ENGAGEMENT AUTHORIZED. STOP

SECTION II

COMMANDER SEAL TEAM EIGHT AUTHO-
RIZED TO BEGIN TACTICAL OPERATIONS
WHEN MISSION CONDITIONS AND RISKS
DEEMED ACCEPTABLE. STOP

ADVISE HQ TIME OPERATIONS BEGIN. HOURLY
SITREPS IAW SOP VIA SECURE COM TO HQ RE-
QUIRED. ADVISE HQ VIA SECURE COM WHEN
MISSION COMPLETE. STOP

SECTION III

ACKNOWLEDGE ON RECEIPT. END
AUTHENTICATION

JENKINS, RADM, JCS J-3 PLANS/OPS

It was the order giving them the go ahead to execute the *Southern Star* rescue mission.

Timmons directed Watson to print two hard copies—one for the team's duty log and one for the *Florida's* captain—and then reached for the phone. He leaned forward, picked up the handset, and punched the top button labeled conn. "This is Lieutenant Timmons in the BMC. Put Commander Davis on the horn—it's urgent."

After being on hold for a few seconds, Timmons straightened and spoke. "Commander Davis, this is Lieutenant Timmons. We've just received the go message from the JCS. Operations are to commence once we're in place and have the SEALs and their equipment ready. Can you give me some idea of when we'll be on station, sir?"

Timmons cocked his head and nodded. "Yes, sir. Four hours and twenty minutes. That should give us plenty of time." He wedged the phone between his shoulder and jaw and jotted a few notes on a pad of paper as he continued to listen. Timmons put the pen down and sat back. "Got it all, sir. I'll be working with your liaison officer and XO on preparations here in the BMC. As soon as we're all set, I'll let you know. Thank you, Commander."

Timmons hung up the phone and turned to the petty officer seated next to him. "Watson, get our mission-planning team in here, pronto. We've got a lot of work to do in the next four hours."

"Yes sir!" Watson responded. He swiveled around and reached for the phone. He picked it up and pushed a button labeled SOFHE, short for Special Operations Force Habitability and Equipment. Pronounced "Sophie" by the crew, it was an area of the *Florida* previously occupied by Trident II missiles now serving as living space. Located amidships on the second level aft of the BMC, it was where the SEALs or other special ops forces bivouacked when on board. It wasn't much—a small berth for sleeping and a tiny personal equipment locker—but it was adequate. The SOFHE was one of the many modifications the *Florida* underwent to prepare her for the new SSGN mission.

During the *Florida's* conversion from boomer to guided missile boat, the two tubes closest to the sail, tubes 1 and 2, became lock-in/lock-out chambers for special operations forces. The other twenty-two tubes would be loaded with seven Tomahawks apiece for a full complement of one hundred fifty-four land attack missiles. If a larger special operations group was required, the number dropped to fifteen tubes with one hundred and five Tomahawks and the unarmed tubes would hold SEAL ordnance and gear instead.

Tubes 1 and 2, sandwiched between the BMC and the SOFHE, allowed the SEALs lots of flexibility. After the lockout chambers had been flooded, swimmers could pass straight through the two thirty-inch hatches atop each tube into the sea. Depending on the configuration and mission, they could push their Combat Rubber Raiding Craft (CRRC) out through the same hatches, move up into a Dry Deck Shelter (DDS), or into an Advanced SEAL Delivery System (ASDS).

In order to accommodate the Dry Deck Shelter and Advanced SEAL Delivery System, the conversion extended each side of the *Florida's* landing deck by four feet. The purpose of Dry Deck Shelters (DDSs) was to transport, deploy, and recover SOF teams from Combat Rubber Raiding Craft or SEAL Delivery Vehicles, all while remaining submerged. The advantage was obvious—the *Florida* and SEAL Team Eight would be invisible, her presence unknown to anyone. That was a distinct advantage they would soon need.

As soon as the SOFHE answered his call, Watson relayed Lieutenant Timmons' instructions. "We just received the go order. Per the OPSO, round up the team and report to the BMC right away." Watson hung up the phone and turned to Timmons. "They'll be here in a couple of minutes, sir," he said with a thumbs-up gesture.

"Thanks Watson," Timmons acknowledged. He stood and started for the other side of the BMC where the final mission planning would be done. "Log the authorization message and continue to monitor the comm. Let me know if anything else comes in—anything at all," Timmons called over his shoulder before he ducked around the corner and disappeared down the passageway.

# 43. A RETURNED FAVOR

*Terminal 22, Port Everglades*
*Ft. Lauderdale, FL*

"What did you find out, Allan? Anything useful yet?" Peter King asked his nephew. Frustration was evident in his voice.

Allan Anderson pressed the cell phone hard against his ear. "I have all of the blueprints and engineering drawings for the *Southern Star* in front of me. So far, I haven't found anything that would be helpful. Her deck is almost forty feet above the waterline. From what I have seen, there is no way to get ropes attached securely to her railings from that far down by a team of divers operating on the surface. The task will be even more difficult if we attempt at night and in rough seas. We'll have to have help from someone topside."

"Damn it!" King exclaimed. "I was hoping you wouldn't say that. Are you sure?" he asked again. "Double check the drawings—maybe you overlooked something."

"I discussed it with the cruise line's chief engineer and he agreed with me. Ropes would have to be secured to the rails and lowered to the water from the deck," Allan explained. "I'm sorry."

"That's going to complicate things quite a bit, then. We have to come up with a way to get between six and twenty-eight SEALs from the sea surface to the *Southern*

*Star's* deck nearly forty feet up. Otherwise, Allan, we can't launch the rescue mission," King conceded.

"Are you in contact with Susan and Murphy?" Allan asked his uncle.

"Not exactly—we don't want to let the terrorists know that they still have their cell phones so we haven't called either of them directly. But we are able to send text messages back and forth," King disclosed. "Why do you ask?"

"Well, I asked the chief engineer what kinds of ropes are found on the *Southern Star*. He told me that it was the usual rigging found on ships of this size—double braided Nylon handling lines that varied from a half inch to one and a half inches in diameter. They were stored in the ship's lockers in one hundred, two hundred and three hundred foot runs. He said the shortest coil weighed fifty-eight pounds and the longest one topped one hundred and sixty-five pounds," Allan explained.

"Good!" King exclaimed. "We can use the one-hundred foot lines then. I'm sure we can contact Murphy so he and another American who is on board can drop the ropes over the side. Once they've been secured to the railings, the SEALs can use ascenders to climb up them."

"No, I'm afraid we can't," Allan advised his uncle. "I thought the same thing until the chief engineer told me that although they are strong and don't stretch like natural fiber lines, they become very slippery when they get wet. He warned against it—even with special equipment."

"What the hell are we supposed to do, then?" King asked his nephew. "I can't believe there isn't a way to get those SEALs forty feet up to the deck of that damned ship!"

"I think there is," Allan suggested. "What I'm proposing is going to sound crazy, but I really think it will work."

"What the hell," King sputtered, "At this point, I'll listen to any idea. Who knows? It might work. What is it?"

"Bed sheets," Allan answered.

There was a long period of silence before Peter King spoke. "Did I hear you correctly? You said bed sheets, right, Allan?"

"Yes, that was it, bed sheets," Allan repeated. "Many prison escapes succeeded using nothing more than knotted bed sheets to form a crude rope. Cotton is a very strong natural fiber—one of the toughest. I figure that ten sheets tied together and knotted every three feet would be sufficient. What do you think?"

Allan's plan had piqued King's interest and he wanted to learn more. "Go on," King insisted.

"Now, here's the best part," Allan elaborated. "The ship's laundry facility is easily accessible from the midsection of the ship. If we can get Murphy and that other man down there, they could assemble the bed sheets and make their way to the fantail to drop them over the side. I checked and each sheet weighs one pound, so these ropes will be relatively light at only ten pounds each."

"Allan, that's splendid!" King remarked excitedly. "Bed sheets! Who would have thought of using bed sheets?"

"Then this will work?" Allan asked.

"I think so," King replied. "Look at the drawings and pinpoint the exact location of the *Southern Star's* laundry facility," he instructed his nephew. "I'll need precise directions and distance from a specific starting point on the ship to the laundry. I have to make a couple of phone calls and send some important text messages.

I'll call you back as soon as I'm done—say in about twenty minutes."

"Will do," Allan responded. "I'll have it ready for you."

"Oh, there's one more thing," King said before hanging up. "The other American I mentioned who is on board that ship—he's Army Colonel Jack Stanton. I'm sure you remember him, since he was the guy who saved your ass at Guantanamo Bay. Well, Allan, here's your chance to return the favor."

# 44. A NEW WRINKLE

*The Oval Office*
*Washington, D.C.*

"Mr. President, I'm afraid I've got some bad news," Jim Conroy said ominously. Brewster, eyes wide, looked up, anxious to hear what Conroy had to say.

Conroy cleared his throat and then spoke. "We've just run the passenger list against our COMPASS databases. Two active duty military officers are aboard the *Southern Star*—a nuclear submarine captain from Kings Bay named Murphy, and an Army colonel named Stanton, who is assigned to Camp X-ray at GITMO."

Brewster sat back and stared intently at Conroy. Neither man spoke. After an unusually long pause, Conroy broke the silence.

"Here's the problem, sir—we don't know if the *Southern Star* was specifically targeted by the terrorists because of passengers Murphy and Stanton, or if it was mere happenstance. In any case, it doesn't matter. Should the terrorists learn that they are American military officers, we believe they could be killed in retaliation for the preemptive strike against Iran by the U.S. a few weeks ago," he concluded. "Is it possible that they already know some of the passengers on the ship are our military men? Are we too late?" Brewster asked sheepishly.

"It's difficult to say," Conroy replied. "Hopefully the answer is no—although I wouldn't rule it out, Mr. President."

Brewster pursed his lips tightly, lowered his head, and rubbed the back of his neck. After a few seconds, he looked up at Conroy again and sighed. "Tell me something good, Jim. Anything," he pleaded.

"There is one thing, Mr. President," Conroy offered.

Brewster gestured with his hand, "Go on."

"Before the Battle of Trafalgar, British Vice Admiral Nelson said, 'When I am without orders and unexpected occurrences arrive I shall always act as I think the honor and glory of my King and Country demand.'" Conroy paused briefly and then continued. "Mr. President, the same thing applies here. We have to assume that these two seasoned military officers—both decorated combat veterans—will realize that the *Southern Star* and her passengers are hostages. Once they figure that out, they'll be clever enough to lie low while they wait for an opportunity to act, whether they do so individually or as a team."

"And if they don't?" Brewster asked pointedly.

"They'll be killed for sure—and probably tortured severely beforehand," Conroy responded.

"Is there any chance that we can send them a message without the terrorists knowing about it?" the president asked, his growing frustration obvious.

Conroy shook his head. "It's doubtful, sir. We have to assume the terrorists have commandeered the radio room and shut down all communications to and from the *Southern Star.*"

Brewster's eyes suddenly widened. "What about cell phones then?" he blurted out. "Do they work on a ship like that?"

"Yes and no, Mr. President. Most cruise ships do have a system of antennas and repeaters that will permit cell phone use when close enough to shore—say a hundred miles or so," Conroy explained. "We've got a team looking into that right now. The *Southern Star* is approximately sixty miles northwest of Nassau. According to our experts, technically, the ship is close enough to land for cell phone operation."

"Then it will work. Am I right, Jim?" Brewster asked.

"Yes, Mr. President, under most circumstances, it would," Conroy acknowledged. "However, as you know Tropical Storm Brenda is tracking due west and heading right for the *Southern Star*. As it gets closer, rain band precipitation will undoubtedly degrade any cell phone signals. Consequently, they may be too weak to provide reliable communication. In the worst case scenario, cell phones on the *Southern Star* may not work at all."

Brewster frowned. "Can anything else go wrong?" he fumed.

"I think we both know the answer to that question, Mr. President," Conroy conceded.

"I'm sorry, Jim. Please don't take it personally," Brewster apologized. "I know everyone is doing their best. It's just that I'm very frustrated by this whole thing."

Conroy nodded. "I know, Mr. President. I feel the same way—helpless."

"Thanks, Jim," Brewster responded.

"There is one unknown that could be a reason for optimism," Conroy said, trying to sound upbeat.

"Pardon me for sounding skeptical, Jim, but that just doesn't seem plausible," Brewster sighed.

"I know this is a stretch," Conroy began, "but let's presume the terrorists don't know Stanton and Murphy are U.S. military officers. Let's say they think they're just plain old American tourists like everyone else on the *Southern Star*. Why shouldn't they?"

The president studied Conroy for a moment, considering what he had said. "Go on," Brewster instructed.

"Very well," Conroy continued. "Now let's assume that Stanton and Murphy team up and formulate a plan to overpower the terrorists. Let's also assume that they're counting on us launching a military rescue effort. I believe that they will do everything they can ahead of time to insure its success," Conroy suggested.

Brewster cocked his head slightly and raised an eyebrow. "Jim, it doesn't sound that far-fetched."

"No, it doesn't, sir," Conroy agreed. "Two of our best tactical military officers are aboard that ship. The combination of their gut instinct and battle hardened know-how is going to be a powerful force to help us neutralize the threat and save the hostages."

"How sure are you?" Brewster asked.

Conroy shook his head. "That's the only way I see it playing out, Mr. President."

The president looked squarely at his intelligence director. "Jim, if you feel that strongly about it, then I do, too," Brewster said confidently.

# 45. NO KIDDING

*Aboard the* **Southern Star**
*Sixty Miles Northwest of Nassau, Bahamas*

"Jesus Christ, Peter! You've got to be kidding me!" Jack Stanton exclaimed.

"I'm afraid not, Jack," King replied. "I know it sound ludicrous, but it's our best bet."

"Ludicrous? That word hardly describes it!" Stanton shot back. "If you ask me, it's insane—absolutely crazy!"

"Jack, I know it's far-fetched," King agreed. "I'll even admit that it sounds a bit preposterous, but I'm telling you that there simply aren't any other options. The only way the SEALs can get from the surface to the *Southern Star's* deck is by climbing up the ropes made from bed sheets."

Stanton continued to utter his disbelief. "For crying out loud," he scoffed. "I've been in the U.S. military for over twenty-five years. I know we have tons of sophisticated hardware and gadgets in the inventory—DOD warehouses are bursting at the seams with that crap. You mean to tell me there isn't a goddamned thing around that can't do the job better than bed sheets?"

King tried hard to calm his old friend. "Jack, please listen. This isn't a typical hostage rescue situation. In fact, this scenario isn't one we've thought of, so no agency has planned for it. We're writing the rules as we go, but I'm going to need your help if this is going to succeed, Jack. Tell me one more time that I can count on you."

"Do I have a choice?" Stanton grumbled. "Peter, I don't know about you, but I'm getting too old for this stuff. I'm supposed to be on vacation, remember?"

"As a matter of fact, I do," King responded. "And it's a good thing for all of us that you are."

"All right," Stanton relented, "lay it out for me."

"Thanks, Jack. I knew I could count on you," King replied. "Okay, listen carefully. Here's the plan: you and Commander Murphy will have to make your way to the ship's laundry and once there, locate enough bed sheets and tie them together to fashion two fifty-foot long knotted ropes that will reach the water from the ship's fantail. So far, so good?"

"Yes, go on," Stanton instructed.

"The ropes won't be heavy—they'll weigh about ten pounds each and will be easy for you to transport," King went on. "But, you'll first have to link up with Murphy and then make your way down two levels to the laundry facility. You'll have to work fast and avoid detection. We can't risk having them catch you. You and Murphy are the key to getting the SEALs on the cruise ship. If you fail—" King stopped in mid-sentence. "Well, you can guess the outcome," he added.

Stanton hesitated. "I'm almost afraid to ask this next question, but where is Murphy?"

"He's not being held hostage in one of the ship's dining rooms with the others," King explained. "We know that because we received a text message from him."

"If Murphy isn't in a dining room, then where the hell is he and how will I find him?" Stanton wondered. "Phone? Text?"

"You can't call him, Jack," King countered. "If Murphy's in the wrong spot when his cell phone rings, he'll be exposed. That will not only jeopardize his safety, but it will scuttle the entire rescue plan."

"What, then?" Stanton demanded. "I simply can't start running around this damned ship hoping to run into him," he snorted. "For Christ's sake, Peter, I don't even know what he looks like!"

"Exactly, Jack," King answered. "This is where you let me do my job. It's not time for you to play a John Wayne part—not yet anyway."

"What the hell is that supposed to mean?" Stanton shot back.

"It's simple," King told him. "You are going to stay put in your cabin and I'll send him a text message directing him to go to your location."

A sudden pause in the conversation signaled trouble over that element of the plan. After a long delay, Stanton spoke.

"Wait, let me get this right?" he asked. "You want me to deliberately sit here in my cabin and do nothing while several hostages are being held at gunpoint elsewhere on the ship?"

"Ye—" King started to reply, but Stanton cut him off with a sharp rebuke.

"I'm not done!" Stanton barked.

King gave in with a sigh, "Okay, Jack. Go ahead, then."

"And," Stanton emphasized the word 'and' as he began, "And while I wait, you send Murphy to my cabin, perhaps leading the terrorists right to me, and then we're both compromised. What will that do you your plan, Peter?"

"You're right, Jack. It is risky," King acknowledged. "But, it's the only way to get you and Murphy teamed up so you can fashion the bed sheet ropes and throw them over the *Southern Star's* stern. Our choices are very limited and this is the best one. I'm sorry."

"Peter, I don't mean to put down your plan," Stanton warned, "but we're not writing some sort of a spy novel or 'good guys versus bad guys' story here."

"Well, Jack," King replied, "actually we are. And you happen to be one of the main characters."

Stanton was clearly annoyed. "Peter, I think you're nuts—all of you—for seeing this merely as some kind of goddamned spy fiction."

King attempted to make his point. "Think what you will, Jack. There's one big difference between this production and similar tales. In tonight's adaptation, we've been kind enough to leave the ending entirely up to you."

King paused briefly and then continued, "I'll be forwarding critical information to you within the hour. In the meantime, you aren't to leave your cabin for any reason, got it? You're a key player here and we can't afford to lose you. It's simple: no ropes, no rescue."

"Okay, I've got it. And don't wish me luck when you hang up, Peter," Stanton chided. "It's going to take more than luck to pull this off. I'm going to need a goddamned miracle!"

# 46. INTO THE LION'S DEN

*Aboard the USS* Florida
*Sixty Miles Northwest of Nassau, Bahamas*

This was the first real show of the Navy's SSGN capabilities and the *Florida* was center stage for the performance. Other converted boomers, namely the *Ohio* and *Michigan*, both homeported at Bangor, WA, forward deployed to the Middle East for nearly a year each. During that time, dual Blue and Gold crews that rotated on and off the boats every three or four months operated the subs. The aim was to have two of the four SSGNs continuously on station to support Operation Iraqi Freedom. Occasionally, the *Ohio* and *Michigan* would perform shallow water recon in and around the Iraqi port city of Basra, a strategic oil terminal, and covert operations in the Straits of Hormuz, south of Iran. Although rarely used, SEALs from both subs were on standby for SOF missions. For the SSGN crews, typically it was nothing more than hurry up and wait. Today, the usual ho-hum routine was about to change.

The small mission briefing room next to the BMC was full—in fact, it was standing room only. Senior Chief Erik Hartman, PO1 Tracy Owens, and the other fifteen enlisted members of Golf Platoon were sandwiched together in the crowded space. SEAL Team Eight's commander, a career Navy O-5 named Pierce, entered. At once, his senior NCO, Master Chief Howe, barked, "Ahhh-ten-shun!"

Everyone in the room immediately sprang out of their seats and came to attention.

Pierce, a rugged, well-built man in his mid-forties, walked purposefully to the podium. His closely cut hair hid the gray that would have otherwise made him look much older. The flattop hairstyle set off square facial features that his intense blue eyes accented. A graduate of the U.S. Naval Academy, Pierce had always been a SEAL. When he was a boy, he took to the water like a fish and began swimming competitively at the local YMCA. Pierce excelled at water sports and set a new high school record for the 100-yard breaststroke event. Pierce dreamed of being a Navy SEAL since the seventh grade and received an offer to try-out for the academy's swim team. Although had been accepted at several top colleges and universities for his swimming talent, the Naval Academy remained his first choice, so Pierce gladly accepted an appointment there because it offered him the best chance to achieve his goal of becoming a SEAL.

"Seats," Pierce ordered in a firm, no-nonsense tone. SEAL Team Eight's combat swimmers and support staff immediately sat in small, folding chairs that were crammed around the podium.

Commander Pierce swept a hand through his brushed crew cut and cleared his throat.

"Gentlemen, I don't have to tell you how import and how terribly critical the success of this mission is. As you all know, we have trained for every imaginable combat and terrorist scenario we could come up with—all but this one." He paused briefly and then continued. "Our nation and the world are counting on us—you—SEAL Team Eight, to save the day. This mission will be extremely dangerous because we don't really know who or what we're up against yet. What we do know is that someone is holding several dozen Americans against their will on a U.S. flagged cruise ship. This deliberate act of piracy is one that must come to a swift, successful end. It is imperative that you rescue the hostages without any loss of life. The president has asked me to convey his thanks. He wants you all to know that he has great confidence in your abilities and will be praying for your success." Pierce stopped and looked over at the SEAL team's operations officer. "Now Lieutenant Timmons will brief you on the details."

Pierce stepped away from the podium and made room for Timmons. Notes and three-ring binders in hand, Timmons quickly moved to the front.

"Good morning, gentlemen. I don't have to repeat what Commander Pierce just said—I think we all understand what's at stake." Heads nodded in unison as Timmons addressed the group. "Then let's get to it, shall we?"

Timmons turned toward a small projection screen that displayed the picture of a cruise ship at sea. It looked like a photo from an advertising brochure—colorful flags flying from the masts, all set against a bright, blue sky. He aimed a laser pointer at the center of the image and began his briefing.

"Gentlemen, this is your objective, the *Southern Star*. Although relatively small as cruise ships go, she is a 574-foot ocean liner with over two hundred eighty-eight staterooms. She has a passenger capacity of five hundred and twelve and carries an international staff and crew of two hundred and sixty. Her cruising speed is nineteen knots with a displacement of 21,667 tons." Timmons clicked the remote control in his left hand to show several more slides of the *Southern Star* from different angles.

"Here's what we know—and this is the good news. She was on a short, four-day cruise from Fort Lauderdale to Nassau with a much smaller than usual number of passengers on board. Rather than her normal capacity, the *Southern Star* is only carrying one hundred and twenty passengers. Now for the bad news: they are all Americans." Timmons stopped briefly and advanced to the next slide, which showed a list of the passengers.

"Unfortunately, their small number means that it will be much easier for the perpetrators to control and monitor the hostages. That could make it difficult, if not impossible, for the hostages to overpower the terrorists. There's one other thing. If you look closely at the passenger list, you will note that two of them are U.S. military officers."

Timmons aimed the laser pointer at two names in bold type on the screen. "One is the skipper of a Navy sub—the same boat that launched the Trident missile at Iran a few weeks ago—and the other is an Army Colonel who's assigned to GITMO as a military police brigade ops officer."

Timmons clicked the remote control again and side-by-side photos of Commander Murphy and Colonel Stanton filled the screen. "If the terrorists already know that—or somehow find out—then the lives of these two men are in jeopardy. Any questions up to this point?" Timmons asked. The room was silent.

"Very well," Timmons continued, "I'll proceed. Operation Second Light has been authorized by the President of the United States to obtain the safe release of all one hundred and twenty Americans on board the *Southern Star*, as well as that of the ship's crew. The president has specifically authorized the lawful use of deadly force against the terrorists in accordance with current rules of engagement.

The goal is to win the freedom of the hostages and crew without loss of life while neutralizing the terrorists. As Commander Pierce said, this will be a difficult and dangerous mission because we have never attempted one like it before. The carefully developed OPLAN accounts for both expected and unexpected events during the operation. Normal contingencies such as air assault or seaborne visit, board, search, and seizure—VBSS—are all but impossible due to the weather conditions on the surface. However, we can use that to our advantage. The element of surprise will be our biggest ally. Our biggest obstacles will be boarding the *Southern Star* and the lack of communication with anyone on board the vessel."

Timmons stopped for a few seconds to let his remarks sink in and then continued. "Any question so far, gentlemen?" He waited for a response. A SEAL seated in the second row raised his hand.

"Yes, Owens," Timmons acknowledged.

"Sir, this may be a dumb question," PO1 Tracy Owens began, "but you said we don't know how many terrorists there are or what particular group they are affiliated with. There has to be some way to scrub the list of passengers and crew to determine that. We're assuming that they are crew members, but what if one or more of them are actually passengers?"

"That's an excellent question, Owens," Timmons responded. "Homeland Security and NSA have done an extensive analysis of the crew and passenger lists. Based on their information, we can rule out any of the terrorists as being from the passenger group. As you mentioned, the critically important piece is for us to know how many terrorists there are. Unfortunately, we don't have that information at present. DHS and NSA are working on it. Unless we find out, we'll be going into this blind not knowing what to expect—sort of like Daniel being thrown into the lion's den."

A murmur broke out as the SEALs quickly glanced at one another. Lieutenant Timmons waited for the buzz to die down and scanned the group. "Any other questions?" he asked.

# 47. LOCK AND LOAD

*Aboard the USS* Florida
*Sixty Miles Northwest of Nassau, Bahamas*

Lieutenant Timmons turned to Petty Officer Erik Hartman, the Platoon Chief. "Chief Hartman will brief you on additional operational details. Good luck, men."

Hartman strode to the center of a small space in the BMC. His hulking physique towered authoritatively over the group of rugged men standing before him. Rather than pause, he got right down to business.

"All right SEALs," Hartman bellowed, "listen up because your lives depend on it. Hold your questions until the end." He moved to the front of the room and continued his briefing. "This isn't your usual VBSS mission. This is a night combat mission directed against an unknown threat. We will be conducting this operation in treacherous conditions. To complicate matters, surface weather has deteriorated due to an approaching tropical storm. Heavy swells and gusty winds will make boarding the vessel extremely difficult. Rain showers have reduced visibility to only a few meters. Once we board the *Southern Star*, we will need to move silently and undetected to avoid alerting the terrorists to our presence. They will be neutralized only after we have determined how many there are and whether the ship has been rigged with explosives. Our number one priority is the safety of the passengers and crew."

"The mission will be conducted with one team of six divers. Weapons for the assault will consist of one M11 SIG Sauer P228 and one MK23 MOD 0 with KAC sound suppressor per diver for close in combat. Half of you will carry the M4A1 carbine and the rest will have M-14 sniper rifles. In addition to the M11 and MK23, I will have an M4A1 with the 870P Masterkey attachment. Each diver will have the usual complement of flash-bang grenades, smoke and tear gas canisters. NVGs will be issued to each diver since we don't know if the terrorists have cut off the *Southern Star's* lights."

The weapons Hartman listed were typical of those used by SEALs during a mission. The MK23 Mod O 45-caliber offensive handgun was a double/single-action pistol with a 12-round magazine developed specifically for U.S. Special Operations Command. When used with the KAC sound suppressor, all that could be heard when the gun fired was the sound of the action. The M11 SIG Sauer P228 was small, light, durable, accurate and easy to conceal. A recoil-operated, semi-automatic pistol, it fired a 9 mm NATO round in both single and double-action modes from a 13-round magazine. The 870P Masterkey was a Remington Model 870 Police 12-gauge shotgun modified to attach to the underside of the M4A1 carbine. Coupled with the element of surprise, the combined firepower from the six men of Golf Platoon could easily shock, overwhelm or neutralize an enemy—which is exactly what this mission called for.

Without losing stride, Hartman continued. "The most difficult part of the operation will be getting from the *Florida* to the *Southern Star*. We will be swimming at night with no communications back to the BMC. Once we climb aboard the SDV and we leave the mother ship, we're on our own. We will be using Dräger LAR Vs during our ingress and egress. Because of the risks associated with the rebreather apparatus, I want to review some safety items. First, I want you to inspect every inch of your own LAR V. Check every fitting, every seal, every hose and every connection. When you finish, I want you to inspect your swim buddy's LAR V. If you see anything at all that doesn't look right, I want you to call a technician. If he says it's bogus, get another unit. We can't afford to have a mishap and end up losing a swimmer—we need everybody. Am I understood?"

"Yes, Chief," came the resounding reply.

The Dräger LAR V Hartman referred to was a closed circuit, oxygen rebreather system. With this type of system, a diver would breathe one hundred percent oxygen. However, instead of escaping into the water as in conventional open circuit systems, the LAR V purified the exhaled gas returned it to the breathing circuit. The exhaled gas passed through a soda lime canister that removed the carbon dioxide and returned it to an inhalation bag as breathable air. With an underwater duration of up to four hours, this system was useful for working in shallow water. Silent and bubble free, the Dräger LAR V was widely used by SEALs, for stealth in wartime and battle conditions. However, use of such rebreather devices was not without its risks.

Hartman picked up where he left off. "Let's review the possible rebreather disorders. First, you can experience a sudden blackout due to hypoxia. Second, oxygen toxicity can cause seizures. Third, excess carbon dioxide can lead to disorientation, panic, headache or hyperventilation. Lastly, if soda lime in the loop encounters seawater, it can result in the dreaded 'caustic cocktail' and can burn your mouth and lungs. It will be important for each of you to monitor your swim buddy for any signs of an LAR V malfunction. If there are any problems, render assistance and then notify me ASAP. Here's the point to remember: If we lose a swimmer for any reason, we scrub the mission. Are there any questions?" Hartman scanned the room. One by one, the SEALs all shook their heads.

"Good," Hartman nodded. "If that's the case, then I'll continue. The *Florida* will be hovering seventy feet below the surface. You will enter the lockout chamber with all of your gear, two swimmers at a time. Once you're clear, rendezvous at the SDV. After we count noses, we'll mount up and head for the *Southern Star*. The cruise ship is drifting so we're going to have a bit of difficulty pinpointing her exact location. I'll receive a final update on her position just before I enter the lockout chamber. The GPS coordinates will be close, but not precise—I'm afraid that's as good as it gets. Our biggest challenge will be getting from the waterline on to the *Southern Star*. Ropes are the preferred method and that's what we'll plan on using. Without a stable platform to work from, the trick will be securing them to the railing or some other ship's structure. The high swells and gusty winds will make it tough to do. If we don't succeed, we'll regroup at the SDV and return to the *Florida* to come up with another course of action. Understood?"

"Yes, Chief," they answered in unison.

"Good." Hartman glanced at his watch. "We move out in one hour and fifty-four minutes. Okay, let's synchronize watches."

As if rehearsed, all fourteen SEALs rotated their fore-arms and turned their attention to the Navy-issue Lumi-nox watches strapped to their wrists.

"On my mark, the time will be twenty-oh-seven in five-four-three-two-one-hack!"

Before issuing his final instruction, Hartman turned to look at Lieutenant Timmons, who nodded his approval.

"All right men, duty calls," Hartman boomed. "We've got a lot of prep work to do and not much time to do it in, so get to it. I'll see you at the lockout chambers."

Golf Platoon's members jumped to their feet and responded with a loud, "Hoo-yah!"

Hartman stepped off the riser and made for the equip-ment room with sixteen eager SEALs close behind.

# 48. TREADING WATER

"Ladies and gentlemen, the President of the United States."

Upon hearing the announcement made by White House press secretary Julie Townsend, the dozens of reporters who were crammed into the crowded space leapt to their feet. President Brewster burst into the briefing room through a side door and quickly walked to the podium and took his place. Hanging on the wall behind him was the iconic blue curtain, the familiar backdrop seen by thousands on national television or in newspaper and magazine photos.

Brewster's greeting was terse and his tone all business. "Let's begin. Before I take your questions, I'd like to provide you with an update on the hostage situation aboard the *Southern Star.*" The president didn't pause or even look up at the reporters seated before him. He simply continued with his prepared remarks.

"As you all know, the recent hijacking of the *Southern Star* has shocked our nation and the world as well. This terrorist act is without justification and placed the lives of many innocent people at risk. Ensuring the safety and well-being of the crew and passengers is of paramount importance. Our goal is to obtain the release of those on board and then get this ship out of harm's way. Unfortunately, for obvious reasons, I cannot say whether we are planning any unilateral or coordinated response to deal with the situation. I can tell you that we are currently working with the other members of the United Nations Security Council, our close allies and other international partners to formulate a proper response."

Brewster stopped speaking and looked up at the gathering before him. "Now, I'll take a few questions." Before the president had uttered his last word, dozens of hands shot into the air as the reporters clamored for a chance to ask him a question. Brewster studied the crowd of journalists and searched for a friendly face among the group. Moments later, Brewster pointed to a correspondent seated in the front row. "Helen, I'll begin with you."

On most days, the president smiled as he called on reporters from the press corps—but not today. As he stood before the assemblage, Brewster appeared to be quite uncomfortable He constantly fidgeted with his notes and glanced furtively around the room, avoiding eye contact with most that were present. Combined with a weary look that was often associated with worry or lack of sleep, the president wore a fatigued expression.

Seasoned veterans of the White House beat like Helen Martin knew the origins of the Press Briefing Room. Some of the newcomers did, too. However, much of the meaning and rich history surrounding its evolution had been lost on the dozens of rookie reporters assigned to cover the White House. For the lucky few like Martin, who knew the details, it was a fascinating story.

The West Wing Terrace area, where the press resided for thirty-seven years, was part of the original construction of the West Wing by President Theodore Roosevelt. It initially served as a laundry area, icehouse, servant's quarters and space for groundskeepers. In 1933, President Franklin D. Roosevelt built an eight-foot deep, fifty foot by fifteen-foot indoor swimming pool in one section. At that time, the other portion of the West Wing Terrace housed a florist shop, changing rooms and massage rooms, with another part reserved for presidential pooches.

A year later, in 1934, a West Wing renovation created a press lobby in the northwest corner of the building, just off the visitors' entrance lobby. In 1970, President Richard Nixon's staff proposed moving the press corps from its lobby location to the ground floor of the nearby Old Executive Office Building across the street. However, reporters liked being adjacent to the visitors' lobby. Nixon, who preferred using the White House's basement bowling alley to the West Wing swimming pool for recreation, covered it over and housed the press corps there instead. That action required twenty-eight cubic yards—over three truckloads—of concrete for the pool slab that became the Press Briefing Room floor.

The James S. Brady Press Briefing Room—named for the man who served as President Ronald Reagan's press secretary and took a bullet during an attempt on Reagan's life—sat in the West Wing of the White House between the workspace assigned to the White House press corps and the Office of the Press Secretary. In actuality, it was a small theater where the White House Press Secretary gave daily briefings to the news media.

Occasionally, the President of the United States addressed the press here and quite often spoke to the nation during televised broadcasts from the same location. To give it a more formal look when the president made an announcement or held a news conference in the Press Briefing Room, the backdrop included a pair of white columns. The result of recent upgrading under President George H. W. Bush, the press corps workspace now featured 570 miles of fiber-optic cable and two 45-inch LCD screens to display the presenter's charts and graphs among other enhancements.

The podium where the press secretary and president usually stood was over the deep end of the former swimming pool. Reporters joked among themselves that the press secretary was "way in over her head today," or that the president was "treading water," or that the press secretary was "all wet." Those remarks weren't disrespectful. They were simply a wonderful play on the room's past and the vernacular. Many a press secretary—including Brewster's current choice, Julie Townsend—often quipped when fielding tough questions from a crowd of demanding reporters, "As you can see, I'm standing in the deep end today."

Martin stood and looked squarely at Brewster. "Thank you Mr. President," she began. As the longest serving member of the White House press corps, Martin had covered every president who occupied the Oval Office since John F. Kennedy. She had seen a lot during the last fifty years, and the experience and skills she had gained over that span gave her a distinct edge.

"As you know, America has never experienced a terrorist incident of this sort. Can you tell me if this kind of threat was anticipated in any way, and if so, what response might we expect from the government?" Martin held her pen at the ready over a page of her stenographer's notepad and waited for the president's answer.

"Thank you, Helen," Brewster began, "This hijacking incident is a very complicated issue. To answer your question more to the point, Helen, the Department of Homeland Security continually assess all manner of threats to U.S. citizens here at home and abroad while the Transportation Security Administration specifically analyzes the risk to travelers by rail, plane, bus, and ship. Prior to the actual event, there was no credible threat. The *Southern Star* is currently in international waters. However, she is close to the Bahamas, which are part of the British Commonwealth. Several branches of the U.S. government are coordinating with the agencies from the Bahamas and the British government. With regard to possible actions by this or any other government, as I said before, at the moment I have no details to release nor can I comment on any plans to attempt a rescue of the hostages and crew."

Martin's pen skittered across the page of her notepad as she captured every word spoken by the president. Martin stopped writing and glanced up at Brewster. "Thank you, Mr. President," she nodded and then sat back down.

Brewster scanned the room and pointed toward a man seated in the back row. "Go ahead, Bill," he called to the reporter.

Before following the other correspondent's question, Martin quickly jotted a few more words near the bottom of the page. They read, "In the deep end and treading water."

## 49. RENDEZVOUS TIME

*Near the promenade deck*
*Aboard the* Southern Star

Murphy and White were making their way down from the bridge deck to the presumed safety of the covered promenade deck when the buzzing of Murphy's vibrating cell phone startled both of them.

"Jesus!" they both exclaimed.

Murphy snatched the phone from its holster and silently read the message. It was very short and looked simple enough: "its king g2 #3oh3 asap n stby dnt txtb"

"What did it say?" Evan White asked.

"It's from Peter King, the CIA man," Murphy replied. "I think he's telling us to go to cabin 303 right now and standby. Also, he doesn't want us to text him back."

White extended his hand. "Mind if I have a look?"

"Not at all," Murphy said, placing the phone firmly in White's upturned palm.

"That's what I make of it. Go to 303 right now and wait, and don't bother to text him back," White nodded. "I wonder what's in cabin 303?" he added.

"Probably not 'what,' but 'who' is in number 303," Murphy suggested.

"Since we're on the move, let's head there now," White proposed. "After all, that's what King instructed."

"Sure, thing," Murphy responded. "You lead the way, Evan."

Cabin 303, like Evan White's office, was located on the Atlantis deck, one level below the promenade deck. It was a Category D cabin with an outside porthole. This type of stateroom wasn't as spacious as some on the upper decks were, but they were nonetheless quite comfortable. They were always popular with passengers because of their central location and proximity to all of the *Southern Star's* amenities.

To reach cabin 303, White and Murphy would first have to make their way to the promenade deck. Once there, they would proceed aft until amidships and then follow the main stairwell down one level to the Atlantis deck, where they would emerge near the Shore Excursion Office. From there, they would go past the purser's office and straight down the corridor to cabin 303.

White and Murphy crept down the stairway that connected the boat deck and the promenade deck. The pair stopped every few feet and listened for footsteps or other sounds. When they reach the landing, they paused before entering the covered promenade deck to head aft.

White turned toward Murphy. "I don't hear anything, and that worries me," he whispered. "I wish we knew how many intruders—I mean terrorists—we were dealing with."

"Me, too," Murphy replied softly. "I just hope that we don't bump into any of them on our way to 303."

White nodded and then tiptoed to the edge of the stairwell bulkhead. He craned his neck, straining to hear footsteps coming from either direction along the teakwood deck. After a few seconds, he gave a Murphy thumbs-up, signaling that everything was all right. He stepped onto the promenade deck and motioned for Murphy to follow.

Although covered, the promenade deck was open to the elements at its sides. As White and Murphy hurried along, wind-driven rain from the advancing storm rushed through the wide opening and splattered across their faces. Without breaking stride, they wiped the water from around their eyes and marched on. Normally, foul weather was the mariner's bane. Today, however, it would prove to be a friend.

White stopped and put his back tightly against the bulkhead in order to minimize his profile, motioning for Murphy to do the same.

"Ordinarily," he panted, "I don't like this kind of weather when we're out." White swept beads of rain from his face and forehead. "Right now, though, I rather welcome it."

"Not being a top side sailor," Murphy apologized, "I can't say for sure. But I'm certain that this weather will keep everyone off the decks and inside—perhaps even the terrorists."

"I hope you're right, Bill." White gave a weak smile and darted off.

Murphy fell in a few steps behind White as the pair jaunted toward the main stairwell. They reached the entrance and ducked inside. Again, they paused and listened for footsteps or other sounds that would warn them if someone were nearby. Hearing none, White leaned close to Murphy, the concern evident on his face.

"Bill, at first I thought that hearing or seeing no one was a good thing. Now, I'm not so sure," he said in a barely audible whisper.

Even at this time of day, the ship's crew would be busy preparing for the day's entertainment activities, performing maintenance and doing housekeeping. Stewards and housekeepers should have been crisscrossing the ship up and down its corridors, moving in and out of the service areas, but they were not. To the *Southern Star's* purser, Evan White, the absence of such activity suggested only one thing.

"I'm afraid that the entire crew has been rounded up and is being held captive somewhere—maybe along with all of the passengers, too," White suggested.

The grim expression on Murphy's face indicated that he understood that what White was proposing was probably correct.

"Oh, my God!" Murphy mumbled faintly, "That means they've got Susan!"

# 50. GIDDY UP

Under the direction of the diving officer, the *Florida* had reached her ordered depth of seventy feet for the SEALs' egress. Next, the officer of the deck rapidly issued speed orders to get the boat at two knots in order to engage the Hovering System. When operating, computers would analyze the difference between actual and ordered depth, the rate of depth changes, and depth acceleration. Using this information, electrical signals caused massive valves to open or close, and ballasting water would be flooded or drained from the tanks as necessary to maintain depth and pitch.

The *Florida's* helm crew carefully monitored the system for any sign of trouble as the ballast tanks were automatically trimmed to keep the nearly 19,000-ton submarine nearly motionless twelve fathoms below the surface of the ocean. That was deep enough to eliminate rolling action from the winds and waves above, yet not so deep that the combat divers couldn't operate safely.

The SEALs that would accompany Hartman on this mission stood next to Tubes 1 and 2.

Reconfigured as lock-in/lock-out chambers, they allowed SEAL swimmers to pass straight through two thirty-inch hatches atop each tube into the sea or onto the *Florida's* landing deck above. The side of the converted eighty-seven inch-diameter missile tubes contained show-erheads and faucets that allowed returning swimmers to rinse their gear of saltwater and then hang it on a powerful dryer down below.

The converted SLBM tubes could accommodate up to five SEALs. Even at eighty-seven inches—more than seven feet—in diameter, with all of their combat gear, things would be rather tight for the SEALs. There was no need to squeeze into the tubes as if they were sardines crammed in a tin can. Hartman had decided the team would utilize a single tube and exit two at a time in dive-buddy pairs up into the Dry Deck Shelter stop the *Florida's* turtle deck.

Hartman turned to the five other SEALs who would accompany him on the raid and gave the go signal with his right hand. "All right men, this is it," he shouted. "It's show time!"

"Hoo-yah!" they responded enthusiastically, slapping one another on the back.

"And remember the SEAL motto," Hartman called as he stepped into the lockout chamber, "The only easy day was yesterday!"

"See you at the SDV," Hartman quipped with a sly smile. He and Owens entered the lockout chamber with their fully loaded weapons, LAR V rebreathers and other SEAL gear attached to their wetsuits. They had already donned their fins and gloves. To get ready for the next phase, they slid their masks down over their faces.

"Do it," Hartman nodded. "Flood the chamber."

They stood side by side and placed the LAR V's breathing tube in their mouths. Owens spun a large red wheel labeled FLOOD VALVES in a clockwise direction. As he did so, the sound of seawater rushing into the tube replaced the chamber's stillness. Saltwater quickly rose past their ankles, then their waists, and above their shoulders. The cold, salty brine covered their mouths and noses until it was finally over their heads. Satisfied that the lockout chamber was fully pressurized, Owens reached up and turned the large wheel to crack the hatch that led to the DDS atop the *Florida's* landing deck.

Owens took a deep breath from the LAR V and pushed the door all the way open to reveal the dark, vast ocean depths. He slithered up and out of the tube. Although numb with shock just seconds after hitting the cold ocean, Owens' body moved into action with an instinct born of countless hours of training. With a quick thrust of his legs, he spun around and plunged downward toward the lockout chamber's opening. Moving with the confidence of a man who knew exactly what he was doing, Owens quickly oriented himself.

It was nighttime and nothing was distinguishable to Owens as he peered into the inky void, but he had trained for such conditions. As a signal to the others, Owens reached for a chem light stick attached to a short line on his waist belt and quickly snapped it. He released it and the faint, yellow-green luminescent blob floated eerily near his midsection. Owens spun around and returned to the lockout chamber's opening. He pulled the chem light to him and made a circular motion with it to signal Hartman that it was okay to emerge.

Although the lockout chambers were nearly eighty-seven inches in diameter, the hatches atop the tube were only thirty-two inches wide. For a large, muscular man like Hartman, it was always a tight fit, especially when decked out with a LAR V and combat gear. Owens hovered near the opening and watched as the Hartman poked his head through. The hard part was next. Hartman rocked back and forth, as his broad shoulders encountered some resistance from the narrow opening. He continued to work at it and finally wriggled through. Once free, Hartman reached for Owens' wrist and gave it two firm squeezes that signaled, "I'm okay."

Hartman followed suit and snapped a chem stick to provide a reference for the other combat swimmers as they emerged from the lockout tube. He took up a position alongside Owens near the opening of Tube 1. Inside the Dry Deck Shelter's middle compartment a couple of feet away, the yellow-green glow from a pair of chem sticks marked the position of two divers that had emerged from Tube 1. Hartman and Owens lifted the hatch and swung it downward. It closed with a thunk.

Minutes later, a muffled clunk told Hartman and Owens that the second swim pair from Tube 1 had closed its hatch. They looked up to see the yellow-green blobs from those divers' chem lights getting closer. Down below, the last two combat swimmers emptied the tube and entered it with their combat gear and the other mission essential equipment. In a matter of minutes, all six SEALs would be atop the *Florida* and making their way to the SEAL Delivery vehicle (SDV) nested inside the Dry Deck Shelter (DDS).

While they waited, Hartman, Owens, and the other two divers quickly inventoried their gear and checked it for proper operation. *Weapons, checked; Ammo, checked; Combat knife, checked; Flash Bangs, checked; LAR V pressure, checked; Swimboard, checked.* According to SOP, no communication with the team leader was required if all the gear and equipment checked out. Swimmers were only to report if their gear was damaged or malfunctioning. During the course of the inspection, no one had approached Hartman, which meant so far, so good.

The group of four divers huddled around Tube 1 and watched the hatch intently. After a few minutes, it swung open and a diver emerged. Shortly afterward, a second diver followed. The two divers quickly closed the hatch, popped a chem stick, and inventoried their gear. No malfunctions. Hartman glanced at his Luminox watch. The team was ahead of schedule.

All eyes were on him as he made a circular "giddy-up" motion with his chem stick. With the skill and grace of a practiced diver, he rolled upward and to one side and began swimming rapidly toward the DDS. Had he turned around to look, he would have seen five SEALs following closely behind him. The mission was on.

# 51. ON THEIR OWN

*Aboard the USS* Florida's *SDV*
*Submerged Near Nassau, Bahamas*

The Dry Shelter mated to the *Florida's* turtle back was an engineering marvel perfected by the Navy over the years through countless tests and sea trials. It consisted of three interconnected compartments made of heavy steel, each capable of being independently pressurized to a depth of one hundred and thirty feet. The spherical, forward-most compartment was a hyperbaric chamber used to prevent or treat decompression sickness in divers. Commonly called the bends, it was a painful and sometimes fatal affliction caused by breathing nitrogen or other gases under pressure not metabolized by the body.

The middle compartment served as a transfer trunk that allowed divers to enter and exit the submarine through a lockout chamber that had once served as a missile tube. From there, they could pass to any of the other shelter sections. The third compartment served as a hangar to house the SEAL Delivery Vehicle (SDV). This portion was cylindrical in shape with bulbous, elliptical ends, one of which was a large door that swung open to the sea that permitted launching and retrieval of the SDV.

SEAL Delivery Vehicle Team Two (SDVT-2), which like SEAL Team Eight was also based at Little Creek, VA, would be supporting Hartman and his assault team tonight. SDVT-2 was an operational element employed to plan, coordinate and command submersible systems operations from specially configured submarines equipped with Dry Deck Shelters like the *Florida*. As with all SDV operations, the DDS platoon commander, in this case a Lieutenant j.g. named Marsh, reported directly to the submarine's commanding officer as a department head. The *Florida's* communications room gave Marsh the go ahead to launch the SDV as soon as it received the president's execution order.

SDVT-2's divers had exited the *Florida* fifteen minutes before Hartman's team did so they could ready the SDV for the SEALs. The DDS hangar was equipped with open-circuit "hookah" stations that allowed the DDS crew to breathe off while working. To help them see, the divers used hand-held rechargeable lights while they worked. Based on the latest in high-tech LED applications, they weighed nearly four pounds and lasted one hour between charges.

The miniature wet submersible Hartman and his SEALs would use sat on a cradle within the DDS hangar until ready for use. The steps that SDVT-2 used to launch the craft were very logical and executed in precise order. After flooding the hangar and equalizing it with outside water pressure, the DDS operators from SDVT-2 had opened the hangar's large outer door and moved a track out onto the *Florida's* landing deck.

SDVT-2's divers next extricated the SDV from its mooring inside the DDS. The nearly twenty-two foot long SDV was chained to a cradle inside the DDS's protective cover. The hangar-like structure mounted on the *Florida's* turtle back was forty feet long, ten feet high, and ten feet wide. The SDV itself was nine feet wide, so there was no room for error. Under normal circumstances, removing the SDV from the hangar was no easy task. Although it had been practiced dozens of times before, the nighttime conditions the DDS crew was operating under presented a new set of challenges for them. One wrong move by the DDS crew, and the damage to the boat-like craft might and render it unusable. It was an extremely delicate maneuver and required the utmost skill and patience.

The DDS hangar supervisor closely monitored the operation as the DDS deck crew slowly pushed the cradle-mounted SDV along the track out onto the *Florida's* landing deck. The tedious operation had taken nearly twenty minutes. Now that the cradle and SDV were on the track, the SDV could depart. The crew loosed the chains one by one, nearly setting the SDV free. The final step of launching the craft remained.

With Hartman in the lead, the small group of divers followed him over to the hangar area where the waiting SDV was located. Its pilot, a fifteen-year Navy lifer named Dickinson, checked the bowline to buoy line connection and stood by for the launch signal. Next, the DDS hangar supervisor watched as the DDS deck captain and deck crewman released the SDV from the DDS track and cradle. After it had cleared the cradle, the DDS deck captain made a large circular motion with a chem stick  As soon as Dickinson saw the launch signal, he let the SDV drift up and out of the *Florida's* slipstream and into the underway current that was flowing barely at one-knot.

Instantly, like minnows swarming around chum, the SEALs began to dart around the vessel as they readied it for the rescue mission. Because of its sleek, torpedo-like shape, SEALs often referred to the SDV simply as "the sled." The vehicle's advanced lithium-ion batteries had been on constant charge ever since the *Florida* left Kings Bay. An intercom system would allow the divers to talk to one another while underwater and compressed air on board extended the range of a swimmer's own air tank or rebreather. Hartman and his team hastily stowed non-critical mission gear in the two small lockers located on top of the craft. They would secure weapons and other essential items to their dive suits.

Depending on the type and duration of the mission, DDS operators would return to the submarine or remain outside. SEAL Team Eight's rescue mission was going to be a long one, so the DDS crew would reenter the *Florida* through the lockout chamber and wait it out there. After conducting their mission, the SEALs would locate the submarine using active sonar pings. Once the SDV returned to the *Florida*, the DDS crew would secure it to its cradle, winch it back into the DDS, and shut the hangar's nine-foot outer door.

As directed by Chief Hartman, the SEALs had checked their personal equipment and found every piece in working order. Hartman, Owens, and the four other SEALs climbed aboard the SDV. Owens would serve as navigator and assist Dickinson, the pilot. GPS signal reception underwater wasn't possible, so the team would rely instead on a Doppler-based inertial guidance system to get them close to the hijacked cruise ship. Once they reached that spot, they would leave the SDV, surface, and swim the rest of the way to the *Southern Star*.

After its launch, the SDV had drifted further and further from the *Florida* and into the black nothingness of the night ocean. Their part of the mission completed for now, the DDS crew had extinguished their diving lights and the faint greenish glow given off by their chem sticks had long since faded away. That made it impossible to tell where the submarine was located. It didn't matter. By now, SDVT-2's divers were back on board the submarine.

Hartman, Owens, Dickinson and the other three SEALs on the team were all alone and on their own. From this point on, the mission's outcome—successful or not—depended entirely on them. Owens reviewed the data provided to him by Lieutenant Timmons moments before he left the *Florida* and carefully entered it into the vessel's navigation system. Satisfied, he squeezed Dickinson's forearm twice signaling that it was okay to move out. Dickinson pressed the throttle and the sled began its journey toward the coordinates that marked the last known position of the *Southern Star*.

# 52. MOVING FORWARD

*On the Atlantis Deck*
*Aboard the* Southern Star

A queasy feeling swept over Bill Murphy as he thought about his companion, Susan Anderson, whom he left behind in the Miramar Café when he and Evan White decided to investigate why the *Southern Star* had stopped. He tried to suppress it, but couldn't.

*I should have let White go alone,* Murphy scolded himself. His mind turned to more sinister thoughts as he considered the danger she might be facing. He felt a hand on his shoulder.

"Bill! Bill! Snap out of it!" White pleaded, gently shaking him.

Murphy, clearly embarrassed, apologized. "Sorry," he said, "I was just thinking about Susan. What if they're holding her and the other passengers as hostages?"

"Good question," White replied. "Fortunately it's not like an airliner, so they can't fly it into a building. Let's hope that this is a Somali pirate scenario being played out here in the Caribbean and all they want is a large ransom."

Murphy nodded in agreement. "Yes, that would be an easy situation to resolve, wouldn't it? Just give them their damned money in exchange for releasing the ship and everyone on board."

"Maybe we'll find out more when we reach cabin 303," White reasoned. "At least I hope so," he added.

"Me, too," Murphy said.

White pointed downward. "Okay, then, let's go."

The pair began their descent toward the Atlantis deck. This stairway was the widest one on the *Southern Star*. Designed to accommodate dozens of people traversing in opposite directions, it was void of the normal hustle and bustle of passengers and crew going about their routines. More cautious now than before, White and Murphy stopped at every other tread and listened intently for telltale sounds. They crept along and eventually found themselves in Atlantis deck's main foyer directly across from the purser's office.

White quickly scanned the area. Satisfied that they were alone, he turned to Murphy and whispered, "I feel better because now I'm on my turf."

Murphy gave a nod and smiled reassuringly at White.

The unexpected sound of approaching footsteps caught their attention. White and Murphy froze. A sudden, adrenaline-fueled "fight or flight" mode caused their muscles to tighten and hearts to race. The thump-thump-thump grew loader as the unidentified person drew closer.

Without warning, White thrust his hand toward Murphy and firmly clutched him by the forearm. In a swift, fluid move, he and Murphy flew into the purser's office and dove behind the massive service counter. A surprised Bill Murphy stared at Evan White, whose sole response was an extended index finger pressed against his lips. The only reaction Murphy could muster was a difficult swallow.

The footsteps grew fainter and fainter until they couldn't hear them anymore. Murphy, still visibly shaken, managed to pose a question.

"Friend or foe?" he asked in a hushed voice.

White shrugged his shoulders. "Can't say for sure. Could have been either, but I'll bet foe."

"Me, too," Murphy replied. "All the more reason to get to 303 right away."

With White leading the way once again, the pair left the safety of the purser's office and stepped into the long corridor. Before moving forward, White pointed to his left, indicating the side of the passageway cabin 303 was on, then held up three fingers and mouthed "third one" so Murphy would know they didn't have far to go. Without waiting for a nod or thumbs-up from Murphy, White darted down the corridor.

A few yards from the Atlantis deck's main foyer, ship's purser Evan White and US Navy Commander Bill Murphy found themselves standing in front of cabin 303, just as Peter King had directed. Not knowing what to expect next, the two exchanges glances before White knocked lightly on the stateroom's brass and mahogany door. There was no answer. After a few seconds, they looked at one another and shrugged. Their anticipation turned to disappointment when a second knock brought no response.

They were about to leave when the door opened a crack. Through the narrow slit, White and Murphy saw an eyeball staring out at them. The gap widened, providing just enough space for them to slip inside. One after the other, Evan White and Bill Murphy slid through the opening into cabin 303 as the door closed behind them with a soft thunk.

Evan White and Bill Murphy stood side by side looking at the occupant of cabin 303. He was a man whom they both judged to be in his mid-fifties. Clean-shaven and sporting a gray crew cut, he appeared to be physically fit. Before they could make introductions, he broke the silence.

"What took you so long?" he quipped.

Left speechless by his question, they glanced at one another and then at him.

Murphy was the first to respond. "You're kidding, right?" he snorted. "Do you have any idea what's going on here?"

Then White chimed in, "Obviously, you don't know what's taken place, do you?"

"Actually, I do know what's happened. Stanton's the name. Jack Stanton," he replied. "Right now, I probably know more than either one of you do, but that's not the point." Without waiting for their response, Stanton motioned toward a large upholstered seat in the center of the room. "Sit," he insisted.

White and Murphy plopped onto the sofa while Stanton settled into an overstuffed chair opposite them.

"Let me bring you up to speed," he offered.

Stanton began with details about his own background why he was on the *Southern Star*. Then he spent the better part of an hour filling White and Murphy in on everything that had occurred with airliners and other presumed terrorist incidents in the U.S. and around the world during the past twenty-four hours. They listened intently, soaking up every detail. When it came to the *Southern Star*, they were all ears and very eager to tell Stanton what they knew.

As Stanton gathered more information to use in formulating a plan, he turned to White.

"So, you believe that there are two terrorists on the bridge?" he asked.

"Based on what I heard up there, I'd say that's accurate," White replied.

"What about other parts of the ship?" he continued. "Any idea?"

"We don't really know how many of them there are," White explained, "but they don't know how many of us there are, either—and since I prepare the ship's manifests, I do!"

# 53. EYES ONLY FOR POTUS

*The White House Residence*
*Washington, D.C.*

Inside the White House, an aide hurried down a wide second-floor hallway toward the Master Bedroom, which was located in the southwest portion of the official residence. He gripped a thin, black leather satchel tightly under one arm. It was the middle of the night, but since it was his scheduled shift, the courier had been awake for hours. Dispatched from the Situation Room on the ground floor of the West Wing minutes earlier, he was now heading straight for President's Brewster's sleeping quarters.

He scurried down the broad corridor appropriately dubbed the Center Hall, marked by tasteful decorations of period American furniture pieces and artwork from a sweeping renovation undertaken by First Lady Nancy Reagan. On his left, the aide passed the Yellow Oval Room that led to the Truman Balcony above the South Portico and overlooked the South Lawn. Next, he passed through a large opening that was framed with white columns on both sides and topped by a stylish arch window and entered the West Sitting Hall. Fitted with comfortable furniture for relaxing or entertaining by the First Family, this space was less formal than the Center Hall but was still elegant. The lights of the Old Executive Office Building across the street played along the top of the West Wing and shone in through the large, graceful half-moon window at the end of the passage.

The aide marched down the West Sitting Hall and stopped outside the president's bedroom. Two Secret Service Uniformed Division officers and two plainclothes Secret Service agents flanked the large wooden panel doors that led inside. Nearby, the military officer who carried the football—the briefcase that contained the nuclear launch codes—sat quietly in a straight back chair along the wall. The uniformed officers were well armed. Each wore a thick, bulletproof vest under his white shirt and tie and held an Uzi sub-machine gun held at the ready. Slung over a shoulder, each man carried a black canvas bag that contained special masks designed not only to protect him, but the president and first lady as well in the event of a chemical or biological attack on the White House.

Because of their duties, the plainclothes Special Agents traveled light—they wore business suits, carried SIG Sauer P229 service pistols, handcuffs and communications devices—that was it. It was impractical for them to carry bulky gas masks like their uniformed counterparts, so the Department of Homeland Security came up with another option. Special Agents had escape hoods outfitted with thin carbon filters inside to scrub the air of toxic smoke, gas or biological substances. Intended for short-term use—about ten to fifteen minutes—the unit measured only four inches wide and eight inches long and easily fit inside a suit coat pocket  In the event of an attack, they could pull the hood out and don it as a means to go safely from a contaminated area back to a secure area.

Before the aide could speak or show his credentials, the four Secret Service agents had quickly closed ranks and moved in front of the door to block access. They studied the courier briefly and then one of the uniformed officers challenged him.

"State your business," he commanded.

"Schwartz. I'm on duty in the Situation Room. I have an important 'Eyes Only' dispatch for POTUS."

He held his credentials out for the agents to see. One of the plainclothes agents scrutinized the ID and compared the likeness of the man standing in front of him to the photo on the badge. The agent brought his left hand, which contained a concealed microphone for his radio, close to his mouth. He spoke into his clenched fist.

"Control, this is Binder. We have a staffer from the Sit Room here in the residence with a dispatch for POTUS. Can you verify?"

A moment later, the agent cocked his head slightly as he listened to the reply from the Secret Service command post that came through his earpiece. The agent lowered his hand and stepped back.

"Okay, Schwartz," he said. "You've been verified. You may proceed."

One of the agents stepped aside, and allowed Binder to approach the door. He knocked loudly enough to wake the president and waited for the door to open. Less than three minutes later, President Brewster, decked out in slippers and a dark blue terrycloth bathrobe, was standing in the doorway.

"Good morning, gentlemen," Brewster said in a groggy voice. "At least I presume it is morning, since you are still here and I am yet in my slippers and robe," he joked.

"Sorry to disturb your night's sleep, Mr. President," agent Binder apologized. "Mr. Schwartz has a dispatch from the Sit Room for you," he explained.

"Very, well," Brewster replied. He turned to Schwartz, "I'll take it then, Mr. Schwartz."

Schwartz stepped forward and approached the president. He removed the satchel from under his arm and held it out for Brewster. The president accepted the thin, zippered black bag from Schwartz and nodded.

"If you don't mind, gentlemen, I'll read it here. I don't want to disturb Mrs. Brewster further," he explained. "I hope you don't mind."

Binder spoke for the group, "Not at all, sir."

Brewster fished his reading glassed from one of the robe's deep pockets and wriggled them onto his face with one hand. Next, he grasped the leather satchel, jerked the zipper open, and removed a manila folder that had EYES ONLY- POTUS stamped in big red letters on it. Brewster flipped the folder open to see a single typewritten sheet tucked inside. The message was in standard military format. It might have been difficult for a novice to decipher, but Brewster was an experienced hand at this and needed no help in translating its contents. He began to read it silently to himself while the Secret Service men, Schwartz and the military aide all looked on.

MSG #0493284G6745WOPQRINV    UTC 0542Z

PRIORITY FLASH//LEVEL ONE

CLASSIFICATION TOP SECRET

FROM JCS J-3 PLANS/OPS

FOR COMMANDER IN CHIEF

REF OPLAN ALPHA-FOUR-ZULU//OPERATION SECOND LIGHT//

SECTION I

SEAL TEAM EIGHT COMMENCED REPEAT COMMENCED TACTICAL OPERATIONS // OPLAN ALPHA-FOUR-ZULU OPERATION SECOND LIGHT. STOP

SECTION II

COMMANDER SEAL TEAM EIGHT REPORTS MISSION UNDERWAY AT UTC 0540Z. EXPECT FURTHER UPDATES AS AVAILABLE. STOP

SECTION III

CINC ACKNOWLEDGEMENT NOT REQUIRED.

END

AUTHENTICATION

JENKINS, RADM, JCS J-3 PLANS/OPS

After Brewster had finished, he looked up and closed his eyes for a moment. He opened them and turned to agent Binder.

"How many hours difference between Zulu time and local time?" he asked.

Twenty-five separate divisions made up the world's lettered time zones. Greenwich, England, location of the atomic clock that served as the standard clock for international time reference, was letter Z, or "Zulu." In military and aviation parlance, it was simply "Zulu" time. If one traveled west from Greenwich into a differently lettered zone, time shifted earlier; eastward and it shifted later. Depending on whether the U.S. was using Standard or Daylight Savings time, there was either a four or a five-hour difference between Zulu time and local time.

"Spring ahead, fall behind," Binder replied, referring to the folksy memory jogger that helped people remember to move clocks forward in spring and back in autumn. "For this time of year, that would make it five hours here in Washington, Mr. President."

"Yes, I recall that now, too," he nodded. "I guess I've got a lot on my mind. Thanks, Agent Binder."

Brewster glanced at his wristwatch and noted the time. It was 12:53 a.m. The *Southern Star* rescue operation had begun barely thirteen minutes ago. The *Florida* transmitted a message to the Joint Chiefs J-3 section as soon as the operation commenced. The Pentagon instantly relayed it to the White House Sit Room where the duty officer logged and authenticated the message, then gave it to Schwartz.

The ten minutes that elapsed represented the time it took Schwartz to walk nearly one block from the situation room's West Wing location to the White House, take the elevator up to the second-floor residence, proceed down the Center and West Sitting Halls, and check in with the Secret Service detail. Brewster looked at each of the men standing outside the Master Bedroom in the West Sitting Hall. He forced a smile and nodded.

"That will be all, gentlemen. I'm going to try to get a little more sleep. But don't hesitate to wake me again."

"Very well, sir," Binder replied.

The president turned away from the group and slowly closed the door. "Good night," he whispered as it clunked shut behind him.

# 54. A PRESS RELEASE

*The Miramar Café*
*Aboard the* Southern Star

With Ali's permission, Susan sat in front of her laptop computer and began to compose a statement for the *Washington Post*. The back and forth exchange between them sounded more like an interview than casual conversation.

"Tell me why you and your group are doing this," Susan began. "Why did you hijack the *Southern Star* and take its passengers hostage?"

Ali first straightened himself as if proud of his actions and started to talk. "The United States has the power to cause harm and pain," he said. Susan typed quickly as he continued. "But the United States is also susceptible to harm and pain. So if that is the path that the U.S. wishes to choose, then, Allah willing, so be it."

Susan probed deeper. "What specific 'harm and pain' are you referring to? Is it the recent missile attack?"

"Yes, that is one incident. But there are many, many other reasons," Ali replied.

"Such as?" Susan pressed him. "Give me some examples."

Ali shook his head. "No one incident. General American policies."

"Look," Susan pleaded, "I need more—something people can point to."

"Very well," Ali responded, "If the United States doesn't refrain from the foolish policy of backing Israel, occupying the lands of Islam, and stealing the treasures of the Muslims, then all of America awaits the same fate," he said.

"So this is about more that the American missile attack against Iran?" Susan asked.

"Yes and no," Ali answered. "All Muslims are brothers, so an attack against one is an attack against all."

Susan leaned toward him. "Then this is an act of revenge, is that correct?"

"No, it is more than that. It is a warning to the west and to all non-believers," Ali replied ominously. "We do not approve of what America is doing in the Middle East or how it treats Muslims around the world."

"So why seize a cruise ship with dozens of innocent people on board?" Susan demanded. "If your quarrel is with the United States government then that just doesn't make any sense."

"That is precisely the point, woman!" Ali snorted. "It is the only way to make your foolish president take notice. Otherwise, he will simply throw more missiles at our country. Now if he does something stupid, he risks the lives of everyone on this ship."

"What makes you so sure," Susan asked.

"Your president will not want the blood of his citizens on his hands," Ali surmised. "Surely, there would be a public outcry. He would be branded as a criminal for such negligence."

"Then tell me," Susan asked, "What exactly are your demands?"

"It's quite simple," Ali smiled. "The American tourists will not be released unless the United States announces that it has given up its hostile policies against the Iranian people and all of Islam."

"I'm afraid it's not quite that simple," Susan sighed. "Not simple at all. And, I think you know it."

"Oh, but it is, woman," Ali sneered. "The tourists are in good health, but the United States needs to cease all hostilities against Iran and all Muslims to ensure their safety."

"Now it's my turn," Susan said angrily. "I can promise nothing of the sort. I will do only what I said, and that was to get my newspaper to print your statement."

She lowered her head and focused on the laptop's screen. Her fingers flew over the computer keyboard. In a matter of minutes, she had composed a few paragraphs that incorporated most of what Ali had said. She reviewed it twice and ran the spell check program. Satisfied, she turned the laptop around so Ali could see the display.

He leaned over the table and read what Susan had written.

## —Flash—Cruise Ship Hijackers Reveal Demands

By Susan Anderson, *Washington Post* staff reporter on the *Southern Star*

-**Nassau, Bahamas** - In an apparent response to the recent missile attack against Iran by the United States, a clandestine pro-Iranian group has seized a cruise ship near the Bahamas and is holding several dozen Americans hostage.

In making his demands known, the group's leader, who identified himself only as "Ali," said that "if the United States doesn't refrain from the foolish policy of backing Israel, occupying the lands of Islam, and stealing the treasures of the Muslims, then all of America awaits the same fate."

Veteran *Washington Post* reporter Susan Anderson, who happened to be vacationing aboard the ship when it was hijacked, interviewed Ali. He told her, "The United States has the power to cause harm and pain. But the United States is also susceptible to harm and pain. So if that is the path that the U.S. wishes to choose, then, Allah willing, so be it."

When asked what it would take to win the release of the passengers, all of whom are U.S. citizens, Ali's answer was brief and very broad. "The American tourists will not be released unless the United States announces that it has given up its hostile policies against the Iranian people and all of Islam," he said. Ali also warned the Brewster administration that only such a response would ensure the continued safety of the hostages.

Except for the release of this statement to the *Washington Post*, the group has made no other demands. The *Southern Star* is not underway and is adrift in waters off the Bahamas near Nassau. The condition of her crew is unknown. An approaching tropical storm adds urgency to the tense situation. For the moment, the world, like the passengers aboard the *Southern Star*, must wait and hope. – End –

Ali straightened and smacked his lips. A sinister smile crept across his face. He took a deep breath and exhaled it slowly. After a long pause, Ali spun the laptop around toward Susan gave her a one-word command, "Send."

# 55. DEAD IN THE WATER

*Aboard the USS* Florida's *SDV*
*Submerged Near Nassau, Bahamas*

The twenty-two foot long Mk 8 SDV churned through the inky blackness toward its destination at four knots, maximum speed for the craft. A computerized Doppler navigation sonar displayed speed, distance, heading, height above the seabed and other piloting functions. Owens kept his eyes riveted on the SDV's bright, blue-green navigation panel, ensuring that Dickinson didn't wander off course. Even a one-degree heading error over a mile or two might be enough to cause the team to miss the target.

Dickinson stared at his group of instruments and concentrated on piloting the vessel. It wasn't a difficult craft to operate, although it did take some practice to handle one skillfully. As the SDV's pilot moved the joystick connected to the rudder, elevator and bow planes, the sled dutifully responded to his inputs. Its rechargeable lithium-ion batteries gave the SDV a top speed of around four knots and a maximum range of thirty-six nautical miles. There was no enclosure while riding the sled, so cold-water exposure time for the SEALs could be more limiting than the SDV's battery power.

This newer SDV travelled twice as far and fifty percent faster than the previous version and it was quieter, significantly easier, and less expensive to maintain. Overhaul intervals dropped to five weeks from nine months and their frequency increased from every two years to every four years. Although the boats were more than capable of completing their missions, often the men inside reached the limits of human endurance.

Besides the environmental considerations of underwater illumination and temperature, diving with the Dräger LAR V—the front-mounted rebreathing device worn by the SEALs—was the most limiting aspect affecting the mission. If one part broke down, the unit could not function. More hazardous than that, if a LAR V unit flooded, it meant the diver would suddenly inhale a caustic cocktail—a potentially toxic combination of fumes that resulted when the chemicals in the rebreather tank mixed with seawater. At the very least, exposure to the mixture would cause mild burns in the diver's mouth and leave an extremely bad aftertaste. In a worst-case scenario, a diver could die because the caustic fumes burned his lungs.

In case of a caustic cocktail, with any luck a SEAL would able to help his swim buddy to the surface before any serious injury occurred. Because surprise was very important, surfacing during a combat swim was the last thing divers were supposed to do, as it not only alerted lookouts to their presence, but also endangered other, undetected teams. Sharing rebreathers solved the short-term problem and would enable divers to remain below the surface and escape undetected. However, it would also reduce the time that the affected team could stay submerged. That was the chief disadvantage. Of course, there were acceptable trade-offs, but it all came down to this: a SEAL *never* went anywhere without his swim buddy.

All six SEALs had connected up to the vessel's onboard life support system. That would allow them to save their LAR V rebreathers for the rescue mission once the team had reached the planned disembarkation point. They had also plugged into the vehicle's communications system, a state of the art, sound-based intercom that used a closed circuit and no radio transmissions to prevent an enemy from detecting their presence. Since the primary purpose of the SDV was to deliver its passengers covertly, allowing them to communicate among themselves without alerting the enemy was critical. The Navy had spent years and hundreds of thousands of dollars to perfect a system such as this one, known by the acronym LPI/LPD—Low Probability Intercept/Low Probability Detection.

The briefed plan called for the *Florida* to remain at its last position in a hover. The Hover System, which used computers and huge pumps capable of on-loading or off-loading 1,000 pounds (120 gallons) of seawater per second from the sub's ballast tanks, would handle that complicated task. It required constant vigilance, close coordination and dedicated teamwork on the part of the SSGN crew. By remaining stationary, it would be possible for the SEAL team to return to the *Florida* using the SDV's Doppler-based inertial navigation system. Similar to a hiker who carried a handheld GPS, all the SDV's navigator had to do was select Reverse Course and they could retrace their route back to the waiting submarine. Once they were within range, a low-powered active sonar system onboard the sled would precisely locate the *Florida* by pinging it. Since the SEALs were operating in complete darkness, that was a vital tool for a successful recovery back to the DDS hangar.

Hartman requested an update from Owens over the interphone. "Status?"

"Time out, one hour six minutes," Owens responded. "Time to go, twenty-four minutes."

"Roger," Hartman acknowledged.

The SDV had been traveling for a little more than an hour. Without taking into account the current, the craft was roughly four nautical miles from the *Florida*. By the time they reached their departure fix, they would be six nautical miles away. According to the last update the team had received just before entering the sub's lockout chambers, the *Southern Star* was located approximately six and a half nautical miles away from the *Florida*. Once the SEALs secured the SDV, they would swim the last half-mile to the cruise ship just below the ocean's surface.

"Awww shit! Holy shit!" Dickinson, the SDV pilot, exclaimed over the intercom.

Owens chimed in next. "Uh-oh! Goddamn it!"

Hartman could have looked at the square red and yellow lights that had lit up on the SDV's instrument cluster to verify that something was wrong. However, he didn't have to. Like the other SEALs, he sensed that the SDV had come to a sudden stop. It was as if somebody had put the brakes on, but there was no noise, no shudder or no vibration to accompany it. The craft just came to a standstill.

"Status?" Hartman demanded.

"Don't know, Chief," Dickinson answered. "We're dead in the water."

"Navigator?" Hartman continued the questioning.

"We're four-point-oh from home plate and two-point-five from the target," Owens replied. "Either way, it would be a long swim."

Hartman queried Dickinson again. "Pilot, life support status?"

"Two hours and eight minutes," he replied. "Long enough to sit here and wait for help."

"Okay, good," Hartman said reassuringly. "We just might have to. Now let's figure out what's wrong. Pilot, what's the problem?"

"Don't know." Dickinson ticked off the indications for Hartman, "The batteries show an acceptable charge level. No shorts or dead cells. All in the green."

The newer Mk8 MOD 1 SDV Hartman and his team were employing featured a significantly improved electrical power storage system. Previous SDV models relied on silver- zinc batteries that needed more than thirty-six hours to recharge. To support a twelve-hour mission turnaround, each SDV deployed with two to three silver-zinc battery sets. The bigger issue was the battery charging and replacement process. Crewmembers funneled these batteries through numerous hatches and ladder-wells between the SDV and the sub's charging station. Each of the twenty-four silver-zinc battery trays weighed fifty-three pounds. To protect them from hazardous electrolyte exposure, technicians wore Personal Protective Equipment (PPE) and had to keep the batteries upright. That process was inefficient and required over forty-six man hours to charge, remove, and install the more than 2,500 pounds of silver-zinc batteries on an SDV.

The answer that the U. S. Navy came up with to resolve the issues with the silver-zinc batteries centered on lithium-ion battery technology. The newer lithium-ion energy system had a charge-in-place feature so an SDV was always mission ready. Another advantage was the much shorter recharging time of less than twelve hours. This was possible because lithium-ion batteries charged at higher charge rates than the other silver-zinc system batteries. Another plus was more stored power—the silver-zinc batteries had a rated capacity of 60 kWh while the lithium-ion battery had a rated capacity of 100 kWh. There was, however one very significant weakness in the overall design. Since all of the lithium-ion batteries were connected in series, the energy system of the Mk8 MOD1 SDV had a single-point failure. If one battery cell on the string shorted or opened, the boat would have no electrical power whatsoever.

"Any ideas?" Hartman asked.

"Let me power down and bring it back up," Dickinson replied. "Sometimes rebooting everything does the trick. You know how computers can be. Maybe we've got some gremlins."

"All right," Hartman agreed. "Power down and back up as soon as the navigator stores our position in the INS. Nav, advise when ready."

"Roger," Owens responded. "Saving position coordinates now. Standby."

A few seconds later, a white light on the navigation panel flashed indicating that the SDV's position had been stored in the INS computer.

"Position stored. Ready for power down," Owens announced.

"Very well, nav. Pilot, proceed," Hartman commanded.

Dickinson answered with a simple, "Roger," and then the SDV's instrument panel went dark.

Dickinson looked at his Navy-issue dive watch and waited for the luminescent second hand to sweep around two complete times. During that lull, swayed by the underwater currents, the SDV bobbed about. The ballast system would keep the craft from sinking, but the vessel was drifting along, carried by the gentle, northward flow of the Gulf Stream. Without power, there was no way for the team members to communicate with one another. For a full two minutes, the six Navy SEALs remained cutoff from each other and the outside world, enveloped by a cocoon of black seventy-five degree water. They were isolated and all alone.

Since it was completely dark, Dickinson had kept his right index finger on the SDV's power button. Like the other SEALs, he was wearing a diving lamp attached to his mask and had an ample supply of chem sticks. He opted not to use them. One of the things all SEALs learned during training was conservation of equipment and personal resources. "Can't use what you don't have," the instructors drilled into them from their first day at BUD/S. "You are going to be miles from nowhere and on your own. Your equipment will be the difference between success and failure; between life and death, so treat it that way."

Dickinson pushed the power button and the SDV's instrument panel sprang to life. Half a dozen red, green and amber squares glowed eerily in the murky water. Dickinson quickly scanned the group of lights in front of him, analyzed their meaning, and relayed it to Hartman.

"No good, Chief," he said. "She's still dead."

"Damn it," Hartman replied. "Now what? Anything else you can try?"

"I'm afraid not. It doesn't appear to the battery system," he responded. "I think something's wrong with our propulsion mechanism."

"What makes you think that?" Hartman asked.

"Well, for one thing, it's relatively simple system. The batteries provide the electrical power to turn the motor, which then drives the screw," Dickinson explained. "We have plenty of battery power—otherwise, the whole damned panel would be dark. For some reason the screw won't respond to throttle movements. Propulsion—that's got to be it," he insisted.

Hartman pondered Dickinson's explanation briefly and then replied. "Could be, pilot. However, I guess it doesn't matter. Doesn't look like we're going anywhere on this thing."

The SDV still had power and the team could communicate with one another. However, now suddenly stranded miles between the *Florida* and the *Southern Star,* the hostage rescue mission was in doubt.

Hartman tried to make light of the situation's seriousness and added, "Remember the SEAL motto, 'the only easy day was yesterday?' They sure got that right, didn't they?"

# 56. SRS

*USS* Florida *Battle Management Center*
*Submerged Near Nassau, Bahamas*

Lieutenant Brian Timmons, the SEAL team operations officer, sat next to a large digital communications console in the *Florida's* dimly lit Battle Management Center (BMC) with a handset pressed firmly against his ear.

"No, sir. Nothing yet," Timmons said. Timmons was speaking to the *Florida's* captain, Commander Davis. "According to our calculations, Commander, the SDV should be nearing the DP," Timmons continued, referring to the departure point, the spot where the SEALs would leave the SDV and swim the rest of the way to the *Southern Star.* "We should get an update from the team within a few minutes."

Timmons listened to Davis's reply and then concluded with, "Aye, sir. Will do." He placed the handset back in the cradle and swiveled around to the equipment operator.

"This is the toughest part, don't you agree, Watson?" Timmons asked the young petty officer seated next to him.

"Sure is, sir," Watson nodded. "Sitting here just waiting and not knowing keeps me on pins and needles."

"I know exactly what you mean. Sometimes it's downright agonizing," Timmons confessed. "What's their ETA to the DP? I want to be able to let Commander Davis know the minute they arrive."

"Standby, sir. Pulling it up now," Watson replied. He pushed a couple of buttons on the console and watched as a block of amber digits appeared on the screen in front of him. "Two point five nautical miles, Mr. Timmons," he announced.

"Very well," Timmons acknowledged. He reached for the operations log to record Commander Davis's call and jot down some other pertinent mission information. As he leaned forward to grab the clipboard a loud, pulsing alarm suddenly pierced the stillness in the BMC. Nearby, a red lamp on the control panel began to flash.

"SRS, sir!" Watson shouted. "SRS!"

"Aye, SRS. Acknowledged!" Timmons responded. "Implement SDV rescue protocol," he ordered. Timmons pulled his chair close to the workstation and reached for the phone on the console. He quickly lifted it from the cradle and punched the red button labeled EMER. Timmons spoke loudly and clearly into the handset.

"Control, BMC. SRS activated," Timmons announced. "Repeat, SRS activated."

Timmons slammed the handset in its holder and reached for a large red three-ring binder marked SDV RESCUE & RECOVERY PLAN.

SRS was the Navy's acronym for SDV Rescue Signal. The SEALs could use it to signal the DDS-equipped sub—in this case, the *Florida*—that they were in need of help. It was designed to transmit the last know Doppler INS coordinates of the SEAL Delivery Vehicle to the submarine's control room and BMC. That way the sub could easily home in on the SDV's last location to recover the craft and render any assistance to the SEAL swimmers. To prevent and enemy from learning of the SDV's distress situation and position, the SRS used a frequency hopping transmitter that sent encrypted information in a series of millisecond bursts. A sophisticated system, it had several safeguards built into it to keep the nature of the emergency communications secure. However, there was still some risk to activating it, so it was a last resort to initiate an SDV rescue and recovery.

As soon as Lieutenant Timmons hung up the handset, in the sub's control room, Commander Davis quickly hopped into the captain's chair to direct the boat and its crew in the rescue operation.

"Chief of the watch, stand by the general alarm," Davis barked at a nearby petty officer.

"Stand by general alarm, aye," he responded.

Davis picked up the microphone in the conn to the sub-wide speaker system, the 1MC, and keyed it. His words reverberated from stem to stern throughout the *Florida*.

"Now hear this, now hear this. This is the captain," Davis said in a clear, authoritative voice. "SRS activated. Repeat SRS activated. All hands respond. This is not a drill. Repeat SRS activated. All hands respond. This is not a drill." Davis kept the microphone in his hand and turned to the officer of the deck.

"Sound general alarm," Davis ordered.

"Aye, sound general alarm," came the acknowledgement.

"Chief of the watch, sound general alarm," the officer of the deck snapped.

"Aye, sound general alarm," the petty officer acknowledged. He grabbed the large yellow handle for the general alarm and swung it downward.

Immediately, the claxon's loud *Bong! Bong! Bong!* sounded throughout the sub. In an instant, all over the *Florida* crewmen dropped what they were doing and sprang into action, rolling down their coverall sleeves as they scurried through the passageways to their battle station watch assignments. Davis's announcement over the sub's PA system with a "this is not a drill" clarifier meant it was the real deal. SDV rescue and recovery was one of the many scenarios that the crew had practiced. Now, everyone aboard the *Florida* would perform just as they did during countless drills and exercises before. As the old saying goes, practice makes perfect. For this urgent situation, that would be critical. A few seconds later, Commander Davis issued another order directed at the diving officer of the watch, a chief petty officer named Warren.

"Dive. Make your depth one-three-zero feet, this course, ten knots."

"Make your depth one-three-zero feet, this course, ten knots. Dive, aye," came Warren's reply.

"Make your depth one-three-zero feet," the diving officer of the watch commanded the planesman.

The planesman repeated the order, "Make depth one-three zero feet, aye."

Under Warren's watchful eye, the planesman eased forward on the controls to start the *Florida* down toward her assigned depth of one-three-zero feet. The diving officer of the watch supervised the maneuver as the depth gauge started winding down—eighty feet, eighty-five feet ninety feet, ninety-five feet—and kept going. Once the submarine attained her ordered depth of one-three-zero feet, the officer of the deck would oversee the throttleman as he adjusted the sub's speed to ten knots.

The officer of the deck, a seasoned lieutenant named Rivera, took over. "Helm, all ahead standard. Make turns for ten knots. Right half rudder," Lieutenant Rivera ordered. "Dive, make your depth one-three-zero feet. Nav, plot course and speed. All stations report. Acknowledge."

Rapidly, one after another, the stations responded to the officer of the deck's commands as the *Florida* dove and turned sharply to starboard.

"Nav, status?" Rivera called over his shoulder.

"Baffles clear. No contacts. Coming right to course zero-eight five, depth one-three-zero feet, speed one-zero," he replied crisply.

"Very well," Rivera responded.

Satisfied, he turned to Davis. "Captain, the boat is underway, ahead at ten knots. Depth, one-three-zero. Course zero-eight-five."

"Very well, Mr. Rivera," Davis answered from his perch.

The *Florida* still buzzed with activity as her crewmen completed reports and checked equipment in preparation for the SDV's rescue and recovery.

"Nav, time to position?" Davis asked the sub's navigator.

"At present speed and course, time to target is estimated twenty-four minutes, sir," he replied. The last known position of the SDV and the SEAL team relayed by the SRS put it four nautical miles away from the *Florida*. The sub was traveling at ten knots so it would take nearly a half hour to reach the stricken craft and the six SEALs. Davis considered the information for a few seconds and then made a decision.

He turned to the officer of the deck and issued another order. "Officer of the deck, all ahead emergency!"

Rivera immediately acknowledged the command, "All ahead emergency. Aye." He quickly relayed it to the throttleman at the helm who repeated it back to Rivera and advanced the throttles for the *Florida's* powerful twin screws as far forward as they would go. Steam from the SSGN's nuclear reactor gushed into the large turbines that powered her propulsion system as the boat responded to the helm's commands. The submarine weighed nearly 19,000 tons so the acceleration was slow in coming, but nonetheless noticeable for a vessel of her size.

"All ahead emergency, sir," the throttleman announced. He quickly scanned the gauges in front of him and provided the officer of the deck with an update. "Making turns for twenty-two knots."

"Acknowledged," Rivera responded. He turned to Davis, "Speed twenty-two knots, captain."

"Nav, time to close?" Davis demanded.

"Time to SRS coordinates, one-zero minutes," the *Florida's* navigator replied loudly.

"That's more like it," Davis nodded. He lifted the 1MC's microphone to his lips and squeezed the PTT button.

"Attention. This is the captain," Davis's voice boomed. "Rendezvous with SDV in one-zero minutes. Divers prepare to enter the water. Repeat. Divers prepare to enter the water."

Davis returned the microphone to its holder and rubbed the back of his neck. Despite the short distance between the *Florida* and the SDV, it was going to be a very long ten-minute journey.

# 57. IN THE DARK

*The White House*
*Washington, D.C.*

"This can't wait. Inform the president at once!" Secretary of Defense John Ellis ordered. "I'm on the way. On my authority, notify other key cabinet members and have them meet me in the White House Sit Room right away. Advise them it's about Operation Second Light."

Ellis hung up the phone and rubbed his red, tired eyes. He glanced at the clock on the nightstand. It was barely after 1 a.m. He leaned over and kissed his wife gently on the cheek.

"Honey, I'm sorry, but I've got to go," he whispered softly. "I'll be home as soon as I can, but don't count on it being until much later in the day, if at all."

"I understand, John," she replied sleepily. "I love you."

Ellis picked up his secure cell phone, scrolled down through a series of quick dial numbers, and stopped at one labeled Car. He pushed the "call" button. The voice on the other end answered immediately with, "This is the duty officer, Mr. Secretary. How may I help you?"

"I need to be picked up in fifteen minutes and taken to the White House. Priority one," Ellis replied.

"I'm dispatching your car and driver now, sir. Is there anything else I can do for you?" the duty officer asked.

"Yes," Ellis said, "I'd like to you locate Peter King and tell him to standby for a call from me within the hour."

"Very well, sir," the duty officer responded. "Look for a text confirmation on your secure phone once he has been located and notified."

Ellis stood and switched the lamp on the nightstand off. According to the bedside clock, his car would be arriving out front of his home in less than twelve minutes. He quickly shuffled to the bathroom to dress.

‹ ● ›

Ellis's Georgetown residence was conveniently located a little over a mile from the White House just up Pennsylvania Avenue. The driver was on time and the short journey took less than two minutes. Ellis's black Lincoln Towncar turned right in front of 1600 Pennsylvania Avenue, pulled up to the White House's N. W. Gate, and stopped. The driver turned off the headlights and a pair of uniformed Secret Service officers approached the car. Even under normal circumstances, the vehicle and its occupants would undergo carefully scrutiny and perhaps a search. However, given recent events, including the *Southern Star's* hijacking, domestic airline incidents, and the U. S.'s preemptive cruise missile strike against Iran, it was clear that these were definitely not normal circumstances.

Ellis and the driver had both lowered the car's windows so the officers could easily see them. One of the police officers bent down so he could identify the driver and passenger while the other one remain a few feet behind, right hand on his holstered service weapon.

"Good morning, Mr. Secretary," the uniformed officer greeted Ellis.

"Thank you," Ellis sighed. "Frankly, it could be better."

"I understand, sir. The Sit Room called a few minutes ago to tell us you'd be arriving soon," the man advised. "Wish it were under better circumstances," he continued.

"Me, too," Ellis replied.

"Good luck, Mr. Secretary," the officer responded. "You may proceed to the West Wing entrance."

The large, black wrought iron gate rolled sideways across the narrow road so Ellis's car could enter the White House grounds. The driver made his way up the lane, brought the car to a stop in the middle of the circle in front of the portico, and parked next to one of the many government limousines already there.

The driver turned around and spoke to Ellis. "Looks like some of the other cabinet members have already arrived, sir."

"Yes, I see that," Ellis acknowledged. "At least something's going right." He grabbed his leather attaché off the seat, opened the door, and slid out.

"Can't say when I'll be finished. Best plan on a long while—maybe several hours," Ellis called as he closed the door.

"No problem, sir," the driver replied. "I'll be here."

Ellis turned and marched briskly toward the West Wing entrance. Another pair of uniformed Secret Security officers stood near the large doorway.

"Good morning, Mr. Secretary," they said in unison.

Ellis responded with a polite, "Hello."

One of the police officers opened the door and Ellis quickly walked into the West Wing's lobby. He turned right and scurried down the corridor to the elevator near the Vice President's office. Unlike the president, who preferred the short flight of stairs just past the West Wing's Cabinet Room, Ellis liked to save a few steps by riding the elevator down to the lower level. Moments later, Ellis was on the ground floor almost directly beneath the Oval Office. He scurried through the lobby, made his way down a few more steps and entered the White House Situation Room.

Ellis managed a trite greeting as he sat in one of the empty chairs. "Good morning, Mr. President. Fellow cabinet members."

Except for the short acknowledgement of "John" from Brewster, no one else spoke a word. In addition to President Brewster and Secretary of Defense John Ellis, Secretary of Homeland Security David Carter, Director of National Intelligence James Conroy and Secretary of State Adrian Ashe sat around the conference table. Present also were the Chairman of the Joint Chiefs of Staff and Paul McCormick, the president's chief of staff.

Brewster looked grim-faced and weary, and he wasn't alone. The others also looked worn and fatigued. The president, in typical fashion, cut right to the chase.

"All right, John, let's have it straight up," Brewster demanded.

"I'm afraid it's a very bad development, Mr. President." Ellis briefly lowered his head and rubbed his brow before continuing. After a few seconds, he looked up, squarely at Brewster. "Here is what we do know. Less than thirty minutes ago while en route to the *Southern Star's* location, the SDV sent out a distress signal. The *Florida* responded and is currently proceeding to the vehicle's last know position. The sub should be on station with divers in the water as we speak. Conditions are inhospitable and difficult, to say the least. The SEALs are operating in the dark some forty feet below the sea surface. At that depth, the water temperature is only seventy-five degrees. What we do not know is the reason for the distress call and the status of the six SEALs who were aboard the SDV. We are waiting for an update from the *Florida's* captain on the team's condition."

Brewster slumped back in the large padded chair and looked as if some large, several-ton weight rested on his frame. The president said nothing—and neither did anyone else. The group sat huddled around the Situation Room's conference table for a very long while as they considered the gravity of the news delivered by Secretary of Defense John Ellis.

Finally, Brewster broke the silence. "John, what does this mean? Do we have any other options?"

Ellis was very quick to answer Brewster's questions—perhaps he had anticipated them. "I'm sorry, Mr. President, but our options are limited," he explained. "If the SEALs are all right, but the SDV is damaged or inoperative, we'll have to scrub the mission. We have no other DDS/SDV capable subs available. The *Florida* is it." He paused for a moment before elaborating further. "If the SEALs are injured or—" he stopped in mid-sentence, not wanting to use the word "dead."

Ellis cleared his throat and began again. "Sorry, sir. If there are casualties among the SEAL team, perhaps we should consider other alternatives rather than risk additional losses."

The Secretary of Defense slumped back in his padded chair and sighed. "I don't know what else to offer you, Mr. President. I just don't know," Ellis conceded.

# 58. TO THE RESCUE

Stopwatch in hand, Lieutenant José Rivera, the *Florida's* officer of the deck, stood midway between the captain's chair and the helm. He was counting down the minutes and seconds as the submarine churned through the water toward its rendezvous with the stricken SDV. With the cadence of a drill sergeant, he ticked off the remaining time in a steady voice.

"Three minutes, thirty seconds...Three minutes, twenty-five seconds...Three minutes, twenty seconds..."

Commander Davis sat in his padded, steel chair, head cocked to one side so he would not miss any of Rivera's callouts. Traveling at top speed now, the *Florida* was making twenty-two knots through the water. This was the easy part. The challenge for Davis and his crew was coming next. They had to first locate the SDV and then skillfully bring the 19,000-ton submarine to a stop as close to the small craft as they could without colliding with it—a feat easier said than done. The 560-foot long *Florida* was nearly the length of two football fields and had the momentum of a freight train. However, unlike a freight train, the *Florida* had no brakes.

At her current speed of twenty-two knots, the *Florida* was traveling 2,228 feet every minute. The three-minute mark was the point where Davis and the crew would begin the series of countdowns and calculations needed to bring the *Florida* nose-to nose with the SDV. It would require exactly one minute of full reverse power applied from the sub's massive twin turbines and screws to stop the gigantic vessel. The *Florida* was still operating at a depth of one-three-zero feet. Davis had purposely kept her there, nearly one hundred feet below the SDV's planned forty-foot operating depth to help avoid a collision. Once the *Florida's* sonar had pinpointed the stricken craft, he would order the diving officer to adjust the sub's depth so the rescue divers could enter the water and begin their rescue and recovery mission. It would be a delicate dance—like a mother whale searching for her nursing calf.

"Helm, I have the con," Davis barked. "Officer of the deck, continue with silent count and standby."

"Captain has the con, aye," Rivera repeated, ceding control of the *Florida's* helm to her captain. "Continue the count and standby, aye," Rivera echoed.

"Sonar, report all contacts!" Davis ordered. From the moment Davis gave the order to move toward the SDV's last known position, the *Florida's* sonarman had been sending out signals, or pinging, through its bow-mounted antennas in search of objects. The *Florida's* sonar was a newer, highly sensitive version that relied more on the characteristics of the receivers than the transmitters. The result was an advanced system that was less easy for the enemy to detect while still providing several key ranging and targeting advantages for an SSGN like the *Florida*.

"Sonar, aye. One contact bearing zero-one-zero, range two-point-five, depth five-five," the petty officer stated. A moment later, he provided Davis with an additional piece of information. "Contact is stationary and not moving. No other contacts ahead. I estimate the active contact is the SDV, sir."

Davis considered the information and then gave the order, "Helm, all ahead one-third," which was immediately followed by, "Mr. Rivera, what's the count?"

The throttleman spoke first, acknowledging the captain's order. "Helm, all ahead, one-third. Aye." That would give the turbines' transmissions time to slow in preparation for what was next—full reverse.

Lieutenant Rivera, eyes still glued to the stopwatch in his left hand, jumped in with the count as the sub barreled toward the SDV. "Three minutes, zero seconds."

"Range?" Davis called to the sonarman.

He was promptly answered with, "Range, two-point-zero."

"Helm, standby all stop," Davis shouted.

"Standby, all stop. Aye," the throttleman repeated.

Davis moved the 1MC microphone close to his lips. "Mr. Rivera, the count?"

"Two minutes, thirty seconds," Rivera responded.

Davis directed his next question to the senior enlisted man on the *Florida*, who was for lack of another description, in charge of every piece of equipment and sailor on the submarine. If there was one single crewman that every sub captain relied on more than any other, it was the Chief of the Boat, or COB.

"Chief of the boat, status?"

"All stations reporting ready. Engines normal. Bow planes set. Ballast trimmed," the COB replied.

"Very well," Davis acknowledged.

"Helm, standby all stop," Davis said again. "Mr. Rivera, resume the count out loud."

"Standby, all stop. Aye," the throttleman repeated.

Rivera picked up the count with his steady cadence, "Two minutes, ten seconds…two minutes, five seconds… two minutes, zero seconds…"

At that moment, Davis barked a command to the throttleman, "All stop!"

The throttleman responded with "All stop. Aye," and retarded the controls to the last detent on the power quadrant.

Rivera continued counting down, "One minute, fifty-five seconds…one minute fifty seconds…"

Davis keyed the 1MC, "This is the captain. We are approaching out target. All hands prepare for tactical stop in one minute. Brace yourselves. Divers prepare to enter the water on my order." Davis lowered the microphone to his lap and settled into the chair for the stop maneuver. Then he issued another preparatory order to the helm, "Helm, standby all back."

As before, the throttleman acknowledged Davis's instructions.

"Sonar?" Davis called out.

"Same contact, bearing zero-one-zero, range one-point-zero, depth five-five," the sonarman replied.

In the background, Rivera continued the countdown, "One minute, ten seconds…one minute five seconds…"

Commander Davis heard Rivera's "One minute, zero seconds" call and swiftly ordered the helm to place the engines in full reverse.

"Helm, all back full!" he shouted.

"All back full. Aye," the throttleman replied. The petty officer lifted the power levers up and retarded them as far back as they would go.

The *Florida's* forward speed was ten knots when Davis ordered reductions from all ahead emergency to one-third to stop as she approached the sonar contact. The throttleman engaged full reverse and steam from the nuclear reactor poured into the twin turbines, and the transmissions shifted from forward to reverse. The two massive screws on the *Florida's* stern quickly changed direction and accelerated as the turbines wound up. The boat shook and shuddered as her propulsion system groaned under the task. Lieutenant Rivera, still focused on the stopwatch in his left hand, dutifully called out the time. Her forward momentum now considerably slowed, with full reverse power, the *Florida's* speed decreased more and more with each passing second.

"Sonar, range to contact?" Davis called.

"One hundred fifty yards," the technician answered.

"Chief of the watch, speed?" Davis asked next.

The senior chief who stood near the helm's control panel beside the throttleman responded with, "Two-point-zero knots."

"Call speed of one-point-zero knots," Davis instructed.

"Call out speed on one-point-zero knots. Aye," the chief of the watch repeated.

"Lieutenant Rivera never missed a beat, "Fifteen seconds...ten seconds...five seconds..."

"Speed, one-point-zero knots," the chief of the watch announced.

Davis issued a final order to the helm, "All stop!"

"All stop. Aye." The throttleman advanced the levers to the detent marked STOP.

"Sonar, range and bearing to contact?" Davis asked.

"Contact on the nose, sir, for fifty yards at a depth of sixty feet," the petty officer reported. "Contact still stationary."

The *Florida* was no longer moving forward and she was now bobbing some seventy-feet below and one hundred and fifty feet in front the sonar contact, which was presumably the out-of-action SDV.

Davis addressed the officer of the deck who had stopped counting aloud and hung the stopwatch around his neck. "Mr. Rivera, we will stay at this depth. Commence hover at one-three-zero-feet."

Rivera acknowledged the order, "Commence hover at one-three-zero-feet. Aye."

Davis then raised the 1MC to his lips and keyed the microphone. "This is the captain. We are commencing hover at our current depth of one-three-zero feet. The sonar contact is dead ahead at fifty yards, sitting above us at a depth of sixty feet. Divers enter the water. Repeat, divers enter the water!"

# 59. THE ONLY OPTION

*The White House Situation Room*
*Washington, D.C.*

President Brewster and the few cabinet members whom he had summoned to the White House Situation Room remained seated around a large, elliptical conference table. Like Brewster, they had all showed up just after midnight and had not left the area since arriving. They group hadn't yet received an update on the fate of the SDV from the *Florida's* captain and were eager for a report on the SEAL team's condition. Anticipating a long wait, the president's chief of staff, Paul McCormick, had ordered fresh sandwiches and hot coffee from the White House kitchen. The food trays and beverage carafes that delivered a few minutes earlier sat untouched behind the president on a small, stainless steel serving cart.

Barely an hour had elapsed since Secretary Ellis had delivered his preliminary report to those assembled. Afterward, conversation between them had been spotty. Given the circumstances, there wasn't much to talk about—at least nothing to take their minds off the six Navy SEALs and the hostages aboard the *Southern Star*. As they sat there waiting, it seemed as if each one hoped that one of others would say something first. Finally, Paul McCormick broke the silence.

"Coffee, Mr. President?" McCormick asked his boss.

"Yes, Paul, that sounds good," Brewster replied. "The usual—light, no sugar."

McCormick slid his chair away from the table and stood. "Sandwich to go with it, sir?"

Brewster shook his head. "No. I'm afraid I'm not very hungry," he answered.

McCormick glanced around the table at Ellis, Conroy and Ashe. "Anyone else want coffee or a sandwich?"

"Great idea, Paul," Ellis responded. He looked at the others seated near him. "Come on, Adrian, Jim. We're going to be here for a while. How about it?"

"Not for me," Secretary of State Ashe replied. "Thanks anyway."

"I'm sold," Jim Conroy, the Director of National Intelligence, declared. He pushed himself away from the table and made his way to the serving cart.

"You're the only hold out," McCormick said, looking directly at Department of Homeland Security chief David Carter.

"What the hell," Carter quipped, "Count me in. I could use a cup of strong coffee right now." He, too, pushed back from the table and went to the food cart.

McCormick grabbed a large, white ceramic mug emblazoned with the Presidential Seal from the cart and filled it with coffee. He added some cream and stirred it. McCormick plucked a paper beverage napkin from the tray, walked over to Brewster, and placed the mug in front of him.

"Your coffee, sir," McCormick announced cheerfully.

Brewster looked up and replied with a half-smile, "Thanks, Paul."

McCormick had just turned around and headed back toward the serving tray to get himself a cup of coffee, when a soft *Bing bong, Bing bong* interrupted his stride. The tones that came from the nearby communications console sounded more like a doorbell than an alert. However, Defense Secretary John Ellis immediately recognized the signal.

"Gentlemen, we have an incoming priority message," Ellis announced. "Perhaps it's news from the *Florida* about the SDV." He quickly walked to the front of the room, dubbed the "Whisper Wall."

There installed on the wall were two large, sound-equipped video screens. Small cameras and a pair of sensitive, wide-area microphones were mounted above them Using secure relay satellites and two-way audio/video equipment that was deployed around the world, the president and others in the room could both see and speak with practically anyone, anywhere, at any time. Ellis stopped in front of the screens and pressed a blinking white button marked RECEIVE. Instantly, the black display came to life and the image of a Navy officer appeared on the visual monitor. From the picture, it was clear that he was on some type of vessel.

"This is Commander Davis aboard the USS *Florida*," he said. "I have an update on the SDV and the SEAL team."

Ellis didn't wait for Brewster or anyone else in the room to speak and quickly replied before the others had a chance to respond.

"This is Secretary Ellis. Go ahead with your report."

Very well, Mr. Secretary," Davis began, "at 0042 hours the *Florida* received an SRS alert from the SDV and six SEALs on Operation Second Light. Twenty-two minutes later at 0104 hours, the *Florida* arrived at the SDV's last known position and began a rescue and recovery operation. A team of DDS divers located the disabled SDV and SEALs at 0117 hours. I am pleased to report that all six SEALs are now onboard the *Florida* and appear to be in good condition. A medical team is currently evaluating them for possible hypothermia or injury.

DDS technicians are also evaluating the SDV. Their preliminary report indicates that the craft's propulsion system failed. At this time, we don't know if a repair that will return it to mission ready status is possible. I should have an update for you in approximately one hour."

"Thank you, Commander," Ellis acknowledged. He turned to the president.

Brewster took the cue. "Nicely done, Commander Davis," he beamed. "I can't tell you how pleased I am to hear the good news about the successful recovery of our SEALs. I commend you and your crew for your efforts. Please pass along my personal thanks to every one of them. The nation owes you a debt of gratitude for your splendid work tonight."

The president removed his glasses and briefly rubbed his tired, bloodshot eyes. He replaced his spectacles and looked at the screen on the Whisper Wall.

"Now, Commander," Brewster began. "I have one very important question for you. We can't forget about the hostages aboard the cruise ship, so should you determine that the SDV is out of action, what other options do we have for getting SEALs on to the *Southern Star*?" he asked Davis pointedly.

"Since we are very close to the *Southern Star's* position, Mr. President," Davis offered, "We can still put SEALs in the water using what we refer to as MSLO—Mass Swimmer Lock Out."

Ellis immediately noticed Brewster's puzzled look. "If I may, sir," he interjected, "SEALs will enter the water by way of the *Florida's* Dry Deck Shelter. There are some key advantages. First, the swimmers won't be exposed to the cold sea temperatures for an extended period as they would be on the SDV." Ellis paused to emphasize his next point. "Second, we can put several more SEALs in the water instead of just six—all thirty-two from both platoons if needed. That might improve our chances of success on the *Southern Star.*"

"The secretary is correct, Mr. President," Davis agreed, "The MSLO operation does have some plusses."

"I see." Brewster's nod indicated that he understood. He then turned to his defense secretary, "John?"

"Commander, how feasible is that?" Ellis asked.

Suddenly, the other video screen sprang to life.

"This is Lieutenant Timmons, sir. I'm SEAL Team Eight's operations officer and I've been monitoring your exchange with Commander Davis from the *Florida's* Battle Management Center. We are able to conduct a Mass Swimmer Lock Out operation to put SEALs in the water for the hostage rescue mission using the Dry Deck Shelter. We can be ready in two hours."

Ellis looked at Brewster and nodded slowly. "There you have it, Mr. President—your other option."

Brewster considered the information for a few seconds before he responded. He glanced at Ellis and then faced the two screens on the Whisper Wall in front of him.

"Very well, gentlemen," the president affirmed. "Make it so and standby for my order."

# 60. A BIT OF SKEPTICISM

*USS* Florida *Ward Room*
*Submerged Near Nassau, Bahamas*

Life aboard a submarine was an interesting, if not different, experience for Navy SEALs. A SEAL's first onboard deployment could be confining, claustrophobic and confusing. On the plus side, unlike smaller attack submarines, larger SSGNs like the *Florida* had relatively spacious crew bunks and places to work out in the SOFHE, which the SEALs constantly did. The forward torpedo room, where the SEALs stored most of their equipment, was their domain while they were onboard. They spent a great deal of time checking and rechecking their gear to be certain that it was mission ready. However, the SEALs were not isolated from the boat's crew and interacted with them every day.

The experience of having Special Forces commandos on board was equally enlightening and often frustrating for a submarine's crew. The sailors encountered a group of energetic SEALs that seemed to invade every nook and cranny of their boat. To the submariner, it seemed like the SEALs were everywhere and their offenses were numerous. They never secured anything while at sea and always made a mess out of the forward torpedo room, ate what seemed like more than their share of rations and worst of all, it meant that many of the sub's enlisted crewmen had to hot-rack all the time.

The SEALs were used to roughing it, so for them the priorities were different. As for the boat being crowded, to the SEALs, more simply meant merrier. The joke among the SEALs was that the only thing the sailors cared about was their three M's—movies, meals, and mattresses. Yet, despite these obvious differences between the SEALs and the submariners, the two groups formed one of most potent fighting teams in the nation's arsenal. That key fact was one everybody was now counting on.

The *Florida's* skipper, Commander Scott Davis, was busy preparing his one hundred and sixty-man crew for what was arguably the most important assignment of their careers: the second attempt at rescuing the passengers still held hostage on the *Southern Star*. The failure of the SDV's propulsion system during the first effort and subsequent aborted operation was a disappointment to everyone aboard the SSGN, but particularly to Davis since it was his boat. He was not about to let something like that happen again.

Immediately following the video conference with President Brewster and key cabinet members who were holed up in the White House Situation Room, Davis had received orders from Secretary of Defense John Ellis to get the *Florida* ready to conduct MSLO—Mass Swimmer Lock Out—operations.

Davis quickly convened a meeting of his key officers and enlisted men in one of the submarine's wardrooms to plan the operation. He had also invited SEAL Team Eight's CO, Commander Pierce, his operations officer, Lieutenant Timmons, Master Chief Howe, Golf platoon's CO, Lieutenant Warner, and Senior Chief Hartman. Now gathered around a table just yards from the Tomahawk missile tubes, each man was ready to begin. Since it was his boat, Davis was technically in charge of the entire operation. However, as a matter of protocol, he would defer to Pierce and his men for any SEAL-specific operational details and related decisions.

"Gentlemen," Davis began in a firm, confident voice, "I'm sure you are all disappointed after the SDV's failure caused you to abort the rescue mission. However, I think we can all agree that things could have turned out worse—much worse." Davis paused briefly before continuing and, as expected, his audience nodded.

"As you know," he went on, "we're going to make another attempt, and this time we have to succeed. Time is running out. No one is sure what this terrorist group wants because they haven't made any specific demands. That is why the situation is so urgent." Davis leaned forward to emphasize his next point. "The longer we wait, the greater the chance they will start killing hostages. Perhaps some of you remember the *Achille Lauro* hijacking. That's exactly what happened in that incident—random, indiscriminate killing."

He spoke with authority on the subject. Originally from New Mexico, Davis had attended the U.S. Naval Academy and graduated in 1988. Like most of his classmates, he had decided to make the Navy a career. He was due for reassignment after his tour as the *Florida's* skipper and had planned to serve at the Pentagon as one of the Navy's liaisons to the U.S. Department of Homeland Security.

To prepare himself for that role, he had earned a master's degree at the Naval Postgraduate School's Center for Homeland Defense and Security in an eighteen-month program designed to prevent terrorist attacks within the United States and reduce America's vulnerability to terrorism. As a DHS liaison, Davis helped mayors, governors, and federal officials improve homeland security preparedness by planning for real world scenarios.

There wasn't any time to waste, so Davis kept right on going. "Commander Pierce, it's your show now. The *Florida* and her crew stand ready to support you in every way we can. Your success is our success. You have the floor."

"Thank you, Commander," Pierce began. "The captain is quite right. This next effort is our best chance at rescuing the hostages alive rather than recovering dozens of dead bodies. We have to succeed."

Pierce stopped speaking and pointed to his operations officer. Lieutenant Timmons, whose eyes had focused on Pierce, immediately took the cue from his CO. "Yes, sir," he said, and turned to address the group.

"Gentlemen, the *Florida* is equipped to conduct MSLO and launch up to twenty-eight SOF divers in the water. The *Southern Star* isn't a large ship, but this isn't a typical VBSS (Visit, Board, Search, and Seizure) operation either, so I believe that one squad is best for this mission. After reassessing the potential threat, it is my judgment that a full complement of eight enlisted SEALs from one platoon will be sufficient to overpower and neutralize the terrorists."

Timmons explained further, "It will be closer to MOUT (Military Operations on Urban Terrain) except that you will not be on dry land. This mission will involve stealth, surprise, shock, and close quarter combat. Those are some of the challenges. However, the biggest obstacle you will face after you leave the *Florida* will be getting from the sea surface forty feet up to the deck of the *Southern Star.* Now, before you ask me how that will be accomplished, let me tell you that I don't have an answer right now—but we're working on it and I'll have an answer for you before you disembark."

Skepticism showed on the faces of the military men seated around the wardroom table, but it was especially evident in the SEALs' expressions. Senior Chief Hartman, who would lead the mission, joined with the others as they scowled at Timmons. Suddenly he blurted out the obvious question, "And if you don't, sir?"

# 61. ANY PORT IN A STORM

*Aboard the* Southern Star
*Sixty Miles Northwest of Nassau, Bahamas*

After Murphy and White slipped out of the Miramar Café and snuck down to Stanton's cabin, Jack Stanton received a text message on his cell phone from Peter King. It was a critical piece of information that Allan had relayed to King based on his review of the ship's layout. It told Stanton where the *Southern Star's* central laundry facility was located—what deck it was on and exactly how many feet from the passageway to the laundry room's double doors. Stanton and Murphy had managed to reach it. Once there, they had worked fast to assemble makeshift ropes fashioned from knotted bed sheets—just two altogether, each about sixty feet long. Now came their next critical task— to make their way to the ship's fantail, drop the sheets over the side, and secure them to the railings.

As a smaller ship, the design of the *Southern Star* was both a blessing and a bane. She was only 574-feet long and eighty-two feet wide. Most of the passenger cabins, restaurants and entertainment lounges were located amidships on the promenade deck. A narrow corridor on either side of them ran inboard along her entire length. That meant that it would be easy for Stanton and Murphy to move about the *Southern Star* rather than having to wind their way through a maze-like collection of hallways typical of larger cruise ships. Of course, having just two main corridors also meant that there was a much greater chance of them running into one or more of the terrorists. It was a chance they would have to take.

Stanton and Murphy crouched low in the darkness and listened intently for the sound of anyone approaching. Ceiling fixtures spaced every twenty feet or so apart illuminated the *Southern Star's* passageways, so there weren't many places to hide from view. Fortunately, a few shadows from stairways that led from one deck to another gave them cover. As long as no one stumbled upon them, it was enough of an advantage to keep them well hidden. Since neither man was armed, that would be very important.

Satisfied that there was no one else in the corridor, the pair crept out from beneath the stairs and moved slowly down the hallway. Stanton and Murphy each lugged a large bundle wrapped in one of the *Southern Star's* white bed sheets from the ship's laundry. Although not heavy, the sack each man carried was a bit on the bulky side. To make it easier, they had slung them over their left shoulders. The two men hugged the wall and inched their way down the narrow hallway, stealthily placing one foot in front of the other and pausing a second or two before advancing. They stopped every few paces and strained to hear the telltale footsteps that would alert them to an intruder. The terrorists had corralled all of the passengers and crew—except for those required on the bridge—in the Miramar Café. Consequently, anyone who happened into the passageway would have to be one of the terrorists. If they were lucky, there would be no such encounter.

Murphy and Stanton continued to move cautiously down the corridor. Suddenly, a loud clang that sounded like a large metallic object falling to the floor shattered the silence. The two men froze and dared not move. Although the startling noise came from somewhere up ahead, neither one of them could pinpoint its exact origin. Stanton slowly turned his head to look back at Murphy, who was standing barely three feet behind him. It was then that Stanton saw the most noticeable thing about Murphy—his open-mouthed, eyes wide expression.

"Whhhaaatt waaasss thaaatt?" Murphy mouthed, exaggerating each consonant and vowel so Stanton would understand his question.

Stanton shook his head from side to side signifying that he didn't know and then raised an index finger to his lips. It was a signal to Murphy not to communicate further. Next Stanton touched his ear repeatedly with the same finger, indicating that he wanted them both to listen for more sounds. Stanton had scarcely lowered his hand when it happened again—a large metal object struck the floor. This time, the noise had a different tone. It was tinny, and sounded more like a large kitchen pot or pan rather than the thud made by a heavier object.

Stanton's grimace said it all: fear of discovery. Since they weren't armed, a confrontation was the last thing either of the two men wanted or could risk. Stanton motioned Murphy to follow him and began to move hurriedly down the passageway. Whoever was making the noise was sure to enter the hallway soon. If intercepted before they reached the *Southern Star's* fantail, Murphy and Stanton couldn't lower the homemade ropes. There would be no way for the SEALs to climb up to the ship's deck and the hostage rescue mission would be in jeopardy. Stanton had no idea where he was going, but he had to find a place for them to hide until he was certain that it was safe to continue.

Stanton and Murphy, sacks still slung over their shoulders, scurried down the corridor. Stanton scanned left and right, looking for a place to hide. They pushed ahead a few more feet and saw a wall sign for the Mayfair Lounge, which was located amidships. Stanton, with Murphy in tow, kept moving, going past the gift shop, photo gallery and the duty free shop. The Miramar Café was the only other space located between them and the *Southern Star's* stern. It also led to an open-air deck, which would give them easy access to the ship's fantail. That was exactly where the two men needed to go.

Stanton and Murphy dashed along the varnished teak deck. In a few yards, the two men would be outside the entrance to the Miramar Café. The good news was that they hadn't heard any more noises nor encountered anyone in the last few minutes. Stanton dared not go much further for fear of running into to the person or persons responsible for the noises they had heard earlier. However, there were few options left and the odds of coming face to face with whoever had made the noises were increasing with each step they took.

Stanton and Murphy faced a difficult choice. Time was running out and both men knew it. According to the plan that Peter King had shared with them, the SEALs would arrive soon and begin their ascent. However, without the aid of makeshift ropes, there wouldn't be any way for the rescuers to get aboard the ship. The only hope for the *Southern Star's* captive passengers and crew was that Stanton and Murphy somehow managed to safely and surreptitiously get to the fantail, secure the ropes and drop them over.

*Jesus H. Christ!* Stanton thought as he shook his head. He glanced at Murphy. The expression on Murphy's face summed it up. Stanton at once interpreted it as desperation rather than disgust. Murphy's blank stare told Stanton that he was waiting for direction of some kind.

*He's right*, Stanton mused. *We're not helpless, so things aren't hopeless. If we act, we might or might not get caught. If we are caught, at least we tried. If we turn and run, then all is lost. So we have to try. That's the only choice left.*

Stanton leaned close to Murphy so he could whisper in his ear.

"Bill," he began in a low voice, "We're almost there. Since we haven't encountered anyone yet, I think it's worth a try. Darkness and the weather are on our side, so I think we'll be okay. Do you agree?" He paused and waited for Murphy's nod before continuing. "Good. To increase our chances of success, we'll split up when we reach the fantail. That will cut our exposure time in half the time and should they capture one of us, perhaps the other will still be able to get one rope overboard without being noticed or caught. We can do it. Sound like a plan?"

Murphy responded with a thumbs-up and mouthed, "Let's go!"

Stanton and Murphy crept along the deck, hugging the bulkheads as they went. Knowing that time was critical, they had quickened their pace. Stanton reasoned that the faster they accomplished their part of the plan, the faster they could retreat from the fantail. Putting distance between them and the makeshift ropes would reduce the chance of discovery and increase the odds that the SEALs could make a successful ascent.

Stanton was relieved when he could make out the stern a few feet in the distance. As a cruise ship, there wasn't much equipment mounted to the passenger decks, so that made maneuvering for him and Murphy much easier. Because there were few items readily available for cover and concealment, despite the weather and cover of darkness, the two men would be out in the open and exposed for several minutes while they attached the ropes to the railings and tossed them over.

The duo approached the end of the promenade deck's bulkhead and Stanton raised his hand as a signal for Murphy to stop. Stanton lowered the sack he was carrying to the deck and Murphy did the same. He turned to Murphy and pointed to the railing directly in front of them. Stanton made a circular motion with his motioned with hands and whispered, "Tight. Goddamned good and tight. Got it?"

Replying in a hushed voice, Murphy tried to inject some humor into the situation with, "I'm a sailor, remember? I know my knots."

If Stanton found anything amusing in Murphy's response, he didn't show it. Instead, he pointed to the other side of the stern and mouthed, "Me." Murphy nodded that he understood.

Stanton squeezed Murphy's shoulder and whispered, "Meet back here when you're done. Okay, let's go!"

The pair bent down, picked up their sacks, and split up, with Murphy headed in one direction and Stanton in the other.

( ● )

It didn't take long for Stanton and Murphy to fish the knotted ropes fashioned from dozens of bed sheets out of the sacks, fasten them securely to the railings on the ship's fantail and lower them over the side. The sheets were white and that would help the SEALs to find them. The overhand knots tied at three-foot intervals in the dangling sheets were big enough to serve as both handholds and footholds, yet not so large that they would impede the SEALs during their climb.

Their tasks completed, Stanton and Murphy met up at the agreed location and quickly compared notes. This time, Murphy began the conversation.

"Everything went as planned. I secured the rope to the railing with a bowline knot," he explained quietly. "That will certainly do the job. I estimate there's about ten feet of rope in the water and that will be just about right for the swells."

Stanton shrugged his shoulders. "Bowline?" he snorted under his breath. "What the hell is that? I just tied a knot that looked to me like it wouldn't come undone," he smirked.

Murphy winked and whispered, "As I said, I'm a sailor and I know my knots."

Stanton was unimpressed with Murphy's knowledge of knot tying and responded with a somewhat indignant, "Humph."

Under other circumstances, Murphy would have told Stanton that his choice of knots, a bowline, was undoubtedly the best one for this purpose because a load placed on the standing part of the rope caused the knot to tighten, preventing it from slipping. He would have also explained to Stanton that rescuers often used this maritime knot, sometimes called the "king of knots," to lift victims from dangerous situations. Tonight, Murphy's bowline knot would help to extricate him and the others on the *Southern Star* from exactly that: a dangerous situation.

Murphy cast off Stanton's disdain with a subtle shrug. "Sorry, Jack. I didn't mean to brag. After we get out of this jam, I'll show you how to tie a few maritime knots so you'll really be ready for the next time we do this."

Stanton managed a smile. "I'll take you up on that," he replied.

Stanton placed a hand on Murphy's shoulder and "Come on," he goaded, "Let's get the hell out of here. Stay close behind me."

The duo began to retrace their steps, creeping from the *Southern Star's* stern back toward amidships. Again, their concern was a chance encounter with one of the terrorists. All Stanton and Murphy could do was hope that didn't happen. They stopped every few feet and listened for footsteps. If they heard none, they continued. Stanton and Murphy hugged the promenade deck's bulkhead as they snuck along and took advantage of the shadows to mask their presence.

*Clang! Clink! Clank!* The sound startled both men—this time, not because it was surprising, but because of where it had originated. It came from behind them. They just crept past that spot and were still out in the open on the promenade deck. Granted, the corridor was dark and dimly lit, but it was still too risky. Stanton had to act fast. As instructed, Murphy was tight on Stanton's heels and stayed close to him. Stanton continued straight ahead toward a bulkhead near the entrance to the Miramar Café where passageway widened slightly. He headed for an opening that would lead him to a place where no one, terrorist or otherwise, would think to look for them. The sign on the doorway read "Women."

# 62. PHOTO ID

*National Intelligence Headquarters*
*Washington, D.C.*

"Son of a bitch!" Director of National Intelligence James Conroy exclaimed. He placed the folder containing the glossy colored photos on the desk and swung his chair around so he faced the large floor-to-ceiling office window. Conroy gazed out across the Potomac River and the twinkling lights of Washington's nighttime skyline. After a moment, he pivoted sharply back around and looked squarely at the intelligence man seated across from him.

After a brief pause, Conroy tapped the file with his index finger with a deliberate thump-thump-thump. "These are from the reporter who is aboard the *Southern Star*—Anderson is her name, I believe?"

"Yes, sir. That's correct," he replied.

Conroy continued to pepper him with questions. "Hendricks, tell me again how we managed to get them."

"Very well, sir," Hendricks began, "We received them from the *Washington Post*. According to the newspaper, Miss Anderson took them with her laptop's camera and then sent them to her editor. He immediately passed them on to us. Using information from the email's header, we traced the computer's IP address and pinpointed the laptop's geographic location. We determined that it matched the current position of the *Southern Star*. Our confidence is very high that she took these photos. There can be no other explanation."

Conroy pressed for more. "As stated earlier, you're certain that this man is the leader of the London-based al-Muhajiroun organization?"

"Quite certain, sir," Hendricks answered. "We sent these photos to our London station and they confirmed his identity for us. We don't know much about him except that he goes by the name Al-qantarah—the bridge—and took over shortly after the group's founder, Omar Bakri-Muhammed, fled London."

"What else do we know?" Conroy demanded. "Give me something actionable."

Hendricks reached for the folder on Conroy's desk. "May I, sir?" Conroy nodded.

Hendricks opened the file and placed his finger in the middle of the top photo.

"Well, sir," Hendricks began, "See the other two men in this photo, the ones highlighted by the yellow circles?" He pointed to one and then the other. Conroy responded with a simple, "Yes."

Hendricks gestured toward the man on the left. "We don't know anything about him," he explained. A barely perceptible smile crept across his face as he continued, "But the man on the right is working for us."

Conroy sat back. "What's his code name?"

"Sinbad," Hendricks replied.

"Hmmm. That's an interesting name choice," Conroy mused. "Has he been able to give us anything at all?"

"No, sir," Hendricks replied. "We haven't been in contact with him since before the *Southern Star* set sail from Port Everglades.

Conroy raised his eyebrows. "I'm confused. So what exactly is he doing for us then?"

That's an excellent question, sir," Hendricks answered. "I'm afraid I don't know. That operational detail is way above my pay grade."

"I'm sorry, Hendricks," Conroy replied. "I should have known that those aspects were compartmentalized. Don't worry about it—I can easily find out. That will be all."

Hendricks stood to leave. "You'll keep the photos, sir?" he asked.

"Yes, I will. For the time being," Conroy nodded.

Hendricks slid a lined sheet of yellow paper in front of Conroy. "Sign the document receipt, sir, and I'll be on my way."

Conroy reached for a pen and quickly scrawled his signature across the page. Hendricks placed it in his slim briefcase, snapped it shut, and hurried to the door.

"Good night, Mr. Conroy," he called behind him.

Conroy didn't answer—he held the telephone receiver in one hand and with the other, busily dialed a number.

# 63. A GAME OF CAT AND MOUSE

*USS* Florida *Battle Management Center*
*Submerged Sixty Miles Northwest of Nassau, Bahamas*

"Technology is a wonderful thing, isn't it, sir?" the specialist who was seated at the console asked.

SEAL Team Eight's intelligence officer, Lieutenant Junior Grade Jeff Baker, continued to focus on the central display and answered the question with a wide grin, "Yes, it sure is."

"I agree, sir. It's the next best thing to being there," the specialist replied with a chuckle. He was right.

The *Florida's* command center where Lieutenant Baker and his team of Navy enlisted men worked was their high-tech window on the world. It was a state-of-the-art marvel. With the push of a button, they could view high-resolution images anywhere on the globe. They could eavesdrop on international phone calls, monitor suspicious Internet traffic, listen to a hushed conversation in a room thousands of miles away, or direct SEALs to a specific target in any weather on any terrain. If necessary, Baker and his group could launch one of the *Florida's* cruise missiles at a hostile target just around the corner or halfway around the world. They could see, yet not be seen; hear and not be heard; throw a swift punch to catch an opposer completely by surprise. Best of all, no one would know they were doing it.

In January of 2003, the Navy conducted a highly classified exercise named Giant Shadow in the waters off the coast of the Bahamas. Planners developed a scenario to test the viability of the SSGN concept that included a mythical country denying access to weapons inspectors, which resulted in a U. S. military response to identify and neutralize the threat. Before her conversion to an SSGN, the USS *Florida* deployed SEALs to help scout out and destroy the suspected bio-weapons plant. Simulating a high-altitude Global Hawk unmanned aerial vehicle (UAV), a Navy EP-3E aircraft first located the building on a remote island and vectored the submarine toward the target. Afterward, the EP-3E's Big Look radar and small ScanEagle UAVs provided ongoing aerial reconnaissance to the SEALs and the mission managers aboard the *Florida*.

A large remotely controlled unmanned underwater vehicle (UUV) called the Seahorse was launched from the *Florida* and reconnoitered the approaches to the island for the SEALs. More than twenty-eight feet long and three feet wide, the UUV ferried supplies to and from the *Florida* throughout the mission. As its first task, the Seahorse plotted a course for the SEALs through a simulated minefield using forward searching sonar.

Satisfied that there were no mines or other weapons to obstruct their ingress, the SEALs used a raft to simulate the then-unfinished Advanced SEAL Delivery System (ASDS) and made landfall. They approached to within fifty yards of the suspected bio-weapons factory and set up remote monitoring sensors to gather information. Sensors transmitted data back to the *Florida* via a wireless network for analysis. The SEAL team gathered soil samples from rainwater run-off areas and returned them to the submarine via the Seahorse UUV. The *Florida* transmitted soil sample findings to the Pentagon and National Command Authority via a secure satellite communications link after examination in a mock lab that was set up onboard the sub.

Once it was determined to be a legitimate target, the SEALs "destroyed" the so-called bio-weapons factory with mock C4 charges in order to evaluate how well their remote sensors could provide post-attack analysis. The National Command Authority ordered the *Florida* to "strike" the target with cruise missiles. The exercise ended with a simulated cruise missile launch. Dubbed a success by the Naval Sea Systems Command, the Giant Shadow trial validated the capabilities of the Navy's future guided missile submarines, especially when combined with SEAL operations.

Arguably, the key to success in the war on terror was good actionable intelligence. Unlike satellites with their predictable overhead paths, or large airborne intelligence platforms, submarines—particularly SSGNs like the *Florida*—could be anywhere, at any time, in a hostile shallow water environment and remain undetected. Using UAVs, UUVs or SEAL teams, SSGNs could engage in covert reconnaissance and operations inside enemy territory. These specially equipped submarines could then gather and disseminate that information directly to the president and the National Command Authority. In other words, the SSGNs could be the eyes and ears of the president and his advisors, and allow them to respond to key developments by delivering a knockout punch if necessary. That's where the *Florida* was about to show her stuff.

Although it was nighttime upstairs—a term the crew used when referring to the water's surface some eighty feet above the *Florida*—the view from inside in the SEAL command center was remarkably different. Orbiting silently high overhead, a ScanEagle UAV provided constant real-time infrared (IR) images of the *Southern Star* to the submarine via a secure satellite data link. The chief advantage of a UAV such as the ScanEagle was its role as a stealthy intelligence, surveillance and reconnaissance (ISR) platform that could serve as the "eyes and ears" of military planners and battlefield commanders, whether located a few kilometers away or on the other side of the globe.

The images Baker looked at made things seem as though it was broad daylight. The resolution and contrast were amazing. Although in black and white, the feeds were not grainy or distorted. The IR signals were digitally processed and enhanced. The console operator could zoom in, zoom out, pan left or right, and even freeze frame, capturing digital images for later analysis or mission planning. This was the latest gizmo the U.S. military had come up with in the war on terror. Other branches of government, including the U.S. Border Patrol and Immigration and Customs Enforcement, were also using it. Even DEA had found the ScanEagle's capabilities to be useful for tracking drug smugglers.

The UAV pilot, a Navy chief petty officer named Morse, moved the joystick-like control and watched on the large display in front of him as the craft respond to his commands. The nighttime cover was welcome and not an impediment for the ScanEagle because of its infrared camera. However, the visibility on the surface above was poor. A weak tropical depression had formed east of the Bahamas and was sending spiraling bands of rain westward over the *Southern Star's* position. The intermittent showers would keep the passengers and the perpetrators off the decks and inside the ship. Consequently, rain dashed any hopes the SEAL team had of easily observing and identifying the hostage-takers.

The UAV pilot skillfully maneuvered the forty-pound bird in a wide, lazy orbit above the *Southern Star*. Despite gusty winds, the ScanEagle's ten-foot long wings sliced through the rain-filled night sky, its gimbaled IR camera firmly locked onto the ship. Lieutenant Baker stood behind Morse and studied the images, looking for the telltale shape that unmistakably belonged to a human.

Lieutenant Baker straightened and shook his head. "Can you take her down a little lower, Chief?" Baker asked.

"Absolutely, sir," Morse replied. "Let's see what five hundred feet will do."

The UAV had been orbiting at 1,000 feet above the *Southern Star*. Chief Morse eased the joystick forward and the UAV began a descent. The display in front of Morse resembled a flight simulator video game. In the center of the screen was an attitude indicator that showed the ScanEagle's pitch and bank. The craft's airspeed appeared on the left side and its altitude on the right. A cluster of other gauges on the screen provided him with heading, vertical speed and systems status information. In less than a minute, a beep alerted Morse that the ScanEagle was nearing its target altitude and he eased the joystick back. The display confirmed that the UAV had leveled off at five hundred feet above the *Southern Star*.

"Level at five hundred feet, sir," he called to Baker. "Keep your fingers crossed."

"Yeah, I will," Baker sighed. "I'm going to need some luck for this one."

# 64. MISTAKEN IDENTITY

*Aboard the* Southern Star
*Sixty Miles Northwest of Nassau, Bahamas*

The door to the women's restroom swung open just enough for the lights on the promenade deck to reveal the outline of a man standing in the entrance. He slid through the narrow opening and let the door close shut behind him. That was a development neither Stanton nor Murphy had expected or wanted. They split up after they entered the lavatory because Stanton told Murphy he thought it best to move to opposite sides of the toilet stalls. He reasoned they would present smaller targets to anyone who happened to enter and have a better chance of fending off an attack.

A little light managed to leak in around the edges of the doorframe, so the space Stanton and Murphy were standing in was not entirely dark. Nonetheless, their opponent's shape was barely visible in the faint yellow glow. The only sound they heard was the soft shuffle of feet sliding across the polished floor as their foe crept along in the shadows. Neither man spoke. Their hearts raced as they waited for the right moment to pounce on the intruder—timing was everything. He kept coming toward them, slowly placing one foot in front of the other. The distance between them steadily closed. Ten feet. Now eight. Six. Five. Four feet. Finally, only two feet separated them.

*Wham!* As if both men were reacting to a starter's pistol, they lunged forward and quickly tackled him. Stanton had managed to find his face, cupped a hand over his mouth, and muffled the ensuing scream. The two men wrestled him to the floor and as the trio rolled in one direction and then another as their assailant struggled to get free. Despite his desperate attempts to break their hold on him, Stanton and Murphy finally managed to subdue him with their own body weight. Satisfied that they were in control, Stanton switched on his flashlight.

Murphy's mouth dropped open and he cocked his head to one side. He stared intently at the face before him in disbelief.

"Ben!" Murphy exclaimed. "You scared the shit out of us! Worse, you could have been killed!"

"Jesus Christ! You know this guy?" Stanton, a bewildered look on his face, asked.

"Yeah. He's one of the cabin stewards," Murphy replied. "He impressed my companion, Susan, by surprising us with a bottle of champagne and strawberries in our room when we boarded."

Stanton was puzzled. "Why in hell would he do that?"

"That's a good question. I don't know," Murphy shrugged.

Stanton approached Ben and looked him squarely in the face. "What the hell are you doing here?" he demanded.

Ben stared at Stanton briefly and then turned to Murphy.

Without speaking, Ben thrust his arms toward the two men. "Here, take these," he urged.

Cradled in his outstretched hands were two Walther PPK automatic pistols. A German-designed weapon first introduced in 1931, the PPK was reliable and concealable.

It became popular with European police agencies and civilian shooters. During World War II, the German Luftwaffe and Nazi Party officials carried it. Reportedly, Adolf Hitler used that type of weapon to kill himself in the Führerbunker in Berlin as the Allies closed in on him.

Stanton immediately recognized them. "Walther PPKs," he said. "How did you get them?"

Ben began to explain. "I hid them before we sailed and was searching for them a few minutes ago. I happened to see your shadows as you crept by. At first, I thought you were with the others but then I recognized him." He pointed at Murphy.

Murphy looked at Stanton quizzically. "That explains the noises we heard, doesn't it?"

"Apparently it does," Stanton replied. "If he can be trusted, that is," he added warily.

"Please, you must trust me. Let me help you," Ben pleaded.

"Why should we?" Stanton scoffed. "For all we know, you could be one of them."

Ben nodded toward the pistols that were still in each hand. "I have the guns, remember? I could have easily killed you before now if that was my intention."

"He does have a valid point," Stanton remarked. "He's quite right. If he wanted to kill us, we'd have been dead minutes ago."

"Good," Ben responded, "Then it is decided. You will accept my help."

Murphy and Stanton looked at one another and spoke simultaneously. "Do we have a choice?" they asked.

Ben thrust the weapons at them again. "Go on. Take them," he coaxed. "It's okay."

Stanton and Murphy each grabbed one of the PPKs from Ben's hands and tucked it out of sight in their waistbands.

"Oh. You'll probably need these," Ben said. He stuffed their pants pockets with a half dozen magazines, each containing eight rounds.

"Now what?" Murphy asked. We can't take on the terrorists with these puny things." He pointed to the pistol in his waistband.

"No, we can't," Stanton agreed. "So what should we do? Wait for the cavalry to arrive?"

"That would make sense. By then it might be too late," Murphy sighed.

"I have a solution," Ben suggested. "They think I'm one of them. My name is Jamal. I'm a Muslim and I was born in Yemen. I have been living in London for the last several years ever since I graduated from university there. However, I am not like them—even though they believe I am. I don't believe in what they are doing and I can help you win the release of your friends."

"How do you propose to do that?" Stanton wondered. "Take us prisoner and march us into the dining room where the others are being held?"

"Exactly!" Ben answered. "Do you have a better idea?"

Ben reached around behind his back and withdrew another PPK that he had tucked in his pants. He pointed it at both men and gestured for them to raise their hands in the air.

He nodded toward the door with his head. "Come on," he ordered, "let's go."

Stanton and Murphy, hands held high, started for the door with Ben an arm's length behind them. In a few minutes, they would all be entering the Miramar Café.

# 65. THE FIGHT IS ON

*Aboard the* Southern Star
*Sixty Miles Northwest of Nassau, Bahamas*

Hartman and the other SEALs on the rescue mission broke through the ocean's surface a few feet from one another. They quickly assessed their physical condition, inventoried their personal gear, and got their bearings. On Commander Pierce's order, they had entered the *Florida's* lockout tubes tied together in groups of two and exited the submarine. Once in the water, they rallied near the DDS and began their ascent. Now, each swim buddy pair bobbed up and down in the eight-foot swells and waited for Hartman's signal.

Even though it was dark, the large, gray shape that loomed a few hundred feet in front of them was unmistakably the *Southern Star.* The wind and rain from Tropical Storm Brenda had subsided somewhat. However, the wind-driven swells would make the task of swimming to the cruise ship a challenge even for the best of them. On the plus side, the cover of darkness combined with the nasty weather would provide them with an essential ally—stealth.

Light signals would give their position away, so the SEALs relied on another means with lower probability of detection to talk with one another. Dubbed DUCS, and pronounced "ducks," the U.S. Navy s developed the

Diver's Underwater Communication System specifically for secure, yet reliable communications between divers or Special Forces swimmers. The system used ultrasonic, upper single-sideband radio transmissions and operated at a depth of one hundred and thirty feet. It provided moderate range and clear diver-to-diver voice communication for up to 1,500 feet, depending on sea conditions and noise levels. The best features were its lightweight and long life. Weighing less than two pounds and powered by a single 9-volt battery, it would operate for nearly ten hours, which was adequate for most missions.

Hartman began the check-in process over the DUCS to account for all of the diver pairs before moving toward the *Southern Star*.

"This is dolphin leader. Count off," he instructed.

One by one, the crisp replies came swiftly. "Two." "Three." "Four."

Having accounted for all eight SEALs, including himself and his swim buddy, he issued the order.

"Move out!" he barked into the mask microphone.

No acknowledgement was required nor expected. Like a school of large fish, the other seven SEALs followed Hartman's lead and began pushing their way toward the drifting cruise ship. This was where their weeks of tough training and hours of drill paid off. The swells were daunting and it would have been exhausting for each diver to attack the wave like a fierce opponent. Instead, each pair acting as a synchronous unit timed the rise and fall of every successive wall of water to know exactly when to stroke and kick in order to turn the sea's energy to their own advantage.

The divers were still wearing their buoyancy vests, SCUBA gear and masks. They would not jettison that equipment until they began the climb up the makeshift ropes from the water's surface to the *Southern Star's* deck. Until then, they were in an environment that many regard as hostile and unforgiving—a stormy night sea. For the men of Golf Platoon, SEAL Team Eight, this was home. A couple of seconds before a wave crashed down, the swimmers took a deep breath and plunged below the surface. As the wave swept over them, they kicked hard and made a series of forceful, lunging strokes that propelled them forward through the water. Once the wave had passed, they kicked upward, and continued swimming. Repeated with each oncoming wave, the whole process took no more than a few seconds. Hartman and his men kept swimming and swimming and swimming.

Hartman glanced at the SEAL to his left. Like Hartman, the junior diver was holding his own against the walls of seawater as the duo pressed on toward their target. During this phase, according to SOP, no man in the platoon was to communicate via the DUCS unless it was life or death—that meant he was either in trouble or being shot at by hostile forces, although periodic status checks by the leader were permitted.

"This is dolphin leader," Hartman huffed into his microphone between breaths of air gulped from the single air tank strapped to his back. "Check in."

"Two—Three—Four," the swim pairs reported in rapid succession, which told Hartman they were still in the game. According to his Navy-issue Luminox watch, the group of combat divers had wriggled through the *Florida's* lockout tubes forty-seven minutes earlier. Twenty-six minutes had elapsed since they had emerged from the inky ocean depths, surfaced, and had begun making their way toward the listless cruise ship off in the distance. The mission was right on schedule and all was going according to plan.

Ten and a half minutes later, the eight SEALs of Golf Platoon drew near the *Southern Star*. According to the briefing from Lieutenant Timmons, they were to make their way to the ship's stern and look for two ropes—one on either side of her fantail—that had been fashioned from knotted bed sheets and secured to the railing by the friendlies who were on board the *Southern Star*. Unlike larger, modern cruise ships, the *Southern Star's* hull wasn't white. Instead, it was a deep blue color, which would make the white makeshift ropes easier for the team to spot.

The SEALs gave one last thrust with their arms and legs and drifted up to the huge ship. One by one, the swim pairs bumped up against the vessel's hull. Even though there was nothing to hang on to, the SEALs were able to maintain their position by placing their hands firmly against the thick blue steel. That allowed them to ride up and down with the *Southern Star* as she heaved back and forth in the eight-foot swells. As long as they could stay in contact with the hull, they would be able to remain in place.

After one last check in, Hartman issued instructions to the SEALs over the DUCS. They had to understand fully and get every detail right because, in a few minutes, there would be no way to communicate except by hand signals or voice commands. Moments before beginning their ascent, they would unfasten the SUCBA tanks and flotation vests from their bodies, remove their facemasks, and simply drop the gear into the ocean.

"Owens, take your four-man fire team and swim around to port," Hartman instructed. "Find the rope and call me when you locate it. Do not jettison your SCUBA gear or begin the ascent until I give the order. Understood?"

"Yes, Chief," Owens responded.

Hartman continued. "The other three men and I will drift back to starboard and locate that rope. Once we are in position with all equipment ready for the assault, I'll order us up the ropes. Any questions?"

The absence of any reply was just the answer he expected.

"Very well," he continued. "Bear in mind that once we get topside, we have no idea what we'll be facing. We're all a little fatigued, but remember, we're SEALs. We can go to the limits of human endurance and beyond. So, stay sharp, stay focused, and most importantly, STAY ALIVE. Now go!"

With that, four swim pairs of combat divers from Golf Platoon, SEAL Team Eight began their slow, deliberate movement from the *Southern Star's* midsection back toward her stern. The fight was on.

# 66. A BIRD'S EYE VIEW

*USS* **Florida** *Battle Management Center*
*Submerged Sixty Miles Northwest of Nassau, Bahamas*

The ScanEagle UAV continued to circle overhead the *Southern Star* as its pilot skillfully maneuvered the craft so Commander Pierce and Lieutenant Timmons could get a better view. So that President Brewster and his cabinet could see the unfolding rescue mission, the *Florida's* BMC also fed the UAV's real-time video to the White House Situation Room. Morse, the ScanEagle pilot, was back on duty following a brief combat nap. He was the best there was and his skills were about to be put to the test. From their position in the *Florida's* BMC nearly one hundred feet below the *Southern Star*, Commander Pierce or Lieutenant Timmons could do nothing to direct the SEALs' assault. However, it was still a ringside seat and that vantage point would make it easy for them to gauge the mission's progress and likelihood of success.

One of the many advances in battlefield imaging, the ScanEagle's short-wave infrared camera enabled military commanders to see objects more clearly in fog or rain. During extensive field-testing before its deployment on unmanned aerial vehicles like the ScanEagle, the camera recorded clear, streaming video during daytime, twilight and nighttime operations. Able to track both stationary and moving targets, the small, nimble aircraft weighed only forty pounds and was capable of flying above 16,000 feet. Known for long endurance, the ScanEagle could loiter over an area for more than twenty-four hours. Consequently, it was particularly well suited for an observation mission such as this one.

Three officers, Pierce, Timmons and SEAL Team Eight's intelligence officer, Lieutenant Baker, stood behind Morse and stared intently at the video screen. Morse had kept the UAV orbiting in a tight circle around the cruise ship some five hundred feet above it. As the craft continued to fly its route, Morse and Baker watched the monitor for human forms, particularly those that were moving. Using the UAV's infrared camera, they had been monitoring the situation on the *Southern Star* for the last several hours. During their constant vigil, they had not seen anything of significance happen—except for one thing. That happened to be the single most important event of the night.

Two obviously human shapes had been making their way down the *Southern Star's* starboard covered promenade deck toward her stern. Their images had come and gone as the pair passed behind lifeboats and other obstructions that temporarily blocked their heat signature. They completely disappeared for several minutes and then emerged on an open deck area aft of the Miramar Café near the vessel's fantail. However, that event was not significant; rather, it was the one that followed. The two shapes split up and ran to points as far back on the vessel as they could go. Each form huddled in the same spot for several minutes and moved its arms and hands back and forth.

Morse had asked Lieutenant Baker if he wanted him to zoom in for a closer look so they could see what the two were doing. As Morse typed in the command on the operator's keyboard, it became clear to him and Baker what the forms had been doing. Two long gray lines dangled from the *Southern Star's* railings forty feet or so down her hull to the waterline below. Baker instructed Morse to zoom in some more and increase the resolution. Baker responded and the image before them was unmistakable. Although their faces weren't visible, two men—presumably Murphy and Stanton—had just attached what appeared to be large, knotted cords of some kind to the cruise ship's railings and then lowered them down to the water. Baker instructed Morse to capture the images for closer analysis later and then picked up the phone to advise Lieutenant Timmons and Commander Pierce.

Now, the four Navy men in the BMC were looking for a double play. They watched the video feed intently for any sign that the eight SEALs were in the water near the ship or had started their ascent up the bed sheet ropes. Timmons, who like Pierce had not slept a wink since the operation began, rubbed his tired, bloodshot eyes. After he had finished, he reached for a steaming mug of black coffee, the tonic of choice for sailors assigned to long watches like this one.

"What the hell is going on?" he asked Morse. "Where are they? We should have seen them by now, don't you think?"

Morse checked the clock on the console and raised his head to reply. "According to the time hack, sir, we're at ETA plus four—they should have been there four minutes ago. Perhaps the wind and currents were stronger than forecast."

Pierce interjected before Timmons could respond. "They're SEALs and they're all excellent swimmers," he stated. "While they may be somewhat fatigued from the aborted SDV mission, they should be able to handle this. I know Hartman, so I know he is doing everything by the book." Pierce bent over and focused on the monitor again. "Don't worry," he added confidently, "they'll be there soon."

A familiar voice broke the silence. "Commander, this is Secretary of Defense Ellis in the White House Situation Room."

Pierce's reply was swift and crisp, "Yes, Mr. Secretary, what can I do for you?"

Ellis was right to the point, "Commander, we've been monitoring things from here and the president wants to know what the delay is. He is concerned that the mission will not go off as planned and that we're running out of both time and options."

"Mr. Secretary, I can understand President Brewster's concern. However, these men are among the best Special Forces fighters we have in our military," Pierce explained. "I mean no disrespect, sir, but over the years, I have learned that the hardest thing to do when you're in the big tent is to sit back, be patient and let things run their course. Therefore, I am confident when I say that they—no, make that we—will succeed."

"Commander, I just hope—" an announcement from Morse cut Ellis's response short.

"Got 'em, sir!" the UAV operator exclaimed. "Look! There they are!"

Timmons was the first to react. "Holy shit!" He pointed to the left side of the monitor. "Commander, look right there. See?"

Pierce zeroed in on the spot next to Timmons's index finger where several circular white blobs had suddenly appeared out of nowhere.

"Are you sure?" he asked Morse.

"Absolutely," he answered. "The thermal index for the targets indicates an average temperature of ninety-five degrees Fahrenheit. That can only indicate one thing—they are humans."

Ellis broke in on the voice network again. "Did I get that right, Commander? You have spotted the SEALs on the surface?"

Yes, sir," Pierce replied excitedly. "The swimmers have reached the target."

"Do we know if all of them made it?" Ellis demanded.

Morse was way ahead of him and had already zoomed in for a close-up and counted the number of heads that were bobbing in the ocean next to the *Southern Star*. He didn't wait for Pierce to ask him a question.

"I've made the count, sir," Morse blurted out, "and confirm eight, say again, eight, swimmers on the surface. They all made it."

Everyone in the *Florida's* BMC expected a reaction from Secretary Ellis, so when President Brewster's voice was heard over the net instead, it surprised them.

"Thank God!" he cheered.

# 67. THE WAITING GAME

*USS* Florida *Battle Management Center*
*Submerged Sixty Miles Northwest of Nassau, Bahamas*

All eyes in the BMC fixated on the video monitor. The next phase of Operation Second Light was about to begin and those present waited anxiously for the two SEAL elements to begin their ascent up the makeshift ropes. There was some discussion among the mission planners that this wild, harebrained idea had little chance of succeeding—especially since no one had tried it before. Some, including Timmons, thought it might be better to wait until a Navy or Air Force Pave Low helicopter could approach the cruise ship and lower the SEALs to the deck by fast roping. That type of assault wouldn't have had the element of surprise like the waterborne plan that was now underway. However, it would have been a more certain method of getting the SEALs on board. However, Secretary of Defense John Ellis ruled out that option so, like all good military men, Timmons was squarely behind plan B.

Morse skillfully played the joystick and trackball device to keep the ScanEagle and its sensitive infrared camera trained on the *Southern Star's* stern. The operator's console looked like a combination of a computer keyboard, video game interface, and airplane cockpit all rolled into one. The console's main feature was a large screen for displaying the processed images captured by the orbiting platform. On one side was a series of digital instruments that displayed the UAV's attitude, altitude, airspeed and magnetic heading. Clustered in a neat group on the other side were such critical items as time aloft, remaining fuel, and the engine's oil pressure and temperature indications.

Technology developed over the last thirty years now enabled operators like Morse to employ UAVs like the ScanEagle or unmanned underwater vehicles (UUVs) called the Seahorse to accomplish critical tasks such as surveillance, reconnaissance, communications, and launching small weapons from hundred—or even thousands—of miles away. It was a boon for battlefield commanders because they could see things in all types of weather and light conditions that until now would have been all but impossible. Better yet, they didn't have to risk men's lives on dangerous missions to accomplish these critical tasks. Armchair combat they called it.

"On the ascent!" Morse shouted. "SEALs on the ropes!"

Instantly, Pierce, Timmons and Baker drew close to the monitor and bent low for a closer look.

Two of the white shapes that he had spotted earlier were much larger and moving upward on the screen. To Morse, that could only mean one thing—the SEALs emerged from the water and had started their climb to the *Southern Star's* deck nearly forty feet above.

"Christ! I hope this works," Pierce mumbled softly under his breath. Timmons heard the remark and nodded in agreement.

One by one, the white shapes fell in line behind the leader and slowly inched up the cruise ship's hull.

"How far up the ropes are they, Morse?" Pierce asked, referring to the climbers on the starboard side of the ship.

"I'd estimate about ten feet, sir," Morse replied. "They've got a long way to go."

Pierce nervously glanced at his watch. "By the way, how much longer can your bird stay aloft?" he asked Morse.

"Hmmm." Morse thought for a moment and then answered. "Total endurance can approach twenty-four hours. However, I wouldn't count on it, sir. We'll need to recover the craft in approximately five hours."

Pierce straightened, obviously expecting more from Morse. "And?"

Baker jumped in with the details. "We're going to send it to Nassau, sir. The Bahamians have agreed to let us land it there. We don't have a military presence there, but since Customs and Border Patrol uses the same equipment along the U.S.-Mexico border, their personnel who are assigned to the airport in Nassau can do it."

"Very well," Pierce snorted. "Let's just hope this mission is all wrapped up before then. I'd hate to miss the show."

"Aaawwwwwhhhhh shhhiiit!" Timmons yelled.

Pierce wheeled around and locked on to the monitor.

"What's the problem? What's wrong?" Pierce demanded.

"One of the SEALs fell off the rope and back into the water. There's more though—he took his swim buddy with him."

"Christ Almighty! Not now!" Pierce fumed.

Baker barked an order to Morse. "Get in as close as you can. We need to know if they're okay. I want you to take the bird down lower, and when you get there, zoom in full, and then sharpen the resolution."

Morse's hands and fingers manipulated the joystick and trackball with the dexterity of an expert PC gamer.

"I can only go down another hundred feet," he advised. "It's pretty windy out there and I don't want to lose the bird."

"Fine with me," Baker acknowledged. "Any objections, Commander?"

Pierce's reply was terse. "No, just get to it!"

"Now four hundred feet and level," Morse announced. "Zooming now." He played the trackball back and forth and tapped on the keyboard a couple of times. Next, he moved the joystick as if he was stirring a cup of coffee. "Acquiring targets…sharpening resolution…got 'em!"

"Good!" Baker responded. "See them yet?"

"Yes, I've got the count," Morse called out. "I've got them all."

"Great!" Pierce chimed in. "I wouldn't want to lose anyone. This is going to be tough enough with eight SEALs," he added.

"Agreed, sir," Timmons nodded.

"Morse, take the UAV around to port. I want to see how the other squad is doing," Pierce ordered.

"Yes, sir!" Morse maneuvered the ScanEagle to the other side of the *Southern Star*.

"Looks like the last pair is almost there," he announced. "Just a few more feet to go."

Pierce breathed a sigh of relief. "Excellent! Bring the bird back to port for another look," Pierce instructed the operator.

Morse moved the joystick to the left. The UAV responded with a sharp roll began a steep turn back toward the *Southern Star's* starboard side. "On the way, sir."

Fortunately, the swim pair that had fallen off was near the bottom of the rope. Two SEALs, including the team's leader, Hartman, were above them. Once they resurfaced, they simply went to the end of the line and started over. By the time the ScanEagle was in position again, only four swimmers remained on the rope and they had already climbed half way up. That meant that four were on the deck.

"Almost there," Pierce gritted. "This just might work. Let's have another look at the port side."

The UAV arced around to the left and then back to the right. Morse pointed the camera at the ship's hull. The only thing visible was the gray line that was the bed sheet climbing rope.

"Looks like all members of this fire team are on top, sir," Morse announced.

"I see that," Pierce, agreed. "Owens is in charge of that element?"

"Yes, sir," Timmons confirmed.

"Okay, Morse," Pierce directed, "time for one last look at the port group."

Morse complied and the ScanEagle rolled around again and retraced its route to the other side of the *Southern Star*. Morse took the craft away from the cruise ship and then swung it around one hundred and eighty degrees to give the officers in the BMC a clear, head on view.

"Stand by," Morse advised. "Zooming and sharpening resolution." He played the trackball and keyboard. "There you go," he announced. The group stared at the monitor.

Morse slowly turned his head toward Pierce. "The rope is clear, sir. Looks like they're all on board. They did it!"

Pierce stepped back from the console and turned to Lieutenant Timmons. He rubbed his hands together gleefully and proclaimed, "Let the games begin!"

# 68. THE CHARGE

*Aboard the* Southern Star
*Sixty Miles Northwest of Nassau, Bahamas*

A hatch swung open and eight camouflage-clad SEALs led by Senior Chief Erik Hartman cautiously entered one of the *Southern Star's* dark passageways. Their senses heightened and ready for anything, they swept their weapons left and right as they went. The only sound was the whirring of ventilation fans and their own shallow breathing as they crept down the narrow corridor. Any of the terrorists who might have been lurking in the shadows wouldn't have stood a chance against the superior tactics and firepower of the SEALs.

The eight-member element stepped from the dim light of the vessel's aft deck into the dark bowels of the ship. Suddenly, a lone terrorist emerged from the darkness some fifteen feet in front of the squad, his weapon pointed directly at them. He steadfastly refused to place his weapon on the deck as the team had ordered him to do. The SEALs raised their weapons and trained their sights on the terrorist's center mass.

"Drop the weapon! Do it NOW!" Hartman yelled. The terrorist refused to comply. That was his fatal mistake.

All eyes were on the armed fanatic as the standoff continued to unfold. Unnoticed by the terrorist, another SEAL had crept into position against a railing one deck above them. He aimed his M4A1 down at terrorist and fired one round, which struck the perpetrator in the forehead. In less time than it took to say "target down," the SEALs were quickly hovering over the limp body, their weapons trained on his chest in case he was still a threat to them.

"Clear!" a squad leader shouted.

"Good. Keep moving," Hartman ordered. "Be careful, though. The weapons fire had to alert the other bad guys to our presence," he cautioned.

The group formed up in two four-man fire teams— one led by Hartman and the other led by Owens—and continued advancing forward. Team member positioning during a space penetration was a key element of successful tactics for boarding a hostile ship. When the team leader was in position, one person moved forward and guarded the front. Meanwhile, another team member moved behind and then another off to the side, so their 360-degree perimeter coverage was maintained at all times for protection.

In the next phase, a Hartman's element headed into a compartment on their way to secure the *Southern Star's* bridge. Before opening the hatch, they turned off all the lights in the room they occupied. This was to prevent back-lighting, which would silhouette anyone standing in the doorway, and thus make him or her easy targets for snipers who could be waiting around any corner. They made their way through the small chamber without incident and found themselves at the bottom of a spiral staircase.

That was their next obstacle to surmount. It would lead the team into the control room on the *Southern Star's* bridge. Once there, they could regain control of the cruise ship's engines and communications equipment after they neutralized the terrorists. Hartman motioned his team to leapfrog up the staircase in two groups of three. With this technique, two men provided cover while one man moved up the stairway and established a position, then provided cover for the next man to move forward, and so on. In a matter of minutes, the team quickly moved up the stairs and was ready to storm the bridge.

The eight SEALs planned to enter the compartment Israeli style. Using this method, team members shined their lights into the black room, illuminating it and temporarily blinding anyone inside. After a quick look, they turned their lights off, rushed into the room with weapons raised and scattered into cover and conceal positions. Then they unexpectedly turned on their lights again to locate, blind, and target anyone in the room.

On Chief Hartman's signal, the SEALs switched on their lights and quickly played the beams around the room from top to bottom and corner to corner. Just as they had practiced numerous times before, after a few seconds they extinguished their lights, readied their weapons and burst into the compartment. Hartman and another team member came through the doorway last and secured the hatch behind them so that nobody could "six the team" or come up from behind and open fire on the team while those who had entered first were focused on securing the room in front of them.

It was easy to tell the good guys from the bad guys—the *Southern Star's* crew wore traditional white uniforms with shoulder boards. In the darkness, their crisp white clothing would be faintly visible, and therefore easier for the SEALs to avoid targeting them by mistake. A series of shots rang out as the SEALs fired at the terrorists. There was no return fire, which suggested that the first salvo of bullets had killed the armed extremists on the bridge.

However, the tactical situation quickly deteriorated. When the SEALs first entered the room, one of the thugs managed to crouch low behind a cabinet and remained hidden from view. Without warning, he opened fire on the element. Casey, the SEALs' point man, reacted instinctively and quickly fired off five rounds in the direction of the terrorist's muzzle flash. But it was too late—a SEAL team member was down. The shooter continued firing into the doorway using a technique known as slicing the pie—firing around a wall or obstacle at an area in small increments or slices—to get a better shot at the SEALs.

It didn't work. To get a better angle where his line of sight fire would be more effective, the sniper came out from behind the cabinet. As he did, one of the SEALs turned on his flashlight and blinded the gunman. The tables quickly turned in the SEALs' favor as Casey opened up on the shooter with his M4A1 carbine. Several rounds struck the terrorist with a thump-thump-thump causing him to crumple to the floor.

"Now, Owens!" Casey shouted. "I'll cover you. Get our man out!" He trained his weapon on the thug he had just cut down as Owens and his swim buddy, Carlson, grabbed their injured teammate and withdrew to safety.

"Holy shit!" Owens shouted to the group. "Hartman's been hit. I think it's pretty bad."

Owens and Carlson quickly knelt down next to Hartman. Owens switched on his flashlight and the beam revealed the extent of the bullet wound. He shined his light on the injured SEAL's chest where a red patch of blood the size of a dinner plate had already soaked through Hartman's outer battle dress. Hartman made a gurgling sound as he gasped for air. Owens placed his hands over the wound in an effort to stop the bleeding as thick crimson liquid gushed from it. It was a futile attempt. The blood kept oozing and oozing with every heartbeat until it stopped flowing. Owens slid a hand up Hartman's chest to the left side of the fallen SEAL's neck where he desperately probed for a pulse. There was none. He looked up at his swim buddy. Owens said nothing—he didn't have to. His silence conveyed the message. Hartman was dead.

"Top's dead! Hartman's gone." Owens shouted. "I'm going to—"

Owens never finished the sentence. A loud crack accompanied by an orange flash emanated from a dark area of the room. The loosed round struck Owens in the right thigh and he screamed out in pain.

"Arrrggghhh! I'm hit" Owens exclaimed. "Shhhiiitt!" He writhed on the floor in pain next to Hartman's body. As soon as Carlson heard the gunshot and Owens' scream, he had sprawled out on the floor in spread eagle fashion to present a lower profile to the sniper. He reached out with one hand and pushed down on Owens to keep him low and prevent another round from striking him.

Owens and his partner had been focusing their attention on Hartman, so neither he nor his swim buddy had seen where the gunshot came from. Casey, however, had been providing cover and zeroed in on the exact spot. SEAL training dictated that they shoot from cover. After they exposed themselves to fire, they quickly returned to the same cover or, if they couldn't, moved to a different location to confuse the assailants. Perhaps the terrorists hadn't trained as well. It was a gamble, but something Casey was counting on. He pointed his weapon in the direction of the muzzle blast and fired off a burst. The dozen or so rounds from the weapon covered the distance in a split second. Casey was lucky, as they found their intended target. The assailant, however, was not so lucky. Loud dog-like yelps followed the repeated thump-thump-thump of the bullets slamming into a human body.

The whimpering ceased and a SEAL ran over to the spot and verified the kill. "Threat neutralized," he called to Casey.

"Good!" Casey acknowledged. "Bastard!" he added.

"Owens?" Casey yelled. "You okay?"

"I don't know," Owens shouted back. "I'm hit, but I think it just grazed me and is just a flesh wound. I'm going to try to stand."

Owens shifted all of his body weight to the uninjured leg and struggled to get up. Using his weapon as a makeshift crutch, he managed to stand upright, although he teetered a bit at first.

"Son of a bitch!" he yelled, "Damn, it hurts!"

Owens hobbled to a nearby cabinet and propped himself against it. He found the spot where the terrorist's AK-47 round had sliced through his BDUs. It was marked by shredded cloth and thick, oozing blood Although just a surface wound, the bullet left a quarter inch deep gash about two inches long in the middle of his right thigh.

Carlson quickly made his way to Owens and assessed the damage. "Goddamned lucky, Owens," he pointed out. "A foot lower, and it would have shattered your entire knee. Any deeper, and it would have smashed your femur. There's minimal bleeding. I'm going to wrap it. If you can stand the pain, I think you can stay in the fight."

"Well then hurry up, Carlson!" Owens snapped. "Time is critical. We still have to make our way to the dining room. Who knows how these bad guys might react to the sound of our weapons fire."

Carlson reached into his waterproof pack, removed a large, dark green plastic box, and opened it. He removed a half dozen boxes marked "Trauma Pad, 5"x 9" - 1 Per Box" and another box labeled "3 in. x 5 yd. - Cohesive Elastic Bandage." He immediately went to work applying layers of gauze and adhesive bandage over the torn tissue. Periodically, Owens winced as Carlson applied pressure to secure the dressings in place.

"Okay, Nurse Ratched, can't you be any gentler?" Owens chided.

"Sorry, Tracy," Carlson responded. "Doing the best I can."

"Really? Now I know why you're a Navy SEAL and not a Hospital Corpsman. It's because you have zero compassion and lack good bedside manners," Owens joked.

"All done," Carlson announced. "That will hold until you get treatment from a qualified medical professional."

"Gee, thanks," Owens replied sarcastically.

"Try to hide your gratitude next time, Owens," Carlson shot back.

Eager to get back to the task, Carlson and Owens patted each other on the back. "Let's go!" they exclaimed.

As the next senior NCO, responsibility for leading the rest of the mission fell to Owens. He surveyed the room. Satisfied that it was secure, he gave the form up signal. SEAL Team Eight was down one man, but they still had ample firepower, first-rate equipment and superior training to help them get the job done. In addition, they had one more thing on their side: the deep-seated desire to avenge a fallen comrade.

# 69. CLOSE COMBAT

*In the Miramar Café*
*Aboard the* **Southern Star**

Tactically, there was no easy, "one size fits all" solution available to the SEALs for retaking the ship. The team could have split up, with four of them going to the bridge and the other four to the dining room. In the end, Hartman decided that concentrating all of their firepower and know-how on one mission element at a time would improve the odds of a successful outcome. In briefing it that way, he reasoned that sticking together would provide mutual support and protection, thereby insuring the SEALs' survival.

Hartman explained that the terrorists would have to stay put in order to protect their own objectives, in this case, the hostages and the ship's bridge. In effect pinned down by the constraints of their mission, they had no flexibility. That would give SEAL Team Eight the advantage of maneuver. Furthermore, Hartman was confident that the terrorists wouldn't kill the hostages because they would them to bargain their way out if things went against them. The seven remaining members of SEAL Team Eight were about to find out if Hartman was right.

After neutralizing the terrorists in the bridge's control room, SEAL Team Eight managed to work its way down to the Miramar Café to free the hostages. One after the other, the SEALs crept along the promenade deck, making their way aft. Although they had been awake for nearly eighteen hours, the rigors of BUD/S training and grueling daily PT workouts kept them alert and energetic. Owens was in the lead followed by his swim buddy, Carlson, and the other pairs with Hartman's partner bringing up the formation's rear. Owens was managing quite well, considering the bullet wound to his right thigh. Now and then, he favored his leg, but didn't make a sound, choosing instead to grit his teeth, rather than cry out or groan.

Without warning, a hooded figure emerged from the shadows some fifty feet in front of the SEALs and, before anyone in the column could react, the bright orange muzzle flash and the loud crack from an AK-47 pierced the night as the dark form quickly retreated from sight.

Owens' right leg gave out and he crumpled on the wooden deck in a writhing heap. The shooter's bullet had found its mark. "Goddammit!" he cried. "Shot twice in one day!"

Carlson quickly bent over Owens and examined the fresh wound. The bullet had penetrated Owens' right thigh, a few inches above the other wound. He was bleeding, but the round had missed the femur and the leg's major blood vessels. There was a lot of tissue damage and Owens was experiencing a great deal of pain, but the gash didn't appear to be life threatening—at least not yet.

Although the other SEALs had fanned out to provide security for the group while Carlson tended to Owens, they didn't see what Owens did. The hooded figure that fired on Owens had reemerged and was raising his AK-47 to his shoulder, no doubt to pick off another SEAL. Realizing the danger, Owens quickly worked his SIG Sauer P228 from its holster and calculated his next step. Despite the jabbing pain in his thigh, Owens rapidly rolled over into the prone firing position, and let two 9mm rounds fly, which instantly struck their target.

Owens' sudden move startled everyone, especially Carlson. "Jesus H. Christ!" he yelled. "I really appreciate the cover, but did you have to get all Rambo?"

"Aaaahhhh!" Owens cried as a bolt of pain from the leg wound jarred his brain. "Just doing my job," he groaned.

Two SEALs dashed over to the terrorist and confirmed the kill with one word, "Dead."

Carlson resumed doctoring Owens' leg wound and hastily applied a large, tightly wrapped compress dressing to protect the deep wound and control bleeding. If the bandage could slow the bleeding, it would limit blood loss and prevent Owens from slipping into shock and possibly unconsciousness, or even death.

When he finished, Carlson helped Owens struggle to his feet. Owens was breathing heavily as the pain from the bullet wound coursed through his entire body. As Owens' stood up, his leg gave out under his body weight and he faltered. Carlson quickly caught him and steadied his teammate while he regained his balance. Owens kept his arm draped over Carlson's shoulder so he wouldn't fall again. Carlson propped Owens up as he tried to put some weight on his badly injured leg again.

"Jesus Christ!" Owens yelped. "Uuggghh. That hurts like hell," he grunted.

"You going to be Okay, Owens?" Carlson asked.

"I don't know," Owens answered. "It hurts like a son of a bitch. If I can walk, I'll be all right."

"I don't think so. You're still losing blood, so I 'm afraid you won't be able to go on with the team," Carlson said. "I'll stay here with you until we can get more help," he suggested. "We can let the others go on without us."

"No!" Owens countered. "There's no time to waste, especially now that we've initiated the operation. I'm sure our weapons fire has tipped off the terrorists in the ship's dining room. We've got to press on for the hostages' sake," Owens insisted.

"But you're wounded," Carlson reasoned. "You can't go on. There's no way you can fight."

"Yes, I can!" Owens argued. "I can use my weapon, so I'm still effective. Besides, now that Hartman is dead, I'm in charge of the team. So, I have to—it's my duty."

"Go ahead," Owens instructed. "Let go of me." He removed his arm from around Carlson's shoulder and stood, putting most of his weight on his good leg.

Carlson slowly backed away, leaving Owens standing in front of him. Owens leaned to one side as he favored his injured limb.

Owens gritted his teeth. "Carlson, I'm going to do this—even if it's the last goddamned thing I do on this earth."

Owens hobbled toward the middle of the promenade deck, dragging his badly wounded leg behind him. Carlson caught up with his swim buddy as he shuffled along and reached out to steady him.

"Chief," Owens said, referring to Hartman, "I'm doing this for you."

Owens fought off the dizziness as he limped along, Carlson at his side. His mind blurred for an instant as he experienced a flashback to the March 2003 amphibious assault against Iraqi forces in Basra. "For you too, Mike Kidd," Owens blurted out. "For you, too, Mike," he repeated.

Owens shook his head vigorously in an effort to remain conscious, but he was growing weaker with every passing minute. In a low voice punctuated by labored breathing, Owens mumbled the SEAL code that he and Mike Kidd had both sworn to uphold so many years before: "Loyalty to Country, Team and Teammate...Teammate ...Tea..." His voice trailed off and then fell silent.

# 70. OUR TURN NOW

*In the Miramar Café*
*Aboard the* Southern Star

The sound of distant weapons fire coming from the direction of the *Southern Star's* bridge hadn't drawn any of the terrorists away from the Miramar Café, but this new volley from automatic rifles nearby on the promenade deck did. Sensing that trouble was approaching, Ali, the leader, signaled for one of the group's members to go investigate.

Stanton and Murphy had been waiting for such a distraction because it more than evened the odds. Now only two terrorists were in the dining room guarding the hostages and three of the hostages were armed. Stanton and Murphy exchanged a quick glance. A subtle nod by each man told the other that the opportunity to turn things around was at hand.

Timing, of course, was everything. Act too soon and the third terrorist would be close enough to rush back to help his accomplices. Wait too long and he might return just when Stanton and Murphy sprang into action. In either case, after they acted, the sound of gunfire from the two Walther PPK pistols that Ben had given Murphy and Stanton would attract the attention of the third terrorist, and he was sure to return. That part they hadn't figured out.

Susan sensed that Murphy and Stanton were up to something, but she didn't know quite what. Anticipating the worst, she fidgeted nervously in her chair. She lowered her head and stared at the white tablecloth so as not to attract unwanted attention. Her hands began to tremble, so she clasped them together and placed them on the table in front of her cup and saucer. Out of the corner of her eye, Susan noticed that Murphy nodded approvingly.

Fortunately, Murphy and Stanton sat almost directly across from one another. That allowed them to communicate with their eyes, hand gestures and mouthed words. It also gave them a view of the entire dining room so they knew where the terrorists were at all times. Now, one was guarding the Miramar Café's main entry and the other one—the group's leader—was on the opposite side of the dining room positioned between the serving table and the kitchen door.

Once Stanton caught Murphy's attention, he mouthed, "You, by the main door." He had waited for a nod from Murphy before he continued. Instead, Murphy mouthed back, "Me, the door?" This time Stanton nodded. Murphy gave a thumbs-up acknowledgement.

Murphy looked directly at Stanton. "When?" he mouthed.

"I'll yell 'Now!'" was his reply. Murphy's nod indicated that he understood.

Stanton slowly scanned the room as he tried to get the timing just right. To do that, he had to anticipate what the terrorists would do and when they would do it. Fortunately, he had been studying them for a long while, so he had their routine down. The guards repeated those behavior patterns like clockwork so he could predict what would come next. The best way to catch them off guard would be when they shifted their focus from one side of the dining room to the other. As they did so, their field of peripheral vision would also move and create a blind spot that would mask Stanton and Murphy's actions as they drew their weapons—at least that's what Stanton was counting on.

Within minutes of Stanton mouthing instructions to Murphy, the terrorists began to turn in order to focus their attention on a different part of the café. As soon as Stanton determined that he and Murphy were in their blind spots, he shouted "Now!"

Stanton and Murphy leapt to their feet, leveled the Walthers, and each squeezed off one round. Like every good military officer, Stanton and Murphy were expert pistol sharpshooters, so the rounds found the intended targets' center of mass. The two terrorists buckled and fell face down on the dining room floor. In a few seconds, it was over.

Shocked by what had just happened, several passengers began to scream and get up from their seats. Quickly sensing the danger, Stanton tried desperately to gain control.

"Stop! Sit!" he commanded. "We're good guys. We're U.S. military. Get back in your seats, please!"

Alerted by the pistol shoots coming from the Miramar Café, the third terrorist sprinted down the promenade deck and burst into the dining room. "What happened here?" he demanded. "Who did this?" He looked over at Stanton and Murphy, who were still holding the Walther PPKs.

"You?" he screamed. "You did this to my brothers?"

The terrorist approached the table. Stanton and Murphy stood motionless. Neither one spoke. When he was some fifteen feet from the table, he stopped and leveled his AK-47 at the pair.

"You did this to my brothers?" he asked again.

Suddenly, from the back of the dining room, a voice cried out, "No, I did it."

The terrorist quickly turned to see who it was and his jaw dropped in disbelief.

"Jamal?" He shook his head. "Jamal, how could you?"

Jamal carefully laid his pistol on the table nearest him. "It's simple," he replied. "I don't believe in your cause. It's unjust and unworthy. You are all misguided. I'm sorry, brother, but that's the truth."

The terrorist sighed heavily and then began to sob. "No, Jamal, it's you who are misguided. We trusted you and you betrayed us. There will be no glorious martyrdom for you."

He raised the AK-47 to his shoulder, aimed squarely at Jamal's head and pulled the trigger.

"Ben! No-o-o-o-o!" Susan screeched.

As horrified passengers watched, Jamal toppled backward and crumpled lifelessly to the floor. Before anyone could react, the sharp *tat–tat* from a weapon fired near the Miramar Café's entrance set off a collective gasp. Thinking the worst, Stanton and Murphy whirled around to see what had happened.

Standing in the doorway was U.S. Navy SEAL Rick Carlson, M4A1 carbine in hand. He had just fired two shots that took down the last terrorist on the *Southern Star*. The hostage ordeal was finally over.

"Ladies and gentlemen," Carlson announced, "I'm a Navy SEAL. You're all safe now. My team and I are in control of the ship. The captain is safe and we will be heading to Nassau where a U.S. military transport is waiting to fly you back to Florida. We will have instructions for you shortly."

Stanton and Murphy turned to one another, shook hands, and smiled.

"Is this what they mean by joint ops?" Murphy quipped.

"Damned if I know," Stanton replied. "I guess anything's fair in war," he replied.

"And love," Murphy added, glancing toward Susan. "Excuse me, will you?"

Murphy slid around the table, lifted Susan from her chair, and held her in a long, tender embrace. Stanton gave him an approving wink and walked off.

"Ben," Susan sobbed. "They killed Ben."

Murphy tried his best to comfort her. "I'm sorry, Susan. Lucky for us that he turned out to be one of the good guys. Ben was very brave and saved all of us."

Susan responded with a sniffle as Murphy rocked her gently. "We're together and we're safe. That's all that matters now," he cooed.

Through the windows of the Miramar Café, Murphy could see that the wind and rain had subsided and slivers of morning light hinted at a clearing sky. He pulled Susan closer and whispered, "It's going to be a good day—a very good day. I promise."

"I know," she replied, squeezing him tightly as tears trickled down her soft cheeks.

# 71. AN INSIDE JOB

*The White House Oval Office*
*Washington, D.C.*

"By someone *inside* the embassy?" Brewster growled. "Adrian, surely you're kidding. That notion is preposterous. Please tell me it isn't so."

Secretary of State Adrian Ashe cleared his throat before he answered the president's question.

"I only wish that were the case, Mr. President." Ashe scratched his forehead briefly and continued with the details.

"Both the FBI and CIA have confirmed that the information was leaked by someone inside our London embassy," he explained. "The only problem is that they don't know who did it—or why."

Brewster gritted his teeth and pressed Ashe for more information. "And were these agencies—FBI and CIA—made aware of the leak?"

"Yes, sir. James Singleton, chief of MI5's Joint Terrorism Analysis Centre, alerted us about the breach. He personally called Jim Conroy to discuss the matter directly with him. According to what Jim told me, Singleton was deeply troubled by this development," Ashe explained.

"Go on," Brewster urged.

"Very well, sir," Ashe nodded. "Conroy in turn put a CIA counterintelligence team on it right away. However, dozens of employees from agencies besides the State Department work at the embassy and the FBI will need to vet and clear each one. To get the ball rolling, Conroy called David Carter at Homeland Security and also tipped off the Attorney General since the FBI fell under his jurisdiction."

"All right, Adrian," Brewster sighed, "let's go over this again. What information was disclosed?"

"This is what Jim Conroy told me, Mr. President," Ashe began. "For several months now, the CIA, MI5 and Interpol have been closely watching al-Muhajiroun. Officially banned under the U.K.'s Terrorism Act 2006, the group and its founder and spiritual leader, Omar Bakri-Muhammed, fled the country shortly afterward. However, reports indicate that elements of it still exist and are active. Ever since Bakri-Muhammed's disappearance, they have been trying to identify its new leader, but have been unsuccessful so far."

"I don't get it—what's the concern?" Brewster demanded.

"An offshoot of this group—or perhaps an element linked to them—surfaced on the University of Oxford campus, of all places. Known as the Da'wah (evangelism) Society, they distributed leaflets at their meetings that carried a phone number that seemed to link them to al-Muhajiroun. It was nothing more than a recruitment effort conducted under the guise of a sanctioned university organization. The FBI's counterterrorism liaison at the embassy, an agent named Blanton, made contact with a member of that campus organization. Blanton was working to learn the identity of al-Muhajiroun's new leader. As you know, sir, this kind of intelligence gathering is very painstaking and takes time. Apparently, someone inside the embassy tipped off the Da'wah Society that one of its members is an informant. That not only jeopardized the intelligence gathering effort, but also placed the lives of both the informant and our FBI agent in danger."

Ashe looked squarely at the president. "It gets worse, sir. That *someone* also provided the terrorists who held the *Southern Star's* passengers hostage with the names of two passengers that could be considered high value to them—Commander Murphy and *Washington Post* reporter Susan Anderson. That action might have made it more difficult to win the release of the hostages and placed these two individual's lives in grave danger as well."

The grimace on Brewster's face conveyed the anger he felt. "I can't believe one of our own people would do something like that. It borders on treason," the president fumed. "Who are the chief suspects, Adrian?"

"That question is perhaps better answered by Jim Conroy than by me," Ashe replied. "Of course Mr. President, until cleared by the FBI, everyone is considered the source of the leak—even the ambassador himself. But I believe the list of prime suspects has been narrowed down to three individuals: Special Agent Blanton; a young CIA analyst named Allan Anderson; and a British national employed at the embassy, Meredith Wilson, who also happens to be Anderson's frequent companion."

"Who is most likely implicated in the matter?" Brewster asked.

"It's hard to say, sir," Ashe replied. "If I were a betting man, I'd place my bet on it being one of our people—Blanton or Anderson. Miss Wilson simply doesn't have access to that kind of information. Moreover, she doesn't appear to have a motive, either. Singleton's MI5 teams have already done a check of her phone records, bank accounts and recent travel. She comes up clean. As for Anderson, he doesn't fit the MO profile either, especially since the newspaper report is his own sister."

"Hmmm," Brewster mused. "Then it has to be the FBI agent—Blanton, I believe you said his name was, right?"

"It looks that way, Mr. President," Ashe groaned.

Brewster shook his head and then removed his eyeglasses and laid them on the desk. He leaned back in his chair and closed his eyes. Secretary of State Ashe sat patiently and watched his boss, who appeared to be deep in thought. After a few seconds, Brewster opened his eyes again and sat upright.

"Adrian, I want to be kept in the loop," Brewster instructed. "Let me know as soon as you find out anything more. Notify me immediately. Now if you don't mind, I'd like to be left alone."

# 72. UNDER ARREST

*The U.S. Embassy*
*London, U.K.*

The heavy wooden office door clunked shut. Meredith Wilson looked up to see a rather tall, neatly dressed man in a dark suit standing a few feet in front of her.

"Can I help you, sir?" she asked with a polite smile.

He approached the desk. "Yes, you can. I'm here to see Mr. Blanton."

Meredith picked up her boss's appointment book and quickly glanced at it. "Is he expecting you? I don't see anything on his calendar."

"No. Actually, it's an unannounced visit—a surprise of sorts. I'm an old friend."

"I see," Meredith said, studying him closely. He had closely cropped hair that made him look younger than he probably was. He was trim and somewhat muscular. *He couldn't have made it past the Marines and up to this level of the embassy without proper credentials. Military or CIA?* she wondered.

Meredith smiled, "Just a moment, then. I'll let Mr. Blanton know you're here. Who should I say is calling?"

"Rogers. Mr. Rogers," he nodded.

"Very well, Mr. Rogers," she replied. "Won't you have a seat, please? I'm sure it won't be long."

"Thanks, but I've been sitting in a taxi. If you don't mind, I'll just stand."

"As you wish." Meredith reached for the phone and lifted the handset. She pushed the number 1 and waited for an answer.

"Mr. Blanton, it's Meredith. I'm sorry to disturb you, but there's a Mr. Rogers here to see you. He says he's an old friend."

Meredith listened for a moment, and then nodded. "Very well, sir. I'll let him know." She returned the handset to its cradle.

Meredith smiled politely at the visitor. "I'm sorry, Mr. Rogers, but Mr. Blanton says he doesn't know anyone by that name. And in that case, I'm afraid I'm going to have to ask you to leave,"

Rogers sighed and turned for the door. "That's a disappointment." He stopped midway, reached inside his suit coat, and withdrew a pistol. Meredith screamed and reached for the phone. Before she could lift the handset, the outer door burst open and three more gun-wielding men in dark suits swarmed into the office foyer. In an instant, all four of them flew past her and crashed through the door to Blanton's office.

They leveled their guns, pointing them at Blanton. "FBI, freeze!" Rogers shouted.

Still speechless, Meredith Wilson slowly turned around and stared into Bill Blanton's office. He was sitting behind his desk, hands held in the air on either side of his shoulders. Two of the FBI agents trained their weapons on him while another patted him down. Rogers had holstered his pistol and produced a pair of handcuffs.

Standing about three feet from Blanton, Rogers read aloud from a laminated card he held in one hand. "You have the right to remain silent. Anything you say or do may be used against you in a court of law. You have the right to speak to an attorney. If you cannot afford one, an attorney will be appointed for you before questioning. You have the right to not answer questions at any time and request an attorney be present before any questioning continues. Do you understand these rights?"

Blanton looked at Rogers and nodded.

"Okay, cuff him," Rogers said, thrusting the handcuffs toward the agent who had frisked Blanton. One at a time, he took Blanton's hands, swung them behind his back, and fastened the cuffs tightly around his wrists. The clicking sound the ratchet locks made as Rogers closed the restraints caused Meredith to wince.

Suddenly, the outer office door opened. Philip Reeves, Allan's supervisor, and the chief of the Marine guard, a Gunnery Sergeant with a white-wall haircut, quickly entered. Meredith swung her chair around toward the pair.

"Mister Reeves," she asked, "I don't understand. What's going on here? Is Mr. Blanton in trouble?"

"Yes, Meredith," Reeves replied, "I'm afraid so. Now that Mr. Blanton is in custody, please sit tight while he's escorted out."

Two FBI agents lifted Blanton up from his chair and ushered him out of his office and toward the door. Rogers led the way and the fourth agent followed a couple of steps behind Blanton and his two guards. Rogers opened the door, let the group pass, and fell in behind them, pulling the door closed as he went.

Before Reeves or the Marine sergeant could say anything, Meredith spoke.

"Mr. Reeves, I'm not feeling so well. Do you mind if I excuse myself and spend the rest of the day at home."

Reeves smiled, "No, not at all, Miss Wilson. I'm sure this whole event has been very upsetting."

Meredith slid her chair away from the desk and stood. "Thank you, Mr. Reeves. Should I report for work in the morning as usual?"

"By all means. We'll be able to find something productive for you to do. In the meantime, why don't you simply take it easy and come in fresh tomorrow."

"Yes," Meredith agreed, "that sounds like a splendid idea. Thank you."

"In fact, let me walk you to the street," Reeves suggested, motioning toward the door.

Meredith grabbed her purse and draped the light coat she had worn to ward off the morning chill over one arm. Reeves and the Marine sergeant started for the door with Meredith close behind. Once in the hallway, they walked a few yards to the elevator and took it to the first floor. The elevator door opened and the trio marched past security toward the main entrance.

The group, led by Reeves, exited the embassy and made their way through the maze of concrete barriers to Grosvenor Square. For security reasons, most traffic was restricted to all but a few vehicles. The three of them stopped at the street just as a black Austin FX4 taxi approached. Reeves raised a hand to signal the driver. The car slowed and glided to a stop alongside the curb in front of them. Reeves opened the rear door and gestured for Meredith to get in. She slid across the seat and smiled at Reeves as he closed the door.

The driver glanced up at the rear view mirror and addressed his passenger. "Where to, miss?"

Meredith paused for a moment and then blurted out, "Heathrow—and hurry!"

"Sure thing," he replied with a Cockney twang.

Meredith leaned her head back against the seat and closed her eyes. Startled by a loud tapping, she sat up quickly and turned in the direction of the noise. It was Reeves, bent low next to the taxi's side window and making a circular motion with his hand. She rolled the window down and Reeves leaned in. He opened his mouth to speak, but she cut him off before he could.

"I'm sorry to seem impolite, Mr. Reeves," she snapped, "I'm in a bit of a rush. What is it?"

Reeves kept his composure. They locked eyes and he studied her for a few seconds. "Miss Wilson, there's something about the incident in Blanton's office that I failed to mention. You see, it wasn't Blanton we were after," he declared. "It was you."

Before Reeves could finish speaking, the door on the other side of the cab flew open and a trench coat clad Scotland Yard detective jumped onto the rear seat next to Meredith, his credentials held out for her to see. Outside, a contingent of uniformed Bobbies and plainclothes detectives, weapons drawn, had surrounded the taxi.

"Good show, Officer Clark," the detective in the back of the taxi yelled to the driver. "Your timing was impeccable." The police officer turned around and nodded.

Meredith fell back against the seat and let out a heavy sigh. She slumped over and hung her head low. The detective turned to her and rattled off the police caution—Britain's version of the Miranda rights—with the deftness of a practiced stage performer.

"Miss Wilson, my name is Inspector Woolford. I am arresting you on suspicion of violating Terrorist Act 2006. You do not have to say anything, but it may harm your defense if you do not mention, when questioned, something you later rely on in court. Anything you do say may be taken down and given in evidence. Do you understand?"

Meredith Wilson said nothing. Instead, she raised her head and glanced out the taxi's open window, past the police officers clustered around the cab. She saw Philip Reeves and the Marine Gunnery Sergeant making their way back toward the U.S. embassy, accompanied by her boss, Bill Blanton, who was no longer in handcuffs.

Slowly, she turned to the Scotland Yard detective seated beside her, hesitated briefly, and then spoke. "There's no point in it now, Inspector. I'll cooperate. What would you like to know?"

# 73. THE NUANCE OF ILLUSION

*CIA Headquarters*
*Langley, VA*

"Of course your girlfriend, Meredith Wilson, not only knew your sister's name and what she did for a living, but also knew of your plans to take a mini-cruise with Susan from Florida to the Bahamas. She forwarded that information to the terrorist cell operating out of the University of Oxford."

"They quickly figured out that if you and your sister—a U.S. embassy employee and a leading national newspaper reporter—were on the *Southern Star* sailing for Nassau, it would give them two very important things they needed: a high-value hostage for negotiating leverage and a prominent media connection for getting their message out." King paused to let that sink in.

"Posing as a jihadist sympathizer," he continued, "a Yemeni living in London code named "Sinbad" had successfully infiltrated the cell and identified the source of the embassy leaks as your girlfriend, Meredith. Sinbad, a k a Jamal, learned about the hijacking plans and tipped off Bill Blanton. You see, Blanton had been working with MI6 to gain access to that terrorist cell in order to determine their "MO" and objectives. Once we learned from Blanton and MI6 what was going on, we covertly planted Sinbad on the *Southern Star* in case the hijacking plot actually unfolded.

Sinbad spoke fluent Arabic and English, but because of his physical features, we knew he could easily pass as a member of the ship's predominantly Filipino crew. Having Sinbad on the ship would give us someone on the inside to keep us apprised of what was happening. We believed that if this group hijacked the ship, we would be able to rescue everyone on board without losing a single hostage. However, as a backup plan, we would try to negotiate a successful release of the hostages by secretly exchanging them for some Guantanamo detainees."

"Unfortunately, it didn't work out that way," King explained. "You see, they knew that Bill Murphy would be on board. Although a high-value target for them, he presented a huge intelligence risk for us. Although we couldn't afford to let any of you fall into their hands, we certainly could not let them capture Murphy. And of course you know why, don't you, Allan?"

Anderson nodded.

King continued, "What the terrorists didn't know—and neither did we—was that U.S. Army Colonel Jack Stanton would also be on board the *Southern Star*. That was sheer coincidence—although I don't believe in coincidences."

Allan cocked his head. "Gosh, wasn't the entire operation, including a behind the scenes investigation here in London, quite risky?"

"Risky, you ask?" King shot back with a chuckle. "Hell, yes! But we ultimately saved many more lives in the process. The presence of a terrorist mole inside the embassy had the potential to be extremely damaging to our global operations—especially our field teams. That's why we made it look like the turncoat was Blanton."

"Why Blanton?" Allan inquired.

"By 'arresting' him at the embassy," King explained, "we were hoping to make Meredith think that we were on to the wrong person. In the aftermath that followed Blanton's staged apprehension, we were betting that she would act foolishly to save her own skin and in doing so, she would incriminate herself. By attempting to flee the country, that's exactly what she did! Acting on a strong hunch that she was the culprit, we set a trap and caught the rat."

# 74. A FITTING END

*Naval Amphibious Base Little Creek*
*Near Virginia Beach, Virginia*

A steady drizzle fell from the ragged, gray overcast that hugged Naval Amphibious Base Little Creek. Raw gusts blew in off the Chesapeake Bay from the northeast and carried the rain with it. It was hardly typical early December weather for Virginia's Tidewater. Something other than its weather, though, would make this day one long remembered. Rather it was why a group of dignitaries and special guests had gathered in a large building near the center of the base.

Seated at the dais along with President Robert K. Brewster were Secretary of the Navy, Dr. John C. Metcalf, and several other VIPs. Navy PO1 Tracy Owens sat in the front row next to an admiral and NAB Little Creek's commander. Other notables were in the audience, including Navy Commander William C. Murphy and Army Colonel John H. Stanton. A mix of civilian and military invitees filled the hall's remaining two hundred chairs.

Dr. Metcalf stood and moved to the center of the dais. He removed a folded sheet of paper from his suit coat pocket and surveyed the audience. He looked to his left toward the president and began to speak.

"President Brewster, Admiral Flynn, Captain Szemanksi, honored family members, and distinguished guests. As the Secretary of the Navy, I am honored and privileged to welcome you to Naval Amphibious Base Little Creek, home of the U.S. Navy's Amphibious Warfare Center.

We are gathered here today to honor the brave men of SEAL Team Eight for their courage and gallantry in rescuing the hostages who were aboard the SS *Southern Star*.

We are also here today to pay special tribute to one of those SEALs who gave his life during that effort. Additionally, we will recognize a SEAL who was seriously wounded during the operation.

Now, I would like to invite our Commander-in-Chief, President Robert K. Brewster, to make a few remarks."

Metcalf turned to Brewster and stepped away from the podium. The president stood and walked to the center of the dais. He placed both hands on the podium looked out across the audience and spoke.

"Ladies and gentlemen, I stand before you today as your president to express the heartfelt gratitude of a troubled nation. The senseless hijacking of a cruise ship carrying American citizens for the purposes of furthering terrorist aims has caused us all to wonder whether we are safe. As your president, I can state unequivocally that we are.

The brave men and women of our armed forces who have sworn an oath to protect and defend the Constitution of the United States against all enemies, foreign and domestic, proved once again that they would uphold that duty, even if it means they must make the ultimate sacrifice.

That, my dear people, is what we are here to commemorate today."

Brewster paused and motioned Secretary Metcalf to join him at the rostrum. Metcalf stood and moved to the podium. A Navy adjutant emerged from the background and quickly followed. The officer, a lieutenant in crisp whites, stepped to the microphone.

"Mr. and Mrs. Hartman, please come forward."

A couple in their mid-sixties seated in the front row stood and moved toward the dais. A Navy captain, who was dressed in a crisp, white uniform with gold braid on his sleeves and several rows of ribbons on his chest, escorted them. They climbed the steps and the officer accompanied them to the center of the platform. The president and the Navy secretary extended their hands and exchanged a few words with the couple. The entire group turned to face the audience and the adjutant took his cue.

"Attention to orders," he bellowed. Everyone in the room rose and the military men and women who were present snapped to attention.

The adjutant opened a blue vinyl folder and began to read aloud solemnly.

"The Navy Cross is posthumously awarded to Navy Chief Petty Officer Erik F. Hartman. Citation reads as follows:

*The President of the United States*
*takes pleasure in presenting the*

## NAVY CROSS CHIEF PETTY OFFICER

### TO

## ERIK F. HARTMAN

### UNITED STATES NAVY

For extraordinary heroism as Platoon Chief, SEAL Team Eight, during Operation SECOND LIGHT.

As SEAL Team Eight initiated the hostage rescue operation on board the SS *Southern Star*, enemy fighters attacked to prevent the retaking of the bridge and freeing of the hostages. Chief Petty Officer Hartman's repeated acts of bravery in providing close in fire support to embattled SEALs helped collapse the terrorist defenses and provided an opportunity to regain control of the hijacked ship. With total disregard for his own safety, he stormed the bridge and wheelhouse to engage the enemy and pin him down. Placing himself at grave personal risk to intermittent terrorist gunfire, Chief Petty Officer Hartman continuously battled enemy fighters providing cover for his fellow SEALs during the most intense period of combat, having been gravely wounded while doing so. By drawing fire while remaining dangerously exposed, he enabled other SEALs and hostage rescue forces to overwhelm and neutralize the terrorists. Chief Petty Officer Hartman's courage and fearless dedication under intense enemy fire rallied fellow SEALs and ultimately resulted in the freeing of seventy American hostages on board the SS *Southern Star* with no loss of life. By his outstanding display of decisive leadership, unlimited courage in the face of heavy enemy fire, and utmost devotion to duty, Chief Petty Officer Hartman reflected great credit upon himself and upheld the highest traditions of the United States Naval Service.

For the President of the United States, John C. Metcalf, Secretary of the Navy."

After a long moment, Dr. Metcalf stepped forward and leaned close to the microphone.

"Ladies and gentlemen, I cannot think of a more fitting tribute to a man like Chief Hartman, who not only loved the Navy and the SEALs, but also his fellow man, than the one we are about to bestow." Metcalf paused.

After a few seconds, he looked at the Hartman's and continued. "This facility is here and forevermore dedicated to the life, deeds and honor of CPO Erik F. Hartman and shall be known as Hartman Hall. A plaque hung outside the entrance reads,

## HARTMAN HALL

**In memory of CPO Erik F. Hartman,**
**Who gave his life in the service of his nation,**
**Forever Loyal to Country, Team and Teammate.**

Brewster and Metcalf each took the Hartman's hands in theirs one by one, nodded a few words, and slowly withdrew. The Hartman's hugged each other briefly and turned to their escort. The Navy captain walked them to the edge of the platform, down the steps and back to the front row. The adjutant waited until they returned to their places, gave them a moment to reflect, and then continued with the ceremony.

"Petty Officer First Class Tracy Owens, front and center," he barked.

Still standing, Owens leaned on his crutches and shuffled toward the dais. An usher near the front, who was also a Navy enlisted man, started for Owens. Before he could reach him to help, Owens shook his head. "No," he said firmly and continued onward. Owens climbed the three steps to the top of the platform and hobbled to the center. He saluted the president and wheeled to the front. Aided by his crutches, Owens stood more-or-less at attention. The adjutant opened a blue vinyl folder and began to read in a loud, clear voice.

"Attention to orders. The Bronze Star Medal with a "V" for valor is awarded to Petty Officer First Class Tracy Owens. Citation reads as follows:

## UNITED STATES OF AMERICA
## THIS IS TO CERTIFY THAT
## THE PRESIDENT OF UNITED STATES
### *HAS AWARDED*
## THE BRONZE STAR WITH "V" DEVICE
## PETTY OFFICER FIRST CLASS
## TO
## TRACY OWENS
## UNITED STATES NAVY

For meritorious achievement in connection with combat operations against the enemy while Golf platoon, SEAL Team Eight, was engaged in hostage rescue operations aboard the SS *Southern Star* during Operation SECOND LIGHT. As the friendly force attempted to secure the ship's bridge, it was subjected to intense small arms fire from a well-concealed terrorist element. Although painfully wounded in the attack, Petty Officer Owens immediately directed his men to launch a counter assault on the enemy's position. Despite his severe wound and without regard for his own safety, Petty Officer Owens continued to lead Golf platoon until they were successful in securing the bridge. While advancing on the ship's dining room to free the hostages, Petty Officer Owens was again struck by small arms fire and despite his wounds, continued to support his team and fought with valor until he was no longer conscious. His courage, initiative and exemplary professionalism significantly contributed to a successful outcome of the hostage rescue mission. Petty Officer Owens' outstanding display of leadership, devotion to duty, and personal bravery reflected great credit upon himself and upheld the highest traditions of the United States Naval Service.

For the President of the United States, John C. Metcalf, Secretary of the Navy."

The adjutant stepped back from the podium and the president and the Navy secretary approached Owens. The president spoke to Owens in a low voice. Owens nodded and responded in a barely audible murmur. Brewster turned to Dr. Metcalf, who handed him the medal, a triangular red ribbon with a blue stripe down the center and a large, bronze star suspended from the end. Attached to the top of the medal on the ribbon was the "V" for valor device. Brewster turned to Owens and pinned the Bronze Star to his uniform on the left breast above his heart. Owens snapped a crisp salute and the president returned it. Owens made an about face and started for the steps.

"Owens," Brewster called. Owens stopped and then turned to face the president.

"There's more," Brewster said. Owens looked at him quizzically and started for the center of the dais.

"That's all right," Brewster offered. "Let me come to you."

Brewster walked the short distance to Owens with Dr. Metcalf close behind. The adjutant hurried over and handed another vinyl folder to Metcalf. He opened it and handed it to the president. Brewster began to read it.

"Greetings. Know all men by these presents that Petty Officer First Class Tracy Owens, United States Navy, is hereby promoted to the rank of Chief Petty Officer effective this date, with all privileges, honor and accord due him.

Given under my hand in the City of Washington, Robert K. Brewster, President of the United States."

Brewster paused and looked at Metcalf, who whispered, "Yes, now."

"And there's another thing," Brewster continued. "You're being reassigned. Effective immediately, you are SEAL Team Eight's Platoon Chief. Congratulations!"

The announcement caught Owens by surprise. He stared inquisitively at the president who was nodding slowly. Once Owens realized what the president said, a proud smile replaced his astonished gaze. This time, the president saluted Owens. Brewster grasped the SEAL's shoulder and turned him toward the audience. The president took Owens' right hand and raised it high above his head. Amid cheers, Hartman Hall erupted in thunderous applause.

# ABOUT THE AUTHOR

Alan J. Murray holds a bachelor's degree from Saint Michael's College. A career military officer, he has piloted numerous Air Force jets and Army helicopters, including the T-33, EB-57, AH-1, UH-1, and UH-60. Among his many assignments, Murray served with distinction as a UH-60 Blackhawk battalion commander and was awarded the Meritorious Service Medal. He currently makes his home near Dobbins ARB outside of Atlanta, Georgia.